THE POWER OF LOVE

Sarah was sinking, drowning in a sea of unfamiliar sensations. The hard knot of tension in her belly grew, spreading warmth as desire flowed like molten lava.

Golden Eagle heard her plea and froze. His lips slowly pulled away.

Softly, he murmured against her lips, lowering her reluctantly, "Your magic is powerful. You have cast a spell over this warrior. It is too bad we are not alone, or Golden Eagle would not be able to resist teaching you the ways of a man and woman. But when I teach you the art of loving, it will be when there is no fear of interruptions."

Sarah returned to reality with a jolt. His hands still cupped her buttocks. They still stood flesh to flesh. Man to woman. With a horrified gasp, Sarah tore her hands from the strong column of his neck. Pushing with all her might, she freed herself with an anguished cry and stumbled for the bank.

WHITE WIND

SUSAN EDWARDS

LEISURE BOOKS   **NEW YORK CITY**

A LEISURE BOOK®

March 1996

Published by

Dorchester Publishing Co., Inc.
276 Fifth Avenue
New York, NY 10001

Dedicated to:

A young writer I'm very proud of, my daughter Deanna. And my husband Lynn and son Brandon, who are the warriors in the family. Without your love, support, sacrifices, and understanding, my dream of becoming a writer would not have come true.

Friends are the world's treasures. Thanks, Esther, Leslie, and Cindy, for all the wonderful get-togethers—yesterday, today, and tomorrow.

A special from-the-bottom-of-my-heart thank-you to Carole Davis, teacher and listener extraordinaire, for her many words of encouragement. Without you, the Wednesday Writers' Society would not exist. And to the members of the WWS past and present, I deeply appreciate your time and invaluable input along with the humor that makes each Wednesday a bright spot in my week.

The Golden Eagle

The Golden Eagle,
perched high on a mountain,
lonely, barren, forsaken.

Néeding a friend,
surrounded by vast emptiness,
miserable, afraid, dispirited.

Stretching great wings,
lifting high into the air,
searching, needing, calling.

Behind white clouds,
Wings grow still, his cries echo,
tired, dejected, grieving.

The wind answers,
gently lifting the falling bird,
comforting, protecting, guiding.

Soaring high above,
pillowed by wisps of white,
content, loved, fulfilled.

No longer alone,
the eagle and the wind,
companions, friends, lovers.

—Susan Edwards

Prologue

Late Summer 1810

The coyote's howl broke the predawn stillness that had startled Emily awake moments ago. Something was wrong. Terribly wrong. It was dark, the moon hidden behind a cover of gray clouds. Seeking warmth and reassurance, the terrified girl had turned to her companion.

But he was gone, leaving only a cold empty spot where she'd fallen asleep wrapped snugly in his arms. She rose to her knees and peered into the darkness.

Suddenly a small ray of light broke through the blanket of clouds and she spotted a familiar figure moving further into the gray shadows.

"*Wait!*" she cried. Jumping to her feet, heedless of the rocks and branches stabbing the bare soles, she stumbled after the departing warrior.

Emily grabbed his arm, dimly aware of the weapons slung across his shoulders and animal-skin pouches of personal items hanging from a throng around his waist.

11

His nostrils flared with emotion. Eyes as brown as earth refused to meet her questioning gaze.

She stepped close and found herself caught by strong muscular arms and held against his bronzed chest. She threw her arms around his neck and clung fiercely, her head burrowing under his chin.

Rough hands covered hers, forcing her arms down to her sides. Strong hands traveled up her bare arms and feathered over her shoulders to frame her small oval face.

Emily closed her eyes as his head lowered. His lips were firm and warm, yet she sensed his desperation as he gently led her back to the spot where they'd spent the night.

She found herself sitting on a fallen pine tree watching the warrior bend over to pick up a water pouch made from the stomach lining of a buffalo and a bulging parfleche filled with meat, berries and greens. He held them out to her.

Emily took the precious pouches that she'd refilled just yesterday and laid them in her lap, wondering why he was preparing to leave so early this day.

He held out a wooden object. Reaching for it, Emily twisted sideways on the decaying log to let beams of moonlight fall on his offering.

A thick piece of bark formed the top of the crudely carved box. Lifting it, she peered inside. Soft brown rabbit fur lined the interior. Curled on the silky fur lay a necklace.

Emily lifted it out and held it up. She gasped at the beauty of the rabbit claws, feathers and even a prized eagle claw strung on a leather thong. She was honored. But as she turned, her cry of pleasure died. She scanned the area but she was alone.

Looking at the gifts, one dangling from the tips of her fingers, the other resting on her palm, she knew she would not find him this time. He'd said good-bye.

Tears slid from her watery blue eyes, spiking long blond lashes as they pooled and flowed in rivulets down smooth ivory skin.

Her head moved slowly from side to side as she refused to believe her protector, friend and lover had disappeared behind nature's wall of greenery.

High overhead, the stillness was broken as birds chirped and fluttered, waking to greet the light of a new day.

Emily heard none of it. She sat perfectly still. This couldn't be happening! Hadn't she suffered already? Hadn't losing her family in that gruesome massacre been enough?

A rustling from the bushes behind Emily caused her to jump off the log, the precious water pouch falling to the ground, creating a puddle at her feet. Her heart raced. She clutched his gift to her chest. Rounding the large green bush, she scanned the area, sure that he'd come back.

Instead a doe, startled by her sudden presence, flicked her white tail and bounded into the concealing darkness of the woods.

Emily stood still, shoulders slumping in despair, unsure of what to do or where to go. Drawn to the pile of gathered leaves topped with furs, mostly rabbit, she fell to her knees.

The sharp sting of truth hit her: She had been abandoned. What had she done wrong? Had she displeased him? Why had he left? Panic overcame numbness and disbelief.

Fingers with ragged nails covered trembling lips in an effort to choke the screams that rose from deep within and clawed at the back of her throat for release.

"No!" Over and over she screamed, until her voice grew hoarse, refusing to believe that she was once again alone in a harsh untamed land.

Chapter One

Missouri Territory 1828

The bright golden sun sent gentle waves of warmth to the land below. Spring would soon be in full bloom. It ruled the land, slowly replacing winter's barren vegetation with the birth of tender green growth. Spring brought change and the renewal of life. It was nature's promise that life continued, even when it seemed lifeless and hopeless. Nothing could stop it. Not even death.

How symbolic of her life since Pa died, Sarah thought, staring from her loft wistfully. Her eye's shut out the early morning scene as a single tear escaped. Shuddering, she wondered if life would ever be fresh and sweet for her again.

"Oh, Pa, why?" Sarah sobbed, looking toward a small plot of land bearing three carved burial markers. Only the wind answered as a blast of frigid air swept into the room.

Sarah closed the shutters, resting her forehead against the rough wood and drew a deep breath. Tears wouldn't wash away her problems. And since her Pa's death four months ago, her problems had only grown.

Straightening her shoulders, she poured a small amount of water from a chipped pitcher into a wooden bowl and splashed her face. The shock of ice-cold water checked the flow of tears. Today's tears weren't for the death of a loved one. They were tears of self-pity and bitterness.

Unconsciously, she sought comfort and courage from the golden chain that was always around her neck, a last birthday gift from Pa on her 16th birthday. Her fingers found two glass beads, one on each side of the heart-shaped locket that had belonged to her ma.

Daydreams of the young warrior who had saved her life when she was but 12 beckoned, but Sarah resisted. Wishful thinking and daydreams would not help this time.

Peering cautiously from the loft, Sarah saw only Mary busy at the age-worn table kneading bread dough. With a great sigh of relief, she left the safety of the loft and descended into the warm cozy room.

Mary, dressed in a plaid shirt and men's breeches, turned at the slight sound, her gnarled hands stopping the rhythmic kneading. She gathered the yeast-smelling dough and put it above the old stove to rise. Turning, she wiped flour-covered hands on an apron tied around her plump waist.

Refreshing her cup of cooling coffee, Mary took the seat next to Sarah and cursed the fate that had left the child she loved as her own looking so pale and listless.

She'd give anything to see the sparkle back in those downcast eyes and the tilt of that determined chin. More than anything, she missed that mischievous grin. The one that usually meant trouble!

"Come now, Sarah," Mary said encouragingly, breaking off a hunk of hot bread and holding it out to the silent girl. "Have some bread. *He* left early this morning. Ben sent him to check traps. Won't be back till dark, I expect."

Staring blankly into space, Sarah dropped the bread that

15

her fingers were shredding into a pile of crumbs on the table. Her voice was taut with months of suppressed emotions as she buried her head in her hands and moaned.

"Oh, Mary, why did Pa do it? We don't need Willy here. He's caused nothing but trouble for all of us," she hoarsely whispered.

Mary slipped her arm around the thin hunched shoulders and fingered blond curls as she sought the words that would explain John's motives.

"There aren't many women out here, and I know your pa worried about the soldiers from the fort posing a threat to you. They respected and even feared John—Mountain Man John, as he was known to most. By making your guardian a member of his family, he was offering protection."

Sarah's head snapped up as she pushed her chair from the table and started pacing. "Protection! Mary, I have you and your husband Ben to protect me. You've been the only mother I've ever really known. You and Ben are my family, not some distant cousin I'd never even heard of before!" Sarah declared, her boot-clad feet pounding the wooden floorboards. Her voice turned harsh as she flung out a hand. "Ben can protect and provide for me a lot better than that weak lazy Willy."

Both were large imposing men, but Ben had the build and stamina that a trapper developed from a lifetime of living off the land, whereas Willy's body had turned soft from preying on what others provided.

"Thinking of me indeed." Sarah laughed bitterly. "I need Pa's horrible cousin Willy like I need . . . fire in a hayloft!"

Mary frowned and narrowed her eyes in displeasure, ready to defend her longtime friend. "Now you listen to me, Sarah. Your pa thought he was doing what was best for you. He rested easy in those last days after his long-lost cousin arrived unexpectedly."

What Mary didn't say was that she agreed with Sarah.

Willy was useless, and a meaner-looking man she'd yet to meet. There weren't many men out here willing to tangle with him, and she suspected that was one of the reasons John choose Willy as Sarah's guardian rather then Ben.

Mary stood before the angry girl. "Do you honestly think your pa would have made Willy your guardian if he'd known what kind of man he was?"

Sarah lowered her head in shame, but Mary continued. "Remember, Willy convinced your pa that, as a relative, he was the only choice for a guardian. He promised he'd look after you and would even choose a good husband for you. What was your pa to say?"

Sarah raised tear-filled eyes and threw her arms around the motherly woman's neck. "I'm sorry, Mary. I know Pa was trying to help make my life easier, but it hasn't worked out like that." Tears fell as she asked, "What am I going to do? I can't stand much more of this."

Mary gathered Sarah fiercely to her bosom for long moments before leading her back to the table. "We'll think of something. But for now you are going to please an old woman and eat."

That evening, in Sarah's own small cabin, the soft patter of rain dancing off the roof slowed, the spring shower nearly spent. She curled deep into a chair padded by thick fur scraps and covered with a patchwork of old material, as dusk gave way to inky darkness.

She rose to add more wood to the red-orange embers in the hearth. All was quiet except for the occasional hiss or crackle as the embers burst into flames to eagerly lick the newly added logs.

Returning to her chair, she pulled forth a small stool and rested her quilt-covered feet before her. The lantern bathed her in a gentle glow of light as the fire kept the cold at bay.

Sarah stared into the hypnotic dancing flames, drowsiness claiming her as eyelids slowly lowered.

Suddenly, the door to the tiny cabin flew open. With a

17

startled cry, Sarah bolted upright, her head snapping toward the open doorway.

A cold draft crept along the floor, sending shivers of dread down her spine as the door slammed shut. Eyes following the intruder, she watched the large man stumble across the room to stand before angry flickering flames that matched her wildly pounding heart.

"Well . . . lookee what we have here. Sure haven't seen much of you lately, cuz. Haven't been avoidin' me now, have you?" slurred a loud, caustic voice.

"What do you want, Willy?" Sarah asked, carefully keeping her tone indifferent.

Her freckle-covered nose wrinkled in distaste. The noxious, stale smell of alcohol came at her in waves, turning her stomach.

"What's a matter, sweets? Ain't I good 'nough for you?" Willy sneered, eyes narrowing as he studied his ward's cabin.

Embroidered curtains hid closed wooden shutters, brightening the dark room. Steam rose from a blackened pot hanging over the fire, and bread lay on the table ready for the morning meal.

Sarah sat in silence as her guardian paced the room, carelessly picking up objects and tossing them down. Her eyes watered as Willy picked up an old torn quilt made by her ma. It had been draped across bare wooden slats in an area under the loft where her pa had slept and died. That too was tossed to the floor.

"Say—sweetie. Sure is cold out tonight," Willy said.

Silence.

"Sure would be nice to share this here cozy place, seein' how's we's family n' all."

Sarah continued to ignore him, knowing how much he hated the silent treatment she reserved for him.

Out of the corner of her eye, she watched his jaw clench and his face redden as she held her tongue.

Willy cursed and turned to leave when it became evident he'd not receive an invitation to stay.

At the door, he stopped, one shaky hand delving into his coat pocket to pull out a flask of home-brew. Taking a hefty swig, he wiped his mouth on the sleeve of his grubby coat, then turned back to her abruptly.

"Think anymore 'bout wha' I asked ya last time?" Willy demanded.

Sarah shrugged, masking revulsion with aloofness. "What's to think over, Willy? I already told you I wouldn't marry you."

"Damn! Ya thinks yer real smart-like, don't ya?" he hissed, kicking the stool from beneath her feet as he returned to stand before her. "Think you's too good for yer poor cousin Willy. Well ya best think again," he warned as his big beefy hands landed on the arms of her chair.

Sarah leaned back, turning her head to the side to avoid being nose-to-nose with his pockmarked face and sour breath. A small cry escaped her as rough fingers yanked her chin around.

"Listen closely, dear cousin. I mean to have you," he uttered menacingly, inches away from her face. Willy's cold gray eyes narrowed to mere slits and he laughed without humor. "Whoever marries you get's John's share of tha' fur business and the money he stashed away for you. That person is gonna be me!"

Sarah watched his gaze lower to her chest, and shuddered as his tongue snaked out to lick coarse lips as if in anticipation of a treat. A wave of nausea swept through her, and she crossed her arms protectively in front of her.

She didn't dare give in to fear, and desperately grasped at anger instead to give her the courage needed to stand up to Willy.

"I won't marry you, Willy, and you can't make me either." Sarah breathed a sigh of relief as Willy straightened angrily and paced in front of her. Sarah met his rage-filled glare with a scornful look of her own.

Inwardly, she trembled. Willy had never been so bold before. Sarah rose abruptly, intending to flee to the loft, expecting he'd slam out in anger and leave her alone for the time being.

As soon as she placed her foot on the first rung of the ladder, Willy grabbed her arm, spun her about and shoved her hard against it.

"Oh, no, you don't. Yer not walkin' out on me this time." His eyes spewed hatred and venom as he tightened his hold on her arm.

"You thinks about this, missy. You'll be mine whether or not ya marries me. I'll have you one way or 'nother!"

Laughing, Willy narrowed lust-filled eyes and squinted at Sarah's terror-stricken face.

"Ya knows I can take what I want any time, dear girl. Would be wise for you to be nice to ol' Willy. Ya know, be friendly like." He took another swallow from the flask as he continued. "Yep. If you was a mite nicer ta me, maybe I would treat ya gentle like."

Sarah clenched her teeth against the pain from Willy's biting fingers. Her heart thudded in panic. Willy's eyes gleamed with lust, but it was his voice that frightened her most of all.

His shouting, tantrums and whining she'd learned to shut out, but now his flat monotone chilled her to the soul.

Sarah's eyes widened, and she gulped. "You can't—I won't—"

"I can. Ya will," Willy informed her, his eyes hard and menacing. He noted Sarah's rapid breathing. "I ain't takin' no for an answer, and don't look to them ol' folks to help you none. I haves it in me to gets rid of 'em if they turn innerferin'," he warned, tightening his grip. "This here's dangerous territory. Accidents happen out here."

"You wouldn't," Sarah gasped, shocked that he would threaten the lives of the two people she loved most.

Willy's lips curled in a self-satisfied sneer as he released her arm to take another gulp of the amber liquid.

"I would, girl. Believe I would. Of course, Ben does all the work round here. No way am I doin' all that back-breakin' work. Course, before I do away with him, I'd hafta find a way to make Ben tell me where John hid your money. He seems mighty fond of Mary and you, though, so it shouldn't be too difficult.''

Willy studied his ragged dirty nails and rubbed them on his shirtfront. "But if you marry me, the money will be mine, you'll be mine and nobody gets hurt. It's up to you."

"No!" she cried, closing her eyes against the fearful images. Sarah could only stare in frightened silence at the crazy man before her. Willy was dangerous, unbalanced, more so than any of them had thought. She had to get help. Slowly, she inched away.

A hand slammed beside her head, effectively blocking her escape. Sarah froze and swallowed her fear. Hands held palm up, she appealed to him. "Look, Willy, it's late. Why don't we discuss this in the morning? You've had too much to drink and I'm tired. Tomorrow we can settle this.''

Sarah was determined that starting tomorrow she would have Mary and Ben move into this cabin, or she'd move in with them. And she would keep Pa's rifle at her side at all times.

"I ain't drunk. Yet."

Sarah's eyes followed his, and she gulped when she saw the bulge growing under his breeches.

"We's gonna settle this tonight. One way or 'nother." Willy grinned, suddenly confident.

"What do ya think would happen if the soldiers and trappers found out you're a . . . half-breed?" he asked smugly.

Sarah's hands flew to her throat, her eyes widened and she shook her head. "How do you know about that?" she whispered hoarsely. "No one knows."

With the rising feuds between whites and Indians, she would be regarded as a "breed" or "squaw" by most. She would lose the respect her father had worked so hard to

21

secure for her, which was why it was a closely guarded secret. Who would think with her blond hair and blue eyes that one of her parents was an Indian?

The liquor began to loosen Willy's tongue even as it slurred his speech. "The good, trusting 'n loyal friends of John will all find out tha' he married a redskin's pregnant whore. Worse 'n that, they'll find out he's lived his life a lie, that they have the seed of a savage in their midst," he gloated.

Willy flung his hands out and shook his head in mock sympathy. "Why, with all tha raidin' 'n killin' and bad feeling's startin' to build, I just don't see how you're gonna be able to survive out here unless it's as someone's whore."

"But . . . How did you find out?" Sarah stammered. Only Ben and Mary knew of her heritage, and surely they of all people wouldn't have said anything to him.

Willy sneered triumphantly. "Dear John couldn't keep secrets from me, ya know. He and I were such 'buddies' as we was growing up." Shaking his head slowly back and forth, an evil glint deep in his eyes, he continued. "Some of them secrets came in mighty handy in those days."

He shifted his wild-eyed gaze back to Sarah. "Though I'll hafta hand it to him, he sure kept this secret for a long time."

Willy smiled a fiendishly toothy smile. "And like so many of his secrets, this one will be very useful to me, won't it, my sweet?" he said hatefully, running a calloused finger down her soft pale cheek.

"Why are you doing this to me? Why do you hate me so much?" Sarah cried out, flinching from his touch.

Chapter Two

Sarah lay on the hard cold floor, her bruised and aching body huddled in a tight ball. The fire had died to glowing embers long ago, but she'd been unable to summon the energy to move, except to reach for the quilt Willy had tossed to the floor earlier.

Her eyes closed, seeking the comfort of sleep, but it was no good. The reasons for Willy's hatred played over and over in her numbed mind. Though he was no longer in the room to torment her, his voice continued to echo in her mind.

"Emily should've been mine! She belonged to me!" Willy had shouted, grabbing handfuls of Sarah's flaxen hair.

His wild gaze had fallen on the pale strands clenched in his fist. His voice had softened, bloodshot eyes glazed as he reminisced. "She was an angel. My angel. Beautiful and pure. She belonged to me," he'd whispered.

Sarah shivered as she remembered how quickly his eyes had cleared and filled with fury and then how she'd found herself stumbling across the room as Willy paced before her.

"Emily loved a filthy redskin. Spent the summer livin' as his squaw. All this time, I'd thought John had gotten Emily in the family way."

Eyes bulging in a face turned purple with rage, he'd lurched toward the door. "I'll get my revenge on you, you good-fer-nothin' squaw. I'm leavin'. Gonna find me a preacher man. When I gets back ya marry me or . . ."

Sarah moaned and slid into the welcome arms of darkness.

The setting sun sent its flame-hued rays darting across the darkening sky, giving the rolling land below one last burst of color in glorious displays of pink, blue and yellow. The lone rider slowly brought his mount to a halt. Pride swelled within his chest as he surveyed the beauty of his people's land.

What could be more soothing to a weary soul than the beauty presented when the sun sank below the horizon to allow darkness its turn to rule?

Golden Eagle offered a prayer of thanks for the earth below him, the air he breathed and the food that nourished him. He filled his lungs with fresh air, and then horse and man moved as one, appreciating the quiet ending to a successful hunt.

Entering a sheltering belt of tall cottonwoods, Golden Eagle wound his way through thick furrowed trunks as cottony seeds drifted from greenish flowers hanging overhead.

Stopping along the edge of the winter camp, Golden Eagle paused and silently observed the activities of family and friends in his *tiyospaye* or clan. They were the largest of all the *Miniconjou* tribes, with over 20 conjugal families.

Dismounting by the stream where a small herd of ponies grazed peacefully, he turned his prized stallion over to the care of a young brave guarding the herd and heaved the results of his hunting trip over broad shoulders.

"Golden Eagle has returned," he announced formally, presenting the results of his hunt to his mother.

"It is good that the son of Chief Hawk Eyes returned. The spirits have kept watch on you this day, my son," Seeing Eyes replied formally as she accepted the rabbits and prairie chickens. She bent down to examine the fur and feathers that would be made into clothing, decorations and other necessities.

"You have provided well, my son. The tipi of Hawk Eyes will have fresh meat tonight. Golden Eagle is a great hunter," she declared, running her fingers through the soft rabbit fur.

Nodding his head in acknowledgment, Golden Eagle accepted her praise as his due. Kneeling, he selected a fine thick-furred rabbit and a fat prairie chicken and looked to the woman who had borne him. No words were necessary between them as he met his mother's nod of approval.

With valuable meat and fur dangling from each hand, he strode to the tipi of an old widowed woman whose husband had been his great-uncle.

Chief Hawk Eyes watched the exchange between mother and son, and then came to stand behind his wife. His strong fingers closed over her hunched shoulders, massaging joints he knew would be tired and aching. Her moans of pleasure told him that, as always, she'd worked hard this day.

Together they watched their son present the gift of food to Morning Grass. He smiled when he noticed tears of pride gathering in his wife's earth-brown eyes.

Seeing Eyes leaned against her husband's warm solid chest, her eyes moving upward to the loving face of her husband. "Our son is kind, caring and sensitive to the needs of others around him."

Hawk Eyes returned his wife's loving gaze. "Golden Eagle has grown into a fine warrior, wife. He will make a good leader when his time comes. He will provide well for his family and tribe," Hawk Eyes stated as he too observed his son taking time at the end of a tiring day to talk to a lonely old woman.

"Wild-Flower will be well provided for with our son as her mate," he added, nodding his head in satisfaction.

Hawk Eyes felt his wife stiffen at the mention of their son's future wife. He stepped around her, his fingers cupping her face, lifting her gaze to his.

"Our son will be happy, wife. The joining of the two tribes is meant to be. I know this to be true. I could choose no better woman to become our daughter than Wild-Flower. He will grow to love her in time."

His eyes narrowed when his wife looked away, unable to face him with her doubts. For the first time since his pledge to merge the two tribes, Hawk Eyes allowed himself to consider that perhaps he was doing an injustice to his son. Golden Eagle was not happy and his restlessness was becoming more apparent each day.

Closing amber eyes, Hawk Eyes silently contemplated this indecision he felt. Surely the last five years of peace and the peace of the future were important matters to consider. As future chief, Golden Eagle would have a strong ally in Chief White Cloud. Also, White Cloud's allies would become theirs as well. Wasn't all this to help his son when the time came for him to guide their people and keep them safe?

The two tribes had been at war for many years. Long ago a marriage pledge between Hawk Eyes' mother and White Cloud's father had been agreed upon to strengthen and give new blood to the tribes. But before the ceremony could take place, White Cloud's father had fled with a white missionary woman he'd captured, one with yellow hair and blue eyes.

His mother's relatives had finally wreaked their revenge by slaying the warrior and his white wife when they returned several years later, but had not known about their young son, who'd shown no signs of the white blood in his veins. Since then there had been countless raids and warring between the two tribes.

The tribes recognized the need to right the wrongs of the past. The two families must be united by marriage as they should have been in the past. Therefore, it had been decided that the eldest son of Hawk Eyes would take as wife the eldest daughter of White Cloud.

Surely his son would find happiness with Wild-Flower. After all, he reasoned to himself, she was strong and healthy and would bear him many strong sons and daughters. She was well mannered and intelligent.

Yes, she would be good for his son's tipi and tribe. Love would come as it had to him and Seeing Eyes. Golden Eagle should be proud to mate with her, he finally decided. All would work out. It had to. To back out now would most certainly mean war again.

"It will be so," he insisted with depth and authority.

Looking into the glowing amber eyes that gave her husband his well-known name, taking in the fiercely proud angle of his head and stern lips, Seeing Eyes closed her eyes, as though to hide her thoughts.

Hawk Eyes embraced his wife, his arms slipping around her plump middle. Fingering long braids that still held the color of night, Hawk Eyes leaned down to whisper in her ear, "Perhaps my wife would care for a walk along the river tonight?" He planted a gentle kiss on the side of her neck and moved his hips against her in a manner that left no doubt as to his needs.

Seeing Eyes turned in Hawk Eyes' embrace, looped her arms around his neck and looked over her shoulder at her son one last time before turning to her husband's gaze.

Her eyes darkened with desire as she looked into smoldering hooded eyes. She cupped her husband's strong chin in her small work-roughened hands, and her fingers gently traced his firm lips as she replied slyly, "Must one wait for a walk after dark, my most desirable husband?"

Hawk Eyes groaned as the tip of her small pink tongue

flicked out to moisten her full lower lip. Mesmerized, he bent down to catch it between his teeth, and felt her move into the welcoming cradle of his hips. "Ah, how I love you, my most desirable wife. I think I cannot wait a moment longer."

Golden Eagle shook his head, his lips twitching with amused tolerance as he watched his parents disappear into their tipi, the flap lowering behind them.

Out of the corner of his eye, he saw a small figure running toward the tipi, long braids flying behind. Turning, he ran to intercept his young sister. The evening meal would once again be late.

The sky had darkened and stars glittered overhead by the time Golden Eagle sat in his parents' tipi eating a meal of hot rabbit stew and dried berry bread. He found his mind wandering as his father talked of the events of the day and the council's decision to begin preparations for the move to the protective and cool hills.

Once again he was assailed by a growing restlessness from within. Something was missing from his life and, try as he might to ignore it, it wouldn't go away. He found himself wandering further and further from the camp in search of answers that eluded him.

Alert to the sudden silence, he froze, his hand midway to his mouth. He glanced up to find his father frowning.

Hawk Eyes choose to ignore his son's rude behavior and delivered his last piece of news.

"We've had word from the village of Chief White Cloud. They have left their winter camp. Wild-Flower is fourteen winters and is now ready for marriage. The ceremony will take place after the *Ca pa-sapa-wi,* the-moon-when-cherries-are-ripe."

Golden Eagle forced the food in his mouth down his constricted throat. His lungs contracted painfully as he tried to breathe. He was cornered. Trapped. Time had run out. There was no place to run or hide. Duty to his people weighed heavily on his shoulders as he rose to his feet to give his father the expected reply.

"As my father and chief wishes. Golden Eagle will fulfill the agreement of Chief Hawk Eyes and Chief White Cloud. Golden Eagle will bring honor to the tribe of Hawk Eyes and take Wild-Flower to his tipi and bring peace to the tribes," he announced before fleeing into the night.

The moon had risen high into the star-studded sky as Golden Eagle silently entered the tipi that was a gift from his mother. He'd known this day was coming. He'd just wished it hadn't been so soon.

He lay down, hands beneath his head, eyes staring at the twinkling of stars through the smoke hole. Shifting on his mat of thick warm furs, he tried in vain to banish the anger and resentment in his heart.

It ate at him, always there just below the surface, rising occasionally like tonight. And again, he'd had to calm it, bury it, for the sake of his people.

He reminded himself that as future chief, he was expected to fulfill many duties. Some would require personal sacrifice.

He recalled the words his father had spoken after the councils from both tribes had agreed that the joining of the two families was the only way to bring peace.

"I fear for the future of our people, my son. The numbers of whites coming to this land rise each year. There are many who say they will take our land and force us out or destroy us. Already the white man is pushing us further into the hills.

"They take from the land. They kill the buffalo, take the furs and leave life sustaining flesh to rot. The whites do not give to *Maka,* the earth, in return. Our people must stay strong. We must band together if we are to survive. We must unite as one to keep what is ours to pass to our children and to their children, as it was passed down by our fathers, given into their care by *Wakan Tanka,* the Great Spirit."

Golden Eagle once again acknowledged his father's great wisdom. There was no other way for the much needed peace between his tribe and the *Hunkpapa* tribe, both belonging to the *Teton* branch of the great Sioux Nation.

Time was against his people. Wild-Flower had been 9 winters and he 16 when the marriage arrangements had been finalized. Five long winters had passed.

Golden Eagle closed his eyes. What had to be done would be done. Time and hope had run out.

Eyes of the bluest sky, hair as pale as the moon overhead came unbidden to his mind. Sitting, he reached for his medicine pouch. With deft fingers he untied the leather thong and held a lock of pale hair. Fingering the silky softness, he wondered what had become of the young white girl he'd saved from the bite of death while wandering the land.

The summer he'd been sent away to search his soul had taken him to a meadow where warm gentle breezes had flowed.

Council members from both tribes had agreed on the joining. All but him. According to their ways, all members had to be in agreement. Peace between their tribes had fallen on his rebellious shoulders.

The beauty and serenity had drawn his troubled soul, and it was there that he'd found peace and come to terms with what must be done for the survival of his people.

He'd just turned his horse into the concealing shadows of the woods, ready to return to his people, when he'd heard laughter.

With a flurry of movement and wild laughter, a horse and rider had burst into the meadow as one. Alert, bow and arrow at ready, he had dismounted and watched the white girl.

Fascinated, he'd watched as she yanked off her hat and tossed it in the air with a wild whoop of joy. Released from confinement, an abundance of long, silky strands of hair had fallen to swing below small narrow shoulders.

Golden Eagle still remembered his fascination with the pale sun-yellow hair. Hair that shimmered and sparkled with a life of its own in the sunlight as the young girl twirled in circles on the grassy ground. She'd laughed with such carefree abandon that he hadn't been able to stop the indulgent smile at her uninhibited display of joy.

He'd judged her to be around 12 winters, just on the verge of entering womanhood, but still a child in her ways.

Recently, his thoughts had turned to the white girl. She would be a woman now. Was she married? Did she have a brood of little ones? No! He would stop this pointless torture. It did not matter. It would not make any difference to his future.

Putting his treasured lock away, he lay down. As he drifted off, he relived the horror he'd felt when her pony had reared in fright, throwing the child to the ground. He again saw the coiled snake ready to strike before he'd pinned it to the earth with a single arrow. He remembered the child's complete trust in him as he'd helped her to her home.

Bright blue eyes whirled against a golden hazy background as sleep claimed him.

Chapter Three

Willy clenched his fist against the pain. His gut burned, not only from the raw liquor, but with rage toward those who had destroyed his most treasured memory. He burned with the need for revenge. It ate at him from the inside out.

He leaned his head against the tree and closed his eyes against pain and unwelcome memories. All the injustices he'd suffered, every bit of bad luck that'd come his way, he blamed on his cousin John.

All his life, John had been the favorite of the two orphaned cousins, had always managed to be first and always got the best. All *he* ever got was second best. Everyone chose John over him, including Emily.

It was John who'd found Emily alone, hysterical, in a wooded area near the cabin. The old man had welcomed her into the family as she had none of her own. Willy thought back and recalled the small gifts he'd given her, boasting that he would marry her someday.

He remembered when he and their French grandfather had taken a load of furs to one of the trading posts along the Missouri River, John remaining behind with Emily.

When they'd returned, John and Emily were gone. Nine months later, they'd returned from Lac Supérieur with three-month-old Sarah and a marriage certificate.

Angry and hurt that John had once again beaten him to the prize, he'd fled. Later Willy discovered that the old man had known all along of their plans, had even helped John and Emily make their escape.

And now John was dead, and he, Willy, was Sarah's guardian. At first, he'd wanted Sarah because she reminded him of Emily. But now, the girl was an unpleasant reminder of her mother's betrayal. Willy had not known the truth until John's dying confession: He'd married Emily to protect her reputation.

For months Willy hid his hatred of her, his hatred of what she was. Besides, he was greedy. He not only wanted the money that would go to Sarah's husband, but also his share of the money he and Ben had made trapping furs for the American Fur Company.

But he was Sarah's guardian in name only. Ben protected her fiercely, Mary guarded her and Sarah gave him no respect. They treated him like he was dirt beneath their feet, even refusing to let him share her cabin until they could add room for all of them.

That really infuriated him. He was no animal to be stabled. After John died he'd thought the cabin would become his. But no. It was hers. It wouldn't be proper for him to stay with her alone, those nosy folks kept telling him.

"Hell," he cursed beneath his breath. Since when had he ever given thought to what was proper!

"Damn!" he muttered, shaking his head back and forth wearily. He'd figured the girl would be easy to manipulate.

Raucous laughter drew his attention to the dying campfire. "Tenderfoots! Fools! Think to make it rich," he sneered under his breath, watching the three men unrolling their bedrolls. He'd run into the brothers a week ago, and been persuaded to ride with them. They were eager for his experience, especially Tom, the youngest, who hung on to his every word.

Willy listened with half an ear as they griped among themselves.

"Hey, Willy. Where's them women you tol' us about? Sure could use one to warm me bed!" Jack yelled out, his brothers chuckling and joining in.

"Yeah, where's them virgins you was braggin' bout."

Willy pulled his knife from his boot. It glittered in the firelight as he stroked it. Silence descended. "I tol' you, keep yer voices down, you fools. Sound carries. Ya wants to get us all killed?"

His body stirred, reminding him of how long it'd been since he'd had a woman. Just remembering the fear on Sarah's face was enough to make him hard.

A thin line of blood beaded on his finger from the razor-sharp edge. She'd pay. They'd all pay.

The move to higher ground was under way. The tribe would go to *Sapa*, the Black Hills. There they would find plenty of wood for tipis, water from the melting snow and an abundance of game to tide them over until the buffalo were fat and ready for the kill.

The hills also afforded them protection against soldiers until they could meet up with others of their tribe and nation during the summer hunting and ceremonies. During the summer festivities their combined numbers were such that no enemy would think to attack.

Following the many small rivers and streams across the rolling prairie, they traveled for several days, stopping only when darkness fell.

Golden Eagle rode back to join his father. "There is a good place to stop ahead. There are no thick stands of trees for our enemies to hide behind, and there is plenty of water for our people and animals. It is a good place to let our elders and young rest." They preferred to camp out in the open, having a healthy fear of ambushes.

Hawk Eyes stopped, turned and signaled for all to halt. "We stop to rest. When *Wi* has risen over *Hanwi* three times, we will continue our journey to the Black Hills." His voice rang out, loud and authoritative.

Cheers rang out. The three-day rest was welcomed by all. Guards were posted and a small group of warriors left to hunt for fresh meat. Many young boys tagged along to search for prairie chickens, antelope and rabbits.

Amid much laughter and jesting, the women quickly and efficiently set their tipis up along the river and, finding a secluded spot downstream, took time to scrub the dust of travel from their clothing. Shrieks of laughter abounded as young children kicked and splashed as they were scrubbed clean. None seemed to mind the cold of the snow-fed stream.

Clean and refreshed, mothers and daughters went about their chores of gathering wood, water, fresh greens and roots for the evening meal. All prayed for fresh meat to add to their simmering stews.

The following days were relaxed ones. Occasional spring showers were welcome as women visited and gossiped while sewing. The older men told stories to eager children, and warriors took up the tedious task of weapon making.

During times when his tribe was on the move, Golden Eagle shared his family's tipi, not wanting to burden his mother with the chore of setting up and taking down two tipis.

He sat before the cook-fire in the tipi, peeling bark from smoke-cured saplings that would become shafts for his arrows. Suddenly he stopped and sniffed the air. The smell of roasting meat brought on hunger pangs.

His eyes fell to the browning skewers in front of him, and he was tempted to help himself.

A voice from outside the tipi stopped him. Golden Eagle rose and stooped to leave the tipi.

Stands Tall was outside. His name fit him perfectly. "The daughters of Stands Tall and Singing Sun have not

35

returned," he gravely announced, lines of worry creasing his high forehead. "They went with the other women to gather food. The others have returned."

Golden Eagle went into immediate action. He gave the cry of alarm, gathered his weapons and went to the group of quiet women and girls.

"Bright Blossom," he said. "Where did you last see Two Moons and her sister?"

Bright Blossom's eyes remained downcast in respect as she pointed. "They went to look for *Wanahcha*."

Golden Eagle frowned. He was familiar with the purple prairie clover. He could not recall seeing any within the boundaries of their camp.

An all-knowing voice broke in. "Stupid girls. I told them they should not leave the camp without escort."

Golden Eagle turned and confronted a plump maiden. "As one of the older maidens, Night Star, you should have alerted one of us," he reprimanded her, surveying the group as he mentally picked out those who would go with him to search for Stands Tall's daughters.

Night Star flushed. She was long past the marriage age, and being referred to as an older maiden was an insult. Golden Eagle held up his hand, preventing her from saying anything further.

"Go back to your father's tipi. I have no time for your sharp tongue," he commanded, motioning the waiting warriors to follow him.

Searching diligently on foot, they spread out, going downriver where the girls were last seen. Around a bend, they found woven baskets, their contents of leaves, roots, bark and purplish flowers strewn across the carpet of green grass.

There the grim-faced warriors also found signs of the girls' struggles. It appeared they had been carried through a belt of thick shrubbery on the other side of the shallow stream. Crossing the stream, they followed the tracks of two men.

The trail of footprints led the anxious group further downriver to where two sets of tracks became four, and horse tracks replaced human ones.

Golden Eagle and Red Fox squatted to study the criss-crossing tracks. "These tracks carry our girls," Red Fox stated, pointing out two of the four sets of prints that made deeper impressions in the rain-softened earth, suggesting those horses carried two riders each.

"The horses are shod," Golden Eagle added, their eyes meeting. White men had been near.

"Let us return to the others and prepare to go after them. We will find and deal with those who take what does not belong to them. Come."

Golden Eagle led the swift return to report their findings to the council, and the decision was made to move to a new location that night. It was too risky to remain.

Tipis were quickly taken down, travois loaded and ready meals hastily eaten. The warriors would catch up. Golden Eagle was the chosen leader of the small band. His closest friend, Red Fox, was among the five bravest warriors who would accompany him.

Weapons were made ready, medicine pouches prepared and blessings given from their *Wicasa Wakan,* Holy Man. Prayers were sent to the Great Spirit to guide them and return the mighty warriors with the daughters of Stands Tall.

The moon hung suspended against a star-studded background lighting the way as the tireless warriors followed the trail of fleeing horses throughout the long night. They slowed only when clouds blocked the moon's glow.

It was late afternoon. One day had passed since the two girls had disappeared. They'd ridden long and hard, breaking only to rest and water their horses, when they came upon the girls.

Six battle-hardened warriors stood surveying the nauseating sight before them. Both girls had been raped, beaten and stabbed to death.

Off to one side lay the body of one white male, a crude knife protruding from his evil heart, his life blood drained from his body to soak into the earth beneath him.

Golden Eagle kneeled and removed the knife. It was the type of knife many of the women in his tribe used in their daily tasks. He carefully wiped it clean. He would present it to Stands Tall. His daughter had died honorably. The young girl had bravely fought for her life and managed to kill one of her attackers. But in the end, she'd been over-powered and killed along with her sister.

"Why do they do this?" Red Fox thundered.

Golden Eagle looked to the heavens, arms high over his head, seeking answers. "I do not understand the greedy whites. Our people go out of their way to keep to ourselves. Why do the whites seek our people out? Why do they take and kill? Do they not have enough that they must take from us?"

Taking deep breaths to calm the fury that threatened to choke him, he gave a bitter laugh, his face mirroring the murderous expression of the others. "And whites say *we* are savages!" He spat and turned away in disgust. His people prided themselves on dealing honestly and justly, both within their tribe and with their enemies.

Even death to an enemy was carefully thought out and planned. Chief Hawk Eyes would not allow senseless kill-ings within his tribe, and anyone who did not abide by this ruling found himself cast out.

Golden Eagle swore to avenge the deaths of the innocent girls who'd had their life so cruelly extinguished. Such wastefulness of life was unforgivable, and those found re-sponsible would pay with their lives.

He watched as Red Fox directed the loading of the life-less bodies onto two makeshift travois. Two warriors, each bearing a burden, not only physically but in their hearts, left to rejoin their people.

The remaining four warriors dragged the dead man's body to the water's edge and left it as warning to other whites who might harbor evil intentions. The message of the mutilated body was clear.

Following the remaining three sets of tracks, the warriors rode low, their eyes trained to spot bent grass, broken branches and overturned rocks.

They followed without rest until *Wi* lowered behind the horizon. Darkness made following difficult, but not impossible for the strong surefooted warriors. But both man and beast needed rest.

At nightfall, they made camp for a few hours, each lost in his own thoughts. Long before the first light streaked across the horizon, four unrelenting warriors were back on the trail they had followed steadily for a night and day. They rode in silence.

After hours of hard riding, the warriors stopped when the trail split. Two sets of tracks went east, while the third headed west. Sending two warriors to follow the single set, Golden Eagle took Red Fox with him to follow the remaining two.

They came upon the white men's camp at the top of a ridge in the late afternoon, disheartened to find it deserted.

A gleaming object drew Golden Eagle's attention. Stooping, he used a twig to pick up a round shiny object hidden beneath the rubble of a hastily eaten meal.

Holding up the round disc that hung from a torn chain, he noticed there was a large marking in its center.

Slipping the white man's belonging into a separate pouch, the two weary warriors continued. At the fall of evening they stopped to examine the freshness of the tracks. "We gain on the white dogs," Golden Eagle exclaimed to Red Fox. He pointed upwards to the round fullness of the glowing moon. "We use the light of *Hanwi* to guide us. Our enemy is ahead."

Sarah woke to the sound of restless snorts coming from the horses in the corral. ''Darn coyotes!'' she mumbled, grabbing her rifle. She crept across the room, careful not to wake Mary.

Since her last confrontation with Willy, Mary and Ben had insisted she stay with them until they could get her to Mary's family. Building the addition onto her cabin had come to a halt. That would no longer be enough to keep her safe.

Sarah opened the door and slipped out, her eyes scanning the area for the dark shadowy movement of wild dogs. Three nights running they'd been here spooking horses ready for travel.

She and Ben had caught, broke and trained the ponies. It had been her pa's dream to breed the finest horses, providing fresh mounts to soldiers and others coming west.

She'd planned to trade the ponies at the fort for a wagon and supplies for the journey to Lac Supérieur. There, they would trade the thick pelts of furs collected over the winter and spring for Sarah's safe passage back east to a cousin of Mary's.

Her brows rose in concern when she spotted a horse in the shadows outside her cabin. Ben must be back! He'd left yesterday, early in the morning, to check his traps one last time and bring them in. He wasn't due back until later today. The traps must've been empty, she thought to herself. It was the only reason he'd be back this soon. She heard noise coming from inside the cabin, and decided to see if everything was all right. He probably didn't want to disturb her or Mary in the middle of the night.

''Ben?'' Sarah quietly called, tiptoeing quietly across the porch to peer inside.

Chapter Four

A beam of moonlight slanted across the room and Sarah froze in fear. All hope of escape crumbled. A sinking sensation settled in the pit of her stomach as her hand tried to suppress the tight knot of terror.

Instead of Ben, Willy stood there, unaware of her presence as he grabbed tins of dried meat, sugar, coffee and other supplies from the shelves above the stove and stuffed them into saddlebags.

Footsteps crunched behind her. Startled, she dropped her rifle to the ground as she was shoved forward.

"Hey, Willy. Look what I found . . ."

Willy turned. "Shut yer trap, kid. You got them horses ready?" His glower of anger turned to one of anticipation as he grabbed Sarah by the arm and yanked her away from Tom.

Tom gulped. "Uhh, not yet. I saw her sneakin' round outside," Tom replied, his eyes never leaving Sarah's ashen face. "Is we gonna take and share her too? She sure is easy on the eyes," he said, reaching out to stroke her hair.

Willy slapped his hand away and replied tersely. "We ain't got time. Get them horses ready like I said. If you's gonna ride with me, you'll do what I tells you to do. Now get outta here."

Sarah watched the boy flee, and turned to face Willy. She gasped in horror. There was blood splattered all over Willy's clothing. She tried to break free.

"Now, don't rush off, cuz. I'm afraid we'll have to postpone our weddin' for a bit," Willy taunted, pulling her against his chest.

"Let go of me, Willy," Sarah screamed before his hand covered her mouth. She clawed, kicked and struck where she could with hands and feet. Her fist made contact with Willy's nose and curses filled the air.

"Why you . . ." His palm made contact with her cheek, spinning her around to fall over a chair onto the floor. Before she could recover, her arms were pinned above her head, Willy's massive body halting her struggles.

"Scream and bring them old folks in here and I'll kill 'em right now," he warned, eyes taking on a maniacal gleam.

"Oh, God, no. Don't hurt them," Sarah begged, the pain lancing through her head. If he knew Ben had gone . . .

She swallowed the bitter taste of fear. Once again she was on her own. She struggled to free her arms.

Willy's breaths came in hoarse gasps. "Too bad we can't take you with us. You'd just slow us down. But maybe there's time for a quick sample. Who knows, you may not be here much longer."

He made a grab for the neckline of her gown and yanked the worn material. His eyes widened. "Lookee what we gots here. I gots me another squaw, all fightin' and squirmin'. That's it. Fight me. I'll show you who's the boss, just like I showed them others. You're nothin' but a squaw. You'll see how good it feels to have a white man, a real man, stick it between your legs," he promised.

Sarah fought harder, his words making no sense. Rough

42

fingers ruthlessly pinched and pulled her tender flesh. Tears of helplessness and rage streamed down her cheeks as his head lowered. She would not give in to this. She had to keep fighting.

Just as his panting mouth drew near and she feared she'd be sick, she heard Willy's name called from the front door.

Tom dashed in and frantically grabbed Willy's arm. "What's takin' you so long. The horses are ready, just like you asked. There's no time now. They wasn't that far behind us when we was on the ridge. Gettin' b'tween her legs ain't worth dyin' for. If ya wants her bad 'nough, take her with us."

Shaking Tom's hand off, Willy replied impatiently, "Take them supplies and get 'em loaded. I'll be right out. I gots some good-byes to tend to. An' don't come back in here neither. This won't take long."

Tom stepped back, fear and uncertainty in his eyes. His gaze fell to bared flesh and he grinned, grabbing the bag of supplies as he ran out to do as he was told.

Sarah tore her hands free from Willy's grasp and pushed and shoved as she fought desperately for her freedom and her life.

Smiling wickedly, Willy laughed at her feeble attempts to shove his heavy bulk aside. He shifted slightly, reaching for the ties of his breeches.

Sarah took advantage of the small space that opened between them and with her right hand managed to pinch his fleshy belly, twisting with all her might. She rolled out from under him, scooting under the table as he twisted away in pain.

Jumping to her feet, clutching the ripped front of her night dress, she grabbed the long knife Mary had left on the stove.

Willy backed off with a deep sigh of regret and buttoned his pants over swollen flesh. His wild gaze narrowed as he backed toward the door. "I'll be back, girl," he panted. "We ain't finished. Don't think by stayin' with Ben and

Mary you'll be safe. It's only a matter of time before they're dead. Soon, it'll just be you and me.''

With that parting threat, he was gone. Sarah ran, bolted the door and fell into the nearest chair, the knife clutched tightly in her hand. She sat until her breathing slowed and the worst of her fright had fled.

When she felt it safe to do so, she recovered the rifle outside the door and ran to the loft, ripping the torn gown from her body as she went. Pouring cold water into a bowl, she washed, scrubbing until she felt clean of Willy's vile touch. Nothing could take away the dark bruises already marring her flesh.

Falling across the bed, head buried in her arms, she tried to think. She had to get away from here. And soon. He'd be back.

Her head lifted. How, she wondered, did Willy know she was planning to leave? Was he watching, lying in wait? She sat up, struck by a hideous thought. It would be so easy for him to kill Mary and Ben and take her away. Also, Ben would have all the money that was stashed away with him.

Sarah stood and dressed quickly. How long before Willy would come back? Would he hesitate to kill to get her and what he wanted? She remembered his blood-splattered clothing. He would not!

Sarah squared her shoulders. There was no way she would risk the lives of Ben and Mary. They would die before letting Willy harm her.

She had to go alone, had to leave tonight while Ben was gone and Mary asleep. Sarah gathered a few changes of clothing and other necessities for her trip to Fort Tecumseh.

Golden Eagle motioned Red Fox to halt and dismount. Leaving their horses hidden, they merged as one with the concealing darkness and followed the horse tracks to the white man's house of wood, Golden Eagle leading the way.

His heart raced as he neared the white man's log house.

The trail of the murdering whites had led him to the home of the white girl whose laughing blue eyes and pale hair haunted his dreams.

Alert to every sound and movement, he turned away from the dark silent cabin. Using the light of the moon, he and Red Fox cautiously skirted the house, following the fresh trail of tracks into a wood house for animals. Entering, they found the white men's horses, tired and near exhaustion. Crouching, they searched the dirt floor and spotted new tracks leaving the barn.

Golden Eagle swore under his breath. They were too late. Silent as shadows, the two warriors retraced their steps to where their trained horses waited, two silhouettes blending into the night.

Golden Eagle turned and stared at the homes the white man built. He refused to believe that those who lived within had anything to do with the brutal slaying of the girls from his tribe.

Squatting, Red Fox voiced his thoughts, while drawing his knife. "We attack. Burn white man's home. We kill all who come running."

Glancing into the vengeful painted face of his friend, Golden Eagle shook his head. "No, my friend. We wait for those who have done the wrong." Visions of the spirited child who might still live within came unbidden to his mind.

He knew Red Fox objected, could see it in his eyes, but he was the leader. His word was law.

"How are we to know who committed this crime against our people?" Red Fox demanded.

Pulling out the disk he'd found, Golden Eagle held it up for Red Fox to see and watched the moon's glow reflect off the object. The glimmer of an idea was forming in his mind. "We use this to identify the man."

Golden Eagle decided to take his friend into his confidence. None knew of his experience with the spirited white child.

"Many summers ago, I saved a white girl-child from the bite of death during my wanderings. But she injured her foot when her pony threw her." Golden Eagle paused, remembering how the girl-child had cuddled against him. "She showed no fear. She looked to me for help. I could not betray that trust. I returned her to her people. Before I left, she asked that I return to these trees in the dark of the night. She promised to leave a gift." He remembered waiting at a distance, watching and wondering if it was a trick of the whites.

"That night, the girl-child and her father left a colt beneath these very trees. The whites acted honorably then. I will remain and watch for them," Golden Eagle said, putting away the object. "They will identify the murderers for me."

Red Fox nodded thoughtfully. "The daughters of Stands Tall must be avenged or their spirits will not rest. But you are wise. We must wait for the ones guilty of the crime. We cannot kill those who have acted honorably toward our people." He turned and glanced at their horses.

"At last I know where you got such a fine beast. Great Star has fathered many strong sons and daughters. We will take one of their horses to present to Stands Tall."

Patting the back of his golden stallion, Golden Eagle was pleased that he had reason to remain. He nodded in agreement. "We must hurry. You must be far from here when it grows light."

They made their way back to the barn and quietly led out two horses, leaving the two exhausted mounts in their stalls.

A noise drew the attention of Red Fox. Silently, the warrior handed the lead rope to Golden Eagle and circled the barn.

There Red Fox found a small corral. He stood in the shadows and watched several ponies move restlessly as they caught his scent. "I will return someday to raid the whites of their horses,'' he vowed before rejoining his friend.

Golden Eagle and Red Fox erased all signs of their presence and agreed upon a place to meet when *Hunwi* had shown her face two times.

Golden Eagle settled on the hard cold ground after Red Fox faded into the night. The moon sat high above, the new dawn far off. His mind wandered, full of questions. Was she still here? Would she remember him? Did she still have spirit and braveness? Or would she now be afraid of him?

He compared the white girl to Wild-Flower. She had been full of spirit, the love of life shining in her eyes-of-the-sky. Brave and unafraid.

Golden Eagle grimaced. Wild-Flower was timid and shy. She never looked him in the eye, had never voiced her thoughts or initiated a conversation. He had to speak first, and maybe she would answer. When she did talk to him, her voice was never more than a weak whisper. He shuddered and let out a long sigh. How he wanted a wife of spirit, one who would enjoy life, one who would enjoy being the wife of a fine warrior.

A movement jerked him to full alertness. A door was slowly opening.

He crouched, muscles tensed, as a slight figure silently slipped out into the night and stealthily crept to the crude corral, nervously glancing over a cloak-covered shoulder.

From his concealed vantage point, Golden Eagle heard a whistle so soft that he wasn't sure he'd heard it. Immediately a black mare trotted over to be led out. His eyes narrowed. This unknown person intended to slip away unnoticed. The two white men had already left. Was this person also involved with the murders and now leaving to join them?

Excited that he might yet be led to the men he sought, Golden Eagle watched the slim figure in breeches, moccasins and a dark cloak lead the horse up a small hill.

He sensed something familiar about the quiet dark figure. He darted. Shadow to shadow. Tree to tree. His heart pounded fiercely making breathing difficult. Not sure what he would discover, Golden Eagle only knew that he had to follow his instincts.

On silent feet he approached from the left, dark eyes observing intently as he neared the small clearing.

Staying down low, Golden Eagle remained hidden at a respectful distance from the white man's burial ground. His eyes never left the boyish figure kneeling beside a wooden cross.

Golden Eagle's breath caught in mounting suspense as two small gloved hands lifted and removed the concealing hood.

Stunned, he stared as long silvery-white hair spilled into the moonlight. It gleamed and shone almost as if it were a beam of light sent from the moon shining brightly above.

It was her, dressed in the clothing of a white man! After all this time, he'd found the girl-child called Sarah again. Only now the child was a young woman, the same one who'd haunted his dreams for so long.

On her knees beside her father's grave Sarah allowed herself a moment of self-doubt. "Oh, Pa, I hope I'm doing right. I miss you so much. Why did you have to leave me? I need you, I need you so much right now."

Her voice breaking, Sarah clutched the heart-shaped locket hanging from her slender neck.

Staring into the inky darkness, Sarah hoped Mary would one day forgive her. She'd left a small white square of paper addressed to Mary on the table.

It was safer for Mary not to know where she was, at least for now. Thank goodness Willy's arrival had not awakened Mary.

Lifting her eyes toward the heavens, Sarah gazed at the full silvery moon through eyes misty with unshed tears. She gathered courage from the bright moonbeams as she slowly pushed herself to her feet.

Pausing beside her mother's grave, she caressed the time-worn cross. "Ma, I don't remember much about you, except the picnics in our meadow. Now I know why you sometimes cried there when you thought no one would see. As a little girl I never could figure out why such a beautiful place made you sad."

Sarah pulled at some grass choking the wildflowers that were beginning to bloom. "Pa told me that was where my father left you and where he found you. I'm going to try to find him, Ma," she promised.

Though her mother had learned to love John, she'd never forgotten her Indian lover. As she had many times since learning of her true father, Sarah wondered about the man who'd befriended her mother and fathered *her*. She thought of the painted box and necklace carefully packed in her bag.

She would hire a scout to find her father's tribe. Some of the trappers had good relations with tribes in the area. Many even wintered with them, trading knowledge of ways and language. Suddenly she needed the comfort of knowing that she had family somewhere. She would find him. Saying her silent good-byes, she squared her shoulders and left the small grave site.

Sarah mounted her coal black horse in one swift fluid movement, and headed toward her meadow for one last good-bye.

Arriving at the quiet wooded area, she slowly skirted the small clearing, a black void in the night. Much like my life these days, she thought wistfully. Would she ever be free to laugh and run with the carefree abandon of her childhood?

Saddened, she silently said her good-byes. She knew it would be a long time before she returned, if at all. All she would have were her memories, good memories.

Stopping near the spot where her Indian rescuer had once

stood proudly, Sarah halted Black Lady. Slowly, she glanced around, eyes searching the darkness surrounding her. A prickling sensation traveled down her spine, almost as though she were being watched. Almost as if he were here, in her meadow, watching her.

Shaking the odd feeling away, Sarah attributed it to the nerve-wracking events of the night and the resulting lack of sleep.

Deciding to follow the river, she pulled gently on the mare's reins and turned, again quelling the strange feeling that she was not alone.

Golden Eagle's excitement faded as he followed the unsuspecting girl, and his brows drew together as suspicions returned. What was wrong? What was she up to? He'd seen tears glistening on her face, had resisted the urge to offer comfort. But where was she going? And more importantly, why?

He pondered her direction. White soldiers had what they called a fort in the direction that lay ahead. He and several warriors had once scouted it to see what threat it posed.

Did she go to get white soldiers to protect the murdering whites? He closed his eyes briefly, thinking. Besides the fort, there were only small trading posts run by whites who spoke what they called ''French'' and some scattered villages of *Arikara* Indians, enemies to his people.

His features firmed with resolve. She must be headed for the fort, he decided. He must stop her. It was too risky for her to bring white soldiers back with her. His people were vulnerable while traveling on the open plains. Guiding his horse deeper into the surrounding trees to conceal his presence, he followed her fast pace. He had plenty of time to see if she met up with the whites.

The sun ruled high overhead, sending fingers of warmth to caress the land below, warming the gentle breeze that cradled bits of white fluff lazily traveling across the clear blue sky.

Sarah wiped her forehead, flapped open her cloak to let the breeze cool her heated flesh and wished she dared to remove the heavy cloak that hid her hair and womanly figure.

Stopping in the cool welcoming shade of the cottonwoods that lined the banks of the river, she slid from her mare. Raising slim arms high overhead, she stretched her cramped, tired muscles.

Strolling toward the flowing stream, she allowed Black Lady to drink her fill before kneeling to rest on the mossy bank. Scooping handfuls of fresh sweet water, Sarah drank thirstily from the snow-fed stream.

Splashing the revitalizing liquid on her face, she shivered as the icy coldness stung, bringing a rosy flush to her unnaturally pale cheeks, soothing the bruise starting to darken one side of her face.

Pushing her hood down to cool her face and neck, hair freed to the rays of the sun, she sat back on her heels, staring straight ahead. A frown marred the smoothness of her features as she contemplated her situation.

"Black Lady," Sarah said to her companion, "am I doing the right thing? Should I have stayed and fought Willy?" Black Lady snorted and moved downstream, searching for tender shoots of greenery.

The first feelings of misgivings assailed Sarah. Heading off on her own had seemed the only thing to do in the bleak, dark, despairing early hours. But now, in the light of the day, she felt overwhelmed at the vast wilderness she was crossing.

"I hope we make it to the trading post by nightfall, Lady." Actually, she thought, I hope we make it without getting lost.

She was relying on the memory of when she had gone with Ben and Mary for fresh supplies. But there were so many twists and splits along the rivers, she was no longer sure if she was headed in the right direction.

Rising gracefully to her feet, Sarah replaced the fur-lined hood of her cloak and turned to retrieve her mare, who had stopped a short distance away. "Time to go, Lady. We'll eat later," she called.

The horse nickered softly, flicked her tail high, pawed the ground and tossed her head as she stared at something beyond her mistress. "What is it, girl?" Sarah asked, whirling about.

Chapter Five

Her eyes widened and her mouth opened, letting forth a shrill scream that pierced the air sending birds, squirrels and other four-legged creatures scurrying for cover. Gloves fell forgotten in the water as her hands flew instinctively to her throat.

She was rooted to the spot, and terror as she'd never known kept Sarah's eyes glued to the silent figure watching her. No one had to tell her that this was no friendly Indian out roaming the land.

The paint and symbols on his body spoke of war, and the term "on the war path" was crystal clear. This fierce-looking warrior standing before her was at war with something or someone. She couldn't move, couldn't think, couldn't breathe.

She dare not make the slightest movement. Against her will, her wide frightened gaze was drawn to his. His eyes narrowed, hiding all thoughts from her. It made him seem all the more sinister, especially with his high cheekbones streaked with mustard-yellow paint and thick black lines.

She couldn't help but notice his proud stance, how he held his head erect with his shoulders thrown back, thrusting his bronze symbol-painted chest forward. Two long onyx-black braids fell over his shoulders, and his muscular legs were planted apart, ready to spring at the slightest movement on her part.

His bulging muscular arms lifted to rest lightly, aggressively on his narrow hips. Clothed only in a hide breechclout and fringed leggings, he looked to be the true savage of every horror story Sarah had heard told over campfires. Never had she been so frightened in her life.

The warrior made a move toward her, and Sarah threw a desperate glance over her shoulder to where her rifle lay tied behind her saddle. She'd never reach it before . . .

Whirling about, Sarah gathered the heavy folds of her cloak and ran for her life. The only chance she had was to cross the stream and escape into the wooded area that lay on the other side.

She eyed the distance—it seemed so far in her panicked state. If she could reach the sheltering trees, perhaps she could find a weapon to use, a heavy branch, rock, anything! Nearly losing her balance on the wet, slippery stones, Sarah stumbled across the shallow stream.

There were no sounds of pursuit behind her, but she felt his presence close behind as she desperately scrambled up the side of the steep rocky bank. In her haste, she tripped over the hem of her cloak and fell flat on the rocky ground.

Her breath coming in harsh gasps, chest burning, Sarah crawled, scrambling for firm ground. "Almost, almost," she breathed as she neared the top.

Suddenly, she felt herself slowly slipping backwards. "Nooo!" she screamed as strong hands wrapped tightly around her slim ankles halting her escape, dragging her down the slope.

She threw her arms out, seeking anything to grab onto. Her fist closed on rocks, and she flipped over to throw them at her captor. "Let go, you beast!" she shrieked, throwing rocks blindly and as fast as her fingers closed upon them as she continued to struggle to regain her freedom.

Loud curses filled the air as the Indian ducked his head, rocks tumbling harmlessly to land with a soft plunk in the stream. Before she could fire more rocks at her captor, her wrists were grabbed, squeezed till she released the small boulders in each one.

Sarah gasped. Sheer black fright swept through her as the harsh bronzed face loomed close to hers. It didn't seem fair. First Willy, now this savage.

Despite her efforts to free herself, Sarah found her hands pinned above her head while strong firm thighs held her legs immobile, preventing her small feet from inflicting any damage. Her struggles were brought to a grinding halt.

She closed her eyes, the lids squeezing tightly together to block the sight above her, tears of helpless frustration seeped from beneath her lashes. How could she have been so naive, so foolish? Her impulsiveness had landed her in trouble once again.

Golden Eagle allowed his eyes to feast on the silent fight-worn girl lying beneath him.

Her eyes, he'd noticed, were the same wild deep blue that haunted his dreams, and like butterflies wings, her feathery lashes quivered in the golden sunlight.

He ran the tip of his finger down the bridge of her slightly upturned nose, then caressed petal-soft cheeks with the backs of his fingers, tenderly removing a single teardrop.

Her lips trembled, but still, she refused to open her eyes to him. The tip of her tongue darted out to moisten her lower lip before she drew the soft flesh into her mouth and he sensed her terror.

Golden Eagle noted the changes from girl-child to woman. His gaze fell to her heaving chest, pale swells peeping from her torn shirt. He shifted, aware, uncomfortably so, of the firm, tensed muscles of her thighs quivering beneath him. His body trembled in response.

This was the woman who haunted his dreams each night. He returned his hungry gaze to her tear-streaked face. She was his. Their paths had once again crossed. Hadn't he been led to her not once, but twice?

He would not part with her this time. He would keep her, use her to cast off the spell she had woven over his mind and body long ago. Maybe then his restlessness would flee and he would be free of her strong magic.

Silent tears continued to roll past small shell-like ears, and Golden Eagle realized he could not take her just to use her.

Once, long ago, she'd trusted him. He could not betray that trust. Yes, he admitted to himself, he wanted her, but more than that, he wanted this woman to want him as much as he desired her.

Leaning forward, he fingered the softness of silky blond hair as it lay in disarray, glittering in the sun's bright rays. He reached into a small pouch tied to his breechclout and pulled out a matching lock of hair. Holding it between long brown fingers, speaking in *Lakota,* he commanded the white girl to look upon him.

Sarah broke out in a cold sweat as minutes went by and nothing happened. What was he waiting for? Was this some sort of game? Some sort of savage torture? Her nerves were stretched to their limit.

She flinched and bit her lip to keep from crying out when his fingers touched her. But instead of revulsion, her skin burned where his finger trailed a blazing path.

Startled, she opened her eyes when he spoke with command in his voice. Eyes wide with terror, she expected to see a knife or other weapon held poised over her. Instead, a lock of pale hair dangled above her face. It was the same shade as hers, but much shorter. It was familiar.

Memory of another lock, given in another time, flitted through her mind. Her eyes flew to the warrior's face. It couldn't be, could it?

Drawing her brows together, Sarah rapidly blinked the tears from her eyes so she could study the face above her. Could this fierce-looking warrior be the same one she had woven so many romantic dreams around?

Ever since her encounter with the young Indian, her fantasies had grown and centered upon that strong, proud warrior. Sometimes it seemed as if a part of him had remained with her.

Looking into ebony eyes, she finally recognized the glint of humor lurking deep within, the lips that twitched with amusement.

Golden Eagle released her hands and sat proudly, arms folded over his chest, as he chuckled and spoke in her tongue. "Holy snooks! We meet again, my pale-haired friend."

Sarah gasped. It was Golden Eagle. Her first words to him came flooding back, a memory sweet as the summer breeze. "Holy snooks, a real live Indian!" she'd exclaimed, excited to finally meet one.

She remembered the fine time she'd had explaining what her words meant after she'd recovered from the shock of hearing an Indian speaking in broken English.

Golden Eagle's humor vanished. "Once again you have been careless, Sarah. You have found yourself at my mercy once more. You did not heed the advice given to you long ago. Women should not travel alone. No longer are you a child who might be excused for impulsiveness. You are a woman. Now you will suffer the consequences."

Sarah frowned as she recalled the lecture he'd given her. Her eyes lowered in acknowledgment. He had proven to be right again. She started to relax now that the danger had passed.

Her lips compressed and she narrowed her eyes on Golden Eagle, his threat of suffering the consequences flying from her mind as her heart slowed its frantic pulsing.

No longer fearing for her life now that she knew who she was dealing with, Sarah felt her senses quickly returning. He nearly frightened me to death, she thought, and on purpose yet.

She glared, anger growing with his unrelenting grin, and she momentarily forgot the predicament she was in. "How could you, Golden Eagle?" she exploded. "Who do you think you are, scaring innocent women like that?"

Her harsh words had no effect on the amused warrior. If anything, his grin widened, and Sarah sensed he was holding back laughter in the face of her anger.

Narrowing her eyes, Sarah fought for control. Her voice cold, she stared directly into the warrior's dark eyes. "You've had your fun, Golden Eagle, now let me go. I have far to go before dark and must be on my way. You made your point." Flashing blue sparks clashed with smoldering black orbs as she attempted to rise.

Golden Eagle's humor vanished in the face of her angry accusations. His head shook slowly side to side and he caught her fisted hands.

"I can't let you go this time, little one. For many moons I have waited and prayed for our paths to cross again."

He laid a finger against her lips and continued. "Many dreams I have had. Many times I resisted the temptation to return to the white man's house of wood and carry you away. I have waited long for the Great Spirit to return you to me."

Sarah's eyes narrowed, but before she could sputter a protest, Golden Eagle boldly declared, "On this day the Great Spirit has granted my wishes. My reward for saving a child's life has been repaid by giving me the women she has become. You now belong to Golden Eagle. I will take you to my tipi."

Sarah couldn't believe what she was hearing. This couldn't be happening, not to her. In a minute, she'd wake up to Mary's wonderful cooking and find this to be no more than a horrible nightmare.

Seeing the set of Golden Eagles jaw, his dark piercing stare, the proud lift of his head, Sarah realized two things at once. This was no dream, and Golden Eagle actually believed he had the right to claim her.

"Did my father not repay you well, Golden Eagle? Has Golden Eagle become greedy with age?" she said.

Sarah hoped her accusations would cause him shame. She'd heard stories from Ben that Indians counted greed a great sin within their tribes, and the white man was considered to be full of greed.

Golden Eagle indignantly folded bronzed muscular arms across his massive chest before realizing what Sarah had done. He spoke in his tongue. "So, you are cunning as well as beautiful. I will show you Golden Eagle is more cunning."

Relaxing, Golden Eagle smiled as he switched back to her tongue. "Ah, but our custom says if a man saves the life of another, that life belongs to him. Golden Eagle did not wish to take a child from her home to serve as a slave. Sarah is not a child nor does she live in the white man's home. She left the house of wood this day. She is now alone, foolishly facing great danger. Golden Eagle will reclaim what was once his."

Sarah's eyes darkened, storms raging in their midnight blue depths as she retorted. "I can take care of myself! I don't need you, and I am not going anywhere with you."

She waited, struggling to forget that moments before his arrival, she'd had misgivings about being alone.

His voice grew deceptively quiet as he said, "You can take care of yourself, can you? The same way you took care of me before you knew who I was? And is this how you protect yourself from other Indians that roam and hunt in this area? Do I need to tell you what is done with white captives, especially white women?"

Golden Eagle paused as Sarah's face paled. Driving his point home, he relentlessly went on. "What about wild dogs at night? Have you ever seen a group of them circle and torment their prey before they kill? What about lonely trappers who roam the mountains, seeking the hides of many animals to trade and sell?''

Golden Eagle held up his hand to forestall her arguments. It was growing late. ''Our paths have crossed this day because two girls were murdered in my tribe. The ones I have followed led me to the house of Sarah.''

Pulling out the chain and silver disc, he held it up, letting the sun reflect off it. ''Does this belong to the father of Sarah? Does the father of Sarah run from those who pursue him?'' his voice coldly demanded.

Understanding dawned. Sarah shook her head in denial remembering Willy's blood-streaked clothing. ''No, Golden Eagle. That belongs to the cousin of my father. My father died during the winter. My father's cousin is now my guardian.''

She trembled in fear. Golden Eagle was all warrior now, humor replaced by chilling anger. Sarah tried once more to explain. ''I did not know what happened. Willy came home late last night, covered in blood. He took supplies and left. I speak the truth, Golden Eagle.''

''Is Sarah to join this Willy where he hides?'' Golden Eagle barked.

''No. I left my home because Willy is cruel, and I fear for my life.'' Unconsciously her hands moved protectively to her bruised chest. ''My father did not know of the evil living within his cousin before he died. Willy holds a grudge against my mother. He hates and resents me for something she did. He becomes meaner each day. I am no longer safe in my own home,'' Sarah finished bitterly, her fingers twisting in the torn front of her shirt, drawing comfort from the locket beneath her fingers.

Hearing truth and honesty in her words, Golden Eagle sighed in relief. He started to grasp her hand and pull her to her feet, but the gleam of something shiny around her neck caught his attention.

Sarah felt fingers brush against her throat as her necklace was pulled from its hiding place between her breasts.

Golden Eagle fingered the blue beads that flanked a heart-shaped locket. "So, Sarah carries her memories with her as well."

He gently tucked the locket back into the valley where it had rested. When his fingers skimmed across her bruised flesh, she let out an involuntary gasp.

Golden Eagle pushed the material aside. "You're hurt," he exclaimed.

Sarah closed her eyes in shame while attempting to cover herself, knowing he was seeing the result of Willy's abuse. "Please Golden Eagle. No. It was not you who . . ."

Her protest was to no avail. Her hands were removed firmly. Silence filled the air as Golden Eagle reached down to gently cup Sarah's chin and turn her to face him. As he did, the sun fell full on her face, part of which had been in shadow. His eyes darkened, black with rage, and he swore loudly when he saw the bruise forming on the side of her face. "Look at me, Sarah." He waited until she complied.

"Who did this to you? Who left marks on your body?" Closing her eyes in humiliation, Sarah could not answer. The emotional pain of her encounter with Willy was still too raw.

He stood above her, eyes glowing with murderous intent. She gulped. Never has she seen anyone look so . . . ready to kill.

"Don't move. Wait here," he commanded, whistling a shrill command to his horse. Suddenly Golden Eagle was gone, and with him, a comforting warmth.

Golden Eagle stood for a moment trying to control the rage coursing through his body. He would kill the evil dog for what he'd done to his woman. Swiftly, he pulled supplies from his parfleche.

Dipping a square piece of hide in the cool water, he returned to Sarah and knelt beside her. He kept his anger checked as he studied the ugly bruises and angry red grooves where nails had left their marks upon her flesh.

"I won't hurt you, little one. Trust me. These wounds must be cared for." His cloth-covered palm gently skimmed tender skin. A piece of cloth brushed against one rosy nipple, and he watched as it shriveled into a hard tight bud.

Sarah gasped. He swallowed hard, his hand stilling. Sarah refused to meet his gaze, and Golden Eagle took a deep breath and quickly finished the torturous job. Taking a small amount of salve, he quickly applied it and tied the torn ends of the cloth with a leather thong.

Taking her hands in his, he pulled Sarah to her feet and watched while she dusted herself off, picked up her fallen cloak, pulled it over her shoulders and looked everywhere but at him.

"As Sarah has no father or trustworthy male relative to look after her, Golden Eagle must believe our paths have crossed for this purpose. It is not right for a female, Indian or white," he declared, "to be alone without male protection." He put his supplies away to give his words time to sink in before turning to continue.

"The Great Spirit has spoken though these events. He led Golden Eagle to Sarah when she was a child in need of help. And once again, Golden Eagle finds Sarah in need of help. This is the way the Great Spirit has joined our paths. Is Golden Eagle not considered to be trustworthy to Sarah?"

"Of course I trust you, Golden Eagle, but . . ."

The warrior nodded. "That is good, because you will come to my village. I will keep you safe from this Willy. He will pay for his evil." Having spoken all that he intended to, he turned away.

Chapter Six

Sarah put her hand to her chest, surprised that the salve had indeed taken the pain away. Even more surprising, his touch had not repulsed her as Willy's had. She flushed, remembering her body's reaction to a simple accidental touch.

Golden Eagle too had been affected, though he'd tried to hide it, but not before she'd seen hungry desire flare in his eyes before he masked it.

She stared at his golden sunbaked back and broad shoulders, which tapered down, where a long piece of deerskin hung from his hips. Each step revealed teasing glimpses of bronzed skin pulled tightly over bunched muscle.

Her voice a soft whisper, she spoke, more to herself. "But who will keep me safe from you, Golden Eagle?"

Golden Eagle heard and retraced his steps. Stopping in front of the spirited girl, he fingered her softly glowing hair.

"I have promised you safety. I cannot promise more than that."

Gnawing at her lower lip, Sarah accepted that he would

not let her continue by herself. He was right, it was too dangerous.

Suddenly the truth hit her. He had been at her home, following her since she left. That explained the feeling of being watched at the meadow. .

Frowning, she worried for Mary and Ben's safety. Were there more warriors there? Would his tribe attack them for crimes committed by Willy?

Voicing her fears, she asked, "Are the warriors of your tribe going to attack my people for what Willy has done? Will you promise their safety if I go with you? They had nothing to do with what Willy did." Sarah knew she had no choice but to go, but she had to try and bargain for Mary and Ben.

Golden Eagle considered her words. "Red Fox, one of our great warriors, has asked that we bring many brave warriors back and burn the evil white man's home."

Tuning toward his horse as if it were already decided, Golden Eagle was without remorse for using her weakness to his advantage.

Sarah stood in shock, visions of her home and dear friends, dead or homeless, flashing through her mind.

A part of her recognized how she'd been cleverly trapped by her own words. But she would not be able to live with herself if anything happened to those she loved. She didn't believe he would allow such a thing, but she couldn't take the risk. She had to be sure.

Running after the sly warrior, Sarah reached out and grabbed his arm, forcing him to turn back to her. Quickly, she released his overly warm flesh.

"Golden Eagle is smart and cunning. I can't let my people be hurt by the actions of one evil white man. I do not believe you would harm my friends, but neither will I take the risk. Deal with Willy as your tribe sees fit, but let no harm come to the innocent. I will come with you if you promise no revenge to my people."

Golden Eagle stepped close to Sarah and cupped her chin

with firm fingers, forcing her to look at him. ''Come with me willingly, promise not to run off, and I promise in return not to harm your people or home. Stay until revenge is ours and the bargain is made.''

''I promise. But only because I have no choice,'' she said as she stared into Golden Eagle's uncompromising features.

Golden Eagle nodded. He lowered his head and his lips brushed against hers, his actions startling her. Before she could react, he had turned once again to lead the way to where the two horses waited.

Golden Eagle looked to the horizon. He knew Sarah would be followed when she was missed. His tracks would also be followed as he hadn't taken the time to hide them in case he lost sight of Sarah. His fingers drummed a silent rhythm on the back of his horse. He needed the fastest way to rejoin his friend.

''You will ride with me,'' he decided, knowing he could go faster without worrying about her. He took the reins from her hands.

Sarah spun around to face him, bringing to mind a wild spitting kitten. Hands on hips she glared at him, standing firm by her horse.

His hands also went to rest on narrow hips as they faced off.

''I will not. I ride my own horse.'' No answer. ''You expect me to just leave my horse here?'' she asked in disbelief. Still no answer, only the narrowing of dark eyes warning her not to push.

''The mare is mine. I raised her myself. I won't leave her. I won't . . .'' Her voice trailed off and she retreated from Golden Eagle's slow approach.

Back at the stream, he'd been excited by her show of spirit, realizing that this was the challenge he needed. Now, he wondered if she had too much spirit. Golden Eagle turned and brought his horse forward, mounting in one fluid motion.

"If she follows, you may keep her. Come. We go."

Sarah turned from his outstretched hand and removed the saddle from her mare, then the supplies and lastly, her bag of clothes.

Golden Eagle enjoyed her graceful movements, and when she stood in front of him, clutching her bag, he grabbed it and tossed it down. "Leave it. I will provide all that you need. You have no need for white man's clothing in my village." He was prepared for her reaction this time.

Glaring, Sarah didn't bother answering as she defiantly tore open her bag and took out one dress, concealing in it the box that had belonged to her mother, the only link she had with her past. Sneaking in a few other small items, she bundled them and stood, daring him to refuse her.

Hoping she would show proper respect in his village, Golden Eagle shook his head and gave in. Stretching his hand, he pulled her up behind him and urged the stallion forward.

Sarah placed her bundle on her lap between them and wrapped her arms around Golden Eagle's waist to keep from falling off when he spurred his horse into a wild gallop.

Her pale hair streamed behind her, whipping her face as she turned to whistle to her mare to follow.

Excitement shone in her eyes. It was the beginning of a new adventure. But would it be one that she'd regret?

Mary paced back and forth, the planks of the wooden porch creaking beneath her agitated steps. She stopped only to scan the horizon for approaching riders. Closing red-rimmed eyes, she prayed. "Oh, Lord, let my girl be found unharmed."

Tears tumbled down her leathery wrinkled skin. Mary reached into her pocket for her ever-present handkerchief, and Sarah's crumbled note fell to the porch.

"Foolish girl," she cried, dabbing at her eyes with the yellowed cloth.

When Mary woke that morning, Sarah was nowhere in sight. Thinking the girl had risen early and had left to start her chores, Mary took her time dressing before heading to the other cabin. She expected to see smoke rising from the chimney, smell the yeasty aroma of fresh bread and find Sarah warming herself with a cup of hot coffee.

But a cold cabin, no bread and no Sarah greeted her. It was then she saw the note on the table. Running out to the corral, she hadn't been surprised to find Black Lady gone. Just in case, though, she'd checked the barn, found the exhausted horses and realized four more were missing. Instinctly she quickly fed and cared for the two that remained.

Ben would be furious when he saw the state they were in. She looked up. The noon day sun blazed overhead. "Oh, Ben, please come home."

Making another trip around the cabins, Mary finally heard a group of men, laughing and singing boisterously. Her eyes searched for and fell on one as they came into view. A head taller, barrel-chested, he loomed over the others, his voice deep and booming. Her Ben was home.

"Ben, Ben." He looked up and the others grew silent as Mary ran toward them. Even from this distance he knew something was wrong. Dropping the reins of the pack mule, he ran to meet her.

"Mary. What's wrong?"

Mary fell into his outstretched arms. "She's gone, Ben. Our Sarah has run off," she sobbed.

Ben held Mary away from him, hands on her shoulders. "What are you talkin' about, Mary? What do you mean? Are you sure?" At his wife's insistent nod, Ben thought a moment.

"Wait, Mary. What about Black Lady? Maybe she just went for a picnic?"

"No Ben. She left this note. She took some of her belongings as well, and Ben, there are four other horses missing."

Ben handed Mary the note. "Read it, wife." Mary read how Sarah explained what had happened when Willy returned last night and her fear for their safety. Mary's voice broke. She wrung her hands and looked to her husband. "What do we do now, Ben?"

Ben looked to the others. He knew he could count on them to help. "Let's go. We'll drop off our stuff and spread out to search for clues to where she went."

He took Mary in his arms. "Make coffee, Mary, and see to the animals. We'll be back."

In the barn Ben found the horses left by Willy, and swore when he saw the condition of the two horses, two of their finest.

One of John's dreams, now Ben's and Sarah's, had been to raise horses and expand into a large prosperous ranch. Already they supplied horses to the nearby fort.

A rifle shot rang out. Ben raced toward the sound. "Jacob, what is it? What have you found?" He arrived beside the kneeling man to lean over to study the tracks. "Are they Sarah's?"

Slowly Jacob raised his head and met the older man's hopeful gaze. "Ben," he whispered, gulping back fear. "Her tracks are here. I followed them from the grave site. They're leading to that place where her and her pa use to picnic."

Grabbing Ben's arm, he pointed. "Look here. There are now two sets of tracks. Someone is following her. The horse's hooves are covered, probably with rawhide. See how faint they are?"

The two men glanced at one another. They knew Indians covered their horse's hooves with rawhide to protect their pony's hooves, silence the noise and hide their tracks.

Quickly they rounded up the others and left to follow, leaving Mary behind with her rifle to signal in case Sarah returned.

The sun was going down when the weary men returned. Ben took his wife gently in his arms and gave her the news.

He told her about the signs of struggle and the saddle, supplies and Sarah's small bundle of clothing they'd found.

All they could do was pray and hope they could find her. The best scout would be hired. Ben and two others were leaving in the morning to search for her. The others decided to stay in case of trouble. From Willy, or Indians. Maybe both.

Kneeling on the soft bank at the water's edge, refreshed by the cool, clear water, Sarah looked up toward the tall, dark hills that seemed to be their destination.

Soaring above, circling the shrouded cloud-covered peaks, golden brown eagles glided gracefully on the currents of air, lazily allowing the breeze to carry them across the stretch of pale blue sky.

With a weary sigh, Sarah stood and returned to their namesake. She was very grateful for the chance to stretch her stiff limbs and quench her thirst as they had been riding all day.

Slowing as she approached man and beast, Sarah stopped and watched with admiring eyes as Golden Eagle tended his horse. Leaning her tired body against a tall pine, she observed the gentle movement of his hands as they caressed the horse's sleek, smooth head.

Cocking her head to the side, Sarah caught the softly spoken words, foreign to her, but not to the horse. His voice was a gentle caress that enthralled both horse and girl. The words enveloped her, soothing her jangled nerves.

Sarah couldn't help the self-satisfied grin that momentarily spread across her worried features. The knowledge that he cared so deeply for the gift she and her father had left for him all those years ago touched her deeply. More so than was proper, she scolded herself, returning her attention to that gift—the magnificent stallion.

From the day of his birth, the golden colt with the white star on its forehead had been Sarah's favorite. On her 12th birthday, he'd been given to her by her pa. Hers to raise and train.

When she'd suggested leaving a horse for her rescuer as payment for saving her life and helping her back to the ranch, her father had agreed. He'd told her that he was very grateful to the unknown Indian for saving her life *and* returning her home.

He'd carried her into the dark barn, and had not argued with her wish to give the just-weaned colt to her savior. It matched the Indian's name, she'd declared when her father questioned her choice.

She felt no resentment giving Golden Eagle the colt. They suited each other. He had done a fine job raising and training him. She turned her attention to study her self-appointed protector.

Of medium height, Golden Eagle was nonetheless very powerful and intimidating. He was now wearing moccasins and breechclout, having discarded his leggings as the sun warmed the air, and his lean, muscular body was exposed for her wandering curious gaze. She swallowed hard. All that bronzed flesh was a bit overpowering.

He stood in a commanding stance, feet planted firmly on the rocky ground, sinewy legs bulging with finely honed muscles. Slowly, Sarah lifted her curious gaze upwards, quickly scanning his nearly bare buttocks before settling on his broad back.

Just thinking how her body reacted to the close contact of that warm male flesh caused heat to creep up her neck and flood her cheeks. Absorbing his male scent while her hands encircled his waist, she realized she'd never seen, let alone touched, such a virile male.

Golden Eagle felt her gaze on him, and shifted slightly so he could in turn appraise her. She was small and delicate in appearance. Her long blond hair and wide blue eyes gave her the illusion of being fragile. But he knew that was all it was. A more stubborn or willful woman he'd not met.

He grinned when her eyes lowered in embarrassment.

Golden Eagle was determined that she would soon do more than look. She was more potent than any woman he'd ever known.

He still felt her touch upon his body. Her softness, her curves pressed tightly against him, slender hands gripping him hesitantly and shyly around his midsection.

Striding toward her with catlike grace, he stopped only inches away and looked into flushed features. Softly, he said, "You have grown into a beautiful woman, Sarah. Why have you not joined with a white man?" he asked, curious. Girls in his tribe would be ashamed to reach her years without marrying.

Shrugging, Sarah looked down and drew circles in the dusty ground with the tip of her boot. "Don't meet many eligible males out here. Usually only old men or soldiers. Haven't found anyone I want to marry, I guess."

Secretly pleased by her reply and not sure it should matter, Golden Eagle said, "Are you ready? We have far to go yet."

Sarah nodded her head and headed for the horses, stopping to rub his horse's sleek neck. "You have raised him well," she said. "He has grown into a fine stallion." Next, she greeted Black Lady. "Are you captive too, Lady?" The stallion kept the mare close beside him.

Standing behind her, Golden Eagle watched as long silky hair brushed her small round bottom tightly encased in her men's breeches.

"He was a fine young colt," he said. "He is the envy of all in my tribe. His name is Great Star and he has fathered many fine sons and daughters. It was a fine gift that young Sarah gave."

Golden Eagle suddenly recalled the angry woman who had greeted Sarah's return that day. "I hope you did not suffer great anger from your outing that day?" he inquired.

Turning around, Sarah smiled. "No worse than I deserved. I was very foolish. Pa was extremely angry with

71

me. But he kept what happened that day our secret. Even Mary wasn't told the whole truth of that day. Smuggling the colt out to the trees and explaining its disappearance the next day was not an easy task. But Pa was very grateful to you.''

Watching her face light up, her eyes sparkle with remembered joy and mischief, Golden Eagle resisted the urge to take her in his arms and kiss those full soft lips. This spell she wove with just a smile was madness.

Turning abruptly, he commanded, ''Let's go.''

Chapter Seven

Night was falling as Golden Eagle slowly picked his way down a steep ridge, leading Black Lady. Great Star had gone ahead, as if he knew the way.

Sarah continued to murmur encouragement to her mare, who if given the choice would turn and flee. Even Great Star snorted his brand of comfort as he stopped and watched their progress.

Reaching bottom, Sarah sighed with relief and found a boulder to sit on, her legs weak and wobbly from the steep downhill descent. "Golden Eagle, wait. Can't we rest?" She was so tired. Golden Eagle had only made short stops for food and brief rest stops. She put her head on her knees and closed her eyes. The only sleep she'd gotten last night had been in Golden Eagle's arms, cradled against his chest to keep from falling off the horse.

Golden Eagle turned slightly. "Not here. We do not have far to go, little one." Groaning, Sarah pushed herself up and stumbled after Golden Eagle.

A short time later, Golden Eagle stopped. Sarah, head

down and concentrating on putting one foot before the other, careened into him.

Golden Eagle caught Sarah by the shoulders, steadying her. "Listen carefully. Remember that you are my captive and must obey me." He held his hand up forestalling her arguments when Sarah started to object.

"You belong to Golden Eagle." He pointed a finger to his chest to emphasize his words. "I have claimed you. Remember this. Keep your promise not to run off and you will keep your freedom, unlike most captives, who are kept in bonds. Do not wander from camp. If you disobey me in front of others, I will be forced to punish you to show my authority over you."

There was no doubt in Sarah's mind that he meant every word. All trace of humor had been replaced by proud arrogance. She swallowed her fear. Somehow, she'd not thought of herself as a captive. Yet that's exactly what she was.

She turned her head to hide her rebellion and dismay. "I would not be so foolish as to wander or run off when I haven't any idea where I am, nor will I cause you any embarrassment," she replied tightly.

Tossing her mane of silvery hair, Sarah met his eyes squarely as she acknowledged her position. Golden Eagle might have physical control over her, but no one controlled her mind or her will.

Golden Eagle understood her defiant look. He hoped he would not be forced to break the feisty spirit he so admired.

"Remember this, my wild one, respect is important to my people. I must have their respect as their future leader. They also distrust whites. You must learn your place or be put there. This I do not think you'd enjoy. In front of others, you will obey me and show proper respect. When we are alone, you may say what you please." Grinning, he added, "*I* have no doubt you will anyway."

With that, Golden Eagle turned, motioning her to keep silent as he listened. Sarah only heard sounds of approaching nightfall as he cupped his hands and gave the call of the great night bird.

Watching the alert body in front of her, Sarah wrapped her arms around her body, and shivered when she realized he was waiting for a signal in return. That meant there were others and she'd no longer be alone with him. Whether that was good or bad she didn't know. She only knew how hungry and tired she was . . . and scared.

Startled out of her musings as his arm grasped hers and pulled her forward, Sarah realized she had missed the return signal, so expertly blended into the night sounds around them. Squaring her slender shoulders, she was determined not to let them know her fear.

Moments later, she peered into the blackness ahead. She could barely make out the dark shadowy shapes of several horses.

Nervously, she watched as one lone figure detached itself from the shadow of a tree and strode forward to meet them. Listening to the two warriors greet one another, she searched for others and found none. Frowning in confusion, she counted at least three horses hobbled beneath the tree.

Feeling hostile eyes upon her, she looked at the fierce painted warrior before her. Swallowing hard, she met his dark brooding gaze before quickly looking away. Wishing she could understand their conversation, Sarah took another look at the horses. They seemed familiar somehow.

"We eat and rest here," Golden Eagle said, then led Great Star to the others, Black Lady following.

Golden Eagle joined Red Fox after seeing to the horses. Together they watched Sarah disappear into a clump of bushes. Golden Eagle saw the tensing of his friend. With a smile, he patted his friend on the back and headed toward the small fire. "Do not worry, my friend, she'll not go far."

Red Fox's raised black brows seemed to question the confidence Golden Eagle displayed toward his captive.

Unpacking food, sleeping mat and water skin, Golden Eagle related all that had happened since they'd parted.

As Red Fox listened, Sarah returned, and wandered over to the horses. He pointed and asked, "What does Golden Eagle plan for the white girl? She would bring you many fine offers. Do you plan to sell her?"

Standing, Golden Eagle met the calculating stare of Red Fox. Softly, a thread of steel running through his words, he warned, "She is not for sale, Red Fox. Not to you. Not to anyone." With that, he strode off to fetch Sarah for the meal.

Sarah's head turned as Golden Eagle approached. With firm steps she met him, hands on hips, and said loudly, "Two of those horses are mine. Has Golden Eagle taken to stealing?"

Golden Eagle grabbed her chin, eyes narrowed to slits. "The horses taken from you will be gifts to the family that lost their daughters at the hands of your guardian. Would you rather give your life for theirs? Would you rather I give you to replace the help those girls gave to their parents? A life of slavery that you would not survive?" He drew a deep breath, ignoring the guilt over the fear he instilled, knowing her life depended on how she was accepted by his people and how well she adapted to their ways.

"Nothing can replace Stands Tall's daughters or ease his pain, but good horses are of much value to our people. They help make our work easier and will help take Stands Tall and his wife's minds off their losses as they retrain them. Owning two fine-blooded horses will give the family pride. Be warned, Sarah. Watch your sharp tongue or you will be punished."

Sarah knew she deserved the tongue-lashing, and bent her head to stare at the ground. "I'm sorry, Golden Eagle. I was not thinking of others. I shouldn't have said anything. The horses will make such a small gift compared to their losses. Pa always said my tongue would get me into trouble. You have every right to be angry with me . . ." She stammered, her voice breaking off.

Cupping her face with both hands, Golden Eagle gently

raised her head and gazed into watery blue eyes. When he saw the hurt and confusion, as well as the emotional exhaustion that threatened to overtake the girl, his anger fled.

"The day has been long. Come. Sit and eat. We rest for a short time."

By the end of the third day of hard, grueling riding, the trio arrived at the base of the hills. Knowing Sarah had reached her limits, Golden Eagle stopped early for the night. Tomorrow they would reach his tribe. He knew where they would be even though they'd been separated many days.

After taking care of the horses, Red Fox left to hunt their evening meal while Golden Eagle led Sarah the short distance to water.

Sarah stood at the edge of the gentle flowing stream, the clear inviting water slowly turning inky as daylight faded.

Turning in frustration, Sarah sighed and tried one last time to reason with her newly appointed guardian. "Be reasonable, Golden Eagle. You can't expect me to bathe with you standing here. I gave you my word that I wouldn't leave. I won't go far or stay in too long. Please . . ."

Golden Eagle leaned his back against the rough bark of a large tree near the edge of the stream. He leisurely scratched his back and folded his arms across his dusty chest. "Do you wish to clean yourself or not? We don't have much time before Red Fox returns with our dinner."

Sarah turned her back on Golden Eagle and looked over her shoulder. Her chin lifted as she coldly said, "The least you could do is turn your back if you do not have the decency to leave." Her eyes dared him to refuse this small courtesy.

Golden Eagle turned his back on the suddenly shy white girl, shaking his head. Why the whites felt shame over their naked skin, he'd never understand. Only in the cold of winter did his people feel the need for much clothing to cover their bodies.

Hearing a quiet splash behind him, he turned, stretching his arms high above him before crossing his ankles and leaning back against the tree. His sharp eyes quickly spotted Sarah in the twilight.

He found himself mesmerized by the sight of her. Silvery hair turned to liquid gold as the strands flowed with the current of the water when she dipped her head back. The smooth softness of her throat lay exposed to the moon's kiss. His eyes were drawn to the pale flesh of her back, gleaming in the moonlight, shiny and sleek from the water.

Golden Eagle's hand lifted with the urge to reach out and stroke the soft silky flesh. He glanced down at his own dust-covered body, and grinned. He quickly shed his breechclout and moccasins and silently sank into dark cold, swirling liquid.

Washing dust, bits of leaves and twigs from her long hair, Sarah was careful to keep her back toward the bank. Closing her eyes, she savored the moment alone, knowing she'd not be able to remain much longer. Already her teeth were starting to chatter with cold.

She wouldn't put it past him to fetch her out if he thought she was taking too long. But the cold water felt so good to her worn and sore limbs. Every joint, muscle and bone in her body ached. She swore she'd never voluntarily mount another horse in her life.

Rising slightly after rinsing her hair, she straightened and opened her eyes.

A gasp of shocked outrage escaped when she saw Golden Eagle standing before her, eyes riveted on her bared breasts.

Cheeks flaming and her heart hammering against ribs, Sarah crossed her arms and sank into the concealing darkness below, the water lapping against her quivering chin.

Furious with herself for thinking she could trust him, Sarah clamped her chattering teeth together and turned without a word to flee to the safety of the bank and her waiting clothes.

She took no more than a step before she felt herself gently tugged back by strong fingers tangled in her flowing hair, a firm hand circling her slim waist, pulling her against his torso.

"Let me go, Golden Eagle," Sarah shouted, trying to twist away and hide her nakedness from his soft gaze.

Golden Eagle drew the embarrassed and furious girl against his chest, flesh to flesh, softness to hardness. He cupped her face and forced her to meet his passion-filled eyes.

"You are beautiful, Sarah. Do not be ashamed." Slowly and seductively, his gaze slid down to rest lingeringly on her parted lips. "I won't hurt you," he promised.

Sarah looked into his dark eyes filled with desire, and shivered, not from cold, as his head slowly lowered. Unsure of herself, she turned her head and unsuccessfully pushed against his warm, enveloping body.

"Please don't," she whispered, even as she felt herself melt against him.

Arms of steel held her prisoner, so male, so bracing, as one caressing hand settled in the small of her back. His breath fanned her cheeks as his lips hovered, as if not sure where to kiss her first.

Holding Sarah's moon-bathed body tenderly, Golden Eagle lightly kissed the tip of her nose, her eyes, the small cleft in her chin. Slowly, he nibbled, stroked and tasted.

Sarah's eyes closed, his warmth and nearness caused such trembling within that she wrapped her arms around his neck to keep from sinking into the dark depths swirling around the two of them.

Golden Eagle continued his gentle teasing. First he planted tiny feather-soft kisses on the corners of her trembling lips. Then his tongue stroked the shape of her upper lip before moving to explore the feel of the lower. As his lips played over her, Sarah felt an urgency deep inside her.

A sudden need to be close drew her closer into his warm safe embrace. She needed more, wanted more than this light teasing. Her lips parted with a moan and she gladly succumbed to the domination of his lips.

Golden Eagle heard Sarah's plea, and tipped her head back, his lips taking hers fully, his tongue stroking and probing as her lips parted in wonder.

Sarah clutched Golden Eagle tightly to her. Never had she dreamed a kiss, the simple meeting of lips, could be so arousing, so demanding. But what he was doing with his tongue made her giddy and close to fainting.

Frozen by the unexpected pleasure of his touch, Sarah allowed him to explore the inside of her mouth, savoring the feel of the roughness of his tongue twining with hers.

Lost in the sweet embrace, she forgot all else as Golden Eagle skimmed his fingers down her throat, leaving a downward trail of heated flesh before gently cupping and lifting one breast. Sarah sucked in her breath as he continued to caress and stroke, her flesh filling the palm of his hand.

She moaned as waves of pleasure surged through her, and her legs moved restlessly as her body began to vibrate with passion. The gentle flowing water lapped against her sensitive flesh, heightening an aching need that settled at the juncture of her thighs. Her head lolled back, opening a small distance between them.

As Golden Eagle's finger and thumb gently rolled one taut rosy bud, her back arched, hips thrusting forward to nestle in the cradle of his hips. The hand at the small of her back slid down to knead the flesh of her buttocks, pulling her against his pulsing flesh as they rocked together.

Her moans became his and his hers, blending as one. They gasped for air, each breath fast and shallow. Caresses became frantic and the cold long forgotten.

Sarah was sinking, drowning in a sea of unfamiliar sensations. The hard knot of tension in her belly grew, spreading warmth as desire flowed like molten lava.

Golden Eagle's hand seared a path down her abdomen, coming to rest against her quivering thighs. Sarah gave a startled gasp of surprise when she felt herself lifted to rest on top of Golden Eagle's hard maleness.

Her hips moved of their own accord, seeking release from the tormenting heat building between them. She moaned, her lips against his. "Please Golden Eagle," she begged, but not knowing for what.

Golden Eagle heard her plea and froze. His lips slowly pulled away.

Sarah's eyes opened slowly in confusion. Golden Eagle's groan of pain rumbled deep in his chest as his hand rose to caress her smooth cheek.

Softly, he murmured against her lips, lowering her reluctantly, "Your magic is powerful. You have cast a spell over this warrior. It is too bad we are not alone, or Golden Eagle would not be able to resist teaching you the ways of a man and woman." He spoke huskily, his voice thick with unfulfilled desire. "But when I teach you the art of loving, it will be when there is no fear of interruptions."

Sarah returned to reality with a jolt. His hands still cupped her buttocks. They still stood flesh to flesh. Man to woman. She, resting against his. . . .

With a horrified gasp, Sarah tore her hands from the strong column of his neck. Pushing with all her might, she freed herself with an anguished cry and stumbled for the bank.

Chapter Eight

Sarah sank to her knees, her emotions a jumble of desire and confusion. She welcomed the discomfort of the hard cold earth as she willed the feel of his hands upon her flesh from her mind.

She sought to calm the dizzying current racing through her veins as goose flesh rose on her body. Teeth chattering, Sarah hugged her clothes tightly to her damp body and groaned, mortified by her actions.

Unconsciously, her fingers traced her swollen well-kissed lips. Never in her wildest fantasies had she imagined the simple act of kissing to be a soul-shattering experience. And his tongue—her skin grew warm as she remembered the things he'd done with his tongue. She should have been disgusted, but it had felt so good, so right.

Sarah closed her eyes. Never had she felt so wild, so wanting, and been left so unfulfilled. Standing, she struggled into damp clothes, trying to convince herself that she hated Golden Eagle for taking advantage of her, that she'd received no pleasure in his lovemaking, that he'd merely taken her by surprise.

Sarah vowed to be on guard against his touch. She would keep her distance from now on.

How could she go back out there and face him? Knowing she must or he'd come for her, Sarah hesitantly stepped out of the concealing bushes.

Spotting him leaning against a tree, she felt her face flame as she recalled where his hands had been. God help her, she'd be better off if she had found his touch as repulsive as Willy's, but she couldn't deceive herself. She hadn't. And on top of it all, she found herself longing to feel his flesh against hers again.

Sarah slowed, waited, her eyes focused at some point over his shoulder, thankful that the semi-darkness hid her embarrassment.

Golden Eagle reached for her, but Sarah hastily stepped back to avoid his touch.

Focusing on anger, it being the easier emotion to deal with, she blurted out, "Don't touch me, Golden Eagle. You had no right to—to—"

Golden Eagle pulled Sarah to his damp chest, his finger lifting her shame-filled gaze to his.

"Come. You would tell me you did not enjoy it?" he mocked, one brow rising, daring her to deny what had flowed between them.

Raising his hand, Golden Eagle prevented Sarah's angry denial. "There will be no lies between us, Sarah." Dark eyes were pitted against blue. "We both know there is strong magic between us. That is why I carry a lock of your hair, and you carry beads that I once wore in mine."

Releasing her before Sarah could reply, Golden Eagle sniffed the air, a grin appearing that matched the sparkle of laughter deep in his eyes. "Come. Red Fox has our evening meal ready. Some hungers can be satisfied now. Others must wait."

Sarah gasped. To her dismay, she found he had indeed left her with an aching hunger, a hunger that had nothing to do with food. She spun out of his arms and hardened her heart, ruthlessly driving out all thought of what had passed between them. But in truth, she only wanted to be back in his arms and have him extinguish the smoldering fire he'd ignited.

Lost in dreams, Sarah snuggled deeper into the cocoon of warmth surrounding her as flashes of past carefree days flitted across her mind. Days when she'd had the freedom to run through meadows filled with wildflowers or lay on her back to dream as clouds floated by. Days when she rode Black Lady to her heart's content through tall grass, as she explored the land she loved.

She tried turning, and found she couldn't move. A frown marred her features, and she became aware of a heavy weight draped across her shoulders. She woke in a panic.

In seconds, she remembered she was on the hard floor of the forest. Slowly, she turned her head and discovered she was nestled against Golden Eagle. His arm was draped possessively across her shoulders, the warmth of his breath mingling with hers, his sleep-relaxed face only inches away.

Holding her breath, she tried to move from under his arm, but Golden Eagle shifted, his arm tightening.

Sarah stiffened, watched and waited. His breathing remained even and she sighed with relief. Not daring to move in case she woke him, she let her thoughts wander to the night before.

She'd never met anyone like Golden Eagle. He was hard, demanding and stubborn, but she'd also caught glimpses of the caring and sensitive warrior she'd once known.

Unlike Red Fox. She shuddered, thankful it was Golden Eagle who'd found her. Red Fox glared at her, hatred burning from his dark eyes whenever she chanced to glance his way.

When they had returned from the stream last night, Red Fox had had a warm fire glowing and fish cooking on long sticks. Golden Eagle had led her to the warmth of the fire and before he would let her eat, he'd combed and dried her hair.

Despite her protest that she could do it herself, he had gently untangled the long wet tresses and braided her hair into one long braid to hang down her back.

She'd been thankful that the darkness hid her flushed features as she'd been intensely aware of his bare thighs cradling her, his heat surrounding her.

Now, looking at his smooth strong chest, Sarah blushed as she unwillingly recalled his sleek naked body gliding against hers. Her body had reacted with a mind of its own, inviting his touch, begging for his caresses.

Her lips had welcomed his, slowly opening for his searching tongue. Only inexperience and an overwhelming shyness had prevented her from returning his bold advances.

Sarah's eyes moved to his lips just a breath away. Full. Soft and slightly parted in sleep. She itched to stroke the soft fullness. Her fingers rose, hovered. Dare she? He was asleep, it was still dark.

Soft as a butterfly's caress, her fingers fluttered along the length of his bottom lip finding it warm, soft and moist. His arm twitched, and she froze as Golden Eagle moved toward her, forcing her to her back as his arm fell across her chest. Sarah held her breath, a quick look confirming he was still asleep.

Now what? she thought, trying to ignore the touch of his arm lying across the top of her breasts. Her eyes closed as her breast swelled, nipples hardening in response to his warmth. She couldn't help remembering his large hands upon them, fondling, caressing and teasing. Nothing like Willy's rough mauling. No pain, only a sweet longing followed by a driving need for more.

Willing such thoughts from her mind, she concentrated

on calming her rapid breathing, reminding herself that she needed to keep her mind sharp, not let her guard down.

While a part of her did trust Golden Eagle, she did not trust Red Fox, and had no idea what to expect from others of their tribe.

And how could she convince Golden Eagle to release her? Last night had shown her there was more at stake than just finding the one who sired her. Sarah had the feeling that if she remained with Golden Eagle, she would lose a lot more than just her virtue.

The warm spicy scent of Golden Eagle became too much for her overwhelmed senses. Not caring if he woke, Sarah turned to slide out from under his arm and away from all that distracting maleness. She was therefore startled to find herself pulled on top of his chest, his arms holding her captive.

She stared into his smoldering eyes and saw amusement shining from within. The corners of his mouth were up-lifted, softening his harsh features in the gray light of morning.

Like a magnet, her fingers itched to explore what her eyes beheld.

Flushing, she wondered how long he'd been awake, watching her.

Golden Eagle spoke, his voice low and husky. "What thoughts go through your mind so early to bring the color of a new sun to your face?" he teased, trailing one long brown finger across her bruised cheek and over her parted lips.

Cursing his ability to read her mind so accurately, Sarah clamped her lips together and pushed away from him.

"That is none of your business, Golden Eagle!" she informed him as she jumped to her feet and stalked off.

Golden Eagle lifted himself to lean on one elbow as he watched Sarah shove through low-growing bushes. He laughed out loud and found himself looking forward to the new day. Lying back, hands under his head, he watched darkness slowly give way to the light of the new day, and realized the restlessness that had plagued him of late was gone. In its place was a burning need for the woman he'd helped as a child.

He ignored the guilt of his upcoming marriage. Somehow, he would find a way to keep Sarah with him always. For he truly believed she was a gift from the Great Spirit. That decided, he rose to his feet in one smooth lithe movement.

Deep in the *Paha Sapa*—Hills of the Shadow—another pair of eyes were directed toward the morning sky peeking through the top of the tipi. They were unaware of the streaks of pink that heralded the rising of the new sun. They saw only images flashing across her honey-brown eyes.

In her dream state, the woman saw her son standing tall and proud at the top of Great Gray Rock. His feet were planted firmly apart, his head held proudly as he surveyed the land below that would one day be his to guide. His hands came to rest arrogantly on lean hips.

The images continued to play out as arms wrapped themselves around her son's waist from behind. A head appeared and, standing on tiptoe, a young woman rested her small pointed chin on his sun-warmed shoulder. Eyes as blue as the sky above sparkled with happiness. The wind lifted her pale hair, sending silky strands toward the soft, fluffy clouds that hovered above the young carefree couple.

Turning, the mighty warrior pulled the laughing girl into the warm protective haven of his arms. Black eyes met blue. Hard firm lips met soft pink ones, before the girl turned and leaned against the golden warrior. There they stood, looking out across the wondrous view before them.

The woman watched an eagle far above in the clouds. She watched it glide on the cool gentle breeze as it called for its mate. Clouds swept by and swallowed the great golden bird, hiding it from the world below. Only its cries could be heard, carried by the strong wind.

What was it saying? the woman wondered. The wind carried the cry closer. It seemed as if the wind were whispering, trying to tell her something. A name perhaps. The name of the eagle's mate?

Frowning in concentration, Seeing Eyes woke. Sitting upright, she waited for her eyes to clear before quietly making her way to the closed flap of the tipi. Silently, she slipped out and headed though the trees and bushes that sheltered the sleeping village. She came to the gentle flowing stream and knelt. Reaching into the water, she splashed cold liquid onto her face, neck and arms.

Rising, she sat on a large flat rock, watched life stir around her to start a new day and reviewed her dream.

The Great Spirit had once again revealed the future to her through dreams. He had confirmed the mate for her son. A white woman with hair the color of the sun and eyes the blue of the sky. This was the girl the Great Spirit would send.

Closing her eyes, she searched her mind for other messages. Something was eluding her. What was it? She remembered the wind as it blew the girl's hair. Seeing Eyes sought to remember.

The wind. It seemed to whisper a name. Struggling to remember, Seeing Eyes finally gave up. It would come to her in time. It always did.

Understanding the difficulties that lay ahead and the pain for her son, she sent a prayer of thanks to the Great Spirit for revealing to her his wishes.

Unaware of her husband's approach, Seeing Eyes gave a start of surprise when Hawk Eyes came from behind, drawing her into his arms as he asked, ''Why does the wife of Hawk Eyes sit here alone instead of waking beside her husband? What troubles you, wife?''

Seeing Eyes didn't answer. How could she tell him what was to be? He would think her dream was because she opposed Wild-Flower as a daughter. No. She could not. It would do no good to tell her husband these things now. Better for him to accept on his own. The will of the Great Spirit would be done as always, regardless of one's wishes.

Receiving no response, Hawk Eyes gently turned Seeing Eyes to face him, lifting her chin with the tip of a calloused finger.

Staring deep into her eyes, Hawk Eyes recognized the distant look and drew her into his arms, waiting for her to speak.

"Dreams, my sharp-eyed Hawk. I have seen again. The Great Spirit has spoken to me." Falling silent, she glanced over her shoulder to see her husband's raised brows.

Seeing Eyes shook her head against the silent question. Reaching up, she cupped his strong chin. "Change, my husband, my chief."

Standing, Seeing Eyes waited for her husband. Chief Hawk Eyes rose. He knew from experience that this was all he would be told.

Hand in hand, Hawk Eyes led his helpmate back to the village, both absorbed in their own thoughts.

Chapter Nine

Huddled close to Golden Eagle, her cloak wrapped tightly around her, hood pulled low against the driving rain, Sarah swallowed a groan of pain. She was drenched to the skin, and painful raw patches made their presence known on her inner thighs as her soaked breeches clung tightly, rubbing against her tender flesh.

One arm remained wrapped tightly around Golden Eagle's slick waist as Sarah let go of the hood to impatiently wipe the moisture running down her face. As she shoved at the hair plastered to her cheeks, the wind blew the hood off her head. Again.

Resigned, she closed her eyes. I give up, she sighed. My hair is soaked. I'm tired. I need to change my clothes and I'm sick of traveling. And with each stride of the galloping horses she grew more apprehensive. Soon, they would arrive in Golden Eagle's village. Would his people be friendly? Or would they treat her as Red Fox did—with unconcealed hostility.

She noticed the rain had no effect on either warrior and

that neither one seemed concerned with her misery.

Mid-morning brought relief from the storm as it dwindled to a light drizzle, then faded completely as the trio arrived at the edge of Golden Eagle's village. All was quiet. Smoke rose from many tipis, and only children and dogs seemed to appreciate nature's shower.

Nervously, Sarah pulled her sodden cloak closer, hiding her wet and tangled hair beneath her hood. She shivered.

Golden Eagle and Red Fox dismounted, leaving Sarah to slide down on her own. Retrieving her bundle of meager possessions, Sarah stood quietly to one side.

Red Fox turned abruptly and glared at Sarah as he spoke to Golden Eagle in their tongue. Taking the rope leads of all five horses, he strode off.

Sarah watched Red Fox go with relief and wondered why he disliked her so. Did he blame her for what Willy had done?

Letting her gaze wander to the village before her, Sarah received her first surprise. Spread before her stood roughly 20 large tipis.

They were arranged in three circles, with the smaller circles inside and all doors facing east. The village had a neat, clean, organized appearance.

She hastily reformed her impressions that Indians were dirty, unkempt and disorganized. She saw no such evidence here. Tantalizing smells mingled with wood smoke, children ran about in what nature had provided them with and heads peered from open flaps of the dwellings.

Golden Eagle turned to Sarah. "Stay behind me. Do as I say and don't speak until spoken to." Not waiting for her reply, he turned and started walking toward the center of the village.

Sarah followed, limping slightly from the saddle sores. To take her mind from the pain, she studied the big clean tipis they passed. They were much larger than she would have thought, and many were adorned with colorful paintings, quills and feathers. Some also had suspicious objects hanging from what looked like hair. Shuddering, she refused to look too closely.

Word spread quickly that the last two warriors had returned with a stranger. Children ran into their tipis and heads peered out as they wound their way between the large dwellings. Many greetings and questions were called out to Golden Eagle.

Sarah looked over her shoulder, saw they were being followed and looked away in embarrassment. A good number of women and girls wore very little clothing.

Sarah stopped behind Golden Eagle near the entrance to one of the largest tipis and waited, pulling the heavy dark cloak around her shoulders.

Golden Eagle frowned when he noticed Sarah's blue chattering lips. Reaching out, he fingered the cloak, felt its wetness and noticed the bottom was caked in mud from the walk to his father's tipi.

It hadn't occurred to him that she was so wet. Requiring little clothing, he was already dry. He tugged at the wet garment. "Take it off," he commanded, pulling the ties to the cloak. "You will warm and dry faster. Soon, you will be able to change." The crowd fell silent and all eyes were on the stranger.

Sarah started to protest, but then she looked into his eyes and remembered his warnings. Full of trepidation, she unfastened the cloak and removed it, her shirt and breeches clinging as a second skin.

Silence descended, then gasps filled the air as all eyes fell to the white girl dressed as a white man. Fingers pointed to her snarled hair that hung loose and wet, the braid having come undone long ago.

They gathered behind her like bees swarming to a new and exotic flower.

Turning back to Sarah after replying to an older man, Golden Eagle nearly knocked her down, she was so close. "You will wait here," he commanded.

Sarah's eyes widened in alarm. The thought of being left

alone out here with strangers who stared and whispered among themselves as they pointed fingers at her was terrifying.

"You will come to no harm. My people are simply curious," Golden Eagle reassured her, careful not to reveal tenderness or concern as he spoke. With that, he turned to his father's tipi and waited for permission to enter.

Seated on the thick fur of a buffalo, consuming his midday meal of dried meat, crushed chokecherries and nuts, Chief Hawk Eyes became aware of the commotion within his village.

He glanced out the open flap, and pleasure and thanks surged through him upon seeing that his son and Red Fox had returned.

He watched and waited eagerly for the news his son would bring. His brows rose, hand stopping midway to his mouth, when he caught sight of the stranger limping behind Golden Eagle.

His gut tightened. Instinctively he felt something was not right. A feeling of foreboding descended when he watched the figure remove a piece of clothing to reveal a very feminine figure and hair of a shade he'd never seen, hair the color of a new moon.

As he watched his son speak with her, he noticed she was not bound, nor did she seem frightened. He discarded his food, appetite gone with the feeling that the white girl meant trouble.

He glanced toward his wife, seated on the other side of the tipi sewing garments made from doeskin, and announced quietly, "Wife, our son returns. He has a white girl with him."

Seeing Eyes did not look up as she replied, "Yes, my husband. I know."

Hawk Eyes narrowed his eyes as he studied his wife, her head bent intently to her task. Her simple reply to an unusual occurrence implied much to the great chief, who pushed such unacceptable thoughts from his mind.

Rising swiftly, he took the couple of steps needed to stand before her.

Squatting, he lifted the softened doeskin garment from her fingers. He held it up, for once oblivious to the workmanship that was the envy of many and a great source of pride to him. The dress was nearly complete. It was far too small for his wife and far too large for his daughter.

Dropping the garment as if it burned, Hawk Eyes turned without a word to step out into the gray day made even more dismal as he now knew what Seeing Eyes' last vision had been.

The crowd hushed and grew watchful as Chief Hawk Eyes stepped outside and greeted his son, noticing the determined set of his jaw. Shifting his attention to the girl, the chief was surprised when she met his hostile stare with an unflinching proud stare of her own.

In her eyes-of-the-sky, he saw pain, uncertainty, curiosity and an unquenchable warmth, but not a trace of the fear he'd expect from one in her position. He frowned. There was something familiar about her eyes. He shook off such thoughts.

Now he knew his first thought of trouble was correct. Burying deep within his mind his wife's prediction of change, the great chief motioned his son to enter, and returned to his place, sitting stiffly to await the explanations he would have.

Golden Eagle entered and waited for permission to sit and join his father on furs scattered around the fire.

He stood, tall and proud, his dark gaze meeting the comforting warmth of his mother's nod before she respectfully lowered her head back to her task. Gaining confidence, he addressed his silent father formally.

"Red Fox and Golden Eagle have returned safely, my father and chief. Golden Eagle has much to speak of."

After studying his son for what seemed an eternity, Chief Hawk Eyes at last motioned his son to sit. Delaying the topic of the white girl, Hawk Eyes asked for news about the white men. The other two warriors had found and dealt with the one white man they had followed.

Sitting across from his father, Golden Eagle spoke of all they had discovered and done. He related how one white man had been killed by one of Stands Tall's daughters and the escape of three others. He described the home the whites had led him to.

Hawk Eyes leaned forward eagerly. "And the white men. What of them?"

Meeting his father's piercing stare, Golden Eagle shook his head in frustration. "We arrived too late. The two escaped. We could go no further without risk as they headed in the direction of the fort of the white soldiers. They have escaped us for now."

"So. The white men remain free." Hawk Eyes spat angrily, his need for revenge great. Without it, the spirits of the two girls would be doomed to roam restlessly.

"There may yet be a way." Golden Eagle brought out the medallion he'd found and handed it to his father to examine.

Hawk Eyes glanced up from studying the strange object. "Speak, my son," he commanded.

"One that we seek is the guardian of the girl I brought back with me. I followed her when she left in the dark of the night, thinking she would lead me to those we sought. Speaking the white man's tongue, I discovered she was running from the same evil white." Golden Eagle told of what Sarah had told him and of the bruises he'd seen himself.

"The people of Chief Hawk Eyes have always dealt fairly with their enemies," Golden Eagle said. "We do not take revenge upon innocent people. There are two others she lives with. The one called Sarah bargained for their safety and freedom. She will identify the one we search for."

Hawk Eyes nodded. It would make revenge easier for

them if the girl helped them. But it also raised his suspicions. "Why would this white girl help us?" he asked, not able to believe the girl would be so willing to go against her own people.

Golden Eagle explained his plan. "I have been told that the one she calls Willy has an affliction in his head. He seeks revenge against her for a deed her mother committed. This girl called Sarah feels the evil-minded one will return to claim her. As I did not cover my tracks when I captured her and left her belongings, all will know that she has been captured by Indians. He will come to us."

"Why does he seek revenge?" Hawk Eyes asked.

Golden Eagle shook his head. "She will not say, my father. Only that we may do as we please with him if we take no revenge on her or the others."

Taking a few minutes to think through all his son had revealed, the chief nodded. "And in the meantime, this woman will be sent to another tribe until we have need of her help," Hawk Eyes said, greatly relieved that she'd not be here among his people for long.

"No, my father. The girl belongs to me. She will remain here, as I have promised protection from the one who will harm her as he did to Stands Tall's daughters."

Chief Hawk Eyes stiffened. His son's response was not what he'd expected or wished. With effort, he suppressed his growing frustration and anger.

"And what reason do you have to bring a white captive to our village? We have had no white slaves among us for many winters. It causes much trouble. We will again have internal fighting and warring. This I will not allow."

"The girl is our link to the murderers. Once we have taken our revenge, the girl can be returned to her home," Golden Eagle shot back.

"I do not understand why all this should matter to us. We can bide our time now that we know where these dogs live. Why bring the girl? Can she not help us from her home? It is not our concern what happens to her. And what of your upcoming joining with Wild-Flower?'' he asked.

Hawk Eyes didn't miss the flash of resentment in Golden Eagle's tightening lips as he continued. "Would it not be better to be rid of the girl? There are others who would take the girl. She could remain in this village to lure the evil white, but as a slave to another."

Rising abruptly, Golden Eagle parried, "Other warriors have taken captives to their tipis in our past. There is no law against this in the tribe of Chief Hawk Eyes. I wish to do the same. I captured her. Is it not my choice to make?"

Determination lent harshness as he answered his own question. "I will decide what is to be done with her. I choose to keep her until she serves no further purpose to us."

Hawk Eyes stood, his face flushed with anger. Never had his son defied him before.

"My joining with Wild-Flower does not take place for many moons. May I not decide then what to do with the girl?" Golden Eagle countered, meeting his father's furious glare.

Golden Eagle watched his father turn away. He knew, as did all in the tribe, that the chief could call a council meeting to decide the issue. And if ruled against, he would have to abide by their decisions.

Shoulders thrown back, feet apart, he took a deep breath and lowered his voice to a respectful level. "The girl's father is not among the living, and her only male relative is one who commits rape and murder. She trusts me and looks to me for protection."

Hawk Eyes had closed his eyes, deep in thought. Amber eyes flew open in disbelief. "Why would a white woman place her trust in an Indian? What is it that my son has not told me? I will hear all. Now." His voice stern and commanding, he motioned his son to sit.

Lowering himself once again to the soft furs, Golden Eagle recounted his first meeting with the white girl.

Finishing his story, Golden Eagle confessed, "And now,

my father, she again places her trust in me. She does not wish to be here, but has no other place to go. I saved her life when she was an innocent child. Her father was honorable and repaid me well. Do we not have many strong horses as a result of his fine gift? The Great Spirit crossed our paths once again. I find I am again responsible for her.''

Hearing no objections, Golden Eagle confidently continued. ''The girl has no one and cannot wander these lands alone. She thinks to go to the white man's fort, but that is where her male relative also heads. I will once again keep her from harm until it is safe for her to return to her white man's house of wood.''

Rising, Hawk Eyes paced the interior of the tipi, his glance falling on his mate, her deft fingers working beads into intricate patterns with skill and speed.

Arms folded across his massive scarred chest, he asked with deceptive softness, ''She has agreed to life in our village? Agreed to learn our ways and live as one of us? Where is she to stay? Is she to sleep in your tipi? She has agreed to this?'' Hawk Eyes rapidly fired the questions, not bothering to wait for a reply.

Rising also, Golden Eagle stated, ''She will do as I tell her.''

Hawk Eyes leaned his head back, eyes drawn to the dark gray clouds gathering overhead. He had a feeling that stormy days lay ahead. ''Bring the girl. I will speak with her myself. Only then will I make my decision.''

Chapter Ten

Sarah found herself jostled further from the tipi that Golden Eagle and his father disappeared into. Looking around at unsmiling faces and remembering the cold glare she'd received from the chief, she wasn't sure her presence here was wise.

Standing on tiptoe, she tried to look over the heads of the crowd, but was unable to see or hear what was going on. What was taking Golden Eagle so long?

The crowd closed in as a few of the younger women became bold, reaching out, fingers touching the strange white girl. Sarah felt hands behind her, stroking her hair. Others pulled at the material of her shirt, fingering the lightweight plaid, exclaiming over its texture and lightness.

Clutching her possessions tightly to her chest, Sarah closed her eyes and prayed that Golden Eagle would return soon. She fought panic as warm bodies pressed in on her.

A small chuckle followed by a sharp tug on her breeches drew her attention downward, and she saw a toddler standing on wobbly, chubby legs. Another tug, and brown arms lifted in demand to be picked up.

Sarah looked around and met sparkling sherry-brown eyes set in a round glowing face. The girl, younger than she, nodded her head. Cautiously, lest she startle the baby, Sarah squatted and lifted the small boy to her chest, ready to hand him to his mother if he cried. This was the first time she'd ever held a baby, and though she wasn't sure what to expect, she found she liked the feeling of his cuddly body in her arms.

Looking into curious brown eyes, Sarah gave a tentative smile. The toddler grinned in return, and reached out to grab a handful of the shiny strands of hair that had drawn his attention.

Laughter and praise of his bravery followed his actions. Startled, he leaned toward the safety of his mother's arms, his newfound bravery gone.

Sarah grinned, released the boy and gently ran a finger down one rounded cheek, amazed at the downy softness of baby skin. Giggling, the toddler buried his head against his mother's chest, suckling at her breast for security and comfort.

Sarah looked away, embarrassed. Many of the women were half naked, wearing only hide skirts to cover their lower bodies.

Laughter at the boy's antics dispelled much of the tension, and she shyly returned their grins. Confident now that these women meant no harm, Sarah relaxed, thinking it might even be fun to be with other girls her age, a pleasure that she'd never experienced living in so isolated an area.

Unexpectedly, a sudden vicious tug to the back of her head forced a cry of pain as she whirled about in confusion.

Sarah found herself facing an angry Indian maiden. Short and plump, lips compressed tightly in a face red with rage, the girl's eyes blazed with hatred. Her fisted hands plopped on wide hips.

Maliciously, the girl advanced as Sarah stepped back.

Her hands shot out, striking suddenly to shove Sarah back.

The silent crowd hurriedly moved away and the girl laughed as Sarah lost her balance and fell to the muddy ground, her belongings rolling beneath the feet of the women.

The Indian maiden spat at Sarah, sneering in halting English, "You white! No belong here! Red Fox not know! You no belong to Golden Eagle!"

Sarah started to rise, and grunted when her attacker's bare foot made contact with her stomach. Gasping with pain and trying to draw her breath, she heard the girl's wild laughter.

Rolling on her sore backside, Sarah caught her breath, her hand lying protectively in front of her chest to ward off another blow. Drawing a deep breath and narrowing her ice-blue eyes, Sarah decided to show this unknown girl she wasn't here to be kicked around. Swiftly she sat up, grabbed the bare brown ankles in front of her and pulled with all her might.

Smiling with satisfaction as the larger girl fell heavily, Sarah scrambled quickly to her feet. She now stared down at the sputtering Indian girl, watching as she struggled to her feet amid the laughter and jeers of her people.

The girl had been caught completely by surprise, and her face reddened with humiliation. She reached for the knife strapped to her thigh and jumped to her feet, teeth bared as she promised, "You die, white whore. You no treat Night Star bad. Night Star kill you, feed to birds of death. Then Golden Eagle be mine."

Sarah threw her hands in front of her, ready to duck to the side as the knife held poised in the air made a downward slash.

Golden Eagle stepped out of his father's tipi and looked into the group of women for Sarah. A flash of metal caught his eye. Heart pounding, he saw the gleaming metal of a knife held high, ready to strike. His mouth went dry and he ran into the crowd, shoving his people aside.

A cry of outrage rent the air as Golden Eagle grabbed Night Star's wrist. Ignoring her cry of pain, Golden Eagle applied pressure until the weapon dropped harmlessly from her fingers.

Paling under the cold menacing anger emanating from the fierce warrior, Night Star tried desperately to save her honor as well as her skin.

Using the *Lakota* tongue, she whined, "Take her away, Golden Eagle. She is evil, no good for our people. No good for mighty Golden Eagle. You be great chief one day. White spirits bad. White girl must go . . ." Her voice trailed off as the face above hers darkened in white-hot anger.

Keeping his temper tightly leashed, Golden Eagle jerked the whining girl's arm behind her, effectively halting her struggles. He ignored her cry of pain. "Who gives Night Star the right to kill the white girl?" he asked in a deceptively soft voice. "Does Night Star now have rights to touch or destroy another's possession?"

Night Star paled, Golden Eagle's words reminding all in hearing that a person's possessions could be freely given, but never taken or destroyed by others without suffering the consequences.

Night Star pointed an accusing finger at Sarah. "Your captive attacked me. I was only defending myself," she lied.

Seeing only anger and disgust in Golden Eagle's eyes, Night Star called to the women in the crowd. "Tell him. Tell our chief's son that his white captive laid her hands upon me."

The crowd moved away, refusing to meet Night Star's wildly accusing eyes.

A warrior stepped through the throng of retreating women. "I apologize for my foolish sister's actions, Golden Eagle. She brings shame to our tipi this day. She will not harm your captive again," Red Fox promised, slapping a hand hard over his sister's shoulders.

Night Star spun around and flinched from eyes that promised retribution.

Nodding his head, Golden Eagle accepted Red Fox's apology. Turning his attention back to the sniveling girl, he felt loathing for the troublemaker. Giving her one last hard glare, he commanded, "Stay away from what belongs to me, Night Star. Harm my captive in any way and you will be punished. All have heard my words." Night Star lowered her head, hiding hate-filled eyes.

"Take her to your father's tipi, Red Fox. Perhaps it is time to arrange a husband for your sister . . . in another village!" Golden Eagle swung around, his long black braids whipping about.

"Are you all right?" Golden Eagle demanded of Sarah. His eyes searched for signs of injury.

Sarah waited until Red Fox led the violent girl away before turning to Golden Eagle. Her heart still raced from the close encounter. "You brought me here to be safe? I would have been safer on my own. Is this what I have to look forward to each day, Golden Eagle?" Sarah glared with reproachful eyes, taking care to keep her voice lowered, mindful of his previous warnings and those who watched.

Her accusation struck home. Guilt crept over him for not being there to watch over her. He'd promised her safety and if he'd been just a few minutes later . . .

"I'm sorry for what happened. Red Fox will punish Night Star," Golden Eagle promised. "No one will harm you now, little one. All now know you belong to me."

Sarah's head snapped up, eyes flashing. "Belong to you, Golden Eagle? I don't belong to you or anyone else. I am no prized horse or other such possession, nor am I a piece of bought merchandise to be shoved around."

Golden Eagle drew himself to his full height and directed his still-smoldering gaze to her defiant blue eyes till they lowered in acknowledgment of his authority. "In my people's eyes, I captured you, brought you here, and that makes you my possession. As my possession you are safe, for we do not steal from our own. You had best learn this now and accept it for your own good. Belonging to me is the only way to keep you safe," he informed his spirited captive, his words cool and clear.

"Come. My father wishes to speak to you." Taking a firm hold of Sarah's arm, Golden Eagle led her to the tipi entrance.

Sarah was about to enter the large dwelling behind Golden Eagle when a soft voice came from behind her. Turning, Sarah watched as the mother of the baby boy approached.

Shyly, the girl handed Sarah her belongings. Speaking in halting English, she explained, "This belong to you. I save for you."

Taking her precious bundle from the pretty young girl, Sarah smiled. She had forgotten all about it. "Thank you," she murmured.

Pleased, the girl turned to Golden Eagle, who'd stepped out to see why Sarah had not entered. "I help. I teach white girl *Lakota*. Teach women's ways." She looked shyly at Sarah. "Maybe white girl teach Bright Blossom better white man's tongue. No use for many moons. Bright Blossom forget many words."

Taking an immediate liking to the friendly, sincere girl, Sarah agreed, "I would be honored for you to teach me, Bright Blossom." Sarah looked at Golden Eagle, letting him know she expected his voice of agreement.

Nodding his head, Golden Eagle was pleased. Bright Blossom would make an excellent teacher and friend. Beckoning for Sarah to follow, he stepped into his father's tipi.

Chapter Eleven

The fragmented shadows of pine, rock and village lengthened and deepened. Merging as one, they came together, a
black cloak draping itself across the land, plunging the village into darkness.

To soften the gloom, glittering stars peered from the
darkened sky. Tiny bright jewels danced and twinkled as if
hung from invisible thread, while the moon rose to reign
in royal splendor, adding its own soft glow to the land
below.

Inside a cone-shaped dwelling, Sarah paced, fighting
waves of exhaustion.

Her eyes fell to her meal, brought to her by Seeing Eyes,
which sat untouched by the cold fire pit. One hand pressed
into her stomach, trying to still the queasy waves roiling
inside her. What was going to happen to her? Where was
Golden Eagle?

Her pacing stopped abruptly as she stumbled and fell.
Too tired to continue, she grabbed a pile of furs and laid
them on the hard floor in front of the doorway. Digging

through the silky softness, she found several rabbit skins sewn together. She caressed the silky softness and wrapped the fur around her shoulders to ward off the chill of the evening.

Lying on her belly, hidden by the shadows within, Sarah pulled a corner of the closed flap aside and peered out into the evening.

Her head cocked to one side as she listened to the comforting activity of night creatures stirring. Owls flew through tree tops, their screeches announcing to the world they were awake and hungry. Insects chirped from beneath bushes and leaves where they hid. And rustling sounds of small scurrying animals foraging for their dinner blended in perfect harmony, nature providing its inhabitants with a special blend of evening music.

Sarah picked out gentle crooning voices mingling with soft singing as mothers held and cuddled their little ones. Relaxing slightly, Sarah found comfort in a ritual that was as old as time itself. The language was different, but a mother's love the same worldwide.

Her eyes dropped wearily as she focused her attention on a fire growing larger near the center of the village. Colorful flames eagerly licked and surrounded the small mound of wood and dried brush, flames leaping high into the air with loud snaps and pops. Sparks soared toward the heavens, then slowly faded out, never to return to the earth below.

A handful of men sat around the fire, talking, laughing and greeting latecomers.

Searching the shadowy faces, Sarah tried to see if Golden Eagle was among them. Peering intently as the shadows were broken only by flickering flames, she groaned in frustration as she could not get a clear view before shadows once again fell.

The group of warriors fell silent as an imposing figure walked with great dignity toward the fire and lowered himself.

Sarah recognized the proud stance of Chief Hawk Eyes, and ducked behind the flap. She bravely peeked out again, her need to see what was going on overcoming her fear of discovery.

As she watched the authoritative chief take control, his hand raised for silence, she unwillingly closed her eyes and relived her first meeting with the forbidding chief.

Golden Eagle had led her into the tipi and after many minutes of being appraised, she'd been commanded to sit, Golden Eagle standing behind her.

She'd sensed at once that the chief was not happy with her presence in his village. Never had she felt so intimidated and scared in all her life. Her insides had trembled as glowering eyes examined her thoroughly. The chief's expression as he looked down his hawkish nose had clearly stated that he found her presence distasteful and lacking. His nostrils had flared and his eyes had blazed amber fire.

The silence lengthened between them, but she forced herself not to squirm. Whether the anger was directed at her or Golden Eagle, she didn't know and had no desire to find out.

Keeping her hands tightly clasped in her lap, her back ramrod stiff, Sarah returned his fierce glare. Blue striking off amber, she waited for what was to come. She would not cower before these people. Nor would she show fear and uncertainty to this arrogant man. If she kept nothing else throughout this ordeal, she would keep her pride.

For long moments, silence reigned as the two of them sat there, staring, each measuring the other's worth. One intimidating, one putting up a brave front.

Sarah could not have known that the first hint of grudging respect was coming her way for her show of fearlessness. To show fear brought scorn. Bravery earned respect, even if one was an enemy.

So intense was the tension between them that when he spoke, his deep voice booming suddenly in the tense atmosphere, she was startled when he addressed her in halting English.

"My son tells me you are here of your own free will. Is this so?" the old chief demanded, almost daring her to agree that it was the truth.

Swallowing hard, Sarah prayed that her voice would not quaver. "Golden Eagle speaks the truth," she admitted, her voice soft, slightly husky, in her nervousness.

"Why?" The question shot forth, echoing loud and sharp like the roar of a firearm.

Sarah wished she'd known what Golden Eagle had told his father. But she had no knowledge of the words exchanged between them. Deciding on honesty, she took a deep breath and blurted out, "Your son offered freedom and safety to my people if I came willingly."

The older man raised bushy eyebrows. His eyes narrowed as he reviewed her words. "Ah, so you are not really here of your own free will. Maybe you were forced to come to save your people?" he mused aloud, a gleam appearing in the older man's eyes. Fixing her with his piercing stare, he offered, "Would you leave now if I promised the same safety to you, with no revenge to your people?"

Sarah saw his expression change, and didn't like the calculating stare directed at her. Now that she was being given a chance to regain her freedom, she wasn't sure she wanted it. Where would she go? She couldn't return home, and trying to travel on her own had proved disastrous.

Perhaps this was where she should be for the time being. Of course, the man standing behind her didn't have anything to do with that decision, she tried to convince herself.

She forced herself to meet the chief's anticipating gaze and confessed, "It is true that I wasn't given much choice, but I was given one. It is due to my foolish actions that I find myself here. I was unwise to attempt traveling alone. I gave my word to Golden Eagle and my father taught me to honor my word. I am bound by honor to the promise I made to your son. Only he may release me from the bargain.''

Suddenly, she found herself very afraid of being told she must leave. While she did not trust Golden Eagle's motives for wanting her with him, she knew he would never harm her.

Chief Hawk Eyes was not pleased by her refusal to take the freedom he'd slyly offered. With an arrogant lift of an eyebrow, he retaliated. ''And if allowed to stay, are you willing to become a slave to my son?''

Sarah's eyes narrowed as she inwardly fought against the thought of being a slave to anyone, but she remembered what Golden Eagle had said earlier.

Sarah also recalled Willy's last attack, and knew it was better to be a slave to Golden Eagle than be under Willy's dominance. So, she gave her nod of agreement.

Still, Hawk Eyes sought to change her mind. ''We have no separate tipis for slaves. As you belong to my son, you shall share his tipi.''

She blushed, the chief's warning veiled but crystal-clear. Unable to meet the chief's mocking eyes, Sarah lowered her head. ''I will do as Golden Eagle says and live where he tells me I must.''

''And what of your . . . guardian?'' The persistent voice continued the grilling, stumbling over the new word. ''Would you bargain mercy for him?''

Clasping her hands in front of her, Sarah declared, ''I promised Golden Eagle I will not interfere in your people's dealings with Willy. My guardian chose his path. If he is caught, he must pay the price of justice. Whether it is from your people or my people, justice will be done.''

Shortly after, she'd been dismissed and Golden Eagle had told her she would be informed later of the chief's decision.

Sarah was still waiting for him to return to his tipi to tell her what had been decided. She pushed to the back of her mind her wild responses to Golden Eagle's lovemaking.

Susan Edwards

She yawned. Her eyes watered from exhaustion, physical as well as mental. Her hand fell from the flap. The toll on her young body finally won. No longer able to hold her head up, she fell into an uneasy slumber.

Several hours later, Golden Eagle nearly stepped on the sleeping girl. Stepping carefully over her still form, he moved silently across the darkened tipi to fashion another bed of mats and furs.

Squatting, he carefully lifted Sarah, cradling her warm sleeping body close to his. Sarah nestled closer to the warmth of his chest.

Unwilling to relinquish her, Golden Eagle studied her peaceful features for a while. Finally, he lowered his lips and inhaled her sweet scent. She smelled of sunshine and wildflowers. He brushed a kiss across her brow and grinned, remembering his father's decision.

He would allow Sarah to remain until his joining with Wild-Flower only because she had no other male relative, and by their customs, Golden Eagle was responsible for her. If she could not be returned to her home, his father expected him to find another home for her.

Golden Eagle knew the chief was hoping he'd tire of his white captive and would then be ready to settle with his new wife.

Only *he* knew how strong his desire for Sarah was. He wouldn't tire of her, but he would not try to convince his father of that now. He wouldn't allow himself to think of being parted from her.

Gently he set Sarah down, and covered her with a soft fur before sliding down to his own pallet. Sleep was a long time in coming. His thoughts kept returning to the girl sleeping so close he could hear her soft breathing, smell her special scent. Close, but not close enough.

Sarah lay writhing and gasping as the smirking toothless face loomed over her, coming closer and closer. She felt

110

the bite of harsh fingers digging into her tender flesh. Willy had come for her, had found her. She fought to free herself, and heard his evil laugh.

With both hands captured and held tightly in one of his, she couldn't stop the clawing fingers of his free hand as they tore at the bodice of her dress. Tears of frustration ran down the sides of her face, and Sarah tried desperately to scream for help. No sound came forth. She panicked and renewed her efforts to free herself.

She moaned as she could not get free from the hands that held her still, and her body went limp. Even caught up in her nightmare, she sensed a change, something different in the arms holding her so firmly.

The sneer on Willy's face faded; the remembered stench of stale liquor and sweat were replaced by the clean scent of tangy pine and wood fires. There was no harsh laughter, jeering taunts and vile threats. Only concerned calling of her name, a soft caressing whisper that repeated itself over and over. Hands no longer clawed at her, but caressed her cheeks and held her tenderly.

Cautiously Sarah opened her eyes to the dark stillness. Frightened, she squinted. She could make out a shape leaning over her. She was ready to scream, until a shaft of moonlight slanted across the man above her. Golden Eagle. Not Willy. Sobbing softly, relieved it had only been a dream, Sarah allowed herself to be lifted and enfolded into strong safe arms.

That small act of kindness, of comfort, was all it took for her to give in to tears too long repressed. Sarah wept for the loss of her father and the security she'd known. She gave in to the resulting fear she'd been forced to live with, and all that had happened since Pa's death. The dam broke loose and all the tears she'd held back flooded.

She cried for what was and what could not be. She cried until the well ran dry and there were no tears left to spill over onto pale cheeks or to run onto a bronzed chest.

Stroking and letting her tears soak his chest, Golden Eagle crooned softly, her display of vulnerability wrenching his heart. His lips moved as he vowed to protect her, to keep her safe.

Golden Eagle knew how brave she'd been, what she'd endured. He'd seen grown men cry over less than what Sarah had been through.

Whispering words of comfort, he tenderly caressed her face, stroked her furrowed brow and rubbed the back of her neck until he felt her sobs subside and her body calm.

Wiping the last of the tears, he turned her face toward his and looked into her wide eyes still brimmed with tears.

"You are safe, little one. It was just a dream. A bad dream. Hush now."

Sarah heard the tenderness in his voice. She relaxed slightly as she reached up to clutch his strong shoulders and stammer, "It w-was s-so real. He f-found m-me. He w-will never leave m-me alone. P-please don't let him find me," she whimpered, the fear in her eyes real as they locked frantically onto Golden Eagle's compassion-filled gaze.

Golden Eagle put a finger to her lips, stilling her quivering flesh. Drawing her tightly against his damp chest, he stroked her tousled head as he comforted her. "You are safe here, Sarah. Do not fear. I will not allow him to touch you, ever again."

Standing, he carried the trembling girl to his mat and lowered her to the softness below. Without releasing her completely, he lay down beside her and pulled her back into the warm security of his arms.

"Hush, hush. Lie with me. Relax. Sleep now. I will keep you safe." Golden Eagle's soothing voice murmured like a gentle breeze against her ear.

Sarah allowed herself to be pulled against the warm safe haven his arms created. Slowly her racking sobs subsided and her breathing settled into a soft, even rhythm. Golden Eagle knew she had finally fallen back into an uneasy slumber. Only an occasional hiccup gave testimony to her flood of tears.

The warrior lay awake a long time, his body painfully aware of Sarah's soft curves that molded themselves so perfectly against him.

Chapter Twelve

Conscious of sensuous sensations enveloping her, Sarah curled on her side, allowing silky softness to cradle her as she hovered somewhere between sleep and awareness. She floated on a bed of fluffy clouds, wisps of warmth touching, kissing, promising.

Waves of heat built along her sloping contours. Starting below one delicate ear, fire blazed a downward path to graze the sensitive flesh along the side of her breast, sunk deep into the valley of her waist before rising to crest a smooth hip and linger for long heated moments on a silky thigh.

Up. Down. Over. Under. The gentle teasing continued, creating ripples of heat that gathered in her center, luring her from her sleep.

She stretched lazily. The strange sensations stopped and Sarah felt an impending sense of loss as she relaxed and continued to drowse.

Faint puffs of warm air caressed the back of her neck.

Sarah squirmed restlessly as feather-soft kisses traveled toward her ear.

Moaning softly, writhing as sparks of pleasure infiltrated her sleep-clouded mind, she lingered in that state of limbo between dreams and reality, not wanting to wake. The new sensations were delicious, incredible, and she wanted to savor them as long as she could. Unconsciously she moved toward the source of this new titillation, seeking more.

Golden Eagle lay on his side, his head resting on a propped elbow as Sarah molded her curves to his hollows. He smiled indulgently, her soft purrs of contentment music to his ears.

It was dark, morning still far off. Golden Eagle had found the need to touch Sarah far too strong to ignore or deny any longer.

Without stopping the movement of his land, Golden Eagle again lowered his head as he continued to caress with his warm breath, his moist lips. The tip of his tongue joined the assault, licking her, tasting her sweetness. Reaching her shell-pink ear, his tongue lightly darted in and around the smooth swirls.

She shuddered beneath him, soft sighs filling his ears. Opening his lips, he drew the soft fleshly lobe between his questing lips and suckled, nipped and tugged. His eyes closed as he planted small exquisite kisses along the line of her jaw, finding the pulsing rhythm in the hollow of her throat.

Sarah's sighs grew louder, her breath came faster, threatening the control Golden Eagle held over his throbbing body, over the desire running swift as an arrow through his veins. He traced the soft fullness of her lips with an exploring finger as he ordered. "*Kechuwa*, my darling, wake."

Sarah's pulse pounded madly and tremors of wild ecstasy rippled across her entire body. Her nerves were raw, sensitive to his every touch, his every command.

115

Lifting passion-heavy lids, Sarah stared, held captive by dark molten depths, desire reflecting, beckoning, igniting an intense longing that struck away all doubts she'd had.

"Shh, do not be afraid," Golden Eagle's voice, thick with need, implored. "I need to touch you. I can wait no longer. You have moved this warrior as no other woman has." Tenderly he held her face between his hands and caressed her cheeks with the pads of shaky fingers.

Sarah was moved by his honesty. She understood his vulnerability, and gloried in his husky admission. He needed her. It was as simple as that. She felt strangely exhilarated as she placed her hands against his firm jaw. Her gaze strayed to his lips. Full and inviting. She wanted to feel again his moist lips against hers.

Sarah admitted to herself that she wanted him, wanted what this golden warrior could give her. She would not fight her attraction any longer, but decided to grab greedily at what he offered. In the past, she'd woven fantasy after fantasy around him. Now she needed reality. She needed her golden warrior.

Keeping her eyes riveted on his parted lips, his breath fanning hers, she whispered, "I'm not afraid. But I don't know what to do, how to please a great warrior such as yourself." Shyly she lifted her eyes to his and nervously moistened her lips with the tip of her tongue.

All restraint fled at her shyly spoken admission, and when her small pointed tongue disappeared, Golden Eagle needed to find it. A low groan escaping, his head lowered, lips flickering over hers. "Ah, sweet Sarah."

Gently, his lips moved teasingly over hers. His tongue stroked and caressed her quivering lips. Slipping between her soft warm flesh, he found his way barred, as before, by small pearly teeth.

Sarah sighed as Golden Eagle lightly nipped her lower lip, drawing it fully into his mouth to savor the soft silkiness. She reveled in his tongue along the inside of her lip, exploring, teasing.

"Open your mouth to me, let me taste the sweetness within," Golden Eagle commanded hoarsely.

Sarah's lips parted, and a ragged sigh escaped. Memory of another kiss in the moonlight guided her. Her mind relived the velvet softness of his kiss. A stab of hunger swept through her as his tongue thrust past her parted lips.

His tongue stroked hers, encouraging her to respond by touching and retreating. Soon her body recognized the ancient rhythm and responded.

Her arms rose to encircle Golden Eagle's glistening neck and her fingers tangled in his hair. She needed to touch him, to taste him as he tasted her. Her tongue came to life as she shyly stroked and mingled with his, lightly touching him, marveling at his rough texture.

When he retreated, she boldly followed, driven by instinct. She pushed her questing tongue past his and drank greedily until he moved to claim her again. With each giving and taking, sampling and tasting, the magical kiss seemed to go on forever.

Gentle kisses rained over her flushed face, her throat, allowing Sarah to take a deep breath of crisp sweet air. Her hands moved to explore the whipcord muscles in Golden Eagle's back and shoulders as her lips melded with his.

Slowly Golden Eagle let his fingers trail down her body, brushing against the outer swell of her breasts through the thin fabric of her dress. He boldly moved his hand to begin an arousing exploration of her full soft flesh.

Sarah gasped. She moaned. Her breasts swelled, the nipples hardening to tight nubs beneath his hand. The gentle massaging sent quivers of need racing to the junction of her thighs. More. She needed more. Thrusting upwards, she moaned, begging for his touch, needing his hands upon her.

Golden Eagle drew a ragged breath and fumbled with the foreign cloth preventing him from feeling and seeing her warm satiny flesh. "I want to see you. All of you," he whispered, his voice deep and husky. Rising above her, he impatiently took her dress in hand and tore the fabric neck to waist.

Encountering another layer of hindering cloth, he disposed of it the same way as he gazed into eyes so dark a blue, he felt he would surely drown in their bewitching depths.

He clutched Sarah to his chest as he rolled over, bringing her to lie on top. Softly, Golden Eagle said, "Kiss me."

Surprised by the quick change of positions, Sarah found herself staring deep into his hot compelling eyes. Bracing her hands beside his head, she lowered her head as she nibbled and teased the swollen fullness of his lips until they opened with a groan of suppressed desire. His breathing became erratic, his body tense beneath hers.

Never had she felt so lost in a sea of unfamiliar emotions. Trailing warm sweet kisses along his hard jaw, she found the softness between his neck and shoulder and inhaled his male scent.

She was vaguely aware of the rushing of cool air over her heated flesh as Golden Eagle ran his fingers up her sides and slipped his fingers beneath her ripped bodice. His calloused palms explored her smooth bare back, tracing the hollow of her spine down to where it gently sloped to meet her buttocks.

Pushing Sarah to a sitting position, Golden Eagle slipped the shredded material down her arms and past her narrow waist, baring her for his eyes.

Her hair hung in pale streaks framing her naked breasts. With her head thrown back, she looked like a pale spirit bathed in the pool of moonlight that filtered in.

Reaching up, he cupped one full breast. Watching her eyes close, he cupped the other and gently fondled them both.

Slipping a hand behind her head, Golden Eagle pulled her back to him. "You are beautiful, Sarah. You are mine. Forever mine."

Resting her palms on his broad shoulders, Sarah gave a

small cry when Golden Eagle latched his mouth onto one rosy tip. His tongue and mouth worked their magic around the sensitive round bud.

Pulling her down against him, Golden Eagle reclaimed her lips as he again switched their positions. Trailing his mouth downward, he gave her other pink bud his undivided attention as he tasted and teased the erect nipple.

His hand skimmed down her side, past her arching hips, to come to rest on her silken belly. Over the firm sloping planes he splayed his hand, savoring the smooth expanse of quivering flesh. Slowly he inched his way lower, pushing down her hindering drawers and what was left of her dress, leaving nothing in the way of his loving gaze.

Gasping and moaning, Sarah clutched desperately at Golden Eagle's shoulders. With each gentle tug of his lips upon her breast, a hard core of tension built deep within her. It started in her belly, an ache that grew, extending in all directions, before settling between her legs, throbbing with need, begging for release. As his hand slipped lower, the feeling intensified, growing stronger, threatening to engulf her.

Reclaiming her lips, Golden Eagle continued his venture downward, finding and resting the palm of his hand on top of her blond mound.

Sarah threw her head back, and clutched frantically at the soft furs beneath her. She felt the thundering of his heart pounding against her breast, his breath mingled with hers, his harsh moans in harmony with her soft passionate cries as her fingers moved across his smooth sweat-slicked flesh.

Sarah jerked and tensed as Golden Eagle slipped his fingers through her soft downy mat of hair and touched the very core of her desire. The magic of his touch overrode her inhibitions as the muscles of her thighs and belly flexed rhythmically.

Golden Eagle stroked on, while her hips, restless, seeking, rose and fell to his slow rhythm as he brought her to the brink of release.

Sarah pleaded for an end to this exquisite torture, her hips lifting in sensuous invitation.

Suddenly the magic touch of his hand vanished. Her eyes opened in pained confusion. Golden Eagle stood above her. With a quick motion, he threw his breechclout to one side.

Her eyes widened at her first glimpse of a naked male body in all its glory. In the pool of faint light, he looked every bit the proud, invincible warrior.

Sarah's cheeks flamed as she stared at him. Excitement mingled with fear because now there was no turning back. She closed her eyes, afraid of his largeness, afraid of the pain she suspected he would bring.

Golden Eagle knelt and stroked the soft silkiness of her inner thighs before leaning forward to caress her heaving breasts. Once again his hand found her moist center, and her hips jerked off the ground as he found her woman's cave with a long finger.

Frightened of the strange wild feelings spreading through her body, Sarah cried out at this new invasion, panic momentarily overcoming desire. She tried to block his hands, clamping her thighs tightly together.

He whispered words, willing her to relax, and his hand stilled, giving her body the time she needed to adjust to his intimate caresses.

Stroking and caressing, Golden Eagle grimaced as his body throbbed and pulsed, begging for release. But he waited until her passion-racked body cried out for him, her legs thrashing wildly as his fingers explored her moist center.

Moving over her, he begged, "Open for me, Sarah. Let me come into you."

His knee nudged her legs apart, and Sarah instinctively bent her knees and opened her legs wide. Golden Eagle rubbed against her arching moistness. Poised and ready, he held her tenderly. Covering her mouth with his to silence her cry of pain, he entered her quickly, his heated flesh searing the guard to her womanhood as he buried his shaft deep within her.

The burning pain, completely unexpected after the unbelievable ecstasy, brought a cry from her lips. Tears of betrayal trickled down her face as she fought against the pain.

Licking and kissing her tears away, Golden Eagle remained still, waiting for her to adjust to his fullness buried deep within her body. "It could not be helped, my sweet one. The first time is always this way. Lie still, the pain will soon fade," he said soothingly.

Lying still as commanded, Sarah gave Golden Eagle a reproachful look as she willed herself to relax. She found to her surprise that the pain had indeed subsided. Gasping when he moved, she braced herself for more pain, but he had spoken the truth. There was none.

The aching need built quickly. It wound its way from where they were joined to the tips of her wildly raking fingers.

Her legs held him to her as she let her body match his in rhythm. Faster and higher they soared. With each deep thrust she felt an overwhelming tenseness seize her, and knew any minute she would surely burst into a million pieces.

"Open your eyes to me, little one. Let me watch you climb the mountain of pleasure." Sarah held tight, drowning in passions as old as the sea until she spiraled out of control. With a muffled cry, she seized Golden Eagle, her lifeline, as waves of spasms spun her into a world of exploding bright stars.

Golden Eagle swallowed her cry of ecstasy as she tensed around him. He threw back his head, and his cry echoed hers as his body gave one final shuddering thrust to spill his seed deep within her receptive body.

Hoarse, ragged sighs of satisfaction filled the tipi and they lay in silence, arms and legs intertwined.

After a while Golden Eagle raised himself up onto his

elbows, relieving her of his heavy weight. Pushing damp tendrils of hair from her face, he planted a gentle kiss on her trembling lips.

Looking into eyes black as the night, Sarah raised a shaky hand to caress his lean brown cheek. "I never knew it would be like this. So wonderful. So powerful. Is it always this way?" she asked, her voice full of wonder.

Smiling tenderly, his eyes shining with amusement, Golden Eagle's lips twitched as he lazily traced circles around one breast. "Only with us. We were meant to come together. It shall always be a magnificent gift we give to one another. There is a mighty force that comes alive between us. One that neither of us can deny any longer. I promise you, there will be no more pain. Only shared pleasure."

Golden Eagle gathered Sarah close and closed her eyes with a gentle kiss. "Let us sleep now. Tomorrow marks your first day and you will need to be rested." Soon her breathing calmed and grew heavy and even.

Golden Eagle rose up on one elbow as Sarah rolled onto her side. He watched her sleep for a long while. Lying back down, he turned slightly and drew her closer, pillowing her head on his shoulder. She was his now. No longer could she deny this attraction. This was where she belonged. She would see this too.

Appeased at having spewed his seed within her, Golden Eagle closed his eyes, content and ready to sleep.

His eyes opened suddenly as a thought came to mind. Not a bad idea, he mused. One that could work, if the Great Spirit was willing.

And on that secret thought, he slept, arms cradled protectively around Sarah.

Chapter Thirteen

Dawning of the new day found the village buzzing with activity. The sky was overcast, thick gray clouds gathered overhead and the promise of rain drifted on the breeze. Meals were hastily consumed inside amid much discussion as daily tasks were assigned. Each individual, no matter the age, would be allotted duties.

Five young braves under the supervision of three aging warriors gathered by the stream for instruction before they left to go hunting. The elders would teach the boys how to use larger bows, arrows and spears. The aging men enjoyed the task. It made them feel useful and it was a source of fun and learning for the boys.

Fathers and brothers rode out to hunt fresh meat, scout for nearby enemies or search for saplings for new arrows.

A group of seasoned warriors gathered to ready themselves for their given task. They were to search for herds of buffalo.

They would then report to the council the locations, numbers and conditions of the great shaggy beasts. The meat from the buffalo provided the bulk of their winter food, warm furs and other needs. It would take most of the summer and fall days to gather and prepare what would be needed to sustain them through the harsh winter months.

Hawk Eyes had also decided that they should pay a visit to the village of Chief White Cloud, delivering many fine gifts of furs and horses to the father of Wild-Flower.

Inside his tipi, Golden Eagle dressed and readied himself to join the others. He wore his plain, everyday moccasins and breechclout and packed formal wear for the celebrating that would be held in his honor.

It was time for him to leave. Past time. He squatted down on powerful haunches beside the sleeping girl and leaned forward to tenderly push a stray lock of blond hair from Sarah's face. She looked so peaceful, so beautiful, that he fought the urge to lay beside her and take her back into his arms.

He debated whether he should wake her to let her know he was leaving. There had been no time the night before for him to inform her. As much as he wanted to wake her, he decided to let her sleep. He knew she was exhausted. The strain of all she'd been through had finally taken its toll. The rest would do her good, he finally decided.

Watching for precious moments, he knew without doubt he was falling in love with this spirited girl who'd been a part of his memories for so long. Swiftly and without mercy, she was piercing his heart. Shaking his head at the predicament he found himself in, Golden Eagle rose with dignity.

Deep in thought, he silently let himself out, filling his lungs with crisp morning air.

Striding purposely to his parents' tipi, he entered and called to Seeing Eyes. He leaned forward to speak quickly. Seeing Eyes gave a nod of agreement.

Pleased with his mother's response, he joined the waiting warriors, ignoring their teasing comments as to why he was the last to arrive. Their grins held a touch of envy. With thundering hooves, they headed into the thick woods that hid their tribe from enemies.

Sarah woke a long time later to laughter, excited yells of children and barking dogs. Slowly she opened heavy lids. It took a few moments for her to remember where she was and why. Turning slightly, she saw she was alone.

Scattered bits and pieces of the night before flashed before her. The campfire, her nightmare and the tenderness of Golden Eagle comforting her. Another dream. One so real, so passionate. Perplexed, she drew her fair brows together. Surely that had been a dream. Hadn't it? They didn't . . . Did they?

Sarah sat, the thick fur fell and cool air brushed against her naked breasts. Her skin flushed pink. Last night had not been a dream. It came back to her clearly. She tried to stand, but fell back against the warm bedding with a soft moan.

The stiffness and soreness she felt between her legs was all the proof she needed of Golden Eagle's lovemaking the night before.

She massaged her aching temples with the tips of her fingers, and scenes from last night replayed in her mind. The feelings and responses this warrior evoked in her didn't bear thinking about. He didn't even have to touch her to start her pulse racing.

Sarah stared into space, determined to close her mind to the ecstasy she had experienced and longed to experience again.

How could she have given herself to him so completely? She silently berated herself. Brooding in her confusion, she could feel her anger rising. With a deep sigh, she closed her eyes in shame as honesty won. It would be so easy to blame Golden Eagle. But it wouldn't be right to do so. She had given herself to him willingly, had even begged him to love her, to take her on that wondrous ride.

"How can I face him after last night?" Sarah groaned

and buried her head in her hands. "I can't. I'll die of humiliation," she cried out loud. She lifted her head, took a deep breath and pushed aside the covers. She needed to get up and dress before he returned. To be naked in the dark was one thing. To be caught unclothed in full daylight was an entirely different matter.

Standing, Sarah looked for her clothing, wondering where Golden Eagle had gone. Surely he wouldn't just leave her alone. She didn't know where to go or what was expected of her. Shaking her head at her conflicting emotions, she muttered to herself, "Sarah, get a hold of yourself! Make up your mind. Either you want to see him or you don't!"

She heard a sound outside. Thinking it might be Golden Eagle, Sarah grabbed the covers and covered herself quickly, looking around for a place to hide. She couldn't face him yet. As there was no place to go, she stood facing the door as the flap was shoved aside.

"So, you wake. Good morning, child. You need bath and food." The owner of the softly spoken words entered the tipi. "I am Seeing Eyes. Golden Eagle my son. He ask I come, take care of you while he away." She explained, talking slowly, as if spending much time choosing and forming her words.

Sarah recognized Golden Eagle's mother. They had not been introduced or spoken to each other last night, but she had noticed the gracefully aging woman sitting quietly in the chief's tipi. As she had last night, Sarah wondered how it was that so many of Golden Eagle's people spoke English. She would ask Golden Eagle when she saw him. Then his mother's words sank in. Golden Eagle was away?

Meeting the older woman's gaze, Sarah felt the fur slip. Snatching it to her chin, she covered her flushed skin as she looked away from those knowing eyes. "You said Golden Eagle is away. Where did he go?"

Clucking her tongue in motherly fashion, Seeing Eyes crossed to the embarrassed Sarah. "My son go to search for herds of buffalo. He be gone many moons. White girl not to worry. You safe with us.''

Setting a bowl of steaming water at her feet, she handed Sarah a small scrap of softened leather and turned away. ''I leave. Bathe now. I return with . . .'' Seeing Eyes stopped to think a moment and grabbed a handful of her deer-skin skirt. ''Dress,'' she finished, a wide grin on her face. She was proud of her English. It had been a while since she'd last spoken the white man's tongue.

Sarah watched Seeing Eyes step out, her heavily accented words registering. ''Wait,'' she called out. ''I have clothes. You don't need to bring . . .'' She stopped in midsentence as Golden Eagle's mother turned and shook her head.

Seeing Eyes studied the white girl her son wanted. ''No, child,'' she patiently explained. ''You not wear white man's clothes here. You dress as one of us.''

Seeing Eyes held one hand up to forestall the argument Sarah was ready to voice.

''Easier for you if you dress as one of us. You be more easily accepted,'' Seeing Eyes finished.

''But . . .'' Sarah swallowed her protest, unable to fault the older woman's logic. She gave in. Suddenly it was important that she get approval from these people.

As soon as the flap shut, Sarah reached for the warm water. Thankful for the privacy, she quickly bathed and wrapped herself in one of the blankets.

She paced around the tipi, careful not to step in the altar behind the fire pit. Golden Eagle had taken only enough time yesterday to instruct her that normally women in his tribe moved to the left side of the tipi, while the men went to the right. He explained that the square area on the floor directly behind the fire was the altar, and pointed out his warrior's equipment that no woman must ever touch.

Sarah wondered what would be expected of her in her new role as she awaited the return of Seeing Eyes. A sigh escaped. She hoped she would not cause shame to Golden Eagle. She owed him that much at least.

Steps outside interrupted her contemplations. The flap moved to admit Seeing Eyes with bundles of clothing slung over her arm. Behind her, Bright Blossom followed, shyly glancing at the white girl.

Laying the clothes aside, Seeing Eyes turned and informed Sarah, "We help you dress." She reached for the tightly held blanket.

The thought of strangers looking at her, dressing her, touching her, was too much. Sarah stared in disbelief and shook her head, taking a step back. "I can dress myself."

Putting hands to hips, Golden Eagle's mother spoke sternly, as one might to an unreasonable silly child. "Come now, child. We women. Do we not look the same? Only skin color different. White girl not be shy. We wish to help. Our clothes strange to you."

With a deep sigh of resignation, Sarah recognized that determined look, the voice that would brook no argument. It was very similar to her son's. Dropping her arms to her side, Sarah allowed the fur to fall from her body.

Picking up the soft doeskin dress, Seeing Eyes slipped it over Sarah's head and guided it over the girl's pale flesh.

The dress, with its V-neck and sleeveless arms, was a perfect fit. Seeing Eyes stood back and gave the white girl a chance to get used to the garment.

Looking down at herself, Sarah studied her new costume. Her love of beautiful pieces of work destroyed her last vestiges of doubt about wearing Indian clothing.

Exquisite bead work, quills and feathers followed the line of the neck. A thin leather thong was cinched at the waist, showing off Sarah's small waist. The bottom of the mid-calf-length dress was decorated with rows of beads above the neatly cut fringe.

Sarah did, however, feel uncomfortable showing so much of her legs and arms. Never had she worn anything so . . . revealing. Surprisingly, though, she found it was very com-

fortable and lightweight. Not nearly as binding as the many
layers of clothing more familiar to her. She twisted around
trying to see all angles. Running her hands down the front
of the dress, she marveled at its incredible softness.

Sarah saw pride on Seeing Eyes' face and remembered
seeing this woman sewing the night before.

"It's beautiful. Thank you," Sarah exclaimed as she fingered the soft fringe. Cocking her head to the side, curious,
Sarah asked the older woman, "You made this?"

Smiling, pleased with Sarah's response, Seeing Eyes replied. "Yes, child. I make. It please this old woman you
like."

"But you made it so quickly," Sarah said, voicing her
confusion. "You were sewing it when I arrived . . ." Her
voice trailed off.

Bending to retrieve the matching moccasins, Seeing Eyes
simply stated, "I saw your coming in my dreams. Please
sit."

Not understanding the strange reply, Sarah did as instructed. Wincing slightly, she lifted a foot and allowed
Bright Blossom to fasten the moccasins around her ankles.

Bright Blossom had seen the flash of pain cross the white
girl's face. Seeking to comfort, she said quietly, "Not
worry, pain go soon. Is always this way for women the first
time our warriors claim us." She spoke in a matter-of-fact
tone.

Sarah's face and neck flamed with shame and humiliation. Rising indignantly to her feet, she exclaimed, "How
did know about . . . Did he tell you what . . ." Sarah stammered, her hands flying to press against hot cheeks, horrified that such a private matter could be public knowledge.

Watching Bright Blossom's smile fade, Sarah felt guilt
creep over her. She was taking out her anger on someone
who did not deserve it.

"I'm sorry, Bright Blossom. I should not have spoken
to you as I did."

Stepping forward, Seeing Eyes intervened. "You have

much to learn, child. My son not say anything. It was expected. When man and woman share tipi they follow nature's path.''

Hearing Sarah's groan of disbelief, Seeing Eyes continued, holding out her hands, palms up. ''In our world, the mating act between man and woman is natural. Not one to be ashamed. What happened last night between you and my son is natural, was meant to be.''

''But there was no marriage. It is not right to . . .'' Sarah shook her head, unable to express herself.

''Do white men always marry women they take to their sleeping mats?'' Seeing Eyes asked the innocent girl.

Shaking her head no, Sarah looked at the two women and confessed, ''This is so different. My people, we do not talk about such matters. They are private. Sometimes, even husband and wife do not talk as freely as this.''

At Sarah's confession, Bright Blossom blurted out, ''But how do they know what each feels? How do you know what needs your mate has?'' Bright Blossom asked, struggling to voice her shock. ''I not mean to anger you. Please, not be mad at Bright Blossom.''

Taking pity on the Indian girl, Sarah smiled. ''It's all right. I can see I have a lot to learn. I will try to be a good learner.'' And with that, she stood and let the two women braid her long hair into two plaits and tie them with beaded thongs.

Following Seeing Eyes and Bright Blossom out into the drizzling rain to face her first day in the Indian village, Sarah needed to know one last thing. Hesitantly, she placed her arm upon Seeing Eyes shoulder and stopped. ''Will your people think badly of me because of . . . last night?''

Stopping to examine the anxious white girl, Seeing Eyes smiled. ''No, child. Here, you be judged on how you work and fit to our way of life. As white captive, you have no choice but to share my son's sleeping mat.''

Sarah nodded and followed the two women. She vowed she would learn all she could. After all, she was half Indian.

Perhaps this new knowledge would be useful, if she ever found her other family.

Riding behind her father and older brother, Wild-Flower observed the group of Indian warriors coming toward them. Even from this distance, she recognized Golden Eagle's great horse.

She glanced at her brother Running Wolf, and received a stern look of warning as he dropped back to ride beside her. Wild-Flower quickly glanced away. She had hoped for more time before having to face Golden Eagle.

Moving closer to his headstrong sister, Running Wolf leaned over and spoke for her ears only. "My sister had best behave as a gentle quiet doe." Hard eyes of earth color met defiant eyes of the same shade as brother and sister glared at each other.

Tossing her head, Wild-Flower sent her brother a contemptuous look. "Do not worry, my brother," she said mockingly, with a low humorless laugh. "I shall not do anything to bring shame to my family or tribe." Wild-Flower dropped back.

She knew he'd watch her every step. Despite their differences, they were close, and only he was aware how she rebelled against the match between her and Golden Eagle.

Her brother thought her crazy, stupid and selfish. How often had he told her so? She knew she was the envy of all the maidens in her tribe. For the son of a great chief to accept her, daughter of a rival chief, as his mate was a great honor for her and her family. She should be happy, proud. But she wasn't. She wanted to choose her own mate.

Golden Eagle spotted the group on their way to meet them. "There, up ahead." He pointed, urging his horse toward the group.

Red Fox watched Golden Eagle greet the chief and his family and those warriors traveling with them.

He could not help but feel envy when he saw Wild-

Flower. Such beauty was rare. She truly resembled a beautiful flower growing free and strong in the prairies. The irresistible urge to pick the blooming meadow flowers matched his need to take and possess the young girl.

He knew of Golden Eagle's feelings on the matter, but couldn't understand his friend. Golden Eagle was regarded as a very lucky warrior. With anyone else, in any other circumstances, he would have challenged for the beauty before him. But he could not. Not with a man who was his best friend. Shaking his head clear of such unclean thoughts, he took his place as the group finished their journey.

Chapter Fourteen

"Tonight, my friends, the tribe of White Cloud will feast and dance in honor of the upcoming marriage of my daughter Wild-Flower to Golden Eagle as was decided long ago. All can see the many fine ponies and gifts he has brought to our tipi. The Great Spirit has smiled upon our humble village this day."

A roar of approval went up. There was much to do this day. It would be a day of preparing for the feast. All other chores would be set aside as warriors left with whoops and yells to find fresh meat.

Women rushed to check their finest garments and those of their families. Each would try to outdo the other. Even the ponies would be decorated with their finest blankets.

Unmarried girls rushed to find a secluded spot for bathing. This would be a night of trying to woo unattached males. More than one had their eye on Red Fox.

Chanting and dancing accompanied the drums filling the air. Golden Eagle and Wild-Flower strolled around the village.

It was permissible and encouraged that the two should spend time with each other. Golden Eagle looked around and saw a few others talking in the shadows, some with blankets thrown over their heads for privacy so none could hear their conversations.

Golden Eagle slowed his pace and tried to show proper interest in his wife-to-be. He knew others watched closely. Much was at stake if the two tribes did not merge. Glancing sideways, he sighed. As usual, Wild-Flower walked with her eyes to the earth beneath their feet, giving him a view of her shiny dark head.

He wondered if he would ever get her to look him in the eye. Many warriors expected their mates to be meek and submissive. His hands clenched. Not him. He was a proud warrior and needed a wife to stand proudly at his side when the time came for him to rule.

Searching for a suitable topic, he tried once again to initiate a conversation between them. "I trust your brothers and sister are well?"

He received a silent nod.

"And your father and mother?" he probed.

Slim shoulders shrugged. "The family of Wild-Flower is well," she faintly replied.

Golden Eagle threw his head back in frustration. They passed another couple and heard the whispering and giggling from under the blanket over their heads. The warrior's gaily decorated pony shielded them.

Stopping in the shadow of a tipi, he looked down at the blanket slung over his arm. He would try one last time to get his soon-to-be bride to talk with him before returning her to the circle where the maidens sat. "Soon Wild-Flower will be wife to Golden Eagle. Does Wild-Flower desire to talk beneath the blanket with her husband-to-be?"

Wild-Flower's head snapped up, eyes blazing with horror and resentment, before quickly lowering. She shook her head side to side. "No, husband-to-be. This maiden has no words to speak of this night," she choked out.

134

Golden Eagle stared in amazement. Had her eyes seemed to blaze with resentment? Telling himself it was just a trick of the moonlight, he sighed. Her eyes were once again lowered, her shoulders slumped. Relief passed over him as he had no desire to share the intimacy of the blanket with her.

Silence fell as they mutually headed back to join the festivities, both engrossed in their own thoughts. Neither knew just how closely matched their thoughts were.

Back at Golden Eagle's village, Sarah spent one afternoon in front of the tipi pounding pine nuts into a paste. Across from her, Bright Blossom also pounded nuts. Sarah looked at the hard ground and groaned as she saw how much had flown from her bowl and noticed that Bright Blossom had no waste.

Vowing to be more careful, she bent her head to her task. Without warning a shadow fell over her and two dead squirrels and a rabbit landed in her lap.

Looking up, Sarah cringed to see Hawk Eyes towering above her. His face remained impassive, his voice stern, as he commanded, "Clean," before turning and walking away. He seemed unconcerned over the pine nuts he'd scattered into the dirt.

Sarah looked at the lifeless bodies and swallowed hard. Panicking, she looked up and found many eyes on her and the retreating back of their chief. The challenge had been given.

Her eyes sought Seeing Eyes. There she found her courage in the confident, knowing eyes of the older woman.

Swallowing the queasiness that threatened to engulf her, Sarah stood, clutching the animals as she looked to Bright Blossom for help.

Bright Blossom nodded and rose to follow her friend to the water. Sarah kneeled at the water's edge, listening and following each instruction Bright Blossom gave her, following her example as she made the first slit into the rabbit.

She gulped, a wave of dizziness overcoming her. I can't

do this, she thought to herself. Bright Blossom whispered encouragement. Voices from the crowd cheered her on. All but one.

"White girl no do. White girl coward. Not brave as Sioux woman. See pale skin. She be sick. Bring shame to Golden Eagle," Night Star jeered.

Silence surrounded her. Sarah lifted her eyes to the smirking girl and found the courage she needed. Taking a deep breath she finished the incision and looked to her friend for the next instruction.

She would do what she had to do. She would not shame Golden Eagle or his mother or Bright Blossom.

When she finished, Sarah stirred a pot of meat stewing with roots and greens that she'd gathered. It was the first meal she'd prepared on her own.

That night she sat proudly, using her fingers to scoop bits of meat into her mouth. She'd done it, to the cheers of the others as Night Star stormed off.

Two weeks later, Sarah left the camp and headed toward the fast-moving stream. Lowering her aching body to the ground, she splashed cool soothing water over her face, neck and arms. Sitting on her heels, she stared at the sparkling water and reflected on the changes in her life.

She'd never thought of her life as easy. There were always chores to be done at home, but never in all her days had she worked so hard as she had the last few weeks.

She now realized how easy her life had really been. Mary and Ben and even her pa, when he'd been alive, had never expected her to do much of the dirty, hard work. It was humbling to find out just how much others had done for her.

Sighing, she sat back and folded her arms around her knees and vowed aloud, "I'll never complain again when Mary needs my help."

Closing her eyes to the still beauty surrounding her, Sarah laid her forehead upon her drawn-up knees. All the canning, baking, drying and tending of their small garden could not equal what she'd been through, not even if she added cleaning, sewing and caring for the livestock.

Whoever had said Indians were lazy, dirty and slothful had never lived among them, Sarah decided with a low moan. Her respect for the hard-working women had grown daily.

Golden Eagle had been gone three weeks now, and Seeing Eyes had insisted she sleep and live in their tipi. It was for her own protection as no young girl lived alone.

Her day started when the sun could barely be seen peeking over the horizon. Sarah was then assigned her tasks over the morning meal. Wood had to be gathered and water skins filled from the nearby stream. Even thinking about carrying the full pouches made her shoulders ache.

Pulling her brows together in a frown, Sarah was so tired she could barely think.

She ran her hands down the front of her dress, and groaned as her chapped hands snagged on the softness. Yesterday she'd been given the task of scrubbing soiled clothing. She looked at her hands. They were still red and raw from the long hours spent kneeling in the cold water.

Sarah also helped Seeing Eyes prepare meals. She'd learned what greens and bark to gather, which ones she must never eat, where the best berries would soon be ready and so much more.

Humming and buzzing filled the silence next to her as several bees darted in and out of tiny flowers. A squirrel leaped from one branch to another, stopped to eye the stranger below him and give her a loud scolding. She smiled at the tiny creature, and looked over her shoulder to make sure no brave or warrior held his bow and arrow trained on the unsuspecting animal.

"You best leave and hide, my friend. Or it's someone's meal you shall become," she warned, shuddering, her smile fading. The one chore she hated was the skinning and cleaning of small animals and fish.

137

But now, she knew what parts to keep for food and other necessities. It still amazed her that there was so little waste. The women were resourceful and clever when it came to finding uses for the innards.

She thought back to her week in the women's hut several days after her arrival. It was the place women went when their monthlies flowed. At first, she'd felt banished, cast away, but quickly learned that the women enjoyed their week away from the hard daily labors. Gossip abounded. While the women waited for nature's job to finish, they sewed. Sarah had learned much that week.

She was surprised at the easy acceptance she met from most. Seeing Eyes had been right when she'd said Sarah would be judged on her performance, not her skin color.

However, there were two in the village eagerly awaiting for her to balk or refuse some task: Night Star and Chief Hawk Eyes. To both she had shown she was no quitter.

A memory came to mind. Ben had always cleaned the animals he hunted. Smiling fondly, Sarah could imagine his shocked weathered old face if he knew she was actually doing this job now and not too badly either.

He'd always claimed, "The catchin' and cleanin' is best left to us menfolk. The cookin' and fixin's is best left to you womenfolk." Of course, Ben was a terrible cook. If not for Mary, Ben would have starved long ago.

Still, she would have a nice assortment of skins and furs to take back and show off. Seeing Eyes had informed Sarah that she could keep the furs of whatever she skinned and use them as she saw fit. But she had to tan and prepare them herself.

And that unwelcome thought reminded her of the reason why her arms and wrists ached. She had helped Seeing Eyes with the tanning of a large antelope hide that afternoon.

Though she was tired and her body ached from the unaccustomed work, she was proud of her new skills and knew she would improve with practice. She thought of her mother. Had Emily done these same chores the summer she'd spent with her Indian warrior?

Sarah smiled. If she found her father, she would go to him with the skills of a plains Indian woman. She would not disgrace his tipi—unless he resented her white blood. Frowning, she put the thoughts of her future from her. She had enough to cope with just surviving day to day.

The breeze picked up, cooling the air. Sarah lifted her face into the wind, feeling it caress her neck and face. On impulse, she reached for the leather thongs that held her hair in two neat plaits. Dropping them into her lap and using her fingers as a comb, Sarah slowly separated the strands until they streamed in a shimmering mass down her back and over her arms.

The wind picked up the silky gossamer threads and playfully tossed the sparkling strands about, turning them white in the bright glare of the afternoon sun.

Seeing Eyes headed toward the water's edge, looking for the white girl. She rounded a bend which shielded the girl from view. Stopping dead in her tracks, the older woman stared in fascination at the sight she beheld.

Sarah sat, legs drawn to her chest, eyes closed, face turned to the warmth of the sun, hair whipping around her head. Seeing Eyes' breath caught. It was the vision of her dream. The girl's pale hair seemed almost to be a part of the wind it drifted on.

Wind. *White Wind.* Her grin widened. Seeing Eyes knew she had the elusive missing part of her vision.

She shook her head. It was so obvious. White Wind was to be Sarah's Indian name. Deep in thought, she backed away and silently retraced her steps, abandoning her reasons for seeking Sarah out.

Leaning into the strong gusty breeze, she became lost in thought as she mulled over what had been revealed to her this day. Seeing the wind lifting and tossing Sarah's hair had been all it took to jog her memory.

She would give the tired girl some time to herself. Since her first morning, Sarah had worked hard without complaint from the time she was called to wakefulness until darkness fell.

No matter what chores she'd been assigned, Sarah completed the many time-consuming and even difficult tasks that made up a woman's daily life in the village. She'd even met skinning the many small furry animals with the same stubborn determination. None could find fault with her.

Seeing Eyes smiled, her eyes shining with amusement as she thought back to Sarah's first attempt at skinning.

It had been obvious to all that the girl had never done this sort of task before, and many doubted that she'd finish her first rabbit as her face went as pale as her hair. But she'd shown them. Gritting her teeth, Sarah had hacked and sawed, clumsily imitating Bright Blossom, until she had a pot full of meat simmering in an old black pot.

None even minded or made comment about the waste of bone and fur. It hadn't mattered. Sarah had shown the people in Hawk Eyes' village that she had courage and determination.

Since that day, Sarah had proven to be a hard worker, willing to learn. Many had respect for the white woman whose skills would improve with practice.

Hawk Eyes glanced up as his soul mate entered their tipi. He raised a questioning brow when he didn't see the white girl behind his wife.

Seeing Eyes responded to her mate's raised brow. "She rests by the water, my husband. I will let her remain for now. She has worked hard this day." Seeing Eyes did not speak of what was revealed to her.

Hawk Eyes went back to sharpening his knife. He contemplated the time the girl had been in their tipi.

His wife had insisted she stay in their tipi while their son was away. On his own, he'd have left her to fend for herself, hoping that she would run off and disappear from his village. But he'd given his word to Golden Eagle to extend his protection to her while he was gone.

Bushy brows drew together. So far, her actions were not the typical white behavior when faced with captivity.

Hawk Eyes did not understand her willingness to learn their ways. He'd expected rebellion, downright refusal to do some of her tasks.

Purposely, he'd returned from a hunt with an armload of animals. Normally, he would not have caught that many in one day. Not because he couldn't. There was simply no need for so much at one time. The reproachful look of his wife had nearly shamed him for his behavior.

Hawk Eyes had been certain the girl would refuse to do her duty. He watched from a discreet distance as she set about her task of cleaning and skinning the animals, almost positive she would disgrace his tipi. To his amazement the weakness he sought to uncover never appeared. When she served his meal that night, she'd shown him a look of pride.

Hawk Eyes shook his head in frustration. His son's white woman was very unusual, and somehow that made it worse! If she'd complained, cried, refused to work, he'd feel better able to cope with her. The last thing he wanted to feel for her was respect. Alas, he was a fair man and knew she was grudgingly earning it.

A short time later, the quiet in the tipi ruptured as squeals of delight and laughter filled the air. With a rush of energy, Golden Eagle burst through the doorway, barely ducking low enough to allow clearance for the small giggling rider clinging to his back.

"He's back! He's back. Golden Eagle has returned," the rider chanted, loud enough for all to hear, as she pulled on long ebony braids. "Again, Golden Eagle, please?" the childish voice begged.

Sinking down to the floor, Golden Eagle allowed his sister to slide down. "No, that is enough for now, Winona.

You will tire your big brother. Then what good will this warrior be?'' Golden Eagle joked.

"My big brother, if carrying me will tire you, then you are not the great warrior all talk about," Winona playfully cried, her hands resting at her tiny waist.

Unable to let that insult pass without retaliating, Golden Eagle gave chase to his young snickering sister. Catching her, he wrestled with her for a few moments, tickling her ribs till she begged for mercy. "My sister becomes sharp-minded as well as sharp-tongued," he teased, standing.

Love shone in Golden Eagle's eyes as he and his father stood side by side and watched Winona lying quiet, an occasional giggle from being tickled still escaping from her "It has been a while since Golden Eagle has seen Winona," the young warrior said. He leaned down and fingered one long braid as she jumped up. "My sister is growing up fast. Soon, this brother will be watching as the braves come to visit."

Watching his two children, Chief Hawk Eyes smiled with indulgence. Winona, meaning First Born Daughter, was the family's pride and joy. After so many long and barren years, Seeing Eyes had despaired of ever giving him more children. They had given up, resigned themselves to only one child to love and raise.

When Seeing Eyes announced she was with child the entire village celebrated, none more than she, who praised *Wakan Tanka,* the Great Spirit for sending her another child. Their daughter was now nearing seven winters, and she had brought love and laughter into his declining years. She made him feel young again.

Chief Hawk Eyes gave his full attention to his son. Briefly, Golden Eagle related to his father the information he gathered: the location of the herds of buffalo, how many there were and their condition.

Nodding his head, Hawk Eyes spoke. "Well done, my son. I will trust your judgment." There was much planning to do before the big hunt and much work to be done after-

142

ward. When all the tasks were finished, the tired people of his tribe would be ready for a period of celebration.

This would be the best time to hold the joining of two tribes. Many tribes of his nation would join for days of feasting and ceremonies. Rising agilely to his feet, Chief Hawk Eyes left the tipi, encouraging his young daughter to trail after him.

Chapter Fifteen

Golden Eagle shook himself dry and dressed. Now that the dust of travel had been cleansed from his body, he would go find Sarah. Walking among the tall grass next to the water's edge, he mulled over his mother's announcement.

White Wind. That would become Sarah's new name. When he thought about it, the name fit. Fit very well indeed. Sarah had reentered his life as unexpectedly as the winds of storms, capturing his heart and confusing his mind. Things had not been the same since she had tumbled back into his life. Yes, White Wind was a very suitable name.

In the three weeks he'd been away, not a day had passed that he hadn't thought of her, worried how she fared, and each night his body burned with longing deep into the night.

Seeing her, he stopped. His breath caught in his throat and his pulse pounded. He took the time to drink in her beauty, and felt the gnawing ache of heightened passion rush through him.

His eyes fell to the leather thong that dangled from his fingers. His hand lifted and he viewed the necklace he'd made for Sarah. The small carved wooden eagle hung with wings outstretched, ready to soar to great heights. Suddenly, he found himself almost afraid of approaching her, unsure of her reaction to him. Did she desire him as he so desperately yearned for her? Or would she deny the magic of their coupling and force him to begin anew?

Memorizing each and every detail, he savored the refreshing sight she made, sitting at the water's edge, completely relaxed and as one with nature.

Sarah sat, legs outstretched, ankles crossed, leaning on her elbows, her fingers absently plucking blades of grass. She sighed, closed her eyes and lost herself in the peace and serenity surrounding her. Water gurgled and splashed, insects hummed as she enjoyed the comforting presence of the gentle breeze caressing her as softly as lover's lips.

Sarah frowned. Why had she thought of that? As she'd done many times since her arrival, she pushed thoughts of Golden Eagle and his captivating touch from her mind.

A small shiver darted up her spine, inducing fine hairs on the back of her neck to rise in defense as she slowly became aware of another presence nearby. A human presence. Sarah felt eyes boring into her, willing her to turn her head.

After several fraught seconds, there was no doubt in her mind who was standing just mere feet away. Only one person could have this effect on her. Golden Eagle had returned.

Unable to resist the silent command that pulled her like a magnet, Sarah opened her heavy lids. Slowly, her head turned.

Involuntarily her jaw dropped as she beheld the glorious sight of Golden Eagle. He stood as the proud warrior, waiting for her to acknowledge his presence.

It was beyond understanding how one person could command such power and authority without the use of words.

She watched him lift a lean brown leg, then place a bare foot on the boulder in front of him. Sarah's gaze lingered, unable to tear her eyes away from this golden, virile male.

She swallowed, filling her memory with each aspect of his appearance. Before they'd made love, she'd been too shy, too unsure, to look at him for long. With her new knowledge as a woman, she studied him now with the eyes of a lover.

His legs, strong and sturdy from his bulging calves to thick thighs, were covered with a faint dusting of dark hairs that glistened with drops of water. He stood tensed, muscles coiled, ready to spring into action if the need arose.

His large hands rested lightly on one raised thigh, one over the other. Sarah's eyes were drawn to his long sensitive fingers that made her squirm with remembered pleasure.

The solid muscular cords in his arms flexed under her close scrutiny, arms that held tenderly, or could become bands of hardened steel.

Her eyes swept quickly past the breechclout that hid his manhood, not quite brave enough to dwell there. Yet. Her hungry gaze slid over his firm flat abdomen, up to his scarred, sun-bronzed, rock-hard chest. There they latched onto twin disks, dusky with small pebbles in their centers.

What would they taste like? What would it feel like to take the round nubs into her mouth, to tease them with her tongue and lips as he'd done to her?

Blushing, she forced her eyes past the strong column of his neck, over his firm chin, lingering momentarily on the hint of a cleft and a jawbone that she'd seen harden with stubbornness and soften with a smile.

Finally, she came to the striking features of his proud arrogant head. High cheekbones, long, straight aquiline nose, down to the full, firm lips that could easily turn her into a weak helpless mass of trembling with just one brush against hers. Under her gaze, the corners of his mouth lifted in an indulgent grin.

After what seemed hours, but in reality was only seconds, she raised seeking blue eyes to his. What she saw from that brief contact had her lowering her lids quickly, hiding her embarrassment as she sat up.

His eyes, dark as a moonless night, smoldered with fire, burning a path to the surface to shine brightly, like stars breaking out of the gloomy darkness with their twinkling flashes of light.

Sparks leapt the distance between them, sending waves of white heat to pulse through her, igniting the desire nestled deep within her.

Golden Eagle had remained still to allow Sarah to explore his body with her gaze. Roaming freely, lingering hungrily, her eyes caressed, invited and inflamed before he made a move toward her.

Sarah watched from the corner of her eye as her warrior neared, then stood over her, his legs straddling hers. Lifting her eyes, she stared at his outstretched hand.

Taking a deep breath, she tentatively put her fingers on his palm. Immediately, her hand disappeared in his firm grasp and she stood before him.

"When did you get back? Was your trip a success? After I fix our meal, you can tell me about it," she babbled, shivering from his heat. She tried to pull her hand free, needing to put some distance between them so she could think.

Golden Eagle held firm, reached out with his free hand to lightly grasp the back of Sarah's neck. Slowly, he lowered his head, planting light feathery kisses on her soft pliant lips as they trembled beneath his.

"Talk can wait. Walk with me." His voice commanded, low and husky with desire.

Unable to tear her eyes away from his, Sarah shook her head. "I have to get back and help Seeing Eyes finish the meal. I . . .'' Her voice trailed off. She was drowning in pools of black, unable to resist his call.

Without releasing her hand, Golden Eagle led her further upstream, away from the village.

Sarah stole a glance sideways. Somewhere, in the back of her mind, warning bells rang. She was taking a risk playing this game, a game she could only lose. Lose what? Stealing another peek at the silent warrior, she knew the answer at once—her heart.

After several minutes, she hung back, suddenly longing for the safety of the village. She concentrated on her duties, anything to prevent this golden warrior from capturing her heart.

Weakly, Sarah protested, ''Please, Golden Eagle, we must return now. Your parents will wonder where we are.'' She met with no response.

Rounding another bend, they followed the winding stream. Sarah noticed the surrounding woods becoming thicker. Coming to a halt, Golden Eagle stopped the flow of words with a single finger placed gently against her warm lips.

''Hush, do not worry, sweet one. My family will not worry. They know you are with me. We will eat later. It is not food for my belly that I hunger for at this moment.''

With that, he claimed her lips hungrily, parting her soft, moist lips, slipping his probing tongue inside. Pulling her against his long lean length, he ran one hand through corn-silk tresses. With his other hand, he stroked her back, molding her body to his intimately, letting her know of his great need for her.

Yielding to the feel of him, Sarah opened her mouth hungrily, allowed him full passage to explore, taste and tease. Her own tongue, stimulated by his, stroked and explored as they danced to their own special music.

As she slipped one hand up his warm chest, her fingers came to rest on his small flat nipples, their tips hard and round. Hesitantly, she flicked each one, amazed that they swelled slightly as she stroked. Becoming bolder, Sarah lightly pinched and rubbed the small pebble between finger and thumb as their tongues continued to frolic in their teasing play.

A rumbling sound filled her ears as Golden Eagle let out a moan of pleasure. Taking advantage of her freed mouth, Sarah shyly lowered her head, giving in to the need to taste and explore his wonderful male body. Where she was softness, he was strength and hardness. She was fascinated.

Cautiously, the tip of her pink tongue darted to his hard brown nub. When a sudden shudder rippled through Golden Eagle, Sarah pulled back, unsure of herself.

"Don't stop. Suckle and taste me as I have you. This warrior likes the feel of your lips upon his flesh." Gently, Golden Eagle pulled Sarah back to his chest, his head thrown back, words of encouragement mingling with hoarse gasps of pleasure.

Sarah resumed stroking his sensitive bud with the tip of her tongue, relishing the thought, the very idea, that she could be the cause of such tremors coursing through Golden Eagle. Moving to the other nipple, she took it fully in her mouth. As she suckled the tiny nugget, her hands roamed over his chest, shoulders, back before stroking and lowering to knead the sculptured flesh of his buttocks under the leather flap.

Golden Eagle's hands tangled in Sarah's hair. "I need you." He groaned, unable to remain passive any longer. His hands lifted her face to his as he pressed his lips to her closed eyes, then down the slender bridge of her nose to its slightly upturned point. Past her mouth, panting for him, to seek the soft pulsing hollow below.

Sarah felt his hands on the leather thong around her waist. With one quick pull, the belt landed in the thick carpet of grass at their feet. Slowly, he reached down and grabbed the fringed hem in his hands. Lifting the garment, he explored the exposed flesh. The backs of his fingers

149

stroked and caressed her inner thighs, his gaze never leaving hers.

Up past silky thighs, over smooth firm twin cheeks he traveled. Sarah moaned and sucked in her breath as his fingers grazed sensitive skin.

Feeling drugged, she lifted her hands over her head. She waited long agonizing seconds before the dress slid up and over her bared breasts, catching on the hardened points. Slowly, ever so slowly, he drew the offending garment over her head, leaving her writhing with longing.

Placing her hands upon broad golden shoulders, Sarah lolled her head back to give Golden Eagle access as his lips and tongue blazed a trail of fire down her throat.

Fingers splayed across her spine as his lips found one breast. Her belly clenched as his mouth claimed the rosy flesh. Sarah whimpered.

Moving to the other waiting mound, Golden Eagle lightly flicked the aroused nipple with his tongue. Back and forth, suckling here, teasing there, until Sarah felt as if she would collapse on legs that shook with need. "Please, Golden Eagle. You're torturing me," she gasped, the deep ache in her belly spreading outward, her hips moving restlessly. Seeking. Wanting. Needing.

Moving his hands to her small bottom, Golden Eagle kneaded the soft rounded flesh before pulling her questing hips tightly against his throbbing manhood, letting her feel the evidence of his strong need for her.

Sarah felt him suck in his breath as she thrust wildly against him, seeking a release only he could give.

"Shh, love. Be patient," he whispered in her ear as he explored the pink swirls with his moist tongue.

Crying out as shivers of desire flowed through her, Sarah let her weight fall against Golden Eagle in weakness and allowed him to lower her to the cool grassy bed beneath them.

Claiming her mouth in a consuming kiss, Golden Eagle slowly stroked his hand downward, letting it rest at the junction between her legs before he gently parted her quivering thighs and stroked her.

Sarah's hips jerked against the heel of his hand, grinding against him. "Please, Golden Eagle. Do not tease me any longer."

Groaning, he slipped a finger within her hidden cavern, inch by tormenting inch, dipping deeper. Finding her hot, moist and alive, Golden Eagle removed his finger and moved over her trembling body.

Her thighs parted wide, legs latching onto him as he thrust deep within her. Cupping her head with his hands, he looked into smoky blue orbs, checking for pain, as she was still so tight that she fit him like a second skin.

Sarah saw his concern. "There is no pain. It feels so good. Please, Golden Eagle, let me fly with you," she cried urgently, pushing her woman's softness against his male hardness.

With a gasp of sheer pleasure, he moved within her, riding her faster, harder as they soared among the clouds, achieving a height of passion neither had thought possible, shuddering as bright flicks of light exploded around them. Two cries rose to mingle with the sounds of nature.

Long afterward, they lay locked tightly in a lovers' embrace. Golden Eagle lifted his torso off her chest, still encased within her pulsing body. Sarah smiled, eyes filled with awe and passion. Golden Eagle moved lightly within her, and Sarah's eyes widened in wonder. He grinned.

"Golden Eagle, you cannot be serious. Again? So soon? Is it possible?" Sarah asked in disbelief.

"Yes, my pale-haired beauty, again, so soon and it's very possible." And with that, Golden Eagle proceeded to show Sarah the truth of his words.

Chapter Sixteen

Tom shoved his way through low-growing brown under-brush. Holding several willow thin branches overhead, he stopped and wiped his forehead with the sleeve of his shirt before pushing on. He flinched from a sharp sting across the side of his bare neck when one of the branches whipped back before he could get out from under it.

He stopped and rubbed the painful raised welt, spewing a string of curses as he dodged on. He mumbled more oaths into the silent air when his foot caught on an exposed root and sent him sprawling head-first into thorny greenery.

Untangling himself, Tom slowed his pace as he continued to pick his way through dense stands of dark pines. Dusk settled, casting grotesque shadows that seemed to move and follow him his every step. As if all this weren't enough to set one's nerves on edge, dozens of buzzing hungry insects seemed to have marked him as their meal.

Finally, and none too soon, he shoved his way past the last barrier, yelling out to the man bent over the small smoking fire, "Hey, Willy, I'm back."

Willy grabbed his rifle, spun around and aimed the loaded weapon. A look of disgust pulled his lips apart as he put the rifle down and waited until Tom joined him beside the fire.

Tom found himself yanked forward, held off the ground by his already torn shirt front, inches from Willy's furious rage-reddened and whiskered face.

"Shut up, ya goddamned fool. We're hidin', remember? You go shoutin' like that and us bein' here ain't gonna be no secret," Willy's voice rasped.

Tom's dull eyes widened, his face turning purple as he gasped for air. Willy tossed Tom aside in disgust.

Rising quickly to his feet, Tom stepped back and warily eyed the older man from a safe distance. Damn, Willy was touchy as of late. Tom didn't dare point out that the fire and smell of cooking food was risky as well. Besides, he was starved and thirsty. He eyed the meat roasting on sticks. He was sick of dried meat and stale bread.

"Sorry, Will. I wasn't thinkin'. It won't happen again."

"That's yer problem, boy. Ya never thinks. You'd be picked clean, hangin' from the boughs of an old oak tree, if it weren't for me," Willy jeered as he shot a stream of spit across the dry, dusty ground.

"Did ya do it?" Willy asked, tired of baiting the sorry figure before him. Squatting, he helped himself to a hunk of overcooked meat.

Tom decided not to mention that if it hadn't been for Willy, he'd be with his brothers now and one brother would still be alive. Eb had gotten himself killed by a mere girl, and his eldest brother had run, not trusting Willy.

Tom watched the older man bite into the tough meat and tear off a huge hunk. His belly rumbled, but he didn't have the courage to help himself. His mouth watered as Willy stuffed his mouth full. With a grimace, Tom thought to himself that Willy looked like a squirrel with his cheeks stuffed full.

Forgetting food for a moment as Willy eyed him impatiently, Tom answered, "Yeah, I did what you said. The boys will meet us tomorrow night as planned."

"Yer weren't followed back here, were ya?" Willy asked through a mouthful of meat. He reached for his flask and took a long swallow of tepid water. A look of disgust flashed across his heavy features as he stared at the container of brackish water.

"Nah. I weren't followed. I was real careful," Tom answered, licking his lips hungrily.

Willy stared at Tom intently for a moment, then motioned toward the burned meat with a flick of his wrist. Leaning back against the trunk of a large tree, he tilted his dirty hat down over his eyes. With a loud smack of his lips, he was asleep.

It was late when Willy and Tom reached their destination. The clouds high overhead cloaked the moon's glow, casting the night into welcomed blackness. Jumping from his horse, Willy grabbed his rifle and circled the small rundown shack.

Satisfied there was no evidence of human habitation or sign that someone had been there recently, he pushed opened the door and thoroughly inspected the inside. Motioning to Tom, he instructed the boy to hide their horses and return quickly.

Peering through a small hole in the side of the rotting logs, Willy watched for the expected arrivals. Then he turned his head and took in his surroundings with a contemptuous glance. The dim lantern light confirmed that there was just a bare room. The only furniture sat in the middle of the room: a table with a broken leg and a couple of rickety chairs lying on their sides. The bed in the corner had long ago rotted and provided nesting material for the many small rodents that had scurried out into the night with Willy's intrusive arrival.

He compared this rundown hovel with John's homey cabin. No, not dear cousin John's any longer, but Sarah's.

How he wished he were back there, sitting in the soft cushioned chair with the caressing warmth of the fire that kept the cold nights at bay.

Stuffing his hands deep into the pockets of his tattered jacket, he shivered with cold. He shook his head when he remembered how Ben had ordered him from Sarah's property. He would get his revenge. He'd make them all pay.

He and Tom had been in hiding for a couple weeks when they'd returned to learn the fate of Sarah and her precious cabin. It had surprised Willy to see everything looking normal. They'd watched for several hours before riding into the open, rifles ready. Cautiously, they'd entered the quiet log cabin and discovered it empty.

Turning to search for Sarah, he'd found himself looking down the barrel of Ben's shotgun. Several trappers, also armed, surrounded him. "Get your sorry hide outta here, Willy. You ain't welcome here no more," Ben ordered. "Walk away, or be carried out. Dead or alive, it's your choice."

Willy's hands clenched, his rifle already taken away. "Don't you be forgettin' who is guardian of that there girl now, Ben. I'm due my share of this here place."

Not backing down, Ben informed him that Sarah was no longer there. "It's your abuse that caused that poor child to leave. Your fault she's been captured by Indians. Far as I'm concerned, you have no more business here. Cabins ain't yours. Horses ain't yours. No Sarah, no guardian. You gets nothin'. You just remove your filthy presence and don't never show your mangy face round here again."

Now Willy shook his head and turned back to stare out the small hole in the wall. The shack boasted only one door. The holes that at one time were windows had long since been nailed shut in a futile attempt to keep animals out.

But now the nails had rusted, the shutters so rotted they barely kept the wind out. The place used to be a small trading post, but now served as an emergency shelter. Glancing around, Willy realized it wouldn't even be good

155

for that much longer. One big storm would probably bring it down, allowing nature to completely reclaim the land.

Straining, he heard a faint whistle. Standing by the door, he peered cautiously into the inky blackness. Softly, he returned the signal. Soon, three men rode up. Motioning to Tom, Willy ordered the boy to take care of the horses.

Single file, the three approached. A tall thin man who went by the name of Hank came first, slapping Willy hard on the back as he passed him. "Missed yer ugly mug hangin' round. Card games just not the same without ya, Will. Too tame." He chuckled, his voice low and rough in the quiet night air.

Hank was followed by his brother, equally tall, but with more flesh on his bones. Dick was commonly known as Red, due to the red hair covering his head and face. Gingerly, he pulled up a chair, rocking back and forth on the uneven legs at the small table while waiting expectantly.

Last, in shuffled a dirty, scruffy, old-looking trapper. Thick layers of bundled clothing and unkempt matted hair made it difficult to tell anything about him. He took his stand by the door. Crossing arms across what appeared to be a massive chest, he stood in silence as his host shut the flimsy wooden door. His bushy gray eyebrows and scraggly beard hid most of his face and all of his thoughts.

Willy moved into the room and sat, stretching his feet out before him as if he were hosting a fancy party, not a clandestine meeting.

Hank spoke at last. "What cha want, Will? Why've you sent for us? This ain't the usual meetin' place." His cold, calculating gleam rested on Willy.

Rubbing his hands, Willy stalled. "All in good time, boys. How 'bout some brew first. Ya bring any?" His eyes gleamed in anticipation as they rested on the bulging pack that Red had dropped in a heap on the dirt-covered floor.

Red reached down, snatched the pack and tossed it toward Willy. Catching it, Willy eagerly searched the contents. Feeling a smooth cool surface, he grabbed and pulled the flask out. Yanking off the lid, he swallowed a mouthful and smacked his lips. "Ahh, that's better. Now listen close, boys, I gots a job for you. I needs your help."

"Wait a minute. First, we wanna know the payment. What's in it for us, Willy? Ya ain't got no money," Hank said, distrust lining his thin face. He knew Willy far too well.

Red chimed in. "Yeah, Will, if you's in hidin' way out here, what's we gonna get in return? What happened to that nice pouch of money you was gonna get your hands on?"

Not noticing the cold stillness that overcame Willy, Red gleefully continued. "Did that young beauty wise up to yore dirty tricks and kick yore hairy butt out?"

Willy seethed, the raucous laughter of the two brothers echoing in the near empty room. He tipped his head back and took another healthy swig of fiery liquid. Carefully he recapped the flask and stuck it in his shirt pocket.

Catching Hank and Red off guard, he lunged forward, his rickety chair flying out from beneath him as he tipped the table and two pairs of booted feet into the air. Standing with hands fisted in front of him, he watched the two brothers, each of whom had been sitting with his feet propped on the table. The chairs, with only two legs on the ground, teetered and fell, tipping their occupants onto the hard cold floor.

Silence thick as morning fog filled the tense room. Hank and Red scrambled to their feet, faces red with anger. Tom stood to one side, nervously fidgeting.

Through the loud angry buzzing in his head, Willy heard harsh chuckles. Turning toward the sound, he saw the old man watching with undisguised amusement. The red haze cleared.

Motioning for Tom to pick up the table, he righted his own chair and sat.

He calmly waited until everyone was reseated at the damaged but still-standing table. "Ya know, boys, one of these days yore flappen' tongues is gonna get you killed.

Best watch who yore messin' with. Now do you want to listen to my proposal or not?'' Willy asked, taking another drink from his flask while fingering his gun.

Shifting uncomfortably in his chair, Hank nodded. "Let's hear what ya got," he agreed, glaring at his brother.

Pleased that he had regained control, Willy announced, "I need you boys to help me track down and locate my ward. Yer payment will be part of the ransom money I'll get from them ol' folks. Ben will give me whatever I wants to get her back," Willy sneered.

Leaning back, he waited for the reactions to his proposal. Harry, the trapper, whom everyone referred to as Old Timer, looked around and asked scornfully, "Where's the girl? Why do ya need help findin' her if you's her guardian?"

"That's right," Red asked, wincing as a sharp booted toe made contact with his shin.

Leaning his thick arms on the table, Willy explained that Sarah had been taken by Indians when she'd run away.

"I want proof that she be alive or not. You, Ol' Timer, you's a trapper, see if you can learn anything from your Indian friends. If some filthy tribe of Indians has her, I want her back. You know the tribes in these here parts and their heathen ways. You can deal with them."

Receiving a small nod of agreement, Willy turned to the others.

"You two—" Willy nodded first at one, then the other—"will travel with him. When he nears a tribe, you stay back. Also, stop at all the tradin' posts. See if anyone has seen her. Find the girl and report back to me. If you can nab her do so."

Seeing agreements all around, Willy stood and warned, "Sarah is mine. Bring her here, unharmed"—he paused, giving each man a fierce glare— "and untouched. If one of you touches her, you're dead . . . understand?"

"Hey, Willy, what if we can't find her? Then how's you gonna get the money?"

All movement stopped, each concerned with his own profit. Willy scowled. "Then we nab the old woman. Her husband'll pay to get her back."

Red scratched his head. "Wouldn't it be easier to go for *her* then?"

"Listen, fools. I want the girl. I don't need you to grab an old woman. I can do that myself. I'm payin' you to bring me Sarah. I gots a score to settle with that bitch."

Looking at each other, Hank and Red both gave their verbal agreements, followed by the silent acceptance of the old man.

"All right, lets get outta here," Willy said. "You know where to leave messages." Quietly, the group of men filtered out into the pitch black night.

Three men headed off in one direction, while Willy and Tom headed back to their hiding place in the dense woods. Spurring his mount in the dark, Willy was eager to get back in front of a warm fire to warm his outside—and with the burning spirits in his pocket, warm his innards.

Uncaring of the cold, a lone figure wept. Kneeling beside a grass-covered grave, Mary ran her fingers over the rough wooden cross. A beam of light spilled across her as Ben came to stand behind her, holding a lantern high. She rose, laid her head upon his shoulder and cried. "Oh, Ben, I've failed John. It's been so long and still no clues to her whereabouts. I'm so worried about her."

"Come now, Mary, there was naught you could have done. That devil was her guardian. Our hands were tied outta loyalty to John. You know we had to go along with his wishes. Short of killing the bastard, we could have prevented none of this."

Ben sighed and ran a hand wearily down his face, tugging at his long thick beard. "Come back to the house, woman. It will do no good for you to take sick. When Sarah is found, she'll need you strong." Ben put his arm around

Mary's shoulders and gently led his sobbing wife to their cabin.

He cursed the recent events. His Mary was beside herself with grief, and now he found himself worried over her as well as Sarah.

He'd hired the best scouts he could find, and still there was no sign of her whereabouts. The only clue they'd had so far was a dead man's body found three days ride from here. They had also found bits and pieces of torn Indian women's clothing and a patch of blood-stained earth a short distance from the man.

Ben knew that Willy had been involved in whatever had happened there. The footprints Mary had found in the cabin had traces of dried blood mixed with the caked mud. It didn't take much to figure that Sarah had been captured by the same Indians who had followed Willy to the cabins the same night that Sarah ran away.

His only consolation so far was that no sign of her body had been found. As long as she was alive, he'd find her, free her and bring her home. He just prayed she was alive and not living a life of torture. Casting out all the horror stories he'd heard about Indians from his mind, he allowed himself to close his eyes and get what sleep would come.

He patted the rifle lying next to him. Willy would never get the chance to set foot here again.

It was too bad that the scouts hadn't ridden back immediately with the report of their findings. He'd have shot the bastard given the chance.

Chapter Seventeen

"Ho! Sarah."

Sarah turned at the greeting, eyes alight with pleasure. She stepped forward eagerly, caught the slight shake of his head and restrained from launching herself into Golden Eagle's arms. Instead she nodded in return and waited until he entered their tipi.

Leaving her cooking fire, she followed, and in privacy threw herself into his arms. "You're back. I was so worried," she cried, holding tightly to him.

Golden Eagle held her for a moment before setting her before him, tipping her chin so she had to look up at him.

Sarah found herself looking into Golden Eagle's serious gaze. "You would insult this warrior? You would imply that Golden Eagle would not return from a small raid? How you crush his honor," he gently mocked.

Sarah recognized the gentle scolding for what it was: another lesson in how an Indian woman viewed her mate. A woman might worry, but she would never express that worry aloud, thus conveying doubts in her mate's abilities to provide and keep her safe.

She also recognized the twitch of his lips as they tried to suppress his humor and indulgence. "You are right, my mighty warrior. Who can harm the mighty eagle as he soars far above others?" she replied, placing her hand in his to follow him out into the cool afternoon.

They stopped and settled on the flower-covered hillside, Sarah nestled securely between Golden Eagle's warm thighs, her back resting against his rock-hard chest, the top of her head resting in the hollow of his throat.

Happy and at peace with herself and surroundings for the first time since her pa's passing, Sarah watched the sun continue its descent. She sighed, her fingers absently stroking the small wooden eagle she wore in addition to her mother's locket and beads as the sky took on a deep rosy glow that matched the healthy pinkness in her cheeks.

There was no need for talk as each enjoyed the quiet end to another day. Staring off into space, Sarah let her mind wander. As near as she could figure, it had been at least six weeks since that day at the stream where Golden Eagle had made his claim on her.

The last few weeks had been so peaceful, so restful to her overwrought mind, that most of the time she forgot about the reasons for her being here.

It was times like this that she found she didn't miss her other life. Of course, she missed Mary and Ben. If she could see them once in a while, she knew she would be content to stay with Golden Eagle for the rest of her life.

She and her golden warrior had fallen into a routine. Each morning he woke her. Sometimes he brought her slowly out of her deep slumbers, her body aroused and ready for his. Other times he'd yank off the warm furs and swat her bare behind, laughing as she shrieked with cold before quickly donning her clothing.

Golden Eagle would then leave. Sometimes he was gone

a few hours, most of the time all day, and occasionally he left for days on end.

She spent her days with Bright Blossom or Seeing Eyes, assisting in whatever tasks needed to be done after seeing that fresh water and dry wood were always plentiful in her tipi.

And each afternoon when Golden Eagle returned, he would fetch her, stopping whatever she was doing to take her to bathe, sometimes joining her. He had cautioned her against bathing alone and leaving the immediate vicinity of the village by herself. There was always the risk of other Indians seeing her and capturing her. Her hair alone, he'd warned, would be worth much. The warning always made her shudder.

Then they would walk, or just sit as Golden Eagle led her to a new or an old favorite spot to watch the sun set. This frequently led to tender lovemaking.

Sarah drew his arms tighter around her. Her hands twined with his. How quickly she was coming to depend on the strong handsome warrior supporting her. How quickly she'd lost her desire—no, her will—to leave him. Her heart belonged to him, as it had since the first time she'd seen him, bow in hand, arrow impaling a snake to the ground a few feet from her.

Her eyes closed as dew gathered. She was at home and at peace with these people. For the first time her life had meaning and purpose. Happiness had come her way after so much sadness and heartache.

Golden Eagle shifted behind her. "You have not spoken to your warrior this evening. What thoughts hold your silence so long, my love? You do not hold fear in your heart, do you?"

Sarah placed her hands over his as they moved to rest on his drawn-up knees. "No, but I'm glad you're back. And even if I shouldn't fear for you when you go on raiding parties, I cannot help it," Sarah replied, turning to look at him, slightly defiantly, before continuing.

"Your woman is thinking how proud she is that she provides nearly all her warrior's meals and tends to most of his needs. Golden Eagle does not have to seek his meals in the tipi of his mother to fill his belly after a long day of hard work."

"The tipi of Golden Eagle always has a warm fire, plenty of good food, and is very clean," he said. "This warrior is proud of your woman's skills. I have also heard from many of our old ones that the one-with-hair-of-the-sun gives abundantly to them. This pleases this warrior."

Sarah beamed with pleasure and leaned on her knees. Whenever he presented the results of his day of hunting, she cleaned and preserved the meat as well as any other woman, with little waste. As there were just the two of them, she gave the excess to others in need.

"And in return, they have taught me how to dismantle and set my tipi up when we seek a new camp," she replied. They'd moved camp just a few days ago, searching for fresh game and food, leaving the fouled one behind for nature to reclaim and to clean the land for the next occupants.

She'd learned from Seeing Eyes that as the summer progressed they would move more often till the time came to join other tribes on the plains.

After which, the time would come when the buffalo would be fat and ready. During the moon-when-leaves turn-brown, they would organize into a massive buffalo hunt which would provide the majority of their supplies for the winter.

"Today, Morning Grass suffered from toothache. I took her some whip plant that your mother gave to me. And this afternoon, Morning Grass sent over a beautiful parfleche that she'd just completed," Sarah proudly announced. Her skills in making usable items out of the leather rawhide were slow in coming.

She thought of the feathers, beads, quills and other necessities for a woman's life she'd accumulated and stored in pouches from the bladder lining of buffalos.

Sarah shook her head as she remembered her shock and revulsion when she found out that she held bladder bags and that the stomach linings of buffalo were her water pouches and cooking bag. She'd been equally amazed that sinew came from muscles and tendons. The sinew was carefully prepared to become strong threads used in sewing and weapon making. Her threads had been carefully braided, wrapped in animal hide and stored in one of her pouches. She'd not yet mastered the art of preparing her own.

"You adapt well to our life, my White Wind. I am proud of you. Each day you become more like one of us. You even look as one of us. Your skin has lost its pale whiteness and is now honey brown. Only your eyes and hair say you are not Indian."

Golden Eagle turned her head to look in her eyes as he asked, "You are happy, are you not?" Golden Eagle pulled her closer to him.

Frowning over the Indian name he used whenever they were alone, Sarah had to wonder if she weren't too happy, too content. She still hadn't told him of her father. She'd been here long enough to learn about tribal wars and the hated Arikara Indians, and didn't dare mention her Indian blood in case her blood flowed from an enemy tribe. And what if they too had the same prejudiced feelings as her own people regarding "half-breeds."

But she couldn't lie as she replied, "Yes, Golden Eagle, I am happy. Your people are good to me. Your tribe lives a good life. Everyone has taught me so much." Except two, but she kept that to herself.

"Even your little sister is eager to show off her knowledge," Sarah said with a laugh. "Of course, I think it's because her small friends hold her in awe that she teaches a white girl what a woman's work is."

Sarah, being an only child, enjoyed the youthful antics of Winona, and the two had formed a close relationship.

Golden Eagle fingered her braided hair and launched into

several stories of his mischievous sister's pranks.

"It pleases me that Winona looks upon White Wind as a sister."

Sarah sighed in frustration. "Why do you call me by that name? It isn't my name. You know I prefer to be called Sarah," she reminded him, looking over her shoulder, brows drawn in displeasure.

Golden Eagle looked away from Sarah's accusing stare. "It suits you. I will continue to use it."

Sarah turned her attention to the quietness before her. She'd found that there was no swaying Golden Eagle when he decided to be stubborn. Deciding not to pursue his use of an Indian name, or possible implications that she wasn't sure she was ready to face, Sarah changed the subject.

"I asked Bright Blossom how it is that some of your tribe speaks my language so well. She told me a trapper stayed in your village. Will you tell me about this trapper?"

Twining his fingers with hers, Golden Eagle told the story that was told over and over again. "When I was ten of your years, a trapper wandered closed to our village. He had been badly injured by a she-bear protecting her young cubs.

"We knew him to be a peaceful man, so we tended to his injuries. When he knew he would live, he asked permission to stay until he grew strong. He offered his hunting knife as payment for his care.

"He stayed in our tipi with my mother tending him. During that time I picked up some of his words, for he loved to tell stories to me, even though I couldn't understand what he was saying. He was lonely with no one to talk to, so I started spending time with him, trying to understand him. He started teaching me his tongue.

"My father, being the clever chief that he is, had seen an opportunity too good to pass. The winter was harsh and long and my father struck a bargain. He would allow the trapper to stay for the winter in exchange for knowledge of the white man's world."

Golden Eagle smiled, plucking at the fringe on Sarah's dress absently. "Each day, the old trapper would gather the older children and instruct us in what you call English. He also taught us some of your customs. When the days grew long and warmed, he left to return to his world.

"He promised to return during the next winter, and he kept his promise. For many years, we welcomed him as a brother into our tipi and he stayed for the winters. Each time he came, he brought furs, beads, pots and other gifts to us in payment for his lodging and food. And each year our knowledge of your ways and language increased."

"What happened to him?" Sarah asked, her respect for the wise chief growing.

"We do not know. One winter he did not come. We were saddened. Under my father's instructions, we continued to practice your tongue. During the long winter days, we still do this. Those of us who speak the white man's tongue instruct the younger ones.

"My father feels very strongly that without knowledge of the white man's ways, we will be destroyed in the future."

Golden Eagle's voice hardened. "The white soldiers speak with false words of peace. They seek and destroy my people. Each year more of our tribe die or are forced to move from their homes by the arrival of the white man. Even we have been forced higher into the hills."

Golden Eagle rose to his feet and stood behind her. "We no longer move along the plains during the warm months as we are too small a band. My tribe needs the shelter of these hills as we have become vulnerable to the white soldiers with their weapons roaming the plains, killing the buffalo for their hides and for sport. Even leaving our winter camps, we cannot be safe from your people."

Turning, Sarah saw his bitterness, his helplessness, and pushed herself to her feet. She knew he was now talking about Willy. Bright Blossom had hesitantly informed her how two sisters, the names of the dead never again re-

167

peated, had been kidnaped while the tribe was moving from their winter camp to the hills.

Her fingers lifted to his face, seeking to ease his pain. "It's such a shame that all men cannot live in peace. Sometimes it doesn't make sense," she said, her voice soft with regret.

Golden Eagle looked into misty blue eyes framed by gold-tipped lashes. "You are right. Look all around." His hand swept in a half circle and pulled her against his chest. "So much land. The Great Spirit provides so much. Yet to some, it is not enough, will never be enough."

Golden Eagle sighed. "Come, let us return. This warrior has traveled hard and longs to return to his tipi today. He is ready for his meal."

Night Star stood in the shadows of the woods watching Golden Eagle's tipi. She would never forgive the white girl for stealing her warrior. Never mind that he was already spoken for. To her, that was an insignificant problem. Once he married Wild-Flower, and peace between the tribes was achieved, she would find a way to be rid of Wild-Flower.

But the white girl posed more of an immediate threat to her plans. Every night she could get away from her father and brother, she came to watch. Tonight, she'd watched the white girl serve Golden Eagle his meal outside, witnessed the tenderness of his kiss before he left to join the other warriors in the council lodge.

Some nights when they walked before retiring, she followed and forced herself to listen to their soft murmurs, the shared laughter of lovers and, on more than one occasion, their cries of passion that made Night Star want to scream and run. But she'd stayed, forcing herself to listen.

She remembered the time she'd left her tipi, unable to sleep. Following the winding stream, she'd discovered them bathing in the moonlight, Golden Eagle tenderly washing the white girl's pale body. And afterwards, Night Star had forced herself to watch the love act that had followed.

Since that day, her fury had grown. Bitterness spread, eating and destroying all reason. That magnificent male body should be hers, not some white dog's! And so she watched, she waited and she planned.

That one memory alone could turn her face red with rage. It strengthened her hatred, kept her fury at a boiling point, for she'd not forgotten the humiliation at the hands of the white girl.

Laughter and sneers greeted her each day from her own people when they reminded her of the girl's cunning. Even her father and brother were shamed by her, for her actions that day had reflected on them as well. Red Fox had publicly shamed her by giving her most prized possessions to the poorer members of the village.

Now she was the laughingstock of the village. "Only an old man would take you to his tipi now," they chanted and laughed until she stormed away in anger and shame. It was all the white girl's fault.

She'd show them. She would become wife to Golden Eagle, the great warrior. Then she'd make all their lives miserable.

Night Star watched Sarah leave her tipi and join Bright Blossom. Her lips curled in disgust as the white girl took the baby from his cradle board and rocked him in her arms.

Her lips twisted in a nasty sneer. Did the white whore think to bear Golden Eagle a son? To be a treasured wife? All knew she couldn't hold the mighty eagle. She was just a convenience until his marriage. A thought came to mind. The entire village knew, but did the white girl know of his marriage plans?

Her eyes gleamed in anticipation. She would gladly take it upon herself to see that the whore was informed of her true position. Laughing silently, she headed back to her tipi.

Chapter Eighteen

Sarah sat among the circle of young women in the shade not far from the village. The noon meal was over and most of the children sat or napped quietly nearby.

Bright Blossom's toddler lay asleep beside her, his belly round and full after going from one tipi to another sampling the meals being served.

"He sleeps. See his belly. He will grow to be big and strong warrior one day," Bright Blossom commented as she returned to the group, taking her place next to her son.

Sarah found the Indian way of raising children fascinating and practical. There was no yelling or rough handling of any child. Starting at a young age, mothers crooned instructional lullabies which included lessons on morals and bravery. Later came stories, lectures on responsibilities and practical day-to-day learning.

A child discovered that consequences resulted from actions. He was asked to help but never told he must. If a youngster refused, reason replaced discipline. There was such pride in being chosen to assist, the young ones sometimes argued over who would do what.

And if a child broke the rules or did not live up to family or tribal standards, he was publicly shamed. Scorn functioned as the social conditions. Parents made sure their children witnessed public shamings. The sight had such an impact that it was usually enough to keep most children and adults in line.

Sarah smiled as she looked at the sleeping toddler. Many times Two Feathers had crawled into her tipi, and she'd always welcomed him, finding something to amuse him.

Sarah glanced up, a skirt and top she was sewing for herself in her lap. "Two Feathers fine son, my friend," she replied in *Lakota*. She was pleased with her growing skills in communicating with the other girls.

Sarah bent her head to her task and concentrated on beading the intricate pattern the girls were teaching her.

Lifting her aching neck and shoulders from her hunched position, Sarah stretched. With a disgusted look at how little she'd accomplished, she glanced up and winced as the glare of the bright sun caught her fully. She shifted slightly. Smiling to herself, she eagerly awaited Golden Eagle's return.

"Look at Sarah. She dreams of man. Hand still, no work," the high-pitched giggling voice teased. Others joined in the good-natured teasing.

Most spoke in various degrees of halting English, as Sarah could not speak or understand enough of their language yet to carry on a long conversation.

A few of the younger girls took the opportunity to practice their English and gain real tutoring from Sarah. They had been too young to learn from the trapper. Their knowledge came from Bright Blossom, Golden Eagle, Red Fox and a few others during long winter days when weather made going out impossible.

Blushing furiously, Sarah met Bright Blossom's spar-

kling eyes. "Pay no mind to silly girls," Bright Blossom
said. "They jealous of attention you get. They know
Golden Eagle come soon to take you away. They wish their
mates were so . . . loving." Bright Blossom grinned, proud
of using the new word.

Smiling in return, Sarah shifted her attention back to her
beading. She ignored the giggles and playful threats Bright
Blossom's words evoked from those around her.

Golden Eagle was so tender, loving and patient that it
seemed each waking thought centered around her golden
warrior. Thoughts of her past and future had no meaning
or importance anymore.

Aware of a quiet hush, Sarah looked up from the frus-
trating work piled in her lap.

Night Star stood behind the circle of women, listening
to their carefree laughter and good-natured bantering. Now
was the time to get even. Now was the time to let that
foolish white girl know a thing or two, one thing in particular.

"So, white girl dream of Indian lover. Does she think
she in love with future chief? Maybe she has thoughts to
marry Golden Eagle," Night Star sneered, eyes gleaming
with malicious intent.

Bright Blossom jumped to her feet in agitation. "Night
Star must not start trouble here. Hold your tongue. Golden
Eagle will be very angry with you," Bright Blossom de-
clared, speaking rapidly in their native tongue.

Circling around Bright Blossom, Night Star stopped in
front of Sarah. The Indian girl snickered and spoke in English for Sarah's benefit. "Me? Make trouble? How mean
of you Bright Blossom." She pouted. "I wish to join fun.
Is funny, is it not, that a white whore thinks to become
chief's wife?"

Exhilarated by the power she held over the hated white
girl, Night Star laughed gleefully, ignoring the stunned
faces and gasps of outrage around her. She was past the

point of caring, driven to burst the bubble of happiness surrounding the white girl. She was furious that most of her tribe had accepted her. Not a day went by without someone singing praises of the white girl.

Night Star smiled wickedly and waved her arms. "All know after buffalo hunt Golden Eagle marry Wild-Flower." She turned and started to walk away.

"Perhaps Wild-Flower allow Golden Eagle to keep whore to be slave. You be chore wife. You see now, white girl? You just a whore to satisfy his man needs till he has wife to love. Wife to give him many strong sons." Night Star watched shock give way to skepticism and disbelief in Sarah's eyes.

"Marriage arranged long ago. Ask others if I speak truth," she suggested spitefully, indicating those in the circle.

Satisfied as Sarah's face paled, eyes glazed with shock, Night Star made her exit. She strolled, a pleased grin plastered across her plump face, the glow of revenge burning bright in her eyes and her laughter echoing behind her.

The silence that followed Night Star's announcement rang loud and telling in Sarah's ears. With wide disbelieving eyes, she prayed for denial, but no one would meet her searching gaze.

Turning to her friend, Sarah demanded, "Tell me she lies, Bright Blossom. Tell me she was being mean and spiteful! Tell me she does not speak the truth," Sarah begged in desperation, her heart pounding painfully against her ribs.

Bright Blossom kneeled beside Sarah and grasped her friend's icy fingers in her own, her eyes begging for understanding. "Listen to Bright Blossom, Sarah. Part what Night Star say is truth." Bright Blossom held tight, not letting Sarah jump to her feet.

"Many winters ago it was arranged for Golden Eagle to marry Wild-Flower, daughter of Chief White Cloud. This

173

joining is needed to bring peace between our tribes. Only this is truth. All else are lies. Golden Eagle not just use you. Bright Blossom and others see the love he has for Sarah. Golden Eagle be very angry when he finds out what Night Star say,'' the anxious girl vowed.

A cold calm cloaked Sarah against her friend's pleading brown eyes as she shook her head. Slowly her color returned as a flush of anger made its marks of two bright spots of color on her cheeks. Sparks of white-hot fury drummed through her veins. The extent of Golden Eagle's betrayal began to destroy the numbness cloaking her from hurt.

"No, my friend. If what you say is true, then Night Star spoke the truth.''

Waving down the protests around her, Sarah stated bitterly, "When he marries, I will be cast aside, no better than a whore.''

Sarah choked back tears as she stressed angrily, "The only difference is I was naive in thinking that perhaps he cared for me. That we had a future . . .'' Her voice broke.

She shook her head and stood abruptly, her garments and beads falling unheeded to the dusty ground. She ignored the protests and pleas as she angrily stalked off. She was furious. Never had she been so angry, so humiliated and shamed. And worst of all was the hurt, the betrayal.

The spoken words, like a poisoned arrow, had struck their intended target with deadly precision. Never in her whole life had she felt such soul-rending pain.

Out of sight of those who watched anxiously, Sarah started to run blindly. Tears of anger and hurt streamed down her face, blurring the scenery as she followed the winding stream higher into the hills.

She ached with a pain so great, it was hard to breathe. The fresh wound lay open, deep and raw, bleeding the happiness from her soul. How could Golden Eagle do this to her? Trust him, he'd said. She had. She had trusted him with far more than her life. She'd trusted him with the greatest gift she could give. Herself. Her love.

Brushing away tears, Sarah cried out as her toe caught the edge of a rock, sending her flying. She buried her head in her hands.

Over and over, Night Star's accusations echoed in her head. "What a fool I've been," she sobbed. "He's made a fool of me, and I've allowed him to. I've made it easy for him to take advantage of me."

She lifted her head, rose onto her scraped knees, wiped the dirt from her face and brushed off her arms. Tears gathered anew. She looked up and saw a pair of eagles flying overhead. "How could I have been such a fool!" she shouted. "I really thought you cared for me. I even thought you might love me." Her voice choked. "Especially when you called me your White Wind."

Never would she have admitted to him her sense of pride, the feelings of belonging that came with the use of such a simple name.

Sarah stumbled and pushed on. After what seemed hours, she gave in to the painful cramps in her side and slowed to a walk, holding her side as the painful spasms increased until she could go no further.

With a moan of pain, emotional and physical, she leaned against a gnarled old tree. Gasping and wheezing, she drew air into her burning lungs. "What am I going to do?" she cried aloud. Her hand went to her throat, seeking the comfort of her mother's locket, and instead encountered a small wooden object.

She looked at her fingers, the small wooden eagle, wings outstretched to catch the currents of the wind, dangling as if in flight. A cry of pain tore from deep in her heart and echoed across the surrounding hills. She yanked the leather thong from her neck, and tossed the necklace as far from her as she could.

Leaning her head wearily against the rough bark, she weighed her options. There was no way of going home on her own. She was smart enough to realize that. It was wandering alone that had landed her in trouble in the first place. She also had no doubt Golden Eagle would come after her as soon as he knew she'd run away. In her hurt and anger she'd left a trail even little Winona could follow.

Pushing away from the sturdy trunk, Sarah squared her shoulders. Lifting her head, she started walking slowly, ignoring the flung necklace resting on a branch by the water's edge that seemed to call out to her. "Yes, my proud warrior. You will come, but I'll not return willingly," she vowed. "I have my pride."

Sarah stopped and took in her surroundings. As she looked at the sun, her eyes narrowed. By her calculations, Golden Eagle would be returning soon. Wiping away all traces of tears from her pale cheeks, Sarah decided that she would not make it easy for him to drag her back.

Heading toward the thick undergrowth, she walked a long distance in, tearing at tree branches, kicking and scuffing the needle-covered ground, ripping bark, before carefully retracing her steps.

Taking care not to leave a trail, Sarah crossed the narrow stream by balancing on small boulders and rocks. Once across, she slowly headed into the bands of trees. She would walk a bit, then find a spot to wait and plan.

She needed time to pick up the scattered pieces of her heart. Time to close the wound in her soul and time to build a defense against Golden Eagle.

Most of all, she needed to stop the flow of pain from the deep gaping wounds left in the wake of his betrayal. Never would Golden Eagle be allowed to know her foolish dreams. Imagine, her, a white girl, thinking she could marry an Indian. A golden warrior at that. Who would be so foolish?

"I would," she burst out. And to her disgust and dismay, tears began to stream down her face, leaving dirt-smudged streaks on her face.

Her head fell to her hands. She had fallen deeply in love

and honestly wished to marry her golden warrior. She wanted to give Golden Eagle a son, full of life, brave as his father and huggable like Bright Blossom's Two Feathers. I've been a fool, she silently berated herself again.

Chapter Nineteen

Golden Eagle and Red Fox returned to the village leading a pony weighed down with the fruits of their hunting trip.

Jumping off his horse, Golden Eagle quickly unloaded the stallion and hobbled him behind his tipi. He returned to help Red Fox unload the game they'd brought back for their own families and for those unable to hunt for fresh meat.

Grabbing several rabbits and a large antelope for his tipi and his parents, he left the rest for Red Fox to distribute.

Golden Eagle was eager to be alone with White Wind. He now automatically thought of her by her Indian name. At his tipi, he dropped the lifeless bodies onto the ground and stepped in, eager for her warm welcome.

He was amazed how quickly Sarah had become a vital part of him, of his life. He'd known from their first meeting there was something special about the child she'd once been. Whenever he looked upon the woman she'd become, gazed into her lively blue eyes, saw how well she'd adapted to their ways, he was convinced this woman was his soul mate. He'd lost his heart to her long ago.

The depth of his feelings surprised him the most. He'd always yearned for a love as strong as his parents', but had given up ever finding it until White Wind.

Golden Eagle was happy and fulfilled. Gone was the restlessness that had seized him. Each day he left found him eager to return. White Wind, he realized, gave a meaning and purpose to his days.

Red Fox teased him without mercy. Golden Eagle frowned. To his sensitive ears there was always a thread of anger or displeasure in his friend's voice whenever he referred to "Golden Eagle's white girl." Could Red Fox be jealous of the time he spent with her?

Sighing, Golden Eagle knew he could do nothing to make his friend accept Sarah. Tonight he planned to tell White Wind of his love, confident she felt the same for him.

It took him several seconds to realized that Sarah was not waiting for him in his tipi. Frowning, he felt a prickling sense of unease go through him. He was certain he'd not seen her outside. Where was she? Maybe she was waiting for him down by the stream. The day had been warm. Perhaps she was fetching cool water for Morning Grass as she often did in the afternoons. He left the tipi with anxious strides.

Red Fox, in the process of removing the hide horse pad from the back of his horse, saw Golden Eagle head for the edge of the village, probably for the stream. He frowned. A nagging sense of uneasiness assailed him. Something was wrong. The white girl was always in the village at this time of day.

His highly trained senses sounded alarms, but he could see nothing amiss. As usual, children scampered happily about, and men sat around mending hunting tools or weapons while they told stories. Most of the older women were laughing and shouting to one another as they prepared evening meals or tended to their sewing and mending.

Red Fox's searching gaze passed over one group of older maidens and young women milling about the tipi of Bright Blossom. His sharp gaze honed in on each and every one. They were quiet, he realized, far too quiet. He watched their anxious heads turn toward Golden Eagle, following his every step.

Sarah could usually be found among them. Laughter always came from that group. Especially when they tried to teach her their language and Sarah in turn corrected their English. The result was gales of laughter at all the mistakes.

Red Fox left the hide horse pad half on and half off. He waited. He had the feeling his horse had more work to do, and leaned against the sturdiness of his mount. From the corner of his eye, he caught sight of Night Star ducking behind their tipi, her eyes fastened on Golden Eagle as he came striding back alone from the stream. He watched his sister turn and run off, smugness etched in her features.

Red Fox straightened. Her pleased grin contrasted with the glowering frowns she'd worn of late. He hoped for her sake she had not been the cause of any trouble, but when he looked over and watched the girls return to their individual tipis as Golden Eagle approached, he knew she'd been up to no good.

Golden Eagle couldn't believe what Bright Blossom was telling him. He was careful to keep his face expressionless, but his anger grew and his eyes hardened as he listened to what had happened that day.

How dare Night Star interfere. He would see that she never caused trouble in this village again. First, however, Sarah had to be found.

He spotted Red Fox waiting by his horse and ran quickly toward him. "I have need of your help, my friend. Sarah's gone."

"Say no more, my brother. I will help you find her."
As the eldest male he was responsible for his sister's actions. If she had committed a wrong, it was his duty to make it right. His father had aged much in the last few years and all family decisions had fallen to Red Fox, including dealing with his difficult sibling.

Together, Golden Eagle and Red Fox rode toward the stream where Sarah had last been seen. The sun peeked through the tree tops as they quickly picked up and followed Sarah's trail. Golden Eagle related what Bright Blossom had revealed to him.

"My sister goes too far this time. She will be punished for her troublemaking deeds," Red Fox stated, angry that Night Star had again cast the shadow of dishonor on the family.

Looking straight ahead, Golden Eagle said, "Let us hope, for her sake, White Wind comes to no harm. I will arrange a meeting with your father. The time is long overdue for Night Star to be married. As she can find no one suitable on her own, we shall arrange a marriage for her. I know of a warrior who is seeking a wife as his wife died during the winter. He will do for her."

Red Fox nodded in agreement as they stopped, the trail ending at the water's edge. Dismounting, Golden Eagle studied the torn and broken branches and scuff marks on the forest floor.

Relieved at having such an easy trail to follow, Golden Eagle suggested, "Wait there. I will follow. She can't have gotten far."

"Go to her, my brother. I will wait with the horses." Red Fox led the horses to the stream for a cool refreshing drink.

No matter his feelings regarding the white girl, Red Fox knew his friend was in love with her. Perhaps he judged harshly after all. You did not always have a choice when

181

it came to your heart, as he well knew. Images of a beautiful young maiden came to mind.

Kneeling, Red Foxed cupped a handful of cold sweet liquid and brought it to his lips. Dipping his hand for more, he froze when his sharp gaze spotted a small faint footprint. Looking closer, he spotted another. Getting to his feet, he followed the nearly invisible trail across the stream, and there saw more prints in the soft dirt leading into the dense growth.

His eyes widened as comprehension hit. Smiling, he chuckled in admiration. "What a shrewd trick." Golden Eagle would not suspect such a ploy from his woman. Red Fox looked toward the bushes where Golden Eagle had gone. He decided to investigate on his own.

Sitting on a fallen log, Sarah stared unseeingly into the green and brown of trees and brush. The snap of a dry twig startled her. Apprehension churned within as she turned, fully expecting to see Golden Eagle. She felt a stab of disappointment when she saw her visitor was only Red Fox.

Sarah tilted her chin, freezing him with her ice-cold glittering eyes, daring him to touch her.

"Golden Eagle will come once he realizes he has been tricked," Red Fox promised, hiding his amusement. "He will not be happy you made a fool of him, Sarah."

Sarah started in surprise. This was the first time Red Fox had ever addressed her directly. She shrugged her slender shoulders. "Now he will know how I feel, Red Fox. A fool fooling a fool," she said.

Red Fox grew serious and straightened. "My sister will be punished for the mischief she has caused."

"Why? Night Star spoke the truth, did she not? It matters not the motive or the method used if what she says is truth."

Frowning at Sarah's reasoning, Red Fox replied harshly, "It was not her place to tell, Sarah. My sister's only motive was to cause trouble and for that she will be punished. Come. Let us return."

Lifting her head, Sarah remained firmly on the log. "No, Red Fox. I'm not going anywhere." She watched Red Fox shrug, then retrace his steps. She prepared herself for Golden Eagle's arrival.

Golden Eagle had retraced his steps, his face a furious mask at being so easily duped by a woman. He returned to the water's edge and spotted Red Fox emerging from the low-growing shrubs across the stream.

Pointing the way, Red Fox warned, "Your woman is there. I've spoken with her. She is very angry. Her pride has been badly hurt. She refused to return with me."

"Thank you, my friend." Golden Eagle, deep in thought, rested his hands on his lean hips and stared at the lowering sun. Finally, he came to a decision. He told Red Fox of his plan, and the two clasped shoulders and went their separate ways. Red Fox headed back to the village, while Golden Eagle went to Sarah.

Sarah looked up when Golden Eagle burst into the tiny clearing in which she nervously waited. Two pairs of angry eyes clashed, neither willing to concede.

Stepping forward, Golden Eagle crossed his arms over his sun-darkened chest. He read the fury and hurt in her eyes and so calmed his own anger, recognizing that she did indeed have reason to be upset. Her pride had been damaged as well, but he had no doubt that he could convince her of his love.

"It grows late. We go and talk before darkness covers our land. No more games, White Wind."

Sarah leaned back on her hands, looked Golden Eagle up and down and said, "I have nothing to say to Golden Eagle. Golden Eagle used Sarah as Willy would have. At least Willy did not pretend with me. There is nothing more to say, except I wish to return home." As an afterthought, she added, "And my name is Sarah, not White Wind."

"No!" Golden Eagle's hand slashed the air. "Your Indian name is White Wind. This is your home now. You belong here. It was meant to be."

"It is you who refuses to see, Golden Eagle," Sarah replied, her voice detached and aloof. "My home is where my people are. I belong there. You have your life, your future wife all picked out and waiting for you. I do not think she will want to share your tipi with your lover, nor would I share your tipi with your wife."

She shrugged her shoulders. "So you see, there really is nothing to discuss—unless, of course, you are not promised to this girl after all, unless you are free to be with me?" Sarah arched her brow, clearly waiting and wishing for his denial.

With a wave of her arm when no such denial came forth, Sarah dismissed him, ignoring the furious anger that waited to erupt. "We will not discuss this any longer, Golden Eagle. You must leave. I wish to be alone. I know the way back and will return when I'm ready." Sarah emphasized each word slowly and clearly.

Golden Eagle compressed his lips tightly and his fisted hands fell to his sides. "You have expressed your anger. I know you have been hurt. We will discuss this matter—now," he thundered. He took two steps toward her, his hands held out, obviously willing to meet her halfway, although his patience was being worn thin by her stubbornness.

He narrowed his eyes and waited for Sarah to rise. When she turned her head away and made no move to stand, his temper nearly snapped.

His hands fell to his side. In a deceptively soft voice, he advised, "Do not defy me, Sarah. You've made your point. Come to me," he commanded in measured tones while pointing to the ground in front of his feet.

Sarah stared at the place where Golden Eagle pointed before moving her gaze up his outstretched arm. Every line in the warrior's body warned of unleashed anger that would soon explode.

If any in his village had been in Sarah's spot, they would have immediately responded, knowing that this warrior wasn't accustomed to being disobeyed or questioned.

But Sarah's hurt and her feelings of betrayal ran so deep, she just didn't care. The look she bestowed upon him said he couldn't possible hurt her anymore than he already had.

"No," she stated, arms crossed as she glanced back at the spot Golden Eagle indicated.

"Get up and come here now." Golden Eagle's slow and menacing words threatened retribution if not obeyed immediately.

"I refused to come to Golden Eagle," Sarah said, scrambling over the log as the angry warrior advanced.

With long strides Golden Eagle stopped in front of the log that Sarah now stood behind. "I warned you not to push me, White Wind." With that reminder, he lifted a foot to the log and leaped over.

Sarah stepped back, keeping out of arm's reach.

Golden Eagle lunged, grabbed Sarah around her waist and swung her up and over his broad shoulders before she realized his intentions.

Ignoring her kicking feet and pounding fists, Golden Eagle stalked through the woods unaware of the low tree limbs that snagged and scratched as he shoved his way through.

"Put me down," Sarah shrieked. Her fists pummeled his back. When that had no effect, she reached down and pinched the flesh near his sides.

A hiss of pain escaped Golden Eagle's clenched jaw. He reached up and smacked the back of her thighs with the flat of his hand. Hearing her squeal of outrage, he cautioned, "Behave."

"I hate you, Golden Eagle. I hate you," Sarah screamed.

Wading through the stream, he deposited her on the ground besides his horse. "Now, do you come with me

185

willing or not?'' he asked, giving her one more chance to change her mind and save her pride.

Crossing her arms and feet, Sarah sat, unmoving. Her defiant and mutinous expression was the sole response to his question.

With a sigh of resignation, Golden Eagle reached down and hauled her squirming figure into his arms. None too gently, he tossed her, belly down, across the back of his horse and mounted behind her.

Golden Eagle was determined to make her understand the circumstances surrounding his betrothal to Wild-Flower. He was angry that she'd not given him the chance to explain.

Pressing one hand into the small of her back to keep Sarah from falling, he held the braided buffalo-hair lead in the other as he ignored Sarah's yells.

Chapter Twenty

Sarah groaned as the horse plodded uphill, winding its way slowly around trees and boulders. She'd never been so humiliated, so badly treated, in all her young life. Her stomach ached from the jarring motion of the horse, her arms dangling over her head were numb and her head pounded. In a word, she was miserable.

Breaking her vow not to plead for mercy, Sarah raised her head. Straining and twisting to see Golden Eagle, she tried to reason with him. "Please, Golden Eagle, let me up. I promise to sit quietly."

Golden Eagle looked down into her pleading eyes, his face impassive to her misery. "No. You had your chance. You were warned. Now you must suffer the consequences."

Using her hands against the side of the horse for leverage, Sarah jerked up as far as she could and threw him a venomous look. "You're a savage animal, mean and heartless. Do you hear me?" she stormed, trying to kick away his hand. "Just you wait, you'll be sorr—"

"You are in no position to make threats, my stubborn wildcat. Be still and sheathe your claws or you will fall on your hard head."

A short time later Golden Eagle drew to a halt. Dismounting, he reached up and pulled Sarah down, letting her land in a heap at his feet.

Sarah groaned, her head spinning dizzily as the world righted itself. Prickly sensations in her arms told her the numbness had left her limbs as the blood flowed. She was thankful to be off the horse. Opening her eyes, she silently watched as the animal was unloaded and hobbled nearby to graze and rest.

She sat, uncaring, as Golden Eagle disappeared behind some thick bushes. With a satisfied expression, he returned and gathered the load that had been lashed to the back of his horse. Again he went behind the concealing bushes. Upon his reappearance, Golden Eagle reached down and scooped Sarah up into his strong arms.

"Put me down, I can walk," Sarah demanded.

Stopping in front of the bushes, Golden Eagle looked into eyes that still blazed with anger. Shaking his head wearily, he commented, "Will you not learn, little one? Perhaps I should toss you over my shoulder again, or drag you by your arms, or hair, as a true savage would."

Sarah lowered her eyes, seething. She knew she was pushing all limits, but she could not seem to stop herself.

Behind the bushes, they came to a dark opening. Sarah could see nothing but a large black void. Entering the darkness, Sarah involuntarily clutched Golden Eagle around the neck, burying her head against his shoulders.

She heard his chuckle, but the darkness had swallowed him as well as everything else. They were in a cave, a large one with a long winding tunnel. Ahead—at least she thought it was ahead—she could see a faint light dispersing the darkness somewhat.

Rounding a slight bend, Golden Eagle stopped. Looking around, Sarah saw they were indeed inside a large cavern.

Her eyes lifted to follow the trail of dust particles floating upward. Through a small hole high up in the top, fading daylight filtered in, which displaced the total blackness in this part of the cavern and left the small enclosure bathed softly in shadowy light.

Sarah examined the cave. The air was musky and cold, but at least it was dry and free from animals—with exception of one, Sarah thought crossly to herself.

Striding toward the back wall, Golden Eagle deposited his armful onto the pallet he'd already laid out. His look cautioned she'd better stay put.

As she watched, he disappeared into the murky tunnel. He soon returned with an armload of small twigs and branches, which he arranged in the center of the cave, directly under the small opening overhead.

With a small fire to ward off the chill, he turned to Sarah, sitting forlornly on his pallet. "Now we talk. We stay here as long as it takes for you to listen."

Hugging her arms to her body, not only against the cave's coolness but what he would say, Sarah leaned wearily against the cold walls. "What is there to say? You did not tell me that you were to be married. You led me to believe . . ." Sarah stopped, unable to confess that she'd thought he loved her.

Golden Eagle kneeled in front of Sarah and placed his hands upon her shivering shoulders. Forcing her to meet his honest, searching gaze, he spoke. "I love you, White Wind. I love you as I love no other. And I know that you love me. We are meant to be. I have told you that. We will remain here until I can convince you of this. You do not understand our ways, but you must understand that I speak the truth when I say I want and need only you."

Looking into his serious love-filled gaze, Sarah felt hysteria build as she cried out, "Why are you doing this to me?"

She swallowed hard, drew her knees to her chest and struggled to contain the deep hurt that threatened to spill out. He must not see. She had to control her anger.

"What you say is not true," she told him. "We both know that soon you will marry. She will share your tipi, cook your meals and bear you sons." She waved him to silence.

"I don't belong here, Golden Eagle. I want to go home." Sarah choked, forcing down the awful urge to throw herself in his arms, desperate to keep herself from begging him to love her as she loved him.

She raised her head bravely as she pushed the heavy lies from her lips. "I don't want you anymore and I don't want you to ever touch me again. And I don't want your false declarations of love."

"No, my sweet one. You want me. You want my touch. Your mind can deceive you, but not your body. You love me." Golden Eagle finished with a grim smile.

Sarah glared at him in frustration. Her arms tightened around her knees, knuckles turning white. There was no way she'd admit the truth to him, admit that all it took was a look and she would melt. She steeled her heart. Giving in now would only let her in for more heartache later.

"I hate what you've done to me, Golden Eagle. You have not told me the truth. I had to hear it from someone else." That bitter thought made her next words easier. "I don't want anything more to do with you, Golden Eagle. I especially don't want your lovemaking. Save that for your wife." Her cold controlled voice formed a barrier between them.

Golden Eagle straightened, clenched his jaw in frustration and moved toward Sarah. Slipping a hand behind her neck, he took her mouth in a bruising kiss, demanding a response.

Sarah willed her body not to respond. She would prove to him his kisses meant nothing to her anymore, that he'd killed all feeling with his betrayal.

Unfortunately, her body did not feel the same way as her mind. As his kiss gentled, fire began to flow in her veins, thawing the coldness she sought to retain. Her dress came off with one swoop and she felt herself lowered.

Her wall of resistance slowly started to crumble. "Please, Golden Eagle, don't do this," she whispered. Her body trembled, ached and any minute now would betray her. She couldn't bear that, couldn't bear his smile of triumph.

Lifting his head, Golden Eagle stared into eyes smoky-blue with desire. "Admit that you want my touch. That you enjoy my kisses. That you need me as much as I need you."

Sarah turned her head. She could not bring herself to say the words aloud. She'd lost. There was no way for her to win. He could so easily prove her words of denial for the lies that they would be.

Golden Eagle shook his head at the obstinate girl, and moved over her, lips leaving feather-light kisses along her contours with tantalizing tenderness.

Moving her head side to side as his lips latched onto her peaked nipples, Sarah moaned and helplessly thrust her firm flesh into his mouth, silently begging for more. Her body had betrayed her after all. Quivers of desire surged from head to toe, but she'd not betray herself by saying the words he wanted. Moving her hands to his shoulders, she squirmed beneath his weight.

"Your body gives me my answer, little one. But I will hear the words from your lips." He whispered into her ear, taking one hand into his, drawing each finger, one by one, between moist lips to suckle. His other hand lightly caressed the rosy tips of her breasts, before moving downward, blazing a heated path across her ribs.

His lips and tongue followed the downward trail, stopping to explore her navel, dipping in, swirling in and around the small crater before leaving lingering kisses on the softness of her belly.

Sarah was on fire. Her muscles contracted fiercely, painfully. Her lips rose silently, begging for relief as only he could give her.

191

She whimpered as he parted her legs, his lips and tongue tasting and nibbling on the softness of her sensitive inner thighs. Anticipating the hardness of his throbbing manhood, Sarah tried to pull him to her, her hips moving in an unmistakable invitation.

Her eyes flew open as the warm wetness of his mouth and tongue found her hidden folds, her hips jerking in response to his explorations.

She lifted her head, and her hands reached out to his dark head buried among her curly blond nether-hairs. ''No, Golden Eagle, not there,'' she protested weakly, dropping back to the soft fur beneath her as incredible waves of pleasure assailed her when his tongue found and stroked her hidden jewel.

He lifted his head momentarily, and his voice washed over her, warm, husky and thick with desire. ''Yes, my love. Here. Like this.''

Moaning softly at the wondrous sensations his tongue aroused, she felt shivers of racing desire take hold. Her hips arched wildly, lifting for more, seeking the fulfillment that only her golden warrior could give her.

Golden Eagle's breathing grew ragged, out of control, as his tongue and lips explored and tasted every hidden crevice.

Whispery mews of pleasure, harsh moans of throbbing desire filled the dimly lit cavern. Voices twined, whispering, begging, pleading, as cries of desperate need swirled around the lovers, bathing them in a pool of drugging passion.

Golden Eagle lifted glazed eyes and moved into Sarah's outstretched arms as he removing his hindering piece of clothing. Holding her head between his hands, he looked into her smoldering blue eyes.

''Tell me, sweet Sarah. Tell me that you want me. Tell me you want my touch,'' he hoarsely commanded as he rocked his hips forward, rubbing his throbbing hardness against her heated softness.

Stalling, Sarah begged, "Please, Golden Eagle. Please love me." Desperately, she thrust her hips forward, trying to capture him in her velvety sheath.

"Tell me!"

With a ragged sob, Sarah burst out, "Yes! Oh, yes. I want you, I need you. Please love me."

Lifting her hips with both hands, poised at her entrance, Golden Eagle whispered, "Do you really hate me?"

Looking into his serious gaze, Sarah groaned. She reached up to trace his full lips with shaking fingers. "No, my golden warrior, I don't hate you. For to hate you would be to hate a part of myself."

The truth was there, on her face, burning brightly from passion-filled eyes though she hadn't said the words. They both knew he could force the words from her. "I'll not force you to tell me of your love. It is here, in your eyes when you look at me." Golden Eagle kissed each lid. "Here in your body that trembles for mine. Soon, you will hold nothing back from this warrior."

Threading his fingers with hers, he took her lips urgently as he thrust deeply, fiercely into her. Savage need ruled as they rode the storm of their mutual passion.

It was late. The chill of the darkened cave woke Golden Eagle. Rising, he stretched his arms overhead, unaware of the play of muscles rippling across his back as he worked out the kinks.

In the faint shadows, he found the small pile of wood and gathered an armful. Soon he had the dying embers licking eagerly at the new fuel as the fire roared to life. The warmth quickly warded off the growing chill and the dancing flames dispelled the gloom, replacing it with the cheerful oranges, reds and yellows.

Pleased with the results of the crackling fire, Golden Eagle walked over to his pile of supplies. He lifted a wrapped bundle and unrolled a pouch of dried meat and fruit. He gathered a small portion and grabbed the water pouch be-

193

fore straightening. As an afterthought, he knelt and reached into another pouch and retrieved an object before returning to the pallet.

Setting the food aside, he reached down, trailing a finger along Sarah's velvety cheek, coaxing her to wake. As he watched, Sarah yawned and stretched her supple young body.

Golden Eagle smiled indulgently as Sarah curled back up, trying to regain some warmth. He pulled her to a sitting position in front of him, closer to the warm crackling fire.

Sarah leaned into his solid warmth and let her head fall to rest against Golden Eagle's shoulder. His arms wrapped around her, embracing her with his warmth. Her eyes closed as she yawned again and sniffed the smoky spiciness of the air. Fire and their presence had long since dispelled the damp, musky smell. Sarah sighed with contentment.

Golden Eagle pulled Sarah tight against his chest and leaned down to rub his cheek against hers. "We must talk, White Wind." He tipped her head back and gazed into her eyes. "You are mine. You belong to me, just as I belong to you. You must see that you were sent to be my soul mate, my life's helpmate. I cannot let you go. I ask that you agree to stay with me. No fighting. No running away."

Sarah stiffened, and turned back to stare at the yellow-orange flames. "I don't want to fight you or myself, but I'm afraid of the future." She closed her eyes against the tears welling there. "It won't work, Golden Eagle. It can't work," Sarah whispered hoarsely.

"It will work. I promise all will work out. The Great Spirit has chosen you for my life's mate. He will reveal this to my father and Chief White Cloud. My mother has already seen this. Her gift is greatly valued among my people. We must be patient," Golden Eagle reassured her.

Securely nestled against him, Sarah leaned her head back into the crook of his neck, her hands resting on his brawny arms as they held her tightly. Letting out a shaky sigh, she spoke softly. "I wish to believe this, my golden warrior.

You know me well. I cannot refuse you, or fight you any longer. I'll stay for as long as I am allowed.''

Golden Eagle's sigh of relief warmed her cheek. Taking a deep breath, she added, ''I have one condition to ask of you.''

''Condition? What condition would you ask of me?'' Golden Eagle's brows furrowed as he anxiously waited.

Choosing her words carefully, Sarah spoke quietly. ''If you must marry Wild-Flower, I ask that you respect my wishes and return me to my home.'' Turning to see Golden Eagle frown in displeasure, Sarah confessed, ''I can't share you with another. It is not our way. It would cause me great pain to see you married to another. Do not ask that of me.''

Pulling her back into his arms, Golden Eagle sat for long moments in deep thought. ''I will not allow you to return to your home unless it is safe for you to do so.'' He held his hand high to forestall her protests. ''In the meantime, I give you my tipi and all within, save my warrior's belongings. Should Golden Eagle have no choice but to make Wild Flower his wife, White Wind will have her freedom and her home.''

Golden Eagle sighed and wrapped his arms tightly around White Wind. ''This warrior promises to find a safe place for you to go to if you must leave. With your own tipi, you would not be considered a slave.'' He felt Sarah's nod as she accepted his compromise, although he alone knew he would never let her go. Holding out his hand in front of her, he opened his palm. There sat the wooden eagle. ''I wish to place this where it belongs.'' He slipped it over her head, pleased with her gasp of pleasure.

Lightly he placed a forefinger under her chin and turned her to him. Looking deeply into her moist eyes, he saw love shining there. ''Does White Wind have words to say to her golden warrior? Words that he longs to hear from her lips, not just see in her eyes?''

Grinning with mischief, Sarah turned in his arms, her fingers wrapped around the much-loved eagle, and placed a finger tip to his lips and traced the fullness. "Are not actions better than words, my brave warrior?" The corners of his lips beneath her caressing fingers started to turn downward, and Sarah hastily added, "I only tease, my love. My golden warrior knows of my love for him."

On her knees, straddling him, Sarah clasped his face between her hands and planted light kisses over his face as she declared, "I love you, Golden Eagle. With all that is me, I love you. Without you and your love, I would be as an empty shell. I wish to show my love to you."

Trailing her lips down his warm body, she eagerly explored his firm flesh. Closing her hand around his swollen flesh, fingers stroking his velvety softness, Sarah lowered her head. Golden Eagle fell back on his elbows as his hoarse moans of pleasure echoed off the walls when she did indeed show her love.

Chapter Twenty-one

Golden Eagle and Sarah remained in the secluded cave for two days, leaving only to take long walks, refill the water and food pouches and bathe. On their last morning they woke late and had a leisurely meal of nuts, fresh berries and pemmican, the shredded dried meat Sarah so enjoyed.

Golden Eagle loaded the horse and by early afternoon, they were set to return. Swinging onto the sturdy animal's back, he pulled Sarah behind him, her arms wrapping around his waist. "Are you ready?"

Twisting around, Sarah nodded. "I wish we could stay longer. But yes, I suppose I am ready."

"We will come here many times. There are many beautiful places Golden Eagle wishes to show you. We will explore them together." And with a quick kiss for her, he nudged his horse forward, Sarah settling behind him as they wound their way downhill, the sun's radiant rays following the progress of the couple.

They weren't far from the cave when Golden Eagle unexpectedly drew to a halt. Without moving his head, he made a slight movement with his hand, warning Sarah to keep silent. He sniffed the air. He felt a prickling sense of unease run down his spine and knew the enemy was behind them.

Golden Eagle tugged Great Star around to face the way they'd just come. He slid one hand to the hilt of the knife strapped to his calf and slowly drew it from its sheath.

Sarah gasped as two figures stepped out from the trees, lances and shields held in their hands, eyes glinting with evil.

Golden Eagle took in their ragged clothing and dirty appearance, and knew these Arikara Indians were renegades on their own. He wondered briefly if there were more.

One of the warriors pointed his lance toward Sarah, clearly indicating what they wanted. Golden Eagle was using sign language to reject their offer to trade when he spotted a movement from the corner of his eye. "Hold tight, White Wind," he yelled as a third warrior appeared behind them, attempting to snatch Sarah from behind. A sharp tug on the reins, accompanied by a terse command, and the stallion whirled about, rearing high on his hind legs, front hooves flailing the renegade warrior.

Golden Eagle watched his enemy fall beneath his horse to lay unmoving as the other two advanced. A bolt of fear struck him, fear not for himself, but for White Wind's life. He knew he must get her away, keep her safe at all costs. If he attempted to bolt, Sarah stood a chance of having a thrown lance pierce her back. He came to a decision.

He turned, placed the reins in Sarah's hands and commanded, "Go. Ride for our village. Do not stop or look back. Get to safety, White Wind." Golden Eagle jumped down with a loud whoop and slapped the flanks of the horse, sending the stallion down the path toward safety.

Sarah made a grab at the horse's long flowing mane to prevent being thrown as the animal lunged forward. She glanced back and saw the two warriors advance, circling Golden Eagle, knives drawn.

"No," she cried, turning back to the stallion, trying to halt his headlong flight. She struggled with the reins until the horse reared in protest. Talking in a low, soothing voice, she finally calmed the animal, yanked him around and prayed it wasn't too late to help Golden Eagle.

How could she go on if anything happened to her golden warrior? She suddenly realized that she would rather see Golden Eagle married to Wild-Flower than have him hurt or worse. She kept her eyes focused ahead, and saw the two warriors and Golden Eagle. The taste of fear flooded her mouth, and she nearly fainted when she saw the amount of blood streaming from gashes on Golden Eagle and one other warrior as knives were viciously slashed into flesh.

Sarah's gaze locked onto Golden Eagle's crouched form. He held his knife in front of him, oblivious to all but the two circling warriors in front of him. She clapped one hand over her mouth to keep from crying out when one warrior's knife made contact with Golden Eagle's arm.

With a cry of outrage, she steered Great Star into the group, scattering the warriors. Spinning around, she felt her blood turned to ice as one warrior ran toward her, his intentions clear, while his friend kept Golden Eagle occupied.

"Run, White Wind," Golden Eagle ordered once again.

"No, I won't leave you," Sarah shouted, preparing to run Great Star at the enemy again. Digging her heels into the sides of the horse, she let out a strangled cry as the Indian feinted to one side and grabbed her leg as she charged by.

Sarah found herself on the ground, flat on her back, the wind knocked out of her. She stared into the grinning face of their enemy as she struggled to get her breath back. As the filthy renegade neared, hunkering down on his haunches, she turned on her side, drew her knees to her chest as she lifted herself on one elbow and allowed a look of helpless fear to overcome her.

Susan Edwards

The Indian tossed his knife to the side with a laugh that made her flesh crawl. His intense gaze burned into her as he leered. Sarah forced herself to remain still in her half-crouched position, keeping an eye on his every move, her heart pounding so loudly she couldn't hear above it. When his hand came toward her, she noticed his thigh muscles beginning to bunch as he prepared to spring.

She sprung first, thankful for the fighting moves Golden Eagle had taught her. Her coiled feet kicked out, making contact with the warrior's groin, as she leapt to her feet and assumed the same crouched position that Golden Eagle and the other warrior were using as they continued to circle and slash at one another.

One of Sarah's hands remained at her side, lost in the folds of her skirt, palm slick with sweat as she concealed the small but sharp knife she used for her chores. She was now thankful she'd taken to wearing her knife strapped to her thigh as the other women did.

The warrior assumed the same crouch, his eyes furious slits, his breathing labored, indicating the pain he still felt. With a loud cry the warrior charged, hands outstretched.

Sarah held her breath, clenched the knife and waited until her enemy was nearly on her before ducking to the left. Her right hand shot out from her side to make contact with the warrior's chest, using his forward momentum to her advantage as the hidden knife flashed briefly before imbedding itself to the hilt in the chest of the attacker.

Breathing heavily, she watched the warrior fall and writhe in pain before gasping his last breath. She glanced over at Golden Eagle, and sucked in her breath in horror as Golden Eagle fell to his knees from a vicious kick to his middle. Each warrior sported several gashes on his arms and chest.

The other warrior laughed and brought his hand high, the sun glinting on his bloodied knife—Golden Eagle's blood, Sarah realized with a sick feeling of dread. Without conscious thought, Sarah yelled and flew toward the gloating

200

warrior, jumped on his back and used both hands to keep him from stabbing Golden Eagle.

Suddenly, the warrior jerked backwards, knocking Sarah to the ground as his legs crumpled beneath him. Sarah screamed as the warrior fell on top of her, his blood soaking her, his weight pinning her to the ground, blocking out the sunlight.

Sarah gasped for breath, fought the darkness closing in on her and shoved, scooting out from under the now-dead Indian. She closed her eyes, shuddering against the grisly sight of the warrior, his innards spilling out from the long slash from chest to abdomen made by Golden Eagle, who still held his blood-dripping knife.

A wave of nausea assailed her and she turned away, retching as the events of the afternoon hit her. Strong arms held her shaking body, soft soothing words finally penetrating her numbed mind as the nausea passed. "White Wind, are you all right? Speak to me," the voice insisted.

Sarah glanced over her shoulder, her eyes locking onto the most wonderful sight she could ever wish to behold. "Golden Eagle," she sobbed, throwing herself into his outstretched arms.

As Golden Eagle held Sarah, he stared at the other two warriors, making sure they posed no further threat. The one his White Wind had taken care of lay dead, sightless eyes trained to the sky above, and the other lay trampled, a deep gash in his forehead from Great Star's mighty hooves.

He continued to whisper his love and praise to Sarah, who had grown quiet—too quiet, he thought. "Look at me, White Wind," he commanded, putting Sarah from him.

As Sarah continued to stare at the ground, shaking uncontrollably, he lifted her chin and stared into her empty gaze. Golden Eagle realized she was in shock. He knew she'd never killed another human before, nor witnessed such gruesome deaths. He drew himself unsteadily to his feet, forced the pain away and concentrated on White Wind.

"You disobeyed me, White Wind. Did I not tell you to go? Did I not command you to seek safety and not look back?" he lashed out, his voice furious. As her head turned to him in disbelief, he continued. "I am angry that you disregarded my orders. You are my woman, you will obey me."

Sarah jumped to her feet, eyes now blazing with anger. "I saved your life, Golden Eagle. How can you speak to me like this? How could I have lived with myself if I had left and you never returned because of my cowardice?"

She turned away, not seeing Golden Eagle's lips lift slightly at the corners. Golden Eagle watched, his eyes shining with pride, as Sarah spun around and came back at him. "You keep telling me we are soul mates. If you die, then I lose my soul mate. I may belong to you, Golden Eagle, but you also belong to me and I will protect what is mine. Do you hear me, Golden Eagle?"

Golden Eagle placed his hands on Sarah's shoulders and drew her close, staring intently into her dark angry eyes. "Golden Eagle hears you, White Wind. White Wind is a true warrior's mate. This warrior is proud of your actions this day. I should punish you for disobeying me, for putting yourself in danger, but I am glad you returned. You saved my life this day."

Sarah threw her arms around Golden Eagle's neck and whispered, "We are even now, my golden warrior." She drew back as he moaned in pain. "You're hurt, Golden Eagle," she exclaimed. "Why did you not say anything?" she demanded, her eyes taking in the many cuts and slashes, two of them bleeding profusely.

Golden Eagle waved aside her concern. "We must leave and return to the safety of our village."

Sarah stepped back and whistled for his horse. Golden Eagle's brows rose at her perfect imitation of his call. Sarah shrugged. "I've been practicing. Black Lady comes when I whistle to her too," she added.

Golden Eagle found himself seated while Sarah checked

his wounds, bathing the cuts from the water left in their water skin. Using his retrieved knife to cut long strips off her skirt, she bound the two deep gashes, one on his forearm and the other in his side.

"There, now we can start back. I will finish tending to your injuries when we return," Sarah said, her tone leaving him in no doubt of her seriousness. He knew from his mother that with the knowledge she'd brought with her and what his people had taught her, Sarah's skills at healing had become highly respected. Many of his people now sought her advice.

Golden Eagle stood, grimacing as stiffness and pain set in. He glanced once more around him before he made the attempt to mount, and noticed the warrior Sarah had killed still had her knife protruding from his chest. He halted Sarah with a gentle pull on the arm. "You cannot leave your knife behind, White Wind. If there are others around, they will know it was our tribe who killed their warriors. You must remove it."

Golden Eagle watched the color drain from her face, and was prepared to go fetch it for her, but Sarah drew herself up and strode over to the dead Indian to do what she had to do.

He watched Sarah pull the knife free and wipe it on the leaves, shuddering as she did so. She then turned, faced him with head held high before replacing the blade in the sheath strapped to her thigh. Returning to stand before him, she indicated that she was now ready to return.

Chapter Twenty-two

They arrived at the village by late afternoon. Golden Eagle stopped abruptly before entering the circles of tipis. A softly uttered curse near her ear startled Sarah.

She turned in surprise, a frown appearing as she noticed lines of displeasure etched about his mouth. Following his gaze, she too saw a large group of people unknown to her. Her eyes settled on one particular girl standing apart from the others.

She appeared restless and wandered aimlessly while her dark eyes scanned the area, as if searching for someone. Blue-black hair hung past her tiny waist, swishing back and forth with each agitated step. Her one-piece dress reached mid-calf, the long fringe brushing against strong brown legs encased in colorful quill-topped moccasins with beaded sides. When she turned toward them, Sarah could only envy the elaborate beading across the yoke of her garment. Row upon row of beaded design covered the entire yoke.

As they neared the girl, Sarah stared into the eyes of the Indian maiden and her mouth went dry. She knew without doubt that this was Wild-Flower. But what puzzled her was the lack of resentment she felt as she stared into the dark gaze of the woman her golden warrior was to wed. She trembled when a flash of recognition ran through her, yet she had never met this girl before. She shrugged the unsettling feeling away. "She is very beautiful, Golden Eagle," Sarah ventured, her voice no more than an awed whisper.

Golden Eagle turned to Sarah. "Not as beautiful as you, White Wind. I'm sorry this had to happen so soon," he said, clearly torn by duties and feelings.

Sarah squared her shoulders and took a deep breath. "We will first tend to your wounds. Then you must greet your guests. I will remain in your tipi. There is much to be done after being away these past days."

Golden Eagle stopped in front of his large tipi to let Sarah slide down from the horse before dismounting himself. He kept hold of her hand as he corrected her. "Your tipi, White Wind. I shall paint your brave act of this day on the outside for all to behold. Tonight, I shall tell all of your braveness."

Eyes glowing with pride, he allowed Sarah to lead him inside as his mother joined them, a bowl full of herbs in her arms as word of his injuries had already spread through the camp.

Wild-Flower continued to scan the village. Where was he? Where had he gone? Full red lips pouted, and her ginger-brown eyes dismissed all men present as she searched for a particular warrior. She paced restlessly, her long hair swinging impatiently behind her.

Narrowing her eyes, Wild-Flower scrutinized the people of Golden Eagle's village intently. She sighed as she spotted the one she sought between two tipis. Her breath caught, and she forgot those around her. He was truly magnificent.

Wild-Flower took several deep breaths and willed her

body to relax. Lowering her head, she secretly studied the warrior through admiring eyes.

He stood on the other side of the village, his dark body smooth and sleek from the laborious work of cutting and stripping bark off the fallen tree. She watched, fascinated, as muscles rippled across his powerful broad chest and his sinewy arms bulged as he ripped another long piece of bark away. Just watching him work was sheer torture.

When Running Wolf had announced he was traveling to the village of Chief Hawk Eyes, she had made excuses to join her brother. She needed to see again the mighty warrior who had caught her eye when Golden Eagle last visited their village.

If only she could choose her own mate. This arranged marriage was not fair. Let Golden Eagle take another to his mat as wife. Wild-Flower bit her lip in frustration.

"Why does my sister stand alone?" a concerned voice asked.

Turning her head reluctantly toward her older brother, Wild-Flower hid her desire and interest for the other warrior. "Do not worry so, my brother."

Chuckling, Running Wolf teased, "Maybe my sister waits eagerly for her soon-to-be husband?"

Flashing her brother a scornful look, Wild-Flower lifted her chin as she advised, "Watch yourself, Running Wolf. You know my feelings on this matter. They have not changed."

Pursing her lips, she thoughtfully remarked, "Have you also heard that Golden Eagle has taken a white captive to his tipi?"

Lifting his head in surprise, Running Wolf asked, "What game do you play now, Wild-Flower?"

Raising her eyes to meet her brother's displeased expression, she stated, "I play no game, brother. Golden Eagle has a white captive and she shares his tipi. I was told this."

"Why would Golden Eagle take a white woman to live

in his tipi? He is soon to be joined with you." Scorn laced his voice. Running Wolf was still not convinced that his sister was serious.

Looking at her brother in amazement and exasperation, Wild-Flower shook her head. "If I need to tell you why, my brother, then you know little of the ways of a man and a woman."

Waving his angry protest aside, she added, "I understand she is very beautiful." Wild-Flower thought back to her friend Bright Blossom's news.

Flushing from his sister's sarcasm, Running Wolf angrily declared, "If what you say is true, I shall speak to Golden Eagle immediately upon his return."

"No! You will not interfere," Wild-Flower informed him, her tone such that even he dared not go against her. If what she'd heard was true, that Golden Eagle loved his white captive and she him, there was hope. Maybe her only hope.

Giving Wild-Flower a speculative look, Running Wolf warned, "You will join with Golden Eagle, my stubborn sister. It was decided long ago. Just remember this."

Scowling, Wild-Flower watched Running Wolf stomp away angrily. Turning her attention back to Red Fox, she was disappointed to see that he had left. Once again she began her search for the warrior who had captured her heart.

As her gaze roamed the village once again, she noticed a male and female just entering the circle of tipis. Her shoulders slumped in defeat with the return of Golden Eagle. She cursed the spirits that worked against her. Why couldn't he have stayed away just one more day?

Her curiosity overcame her frustration and she watched the pair stop in front of Golden Eagle's tipi. Wild-Flower frowned when she saw evidence of Golden Eagle's injuries, but smiled to herself as she witnessed the tenderness that Golden Eagle bestowed upon the white girl before allowing her to lead him into the tipi, followed by Seeing Eyes. The white girl did not look to be afraid or unhappy. That was a very good sign.

Hoping to avoid conversation with Golden Eagle, Wild-Flower turned away and threaded her way through the shady trees. Coming to the water's edge, she found a cool spot and sat. The gentle babbling of the flowing water relaxed her. She had much to think about, much to plan.

Returning from his refreshing bath, Red Fox tried in vain to put thoughts of Wild-Flower aside. He groaned, and his loins tightened with just the thought of the lovely maiden.

He'd felt her eyes upon him as he worked, heating his body to a feverish pitch. Finally, not able to stand any more, he'd left to bathe and cool his body. With luck, Golden Eagle would return today.

Rounding the bend, he came to an abrupt halt. The woman of his thoughts was sitting before him. Perhaps he could sneak back the way he'd come.

Wild-Flower chose that moment to glance up, her innocent gaze meeting his, and he cursed. Out of politeness he could not walk away. Taking a deep breath, he continued on his path.

Wild-Flower smiled before quickly lowering her head in respect.

"Why does Wild-Flower sit here alone?" Red Fox asked.

Looking up shyly, Wild-Flower replied softly, "It is quiet and peaceful here, Red Fox. Wild-Flower enjoys the beauty of your village."

Letting her husky voice wash over him, the soft tones soothing his jangled nerves, Red Fox swallowed his uneasiness in her presence and offered, "It is nearly time for the evening meal. Perhaps you will allow this warrior to escort you back to the tipi of Chief Hawk Eyes."

Wild-Flower kept her eyes lowered and stood. "That is very kind of you, Red Fox. Thank you." In silence, they made their way to the tipi of the chief, Red Fox one stride ahead.

As she sat alone in Golden Eagle's tipi, Sarah's belly rumbled with hunger. The smell of many cooking fires reminded her that she hadn't had anything to eat since that morning, hadn't been able to bring herself to eat since they'd returned.

She'd not seen Golden Eagle since he'd left after submitting to his mother's and her ministrations of packing the deep cuts with chewed *maka skithe,* or sweet medicine, taken from the part of the hop root three feet underground, and then dressing them with a paste made from several other roots and herbs. He'd then declared that his wounds were not serious enough to keep him from his responsibilities.

She too had gone right to work, softening an antelope skin that she had already tanned by rubbing a mixture of fat and antelope brains into the hide and leaving it out to dry in the sun, before gathering wood and water, anything to keep from reliving the horrible nightmare of the attack.

Now, however, she wondered what to do about the evening meal. Normally, she took her evening meals here with Golden Eagle, or occasionally with his family. But with guests visiting, she knew he would be expected to join his family this night. Sarah was loath to join them. The nature of the guests made it seem improper and too uncomfortable.

Crawling over to the parfleche of dried meat she'd prepared, she decided to eat in her tipi. Crossing her legs, she withdrew a piece from the rawhide bag, and was just about to pop it in her mouth when Golden Eagle came through the doorway.

"Why are you sitting here, White Wind? We are ready to eat. You are not still upset from what happened earlier, are you?" Golden Eagle asked, frowning when he noticed the dried jerky Sarah was about to consume.

Looking up in surprise, Sarah pointed out, "Your family

has guests, Golden Eagle. I will eat here. It would not be proper for me to eat with your family this day. I have food here. You must join your guests.''

Sarah did not meet his searching gaze. It was harder than she'd thought it would be to know he would have to leave and join his betrothed for a meal.

"No. You will eat with us as is your custom to do so. Wild-Flower and the others do not change anything, White Wind. Come, let us not hold up the meal.''

"Golden Eagle,'' Sarah begged. "Think of Wild-Flower. My being present isn't fair to her. It will only make things more difficult. Your father will also be displeased. It's only for one or two nights. . . .'' Her voice trailed off as Golden Eagle advanced.

Golden Eagle pressed his lips together, his hands planted firmly on lean hips as he silently stared at Sarah.

Sighing, Sarah knew he wouldn't take no for an answer. Putting away the untouched meat, she stood and followed him out to his parents' tipi.

After serving the roasted prairie chickens and bowls of chokecherries to the males outside, the women went inside to eat their share of the food. Except for the bright chatter of Winona, the three older women sat silently.

Sarah looked upon the child with fondness. Oh, to be so young and innocent. The youngster's eyes gleamed golden as she related her pranks of the day. Such a scamp!

With a smile hovering on her lips, Sarah looked up and caught Wild-Flower studying her, the girl's large eyes filled with curiosity. The two girls stared at one another.

Wild-Flower sat tall and proud, her skin a rich tawny-brown, her features fine and sharp. She was, Sarah decided, the most beautiful, most striking woman she had ever seen. Her long hair hung straight and sleek, emphasizing straight narrow shoulders. Her eyes slanted slightly as she met Sarah's gaze, giving off a certain mysterious air. How could Golden Eagle not love this beautiful girl?

It was easy for Wild-Flower to see why the high-ranking warrior would fall in love with the white girl. Her face was lovely, intelligent and honest. Wild-Flower had also seen the fond look bestowed on Winona, watched the indulgent lift of her lips. She knew that Sarah was a woman not selfish with her love.

Smiling shyly at the white girl, Wild-Flower lowered her head and continued with her meal.

Seeing Eyes also watched the two young women with fondness and a bit of trepidation. She was genuinely fond of Wild-Flower, but had always known this was not the woman for her son. Calling for Winona to assist, Seeing Eyes left the two girls alone, praying that there'd be no trouble.

Two pairs of anxious eyes watched the older woman and her daughter leave. As Sarah and Wild-Flower turned toward one another, an uneasy silence fell. Neither knew what to say.

Finally, Sarah held her hands palm up. Not sure of what to say, but needing to say something, she apologized. "I'm sorry to cause you pain, Wild-Flower. I should have stayed and eaten in my—uh, I mean, Golden Eagle's . . ."

She stopped, not wanting to hurt the other girl by admitting she shared his tipi. "I should not eat here with you." Sarah faltered, not sure if the other girl would understand her words.

Leaning forward, Wild-Flower fingered a lock of Sarah's flowing mane of pale hair. "You very pretty, white girl. I see why Golden Eagle take you. Do not worry. Wild-Flower not angry. It is the way with men. Is this not so?"

"You speak English also?" Sarah asked, surprised.

Wild-Flower laughed and nodded her head. "My father, Chief White Cloud, speaks your tongue. My brother and I both learned to speak it. It is handy to know white man's tongue. Our tribe lives on the Great White River. Many whites come near. Many traders come to trade with my people. Many lie and cheat.'' A sly look came into her eyes. ''White man cannot cheat or steal so easily now. I also speak the French tongue. My mother's sister is married to a French trapper who lives with my people when he is not away,'' she finished proudly.

Impressed, Sarah smiled and held out her hand in a token of friendship. ''My father was also a French trapper, but he died last winter.'' She'd replied in French, and noted the surprised look on Wild-Flower's face. There was something likeable about this girl, and Sarah couldn't shake the strange feeling she'd known the Indian girl for a long time.

Taking the lightly tanned hand, Wild-Flower clasped it with her own darker one, and in that moment a strong bond formed between them.

Leaving the tipi, the two girls walked side by side as Sarah led the way to Bright Blossom's tipi, conversing easily in French.

The watching males each had his own reaction to the sight of two rival women who showed no animosity toward each other.

Golden Eagle watched the two girls talk and laugh. He was proud of Sarah. He also eyed Wild-Flower with curiosity for he'd never seen her so animated, happy and relaxed. He shook his head as if to say he'd never understand the female species.

Running Wolf frowned, for he knew his younger sister all too well. He wondered what she was up to. He too glanced upon the white girl, and had to admit with her fair looks she was very appealing. He understood why Golden Eagle had taken her to his tipi. Any warrior would desire her beneath him on his mat. But he worried over the marriage. He couldn't relax until the joining of the two tribes was complete. For now, he would watch and wait.

Chief Hawk Eyes brooded. He, the great chief, found himself confused in his thoughts. Despite his efforts, and he had fought hard, he had become fond of the white girl. She had taken to their way of life as if born to it, and took care of his son's tipi as well as any Indian woman. His young daughter looked upon Sarah as an older sister. In fact, she tried very hard to emulate the other girl. And now, he had to admire this white woman for her brave deed in saving his son's life.

Red Fox, who had just arrived, fought to hide his anger. How could Golden Eagle treat Wild-Flower in such a shameful way? As he watched Wild-Flower laugh and giggle, he knew she had to be putting on a brave face, hiding hurt and shame brought on by her unthoughtful and selfish future husband. She deserved better. She deserved . . . Jerking himself to his feet, Red Fox stalked away, knowing he had no say in the matter. But neither did he have to witness Wild-Flower's shame.

Chapter Twenty-three

The light of day slowly faded. It should have been a period for rest and reflection. A time to meditate and sort through the day's events, a time to prepare oneself for what tomorrow would bring. But for one young woman, it was a trap, an enemy reminding her that time was running out.

Knees drawn to her chest, chin propped in her hands, Wild-Flower blotted out the laughter and shouting. Her thoughts were too angry and desperate to appreciate the high spirits of those celebrating her presence in their village.

Her eyes closed and she buried her head in her hands. During the evening meal, her brother had announced that they would be leaving on the new sun. When confronted later, Running Wolf had stated that it was time for her to return home. No amount of pleading changed his mind.

Wild-Flower raised her head. Her time in this amiable village was at an end. The next time she saw Golden Eagle it would be the day of their marriage. But what could she do in the short amount of time she had left?

She spotted Golden Eagle walking away from the roaring fire. Wild-Flower took a deep breath, mustered her courage and rose to her feet.

Golden Eagle nearly ran Wild-Flower down on his way to join his father and guests at the council lodge. His brows rose in concern when Wild-Flower lifted misery-filled eyes to his.

"Please, Golden Eagle, Wild-Flower wishes to speak with you."

Golden Eagle's brows rose at her bold request. "Speak. What troubles you, Wild-Flower?" Not a trace of surprise showed in his features, even though it was the first time Wild-Flower had initiated a conversation between them.

Glancing about, Wild-Flower looked at his injuries and asked, "Can we walk? What I have to say is of a private matter."

Nodding his agreement, Golden Eagle turned and walked a short distance from the village. Stopping just inside the sheltering band of trees at the edge of his village, he turned toward Wild-Flower. "Now then, speak what is on your mind."

Wild-Flower's eyes dropped to her quilled moccasins. She cleared her throat and hesitantly began. "We are to be joined soon. I . . . I don't . . ."

"You don't what?" Golden Eagle interrupted, his brows drawn together impatiently, frowning as he sought to understand what it was that had upset her so.

Wild-Flower glanced at Golden Eagle. Taking a deep breath, she blurted out, "I don't wish to marry you, Golden Eagle. I love another." A tremor of defiance crept into her voice and eyes. Chin thrust forward, she awaited his reaction.

Golden Eagle blinked. "Does my hearing deceive me? Did Wild-Flower say she does not wish to join with Golden Eagle?" he exclaimed, afraid to believe what he'd heard.

He was certain it was his own desperation playing tricks on him, or fever from his wounds.

"Yes, Golden Eagle," Wild-Flower answered. Her eyes were wide and filled with trepidation as Golden Eagle closed his eyes.

The silence grew, and Wild-Flower lost her courage. Turning away, she burst into tears, covering her face with her hands.

When he heard her muffled sob, Golden Eagle's eyes flew open. He reached forward and pulled Wild-Flower into his arms, automatically soothing her while his mind struggled with her announcement.

He was so deep in thought that he was unaware of Sarah's approach from the stream, her arms full of eating utensils that she'd washed and now nearly dropped. Golden Eagle did not see Sarah come to an abrupt halt, nor did he see her mouth fall open with shock and disbelief. He did not see the tears glistening in her eyes as she backed away.

Looking down at the black head against his chest, Golden Eagle knew only the great sense of relief soaring through him. There was hope after all. Surely, this was the work of the Great Spirit. Raising Wild-Flower's trembling chin, he gazed into her tear-brimmed eyes. Gently, he wiped away the remaining tears.

Wild-Flower sniffed into the silence surrounding them. "I'm sorry, Golden Eagle. I do not mean to cause shame to you or your tribe. Please, do not be hurt or angry. I did not know what else to do. I thought it only right for you to know my feelings."

Looking away, her fingers twisting together, she fretted. "I should not have said anything. If you tell Running Wolf or your father, I will be punished. I have acted rashly." Wild-Flower shivered as if from the cold. "I will marry you as planned and be a good wife if you will not hold my actions against my tribe," she whispered brokenly.

Golden Eagle smiled and laid a quieting finger over her lips, silencing her nervous chatter. "Look at me, Wild-

Flower. Do you see the face of anger or hurt on this warrior?'' He waited as Wild-Flower slowly lifted her eyes and took a good look at him.

''Wild-Flower is very brave to reveal her true feelings to this warrior. You are much braver than Golden Eagle. I too feel the trap of our fathers' making. My heart also belongs to another. You and I were meant to take others as our mates.''

Searching the face above her, Wild-Flower saw the truth of his words. Golden Eagle's eyes sparkled, his face so handsome Wild-Flower caught her breath.

Nodding her head in agreement, she could only be honest as she admitted, ''You are very wise, Golden Eagle. I am happy for you. However, the warrior I love does not yet know of my love for him. In fact''—she sighed sadly— ''he does not even notice I exist. But now, perhaps I can change that.''

Her eyes narrowed as she thought for a moment. ''Soon,'' Wild-Flower declared with confidence, ''very soon, he will know of my love.''

Chuckling, Golden Eagle beheld her determination. ''This warrior who has caught your eye must be blind not to notice your beauty. But what weapon does a poor warrior carry to fight a female in love?'' he quipped, his lips twitching with humor.

Cocking her head to one side, Wild-Flower studied the warrior before her. ''Or a helpless girl faced with a man's love and strength,'' she added. Her face lit up with relief and joy as she asked, ''Is it true what I have heard, that you love your white captive?'' She had let her naturally curious nature overstep the invisible boundaries laid down by custom.

Receiving his first spontaneous smile and listening to her laughter, Golden Eagle joined in, not in the least offended with her bluntness. ''I think I am finally seeing and hearing the true spirit of Wild-Flower. You deserve to be thoroughly punished for your deceitfulness.''

Golden Eagle watched her face flush with guilt. Taking pity on her, he conceded, "Yes, I love Sarah. I wish to make Sarah my mate for my walk on *Maka*. It is meant to be. However," he cautioned her, "our fathers will not release us from the arrangements just because each of us loves another. There is much at stake between our tribes. Pride and honor will be difficult to overcome. Do not do anything foolish."

Frowning, Wild-Flower paced back and forth like a caged tiger. She stopped, a determined glint entering her eyes as she faced Golden Eagle and declared, "We must find a way. I will think of something."

Shaking his head in wonder, as he had not quite adjusted to the transformation Wild-Flower had so suddenly undergone, Golden Eagle reminded her, "We have time. We will ask the Great Spirit to guide our respective fathers down his path. He will reveal his plan in good time. Meanwhile, now that we have been honest with each other, perhaps we can become friends?"

Wild-Flower smiled, nodding her agreement. "I would like that, Golden Eagle." Turning, they made their way back toward the village. As they parted, Golden Eagle offered words of comfort. "Things will work out as they are meant to do. Do not worry for now."

Wild-Flower stopped, an impish grin spreading across her young features. "You are right, Golden Eagle, but a little help can't hurt."

Golden Eagle watched Wild-Flower head toward his parents' tipi with the look of a warrior who'd been struck by lightning. He tipped his head back and spoke to the heavens. "How could I have misjudged Wild-Flower so badly? How has she been able to fool me with her spiritless nature all this time? Have I perhaps seen only what I wished to see?" There were no answers forthcoming yet.

As the moon soared high, women and children retired to their tipis for the night. Hidden in shadows, Wild-Flower watched Red Fox leave the village. Chewing her lower lip, she wasn't sure if she was brave enough to follow through with her plan. Squaring her shoulders, she made up her mind. She would do it.

Glancing about, she pinpointed her brother's whereabouts and released her pent-up breath in relief as she found him deeply engrossed in conversation with a group of warriors.

Wild-Flower stealthily slipped away and faded into the darkness. He would never miss her. He would assume her to be bedded down in one of the tipis offered to her for her stay.

Wiping moist palms on her gaily decorated hide skirt, she was determined to get an answer tonight. She followed Red Fox, keeping a safe distance behind him. She didn't know what she was going to do yet, but she had to find out if he was truly as indifferent to her as he seemed.

Staying in the shadows of the shrubs, she halted, so lost in thought she nearly revealed herself when Red Fox stopped at the water's edge. She stood, waiting to see what Red Fox was going to do. Then he suddenly stripped off his breechclout and waded into the murky water.

Covering her mouth with her hands, Wild-Flower was unable to tear her eyes away from his naked flesh. She had no idea he was coming to bathe. She clamped a hand over her heart, which was beating so fast she thought it would march off through her chest.

She came to her senses when Red Fox turned toward her, his bathing complete. Wild-Flower quietly backtracked a short distance.

Calculating her timing, giving him time to dry and dress, Wild-Flower casually strolled through the trees toward the water's edge as if on an innocent walk.

She did not have to fake her surprised squeal when she caught sight of his sleek, wet, naked body stretching in the moonlight. Her face flushed with desire, and a longing to know the secrets of a man brought a surge of trembling weakness to her limbs.

When her eyes fell upon his sex, she quickly turned her back in an attempt to hide the raw need that suddenly engulfed her. She had gotten more than she had bargained for in her bold appraisal. What she'd seen of his naked body before he'd turned away from her far surpassed her wanton imagination.

Wild-Flower wasn't the only one trying to regain composure. Red Fox cursed beneath his breath as he struggled with his breechclout.

Wet, but somewhat clothed, Red Fox walked over to Wild-Flower and roughly spun her around to face him. "What are you doing this far from the village, Wild-Flower? It is late. You should not be out, nor should you wander so far alone," he rebuked her, his tone harsh due to his shock and extremely uncomfortable state.

All Wild-Flower's hopes and dreams crumbled. Tears welled in her eyes. He'd never spoken to her so coldly before. She had her answer. Mortified, she turned to flee, humiliated and hurt beyond words. Blinded by tears, she tripped over a large rock jutting out in the darkness.

Too miserable to pick herself up, Wild-Flower couldn't stop the tears from falling or the sobs that racked her slender form. Strong arms gently lifted her, but she kept her head averted as tears continued to roll down her cheeks. She found herself pulled into a sitting position and warm fingers slid beneath her quivering chin.

Red Fox swore into the night air as he held up his wet fingers. "This is all Golden Eagle's doing. I will speak to him tonight. It is not right how he treats you. He has no right to make you so unhappy that you flee the safety of the village. You could have come to harm. He causes you shame with his behavior," Red Fox spat.

Looking at Red Fox in confusion, Wild-Flower corrected the angry warrior. "Golden Eagle has nothing to do with my being here, Red Fox,'' she said, her eyes wide and honest.

Drawing his thick brows together, Red Fox looked in confusion at Wild-Flower, her oval face staring at him with large sad eyes. "If not Golden Eagle, then what is the cause of these tears?" he demanded, softly stroking her damp face. "Is it Sarah? Did she say something to hurt you?" His nostrils flared with anger as his protective instincts surfaced.

Afraid Red Fox would act on his anger, Wild-Flower rose to her knees and clutched his bare shoulders. "No, Red Fox. I am happy for Sarah and Golden Eagle. They are in love. I am not in love with Golden Eagle," she anxiously explained.

"Then why the tears?" Seeing her head lower, Red Fox stood, taking Wild-Flower with him as he again forced her to meet his gaze. "I will know the truth, Wild-Flower. Speak now," Red Fox commanded, his heart beating faster with her confession that she did not love his friend.

Seeing no way out, but refusing to expose her wounds, Wild-Flower mumbled, "I too am in love. But the warrior I love does not return my feelings." Closing her eyes in shame at her admission, she waited.

Red Fox flinched as if he'd been kicked in the stomach. He took a deep breath. "You love another? Who, Wild-Flower? I will know the name of this warrior," he demanded angrily.

Refusing to meet his accusing glare, she shook her head.

Grabbing her arms, Red Fox yanked her close. "You will tell me now," he thundered. Fear of an unknown rival brought jealousy to a rolling boil.

Wild-Flower's eyes flew open. She opened her mouth to ask him to let her go but the look on his face stopped her. She fell against him and whispered, "It is you I love, Red Fox."

The warrior staggered back, catching hold of Wild-Flower, who still clutched him. "Me?" His normally deep

Susan Edwards

voice failed and came out as a high-pitched squeak. Swallowing hard, he whispered, "I am the man who does not return your love?" He stared at Wild-Flower. Groaning, he folded her into his strong embrace.

"Oh, foolish one," he murmured against her smooth honey-brown neck. He held her head pressed against his heaving chest. "You are all I think about, dream about. I cannot get your lovely face out of my head," Red Fox said with a sigh, closing his eyes.

He smiled sadly. "Thoughts of you are with me day and night. But you are promised to another. What I feel is not right. You should not be here with me." His eyes opened as he set Wild-Flower away from him.

Joy flooded Wild-Flower's heart. "Oh, Red Fox, I nearly lost all hope. You are the one I love. You are the one I want to call husband." She stepped forward, her slender arms wrapping themselves around his neck, refusing to allow the warrior to put any physical or emotional distance between them.

Pleading, she cried, "You are wrong. This is right. Hold me, Red Fox. I need to feel your arms around me."

Red Fox searched her smiling tear-stained face and groaned. "I cannot deny anything you ask of me." He wrapped his arms around her slender form, his lips covering hers.

Wild-Flower sighed as he stroked her lips and parted them. She murmured her pleasure, pressing her body close to his.

Red Fox answered her plea with a deep moan of his own. Scooping her up into his strong arms, he strode far into the woods, not stopping until he reached a hidden grassy clearing.

Looking into eyes glazed with desire and need, he cautioned, "I love you, Wild-Flower. Be sure of yourself. If I touch you again, I will not be able to stop."

With the simplest of words, Wild-Flower sealed her fate. "I am yours, Red Fox."

Chapter Twenty-four

It was late, the village quiet, when Golden Eagle stopped outside the entrance to his tipi.

Rolling his shoulders, mindful of the knife wounds from that morning, he worked the tension from his limbs, which were now stiff from the fight as well as spending many hours in the council lodge. For the first time since becoming a member of the council, he'd had to force himself to listen to and take part in tribal affairs. Keeping his mind on the matters being discussed had taken considerable effort on his part.

He needed to see White Wind and impart his good news. Of course, all was not settled, but that would come later. Somehow, he'd make his father see that peace between the two tribes could be achieved without the joining of the two families. After all, hadn't friendship and respect grown over the last few years between members of both tribes?

Lifting the closed flap, Golden Eagle entered the dim interior. Quietly, he secured the flap of hide. He stood for a moment, allowing his eyes to adjust. Walking silently toward his sleeping mat, he removed his moccasins, beaded arm bands and the feathers worn on his head for tribal affairs.

Golden Eagle lay on his side next to Sarah. The curve of her back gleamed in the night as he slid under the fur covering. He remembered her fearlessness that day and how terrifying it had been for her. He recalled too how difficult it had been for her to retrieve her knife from the chest of the enemy.

When he'd recounted her brave act to the council tonight, all had been amazed. Several warriors had even stood and sung songs in her honor for she had counted coup, a feat regarded with high respect by all. His White Wind had not only touched the enemy with an object in her hand, but had laid her hand on her enemy, saving his life in the process.

Counting coup was the ultimate honor, and all in his village would honor her tomorrow with feasting and dancing. He thought of the scalp locks he could have taken for all to see and praise, and he sighed. He had known that Sarah would not have been able to bear witnessing that act of violence, and so had contented himself with the taking of the warriors' weapons.

Gently, his hand gripped Sarah's slim waist as he coaxed her toward him, waking her with tender words of love.

Instead of Sarah rolling over, pulling him to her, she stiffened under his tender touch, resisted him as he tried to pull her close. He sat up and stared at her rigid form with a hurt and puzzled look. He leaned over to try again. Perhaps she was deeply asleep. However, this time there was no mistaking her resistance as Sarah, for the first time, actually edged away from him.

Compressing his lips, Golden Eagle narrowed his eyes as he pulled her on her back and studied Sarah's pale features. With the help of faint filtered light from above, the effects of her bout of tears was visible. Placing his hands on either side of her head, he questioned.

"Why the tears? Tell me what is wrong, White Wind. Is

it dreams again?'' Golden Eagle coaxed gently. He stroked her petal soft cheek as his breath caressed her.

"Look at me, White Wind," Golden Eagle commanded gently, half leaning over Sarah. Concern etched his forehead into many small creases.

Sarah continued to lay still as she sought to compose herself. Her tears had subsided long ago, but she knew her eyes were still red and swollen. She'd struggled to be brave and strong, but her love was as delicate and fragile as a spider's web.

Fresh tears trickled from her over-bright eyes. She'd tried so hard to hide her misery, her fear of the future. She'd smiled and laughed with the other women until she could retire to nurse her wounds. Alone in the tipi, she'd fought to remember her vow to love Golden Eagle for whatever time was left to them.

But she'd failed miserably. Tears had flowed the moment she'd been alone. The sight of Wild Flower in Golden Eagle's arms had been like a knife plunging straight into her heart, draining her life's blood.

How could she bear to see him wed to another? How could she live without her Golden Warrior by her side? He was the air she breathed, the nourishment she needed to live, to grow, the joy of living and loving.

Sarah finally opened her eyes and glanced at Golden Eagle. She saw his hurt and looked over his shoulder, at his strong firm chin, anywhere but at those eyes that saw too much.

The silence grew and lay heavily, tension between them thickening, as neither spoke. Sarah shook her head. Her love for him was so great, so unselfish, that she was unwilling to tell him, unwilling to cause him more grief, so she kept silent. She didn't blame him. He was caught between two women who loved him.

Sarah's eyes fluttered closed, shutting him out, as long thick lashes fanned out, dark smudges on a pale face, lips pressed tightly together to still the quivering emotions. Golden Eagle gently lifted her into his arms. "I will know what is wrong, little one. Who or what has made you unhappy?"

Sarah opened her eyes, a spark of resentment coming forth from watery blue orbs as she halfheartedly pushed against his chest. "Don't you ever take no for an answer, Golden Eagle?" Her voice, hoarse with suppressed emotion, cracked on his name.

Seeing his concerned expression, Sarah sighed. "All right." She gave in, pushing out of his arms. "Be warned. You won't like my answer."

"Tell me."

Looking him straight in the eye, she lowered her voice to a bare whisper. "It is your actions that have caused my tears this night, Golden Eagle."

"What?"

Sarah remained silent.

"Me? How can that be? What have I done to cause these tears?" Lifting himself to his knees, Golden Eagle stared in confusion at Sarah. With effort, he lowered his voice. "You will explain yourself, White Wind."

Sitting in front of him, Sarah placed her hands upon his warm shoulders and curled into his lap, laying her head against his chest, feeling his heart beating against her ear. "Please, let us forget it. Can't we just enjoy what time we have left? I don't want to fight with you. Nor can I fight what will be." Sarah felt her world crumbling around her.

Unable to hold back the tears at the sight of his bewilderment, she felt all her hurt drain away. All she wanted, all she needed, was to hold him and love him for whatever time they had left.

With furrowed brows, Golden Eagle fingered her braids. "What do you mean, our time left? We have our entire lives together. Explain this foolishness. I thought we had agreed that this matter was ended, did we not?" Golden

Eagle asked, trying to understand what had upset her. "Has Night Star bothered you again?"

Looking sadly at her golden warrior, Sarah shook her head. "No, Golden Eagle. She hasn't spoken to me since our return." She reached up to stroke the side of his smooth jaw, and buried her face in the pulsing hollow of his neck and shoulder. "I saw you with Wild-Flower tonight. I saw her in your arms."

Sarah looked up. "I want you to know, I understand her hurt. But it hurts me to know that soon she will have the rightful claim to you. That she will receive your embraces and kisses. That she will bear your children." Seeing understanding dawn in his eyes, Sarah quickly continued.

"I know she must love you as much as I do. All I want is to love you. Please, let me love you, Golden Eagle. Let me pretend that you are mine forever, that you belong to no one else but me . . ." Her voice trailed off and she closed her eyes against tears that sought release.

Golden Eagle smiled tenderly at Sarah. "Look at me, my love." He waited until he had Sarah's full attention. "I love you and only you. You are the woman this warrior needs. Let me explain what happened. Tonight . . ." He stopped in mid-sentence as a firm hand closed over his mouth.

Sarah saw the truth radiating from her golden lover. Keeping her hand firmly placed upon his lips, she spoke, her voice full of desperation, eyes moist with unshed tears. "I know you love me, Golden Eagle, as I love you. But it may not be enough to keep us together. No more words tonight. Please, just hold me and love me."

Not giving him time or opportunity to protest, Sarah removed her hand, wrapped her arms tightly around the strong column of his neck and took his lips hungrily. As his lips parted in surprise at her unexpected boldness, she thrust her tongue between his lips, effectively wiping out any remaining protest.

Golden Eagle groaned. He lifted his head and gave in. He pulled her legs around him as he was consumed by the fire that their bodies ignited within each other.

Far above, countless bright stars twinkled. A crescent-shaped moon seemed to grow just a little brighter as it shined down, sending shafts of glowing light to embrace the lovers as they moved in harmony to nature's strongest demands.

Golden Eagle lay under Sarah, their sweat-slick bodies calm, she so still that he knew she had fallen asleep. He caressed the still-damp skin of her back and coaxed her awake.

She eyed him in the dazed manner of someone waking from a deep sleep, murmured something unintelligible and flopped her head back down.

"Hmmm, you smell so good." Matching actions to words, he buried his face against her throat. Nuzzling and kissing his way to her lips, he added, "You taste good too."

Sarah pushed him away. "You woke me up to tell me that? Golden Eagle, go back to sleep. I'm so tired," she sighed.

Golden Eagle rolled over, ignoring Sarah's protest. Propping furs behind them, he lay back and drew Sarah into the crook of his arm. "We must talk," he said.

Sarah drew tiny circles with the tip of her finger on his chest, stalling. Golden Eagle's firm hands closed over her fingers. She glanced up, sensing his serious manner.

"No more distractions. Listen. I will tell you the truth of what you saw. Wild-Flower came to me tonight to tell me she is in love with another warrior and does not wish to become my wife."

Sarah pulled away and turned to look at Golden Eagle suspiciously. "She what?"

Briefly, Golden Eagle explained why Wild-Flower had sought him out and his conversation with her and why she'd been in his arms.

Sarah sat up and faced Golden Eagle. She shook her head

in confusion. "But this is wrong. Neither one of you loves the other, you each love someone else, and still your fathers will force this marriage on you both?"

Golden Eagle took hold of her hands. He nodded, trying to make her understand. Lifting one hand, he fingered the necklace he'd given to Sarah.

"My people are proud. Our way is based on pride and honor. Both tribes will lose honor if the marriage does not take place. It is the only way to right the wrong of White Cloud's father, and to satisfy my tribe's need for revenge. Only this can restore honor to both tribes."

Sarah frowned as she sought to understand. "If you go back on your word, then you would be no better than the one who started this in the beginning, and if Wild-Flower refuses, it would be her grandfather's shame all over again."

Golden Eagle nodded, pleased that she understood. "So you see, a way must be found where neither tribe loses honor."

He let out a long sigh. "I am ashamed to admit this, but tonight was the first time I've seen the true Wild-Flower. All these years, I've thought her to be spiritless. My talk with her tonight showed me just how badly I have misjudged her."

Sarah smoothed the hair from his face. "Do not feel so badly, my love. You probably saw what she wanted you to see. Wild-Flower is both smart and cunning, as you said. Who is it that Wild-Flower loves?"

Golden Eagle grinned. "She didn't say, but I have thought about this. After all, I want her to choose well. I think it is Red Fox who has captured her heart."

Sarah's jaw dropped. "Red Fox? No, you must be wrong. He is so . . . cold and unfeeling," she exclaimed.

"No, my love. Red Fox guards his heart well. If he returns her feelings, it explains why he has been so short of patience recently. It also explains his resentment of you."

"What do I have to do with Red Fox? I would have

thought if he loves Wild-Flower, he'd be happy that you love me. Do you really think he loves her?''

"If Red Fox felt her honor was threatened, that she was being shamed by you or me, then it explains much, my love,'' Golden Eagle murmured, pulling her down beside him.

Sarah cuddled close to Golden Eagle. "So, my great and clever warrior, now that I am wide awake and dawn is still far off, do you have any ideas on how to pass the remaining time before we must show ourselves to the world?'' she asked, her voice low and husky.

Golden Eagle moved over her. "I have many ideas. How about . . .'' He whispered in her ear before preceding to show her.

Elsewhere, under the same moon and stars, Wild-Flower and Red Fox lay, arms and legs tangled.

Standing, Red Fox pulled Wild-Flower to her feet. Arms twined, they walked the distance to the cold stream. Quickly they bathed, whispering words of love to each other.

Looking into her glowing eyes, Red Fox bent his head, lips lingering, then lifting reluctantly. "We must return, Wild-Flower. It's too risky to remain any longer.''

Watching Wild-Flower step away to dress, he wondered if this was a dream. In all his wildest imagining, he'd never thought his wish would be granted. Maybe he would wake, alone, and find that this had been a cruel dream.

Wild-Flower smiled the smile of a woman who had been well loved. Dressed, she eyed Red Fox with a mixture of love and wonder. Staring at his beautiful body, she laughed, the sound low and husky. "Does my Fox plan to walk back to the village like that?'' Her dainty hand made a wide sweep of the naked body in front of her.

Looking down, Red Fox grinned, not the least bit embarrassed. He grabbed the giggling girl, swung her high into his arms and took her full lips with his, effectively silencing

230

her. As he deepened the kiss, deep shudders racked his body at the same time that guilt overcame him. Lifting his head, he gently set her back on her feet and turned away to dress.

When her arms circled him from behind, Red Fox sighed, turned in her arms and placed his hands on her shoulders, putting distance between them. "I have dishonored you and betrayed my friend, Golden Eagle. We must not be alone again, Wild-Flower."

Wild-Flower placed her hands on Red Fox's chest and leaned forward. "I did not get a chance to tell you before, Red Fox, but Golden Eagle and I talked tonight. He loves Sarah and I love you. We will not marry. Somehow, we will convince our fathers that it would be wrong."

"And if you cannot?" Red Fox asked sadly. He watched Wild-Flower turn and pace.

"Then we shall run away together. If my grandfather could do it, then so shall I."

"No, Wild-Flower. That would cause war between our tribes again. Come, we will talk no more of this."

Hand in hand, the two lovers strolled slowly toward the village in silence. Parting, each entered from a separate direction, hidden by the black shadows of night.

Blackness for evil. White for goodness. Swirling, tangling, like some primordial being, the two forces twisted together. With agonizing slowness, their colors began to separate and take on form. The billowing darkness condensed into the shape of a huge distorted man. Black surrounded him, came forth from him, consumed him and threatened the figure of a woman in white. The whiteness surrounding her began to fade, engulfed by the evil spirit.

In her dream-state, the nightmare, the future, seemed so real. The terror of the woman was so frightening that a scream lodged in the throat of Seeing Eye. Desperately, she opened her eyes. Beads of sweat lined her forehead as she made an effort to escape the nightmarish vision. With shaking hands, she first wiped her damp forehead, then wiped the tears still in her eyes from the haunting dream. She shook her head helplessly. There were times when she resented her gift of sight, times when it became a burden. There was nothing she could do to prevent the events forecast by her dream from coming true.

She could only pray that the spirits would watch over the girl and keep her from lasting harm.

Chapter Twenty-five

Golden Eagle stood next to Red Fox to see Wild-Flower and her brother off the next morning. He glanced sideways at Red Fox. As usual, his friend looked to be relaxed, showing no emotion, just another warrior gathered to watch the important guests take their leave. No one looking at him would guess his true feelings.

But Golden Eagle knew his friend well. He spotted the rapid eye movements that followed Wild-Flower's every move as Red Fox held his hands clenched tightly behind his back. Only Golden Eagle and perhaps Wild-Flower were aware that there had been no farewell salute from Red Fox.

Golden Eagle rolled his shoulders and tipped his head to the serene blue above, seeking courage to confront his father. When the time was right, he would tell Hawk Eyes that he would not marry Wild-Flower.

Turning, the two warriors began to talk of other pressing matters. As was the way with true warriors, they pushed their problems of the heart aside, hidden for the moment, to be taken out later in private and reexamined. Unpleasant matters awaited their attention.

Looking straight ahead, Golden Eagle imparted his news. "I received word from Matosapa of the Oglalas. Matosapa has agreed to take Night Star as his mate. His first wife died last winter. He is a strong warrior who has counted coup many times for his brave deeds and has proven to be a good provider in his village. He should be able to control your sister so she cannot cause more trouble. He is on his way as we speak."

Red Fox came to an abrupt stop and placed his hands upon his comrade's shoulders, relief flooding his solemn features. "That is good news, my brother. I had feared there were no warriors left brave enough to take Night Star. Word of her troublemaking and mean spirit has spread to the other tribes," he confided. His brows rose in concern, lips tightening. "Does Matosapa know of my sister's reputation?" Red Fox asked. "I do not want her to be returned."

Golden Eagle patted Red Fox on the back and moved forward. "Do not worry, Red Fox. Matosapa knows of your sister. He is lonely and needs a woman to take care of his tipi and give him little ones. He looks forward to the challenge of taming your sister."

Red Fox sighed with relief. "Ah, that is good then. Let us go tell my father. He is getting too old to deal with her. It is time she had a family of her own to occupy her time."

A short while later Golden Eagle and Red Fox left the tipi of Striking Snake and went their separate ways.

Red Fox spotted Night Star and approached her, interrupting the chatter of the small group of women. "My sister. You are needed in our tipi. Come," he ordered quietly but firmly.

Night Star stomped after her brother and entered her father's tipi. Placing her plump hands on her wide hips, she glared at Red Fox, completely ignoring her aging father.

"What is it you want that could not have waited, Red Fox," she demanded peevishly. She'd been humiliated when Red Fox summoned her so brusquely. Oh, he'd been polite, but all had heard the command underlining the words, and she'd seen amusement in the other women's eyes as she'd had no choice but to follow him. A brother was given authority over his sisters until that authority was transferred to her husband.

"Sit, daughter." Striking Snake's deep voice thundered in obvious displeasure as he cut off her angry tirade.

Night Star jumped. Her father had not spoken to her so harshly for many winters. A sense of foreboding assailed her. Nonetheless, she raised her chin and defiantly stated, "I will stand, my father. What is it that is so important that I must be summoned as if I were a child?"

Hands on her shoulders applied pressure. "Our father has asked that you sit, sister. Sit on your own, or be put on your sitting mat," Red Fox told her.

Night Star threw a look of hatred over her shoulder and threw herself down, the corners of her mouth drooping with resentment.

Striking Snake studied his daughter's defiant demeanor before looking over her shoulder to his son. "My son, I see that you are very wise. She does not have the look of contentment and happiness. I see bitterness and anger in their place. I have been neglectful in my duties, and for this I apologize."

Night Star sputtered, and would have jumped to her feet were it not for Red Fox standing behind her.

"I have received an offer of marriage for you, my daughter," Striking Snake announced.

Lifting her head high, Night Star looked down her nose, hiding her relief. For a few moments she'd been afraid of something much more serious. This was a problem she could handle easily and quickly. "Who has made this offer, my father?" Night Star asked, struggling for the proper respect due such a request.

"Matosapa of the Oglala tribe has offered for you. He has sent some fine furs and two ponies." With a wave of his hand, he indicated a pile of richly colored furs.

Tossing her head, Night Star stood and kneeled beside the generous pile of furs. She fingered the softness with regret. They were indeed beautiful, thick and rich in color. If only she could keep them without accepting the marriage offer. Turning back to her father, she gave him a sad look.

"No, my father. You will have to send these back. I do not wish to join to Matosapa." She turned to leave, and gasped when Red Fox stepped in her path, blocking her exit.

Rounding on Red Fox, Night Star hissed, "Let me pass, Red Fox. I will not stay and discuss this. You have been given my answer."

Red Fox calmly stated, "I did not expect any different answer from your lips, sister. I know that you bide your time for Golden Eagle."

Night Star gasped. If the rest of the village found out, she would never be able to hold her head up without fear of ridicule. Never mind that it was the truth. She drew herself up proudly, and boldly faced Red Fox. "How ridiculous, brother. Golden Eagle is spoken for. All know this. He is not the reason I turn down Matosapa. I will find a husband when I'm ready. Now let me pass."

Red Fox shook his head and grabbed Night Star by the arm. "The decision has already been made, my sister. It was never a choice for you to make. Our father had hoped you would accept on your own. You will marry Matosapa when he arrives in a few days' time."

Twisting out of his hurtful grasp, Night Star turned to her father. Surely he'd not force her into this marriage. Seeing her father's stoical expression, Night Star felt true fear.

She fell before him and begged. "No, Father, no. Do not force me to join this warrior. Don't make me leave our village. You can't send me away. I am your only daughter," she appealed.

Seeing conviction hardening his eyes against her pleading, Night Star tried a different approach. "What about you? If I leave your tipi, who will take care of you? Who will tend to the women's work here? You need me here." She whined, truly afraid. Here, she could do as she pleased, but in another village . . .

Raising his brows sharply, Striking Snake glanced over his daughter's head and met Red Fox's knowing gaze. He shook his head at Night Star.

"Red Fox is right, Night Star. I have been wrong to let you wait so long. I had hoped that you would choose a mate and settle on your own. The one you choose and would wait for is spoken for and therefore not meant for you," Striking Snake advised his daughter.

Night Star jumped up, all pretense of sadness vanishing as she glared at her brother.

"Your mind and heart are turning bitter and evil, my daughter. You need a husband to guide you during your walk through this life. All has been arranged. Nothing you can say will change the decision that has been made. Someday, you may thank me." Striking Snake signaled an end to the discussion as his voice grew faint with weakness.

Red Fox grabbed Night Star. "Our father tires. We will leave him to rest," he commanded, dragging Night Star behind him.

Outside and away from her tipi, Night Star turned on Red Fox, swinging her arm, aiming a blow toward his face. "I hate you, Red Fox. How could you do this to me?" she raged.

Catching her wrist, Red Fox easily thrust her hand down behind her back. "Be warned, little sister. Do not try that again. I would not hesitate to punish you here and now."

Sternly, he added, "you have caused much trouble in our village of late. You refused to heed the warnings given

237

to you and have disobeyed me and Golden Eagle. This is to be part of your punishment.''

Spitting at his feet, Night Star sneered. ''You would banish your own flesh and blood? You would keep me from my father? Perhaps you plan on taking the white whore to your tipi to replace me when Golden Eagle and Wild-Flower . . .'' Her words broke off abruptly when Red Fox's fingers bit painfully into her flesh.

''Will you never learn to hold your tongue, sister? You should take care lest you find yourself without it one day,'' Red Fox warned.

He sighed, visibly controlling his temper. ''You have not been banished from our tribe. You will be able to come and visit, but it has been made clear to Matosapa that he must accompany you. It is our hope you will not find your new life so bad. That is up to you. You alone are responsible for the path you walk.''

Red Fox released her and cautioned, ''Watch yourself with your new husband. Matosapa is not the kind of warrior who will let his woman strike him or tell him what to do. Golden Eagle made sure he found someone who would be able to keep you in your place. Matosapa will keep you too busy to cause trouble in the Oglala village.''

Red Fox turned his back and walked off, leaving Night Star to deal with her fate. Night Star seethed. Her hands balled into tight fists. She hated him, hated them all. Her fury grew with each passing second, and before she even knew what she was doing, she was running after her brother.

''I'll run away before I marry someone you choose for me,'' she screamed, crossing her arms, oblivious to the shocked onlookers. Night Star's lips curled in a sneer and she laughed at her brother's incredulous expression. She refused to back down as he stalked toward her. She meant what she said.

In a deceptively calm voice Red Fox inquired, as if he had not heard right, ''You'll do what?'' Crossing his arms in his most menacing manner, he and all the others waited for her to back down. Some, by the look on their faces, were thoroughly enjoying the showdown between brother and sister.

Night Star scornfully goaded her brother. "You heard me. Of course, I won't stay away long. Just long enough that Matosapa or whomever else you choose leaves in disgust." Throwing Red Fox a malicious grin, Night Star turned on her heels and stalked off.

Chapter Twenty-six

Red Fox stared open-mouthed as Night Star left. He didn't believe she would actually dare go to that extreme to avoid marriage, but neither would he risk it. Throwing back his shoulders, hands at hips, he stared at the gathered crowd. Determination lent a harshness to his features. She will marry Matosapa and I will personally see to it, he vowed silently.

His mouth tightened angrily as he pursued Night Star. Stopping in front of her, he bent at the waist, grabbed her around the knees and slung her over his shoulder. Straightening under the considerable weight, he called to several young unmarried warriors he knew he could trust to do his bidding. He motioned for them to follow as he stalked toward the sloping bank of the slow-moving stream.

Red Fox turned a deaf ear to the screeches and curses being hurled upon him. All the people of the village stopped what they were doing and eagerly followed brother and sister. Yells and cheers rang loud and clear, many shouting out advice to Red Fox.

Arriving at the water's edge, Red Fox waded into the deep swirling middle. Dumping his heavy load with a splash, he commanded the three warriors waiting for instructions, "You will divide the task of following and watching my sister day and night. She is not to leave this village nor is she allowed near a horse. You will not let her out of your sight for any reason."

Looking directly at his shocked and sputtering sister, he added, "And that includes all her personal needs including bathing," he added. "Perhaps now you will act in a reasonable manner," he told her.

Turning, Red Fox left the stream. Stopping in front of the warriors, he gave a last warning. "You are responsible for Night Star. You will be held accountable if she should run away."

Nodding their heads, the warriors accepted their responsibility. They, like everyone else in the village, had grown tired of Night Star's never-ending complaints and troublemaking. And all three, at one time or another, had been spurned by her as well.

Toward the end of the week, a hot spell overcame the lands. Even high into the hills, the shade offered little relief from the hot breeze. Sarah sat outside, leaning against the tipi in what little sheltering shade it provided.

A makeshift fan made from woven dried grass provided little relief. High above, the bright yellow sun sent its rays down, scorching everything in its path.

She pulled her dress away from her sweat-slicked skin. The dress she wore was the first garment she'd made for herself.

The hide dress was unadorned, being one of her everyday garments. She'd chosen to leave off the yoke, not wanting the added layer of hide in the summer heat. Using the skin of an antelope, she'd simply cut a hole in the center of the hide for her head and stitched up the sides, leaving the sleeves short and loose.

Susan Edwards

Fanning herself vigorously, Sarah tried to muster the energy required to prepare their noon meal, but when she tried to rise, she found herself so weak and lethargic that she remained where she was.

She leaned forward, resting her elbows on her drawn-up knees, her attention on Matosapa and Night Star, his new wife, as they prepared to leave.

Matosapa had arrived yesterday, alone, leading several horses loaded with many fine gifts for his future wife's family and the chief. Sarah could almost feel sorry for the Indian girl. After the scene with her brother a week ago, it was no secret within the village that she had been forced to marry. Many of the younger women, along with scorned past suitors, were openly delighted that Night Star had been watched and followed wherever she went this past week, some even joining in on their own to watch and follow her.

Observing the big Indian, Sarah was amazed at his incredible size. Matosapa, whose name meant Black Bear, stood tall and proud, around six feet in height. His massive body towered over all the other warriors. His air of command and size had Night Star obeying without hesitation.

Closing her eyes to the blinding brightness, she sighed as a shadow fell over her, giving her some relief from the glare. Reluctantly, she opened her eyes to see who had come to call, and found herself looking up at Golden Eagle.

Mistaking his frown of concern for displeasure, she started to rise. "I'm sorry, Golden Eagle, our meal is not ready."

Golden Eagle hunkered down on his haunches and stilled Sarah with hands on her shoulders. "Do you not feel well, White Wind? You are not sick, are you?" he asked, concern lacing his words.

Sarah shook her head. "No, I'm fine. Just hot and tired. Must be this heat." Shading her eyes, she turned her gaze back to the group loading the packhorse.

Golden Eagle tucked a stray damp lock of hair behind Sarah's ear. "Don't worry about her, White Wind. She

242

chose her path. Matosapa is a good man. The rest is up to Night Star.'' Standing, he offered his hand. Pulling Sarah to her feet, he kept an arm around her as she swayed. "How about joining me for a swim? It will cool you and perhaps make you feel better. When we return, we will have dried meat for our meal and you will rest.''

Sarah smiled weakly. This was one time she wouldn't argue with him. "A swim sounds wonderful. Thank you, Golden Eagle." Side by side, they walked along the path that would lead them to inviting cool waters.

Dark angry eyes followed their progress. Night Star watched until Golden Eagle and Sarah disappeared, hate filling her. She blamed her misfortune on the white girl. All of this was *her* fault. She would find a way to get even with both of them.

Turning at the call of her new husband, Night Star paled when she realized all was ready for their journey. There was no way to stall for more time. Soon, she would be alone with the big Indian. Shuddering at the thought of lying beneath her huge husband, she closed her eyes. There had to be a way out. She had plenty of time before nightfall. Without looking at her family, Night Star had no choice but to allow her husband to assist her onto her pony. Warned beforehand of Night Star's reluctance, Matosapa took the lead rope in his hands. Night Star did not look back as he led the way out of the village.

The breeze picked up, drifting lazily, caressing the inhabitants of the Black Hills, and the sun began to lose its fiery heat as it sank on the distant horizon.

The week had been overly warm, and topped with Night Star's black moods, a heavy cloud of tension had hung over the tribe. Nature took pity with the arrival of a welcome cooling breeze that, along with Night Star's departure, relieved the oppressive mood. That night a festive mood abounded in the village.

Too warm to sleep, toddlers and youngsters ran gleefully, finally able to expend some of their energies as their naked bodies frolicked in the night air, taking advantage of their indulgent parents. Older children sat in groups, playing with miniature tipis, dolls, travois and weapons or talking, enjoying the treat of staying up later than normal. Adults sat and gossiped as they kept their eyes on the little ones.

Squirrels scampered through tree tops, stopping to chatter at the noisy humans, as if to say it was late and time for bed. Startled birds rose into the darkening sky to land higher in the tall tree tops, seeking quiet to settle in for the night.

Chief Hawk Eyes was on his way back from a refreshing cool dip in the water. Stopping, he turned his head to the dusky sky above. This was his favorite time of the day. The land grew still, the brightness of the sun faded into colorful streaks across Mother Sky before fading into darkness. It was a time when he could silently enjoy the peace of his land and communicate with the spirits.

Sounds of angry squealing came through the tree tops, followed by the descent of a large nut that hit him in the head. Two pairs of beady eyes peered over the edge of their perch. Hawk Eyes laughed and picked up the fallen prize. He would have it later.

He took no more than a couple of steps before another sound from nearby bushes stopped him in his tracks. At full alert, he frowned, cocked his head to one side and listened. The sound of retching was unmistakable.

Pushing back the green branches, he saw the white girl kneeling hunched over a log, head held between her knees.

A strong inbred sense of duty overcame his reluctance. He returned to the stream, where he gathered some tall grasses and dipped them in the water, then returned to Sarah.

Sarah groaned, her shoulders shaking as another wave of

nausea overcame her. Hawk Eyes placed his hands on her shoulders, holding her braids from her face as another spasm racked her body.

The nausea finally passed and Sarah lifted her head and looked over her shoulder through watery eyes. Her face paled even more when she saw that it was Hawk Eyes standing with his hands resting upon her trembling shoulders.

Silently, Hawk Eyes handed her the bunch of wet grass and watched as she wiped her face, lowering her eyes in embarrassment.

After a few minutes, he noticed the color slowly returning to the white girl's face. He reached down and helped her to her feet. With his hand gripping her elbow, he led her to a large rock. "Sit," he commanded.

Hawk Eyes studied her wan features. "Have you been sick long?" he asked, trying to control the suspicions running wildly through his head.

"No, Chief Hawk Eyes," Sarah replied quietly. "It is the heat causing my illness. It only started this week with the arrival of hot weather. It comes and goes, never lasting long. I am fine now. Thank you for your kindness. I will return to your son's tipi."

Hawk Eyes moved in front of her, blocking her exit. "Not yet. Sit." Startled, Sarah resumed her seated position. "How long have you been with us, Sarah?" He frowned, realizing that he'd called her by her given name for the first time, something he'd vowed never to do. She was the "white girl" whenever he was forced to speak to or about her.

Sarah drew her brows together as she mentally calculated. "Almost three months, I think. Why?" she asked.

Closing his eyes, not wanting things more complicated than they already were, he prayed her answer to his next question would alleviate his suspicions. Drawing a deep breath, the chief boldly plunged on. "When is the last time you visited the women's lodge?" he delicately asked.

He remembered her going there a few days after her arrival in their village. He'd been relieved to have her out of his tipi for even that short amount of time.

Sarah closed her eyes. Her shoulders slumped in exhaustion. "The women's lodge?" Sarah echoed. Just last week Bright Blossom had said the others had missed her in the women's lodge, but Sarah had dismissed the thought, paying no further attention to any possible changes in her body—until now.

Her eyes shot open and flew to his face. She colored, scarlet staining her cheeks as her hands fluttered to her middle. "It can't be," she whispered in awe and wonder.

Crossing his arms, Hawk Eyes closed his eyes for a moment, seeking control of his emotions before he spoke sternly.

"If you have been sharing my son's sleeping mat, then not only can it be, but it is very likely that you are with child. My son's child," he added unnecessarily.

Sarah looked away in embarrassment, but not before he saw the glow enter her eyes. Hawk Eyes put his hand to his forehead and swore beneath his breath as he realized something else. If the white girl were indeed with child, as it appeared she was, then she carried his first grandchild.

Sarah hugged herself and watched Chief Hawk Eyes pace the ground in front of her, mumbling to himself. If anyone had come upon them, they too would have been amazed, for the chief never lost control.

He spun around, startling Sarah. "Do you love my son?" His arms folded across his scarred chest as he stared down at her.

Sarah looked up, her eyes softening, face glowing. "Yes, Chief Hawk Eyes, I love Golden Eagle."

Looking into deep blue pools, he could not deny the truth of her words. He'd seen the same love there many times, but had refused to acknowledge it. Taking a few steps back, he stated, "You carry my grandchild. The life we lead is a harsh one. How long will you remain in our village before

246

you decide to return to your house of wood and the comforts within? Can you promise that you will never want to leave and take the child away to return to your people and way of life? Answer me truthfully,'' Hawk Eyes commanded.

Sarah stood on shaky legs, arms at her side, and looked Hawk Eyes in the eye. "I do not know the future or what it holds, so I would be foolish to promise what I do not know. I can only tell you how I feel." She sank down on the log, struggling to control another wave of nausea.

"Where Golden Eagle goes, I will follow as long as he wants me and I am allowed to stay," she continued in a voice as firm as she could manage. "This is where I belong. I am content and happy living among your people. There will be times, though, when I will want to visit my other home and have my children know of their white heritage as well."

Hawk Eyes took a deep breath, fighting his admiration for Sarah. He stepped forward, unwilling to give in yet. While her words were spoken with spirit and honesty, there was much at stake. He stood toe to toe with Sarah, brows drawn fiercely, hands crossed intimidatingly across his chest. Still, Sarah did not back down. She looked up at him, her chin lifted higher, and unflinching blue eyes meshed with brown.

"I do not doubt that you wish to remain with my son. Nor do I question your feelings. But none of that is important if you cannot endure the life that our women endure day after day, year after year. You are white. Few white women can survive the harshness of our way of life. What makes you think you can survive our way of life?" he asked, contempt of her white blood raining over Sarah as if he'd physically struck her.

Sarah's jaw dropped. Disbelief quickly fled as anger, swift as a shadow, swept across her face and settled in her eyes. Her mouth worked, but no words came out. She pushed herself from the log. Her hands gripped her hips as

247

she turned away for long moments before returning to stand before the stoic chief.

"Chief Hawk Eyes, you are wrong to presume that only Indian women are strong enough to survive in this wilderness. Just because my way of life is different doesn't mean I am inferior or that your women are better. There are many things we can learn from each other to make all our lives better," Sarah sputtered, bristling with indignation.

"Besides. My blood is not all white. My father is an Ind . . ." Sarah stopped, horrified by what she'd nearly revealed, and quickly turned, hiding her fearful expression.

Hawk Eyes had not been paying attention to her outburst, but her last words caught his attention. His hands gripped Sarah's shoulders and spun her around to face him. "What did you say? What do you mean your blood is not all white? What is you father? Finish what you were about to say!"

Sarah stared at her feet and shook her head. "I did not mean anything. I should return now, Chief Hawk Eyes. Golden Eagle will wonder where I am."

Sarah's poor attempt at evasion as well as her suddenly meek appearance did not go unnoticed by Hawk Eyes. One finger lifted her chin, allowing him to look into her eyes. "My son will wait. Were you about to say your father is an Indian? Tell me, Sarah."

Sarah let out her pent-up breath, keeping her eyes on Hawk Eyes. "Yes. My father is an Indian," she announced quietly, simply and proudly.

Hawk Eyes absorbed her words, then shook his head in denial. "My son says your father is a trapper who recently journeyed to the spirit world. Is this not true?" he asked.

"The man who raised me, the one I called 'Pa,' died last winter, that is true. But he is not my blood father. The one who sired me is an Indian warrior," Sarah explained, her pride mingling with fear of the chief's reaction.

Astounded, Hawk Eyes stared at Sarah and staggered back. Incredulously, for the first time in many moons, he found himself totally speechless. It slowly sunk in. The girl before him carried Indian blood. Groaning, he rubbed his temple with his fingers as he wondered if things could get any more complicated. "Does my son know of this story?" he sighed. Nothing from this point on would surprise him.

Shaking her head no, Sarah confessed, "You are the only one who knows of this."

"Why did you not say something of this matter when you first came to us?"

Sarah looked down at her hands, fingers threaded together. "I was afraid to. My people do not like those with Indian blood, especially women."

"You will tell me everything," Hawk Eyes demanded, his voice laced with a new gentleness. He listened intently as Sarah told him of her mother, the little she knew about her Indian father, her guardian and why he hated her. She also told him how others of her race would view her mixed parentage and what her almost certain future would be if they ever found out.

When she finished and glanced at him almost fearfully, Hawk Eyes placed his hands on her shoulders. "I have been wrong in my feelings toward you. You have conducted yourself with pride and honor in my village. I see now why you adjusted so quickly to our ways. You would make my son a fine wife."

He glanced at the stars slowly appearing far above as he conceded, "Yes. I would find much honor in calling you daughter, but like you, I cannot make promises until I meet with White Cloud. Being with child may change things considerably. Certainly your Indian blood complicates matters." Seeing hope shining from her wide trusting eyes, he held up his hand in warning. "All is not settled."

Side by side, they returned to the village, with Hawk Eyes feeling a surge of protectiveness, making sure she did not trip over roots or twigs as he kept his hand on her elbow, guiding her.

Chapter Twenty-seven

Golden Eagle stood deep in the shadows of his tipi scanning the darkened village. All was quiet as most had retired for the night.

He glanced around, looking for White Wind, realizing he'd not seen her since their evening meal. He turned and headed for Bright Blossom's tipi. Most nights, if he was called away on tribal business, she went there, the two women keeping each other company until their warriors returned.

Halfway there, he spotted White Wind and his father leaving the shadowy protection of the woods. He started to head in their direction, but stopped when he noticed how deep in conversation they were. So absorbed were they, neither one noticed his presence.

Their heads bent together as they moved toward the tipi Sarah shared with Golden Eagle.

Golden Eagle followed, staying in the shadows. At his tipi, Chief Hawk Eyes waited outside while Sarah ducked inside. Moments later, she reappeared and handed his father an object. Hawk Eyes took his leave and Sarah reentered the tipi, lowering the flap behind her.

Sarah danced around and resisted the impulse to shout her happiness. She was going to have a baby. A baby like little Two Feathers. A baby of her own. Her's and Golden Eagle's. Her fingers splayed across her belly, a look of wonder overcoming her. Tears of happiness and joy trickled down her cheeks. A baby. They were going to have a baby!

She was standing with her back to the doorway when Golden Eagle entered. At his entrance, she twirled around and flew at him, throwing her arms around his neck.

Golden Eagle wrapped his arms around her and held her. Putting Sarah aside, he wiped the moisture from her flushed skin. "*Kechuwa.* What is wrong? What did my father say to upset you?" he asked, an edge to his voice, his lips tightening in anger.

Sarah's lips curved into a secretive smile. It was nice to know he watched over her and cared. Mary had always done a good job watching over her, but it wasn't the same. She knew Golden Eagle did not like it when his father went out of his way to torment her. Only at her insistence that he not interfere did Golden Eagle agree to let her handle Chief Hawk Eyes on her own.

Sarah grabbed his hands and held them gently in hers as she led him further into the tipi and quickly reassured him, "I'm fine, Golden Eagle. I've got something wonderful to tell you."

Needing to be closer, Sarah placed her hands on his shoulders as she shyly revealed, "Your seed grows within my body. I'm going to have your baby, Golden Eagle."

She giggled as Golden Eagle's features changed instantly from dark and foreboding to awestruck silence before he dropped to his knees. Opening his mouth, Golden Eagle gulped a breath of air and his lips moved, but no sound came forth.

Looking down at her speechless warrior, Sarah gave a

251

nervous laugh, her hands tightening on his shoulders. "You are pleased, aren't you?"

Running his hands down her flat abdomen, Golden Eagle pulled her head down to his. Planting a feathery kiss upon her brow, he replied, "A babe? You're giving me a babe?" At her shy nod, he grinned. "Yes. I am very pleased. I can't believe it. You have made me very happy." Drawing his brows together, he asked, wanting to be sure, "You are positive of this?"

Sarah's fingers stroked his cheek. "Your father is," she replied, her tone light and teasing.

Golden Eagle was still looking for signs of life when her words registered. "My father? What has he to do with this?" His head snapped up.

Briefly, Sarah told Golden Eagle how his father had found her and the resulting conversation that led to the reason for her sickness.

A light scratch from outside and a voice bidding permission to enter halted further conversation.

Golden Eagle stood and called out permission for his mother to enter. The flap was shoved aside to admit Seeing Eyes.

Looking from one to the other, Seeing Eyes nodded approval. "You have told him." She directed her approval toward Sarah. "That is good. I have special drink for you. Take away sickness."

Seeing Eyes set the bowl down and gave each a swift hug before quickly departing, leaving the couple alone to share this special time together.

Cautiously Sarah sipped the brew. Finding the taste not too bitter, she finished and handed the empty bowl to Golden Eagle. Golden Eagle quickly laid out their sleeping pallet and led her to the center.

With reverence, he slowly removed each piece of clothing as if he needed to see where his child lay nestled within its mother's womb. Not taking his eyes from her slender body, he grinned and placed a small tender kiss on the soft skin of her abdomen. "Soon, you will grow big with our child." He spoke with reverence.

Sarah needed to tell him everything, wanting nothing left between them. Stepping away from his gentle embrace, she sat, covering her nakedness with a fur around her shoulders. Not wanting him to get the wrong impression, she reached out, took his hand in hers and placed a kiss in the touch center of his palm.

"There is more that you need to know, my golden warrior. I cannot seem to talk when you are touching or looking upon me."

Motioning him to sit, Sarah repeated her story about the summer her mother was in the care of an Indian warrior and why Willy sought revenge against her.

Finishing her story, Sarah waited for Golden Eagle's reaction, chewing her lower lip and fingering her locket as he remained silent for so long.

Like his father, Golden Eagle found himself incapable of speech. He could only stare at Sarah as he digested her announcement.

Sarah watched his eyes settle on her high cheekbones before moving over her limbs. She knew he was studying skin that had once been a pale honey, but in the last couple of months had turned to a golden brown. He, as his father had done, was now seeing signs that had always been there.

Next, she watched Golden Eagle glance around the tipi. He eyed her handiwork, all of which she'd learned so quickly. She sighed, knowing he'd come to the same conclusion as his father as to why she'd adapted to his way of life with a stamina and courage. She'd never be able to convince either one of them that just maybe, Indian blood or not, she had adapted to their way of life because she'd wanted to.

Sarah watched the emotions chase across his face. Her nervousness had fled, and she was beginning to enjoy herself. She didn't see him speechless very often, let alone twice in such a short period of time—and his father as well.

The two of them in one short night! She'd better enjoy it. It would probably never happen again.

"You have Indian blood flowing within your veins." Lifting his hands to her blond hair, he fingered it in amazement. Looking into her laughing eyes, he asked, "My father? He knows of this too?"

Nodding her head, Sarah laughed and told her stunned warrior of his father's reaction and his promise to try and locate her father.

"Why didn't you tell me this?" Golden Eagle asked.

Sarah shrugged. "I didn't say anything before about my Indian parentage because I didn't know anything about Indians or the way they lived. I was afraid to mention it. Most whites feel strongly about mixed blood. Children born with an Indian parent are called 'half-breeds' and are treated with contempt for something they had no control over. I was afraid you would think the same."

Interrupting her, Golden Eagle said, "Never would I have turned against you because you carry mixed blood."

Sarah stroked his cheek and replied gently, "I know this now. My plan was to try to find my father first and decide if I should make my heritage known. I was going to hire a scout to find him. After I came here, I found I didn't want to leave you and was afraid if your father knew I had an Indian father, he would find him and force me to leave. A small part of me is still afraid," she confessed. Hawk Eyes' apparent acceptance of her still seemed too good to be true.

Tenderly lowering Sarah to the soft bedding, Golden Eagle broke out into another silly grin. He bent his head to place another kiss on her belly. "Soon I will feel the strong kick of our son or daughter." Trailing his lips upward, he blazed a sensuous trail.

Reaching forward, Sarah held his long braids in her hands, and quickly undid them. Using her fingers as a comb, she separated the silky strands, until his hair fell forward, a dark waterfall spilling from his head, to pool onto her chest.

Moaning his name, Sarah urged him over her, needing
to feel him buried deep within her. Fumbling, she untied
the offending piece of leather hindering her questing fingers
and tossed it aside. Gently she wrapped her fingers around
his hardness, thrilling as it filled her loving hands. Stroking
the velvet-soft tip, she wiped away a drop of dew and
coaxed his throbbing shaft to her hot moist center, letting
him feel her readiness.

Golden Eagle entered her slowly, carefully. His voice
hoarse, he whispered in her ear, ''I'm afraid I'll hurt you
or the babe, my sweet White Wind.''

Tightening her legs around him, Sarah twined her arms
around Golden Eagle's taut neck, and reassured him, ''You
won't hurt me or the baby. I love you, Golden Eagle. Take
me now. I can't wait any longer.''

As he listened to her whispery pleas, all restraint and
fear fled. Together they soared, carried by forces as old as
time itself, until they lay satiated in each other's arms.

Before falling asleep, Golden Eagle lifted himself onto
his elbows, relieving Sarah of his weight as he looked
closely, concern etched in his features. He searched for any
sign that she was in pain, but saw only the warm afterglow
in Sarah's eyes as she snuggled next to him, pulling him
down beside her.

Golden Eagle relaxed when he realized that he'd not hurt
her or his baby. He turned to his side. ''And you, White
Wind? Are you happy about our babe?'' he asked, needing
to hear the words from her lips.

Fingers stoked him from the side of his face down to his
bare chest as Sarah stared at him through sparkling eyes,
her lips smiling softly. ''Yes, my golden warrior. I am very
happy to carry your baby.''

Golden Eagle pulled Sarah close, his shoulder pillowing
her head. He listened to her breathing as it grew slow, and
kissed her forehead lightly, vowing no harm would come

to her. He gave silent thanks to the spirits and asked them to watch over his love and baby.

A baby . . . He was going to be a father. What would their child look like? Would he have a son who would one day lead his people with courage and wisdom, or would their first child be a miniature of White Wind, with hair of the sun and eyes of the sky? Brown eyes or blue, white skin or bronze, it didn't really matter to Golden Eagle. He knew their children would be special. How could they not be with White Wind as their mother? A smile played on his lips as dreams of fatherhood lured his eyes to close and sleep overtook him.

Chapter Twenty-eight

"Hey," Hank yelled, spurring his horse forward. "When are we gonna reach the next tribe of savages? I'm gettin' tired of all this ridin' round fer nuthin.'' He stood in his stirrups and lifted his sore seat from the saddle.

Pulling on his reins, Harry whipped around, moving much faster than it appeared his bulk would allow. Startled, Hank fell back into his saddle with a moan of pain, pulling abruptly on his reins as he did so and nearly lost his seat as his horse reared to let him know he didn't appreciate the rough treatment.

When Hank regained control of his horse, Harry's bushy brows pulled together, his face a cold mask as he lashed out at Hank. "You watch yore mouth, young fella, unless you want to get us all scalped. They could be watching us now. I'll be at the village by afternoon," Harry informed both Hank and Red before turning to continue onward.

"Wait a sec, ol'-timer. We's goin' with ya this time," Red declared. "We's tired of stayin' behind while you goes to eat and enjoy yourself. Hell, we'll never find that brat for Willy,'' he grumbled.

"I agree with my brother," Hank said. "We all go together this time. For all we know, maybe you're getting all them squaws too. I'm ready for a woman. Even a squaw will do." He snickered.

Muttering about young fools who would get them all killed, Harry gave in. In a way, he couldn't blame them. If any of them had guts, they'd return and tell Willy they had failed. But he didn't want to face Willy's wrath. Not yet anyways.

Stopping a short time later on the pretense of resting, he warned his companions they were under observation. In a low voice he gave his instructions.

"Go sit and relax. But leave your guns on your horses and stay calm for Gawd's sake! They's approach us here, we must be convincing as trappers if we want to get into their village. Do only as I do and for Christ's sake, keep yore traps shut and let me do any talking."

"Why don't we just ride into the village? Why's we gotta sit out here like sittin' ducks?" Red complained, glancing over his shoulder.

Closing his eyes, Harry forced himself to remain calm. Turning to Red, he hissed in a low tone, "You don't just ride into an Indian village, you stupid fool. They are well guarded. They know you're in their territory long before you find the entrance to their villages. Now shut up and do as you're told, or I might just let them savages have at you."

Watching Red and Hank lower themselves beneath the shade of a large pine tree, he followed, grumbling he should've left those two fools behind and come alone as he'd done countless times since leaving Willy that night so long ago. He sat, a bundle of pemmican in his hand. Looking at each other, the brothers followed suit and started to eat.

Sure enough, they had barely finished eating when they were approached and surrounded by several warriors, their faces and chests streaked with slashes of paint, sharp lances held ready to throw in one hand, shields held in the other. Harry slowly got to his feet and used the hand signs for friends and traders.

Harry conveyed to the distrustful warriors that they meant no harm. They were only there to trap and trade. Waving his hand toward the heavily loaded pack mule, he invited them to inspect his goods.

The leader motioned to his warriors. Immediately, their horses and goods were inspected. Hank and Red sat, too afraid to move or speak. They cringed when the leader pointed his spear at them and looked to Harry, a question in his black eyes.

Hank and Red turned their wide eyes toward Harry. Unbelievably, Harry sat relaxed, as if this were an everyday occurrence. Next time they would stay back, their looks to each other said.

Harry didn't have to understand the Indian's language to understand his unspoken question. Once glance at Red and Hank was all it took. The two quivering dummies didn't look like seasoned trappers or traders. Hopefully, they wouldn't get them all killed. Harry forced a laugh and again used sign language. He explained that the two were his sister's sons, his nephews. Using the sign for children, he explained they were like children learning, and he was their teacher.

He also signed to the warriors that they were slow learners, not very bright, but his responsibility. He pointed to his head, and shook his head.

The leader laughed and shook his head to show his contempt at grown men who cringed like babies. Conversing with the rest of his party, the mighty warrior motioned them to their horses.

Back in his saddle, Hank leaned over and asked what was going on. Unable to resist passing on the insult, Harry told the boys what had been conveyed. Watching their faces turn the color of Red's hair, he advised, ''You two big tough boys continue to act scared and green. It may be the only way you get out of their village alive. Follow my lead, and for Gawd's sake, stay away from their women. If you get into trouble, I won't be able to help you.''

Entering the large village later, they were immediately surrounded by the people of the tribe. The chief and his family came to meet them. The others hung back. Talking to the leading warrior, the chief nodded his head. Walking forward, he silently went through the goods laid out on the ground for their inspection. Choosing what he and his family wanted, the chief walked away without a single word.

Seeing the confused expressions, Harry explained that was the price and the signal from the chief to trade with his people.

For the next hour, hot bodies pressed close together, each trying to find the best bargain.

Sulking in her tipi, Night Star peered out to see what the noise and commotion was about. She stared with envy at the silky furs and shiny trinkets the other women were carrying back to their tipis. It had been a long time since she'd seen a trader. Her old village stayed so far up in the mountains that they didn't get visitors.

Unable to resist, she stepped out. She didn't have anything to trade with, but she could look. She chose to ignore the fact that she was banned to her tipi for disobeying her husband. She scowled. Matosapa thought he could order her around like a slave. She ignored the fact that he was kind to her most of the time and had not forced himself on her. Night Star resisted the softening of her hate. She didn't want to like anything about him or his village. The other women ignored her as she picked at the remaining furs and shiny baubles.

Unknown to Night Star, Harry's sharp beady eyes watched her closely. He saw the lips twisted with bitterness, eyes that burned with unhappiness and hatred.

Harry approached her, noticing the way she fingered the

small fur trim in her fingers. Speaking aloud, as well as using his hands, he told Night Star. "Take. I give to you a gift of friendship."

Night Star glanced around, seeing that most of the others had finished. She threw the fur at the white man. "No. I not take white man's gifts. Give to your white-girl dogs." Night Star spat at his feet contemptuously. As much as she wanted to accept the gift, her pride would not allow it.

Harry raised his brows at her broken English as well as her hatred. He played along, sighing loudly. "But I do not have a white girl to give beautiful furs to. Perhaps you know of one that would like gifts of furs and trinkets?" He reached down and brought up a large soft pelt and fingered the silky fur.

She narrowed her eyes, and a gleam of evil lurked as a plan formed in Night Star's mind. Looking appraisingly at the old trapper, she slyly asked, "How bad you want white girl, white man? Bad enough to steal from Indian village?"

No emotion showed as the wise old trapper shrugged. "Depends on how pretty she is." He sighed. "I do have a weakness for young yellowed-haired beauties, however. Do you know of any such women?" Harry asked nonchalantly.

"Maybe, white man. Maybe. If I know of one, and if I choose to tell you, it will cost you much," Night Star hissed. She'd show these stupid women and get even at the same time.

Pretending to consider, Harry chose his words carefully. "I will take a chance. Describe this girl to me. If I likes what I hear, I will pay you many furs and beads." Taking a bag from deep within his many layers of clothing, he held it so only she could see.

Greedily, Night Star eyed the small bag of treasured pony beads. She'd make herself many beautiful garments with those. Quickly she gave him the description of Sarah without taking her eyes off the bag he swung in front of her.

Tossing the girl the bag, Harry squatted next to the

picked-over pile as if showing Night Star more furs, and handed her a short stick.

Night Star glanced over her shoulder and drew a rough map of the area in which he would be able to find her village.

Standing, Harry tossed Night Star an armful of furs and cheap baubles.

Looking at her armful of goods, Night Star fled to her tipi. She had to hide her bounty. As she buried them among her belongings from her village, her face grew grim. If Matosapa found them, she would tell him they were her treasures and that she'd brought them with her. Lying came easy to her.

She peered out of her tipi when she heard the traders take their leave. Laughing, she danced with glee. She had not gotten Golden Eagle, but now the white girl wouldn't have him much longer either.

Night Star had just barely concealed her goods when the flap flew open and Matosapa stormed into the tipi. "You were told not to leave this tipi, wife! You have disobeyed me again. Why can you not act as other warrior's wives? Where are the things you got from the traders?"

Night Star's heart pounded both from the fright he'd given her and the sheer handsomeness of her husband. Her face flushed with guilt, but she sent a look of disdain toward him to hide her growing awareness. "You startled me, husband. What are you talking about? I went out to relieve myself."

"I was told that you returned from a conversation with the trappers with many furs in your arms. Where are they?" Matosapa towered over her, red with rage.

Night Star shrugged. "Then you were informed wrong. I only stopped to look on my way back from the bushes." What she wouldn't give to know who'd told her husband.

"Very well, Night Star. You were given the chance to be honest with me." Matosapa went to his wife's pile of belongings and started to rummage through them.

Night Star jumped to her feet. "Get out of my belongings, Matosapa. These are my belongings from home and you have no right to go through them." She tried unsuccessfully to pull her husband's large bulk away, but found herself put aside.

"Ah, what have we here?" Matosapa exclaimed triumphantly, holding up a leather pouch. Opening it, he dumped the contents onto the hard earth floor, watching as the colorful beads scattered over the hard-packed dirt. Next, his searching fingers latched onto the many fur trims and pelts, and he threw them at her feet.

"Brought from the village of Chief Hawk Eyes, you say?" He held one up, eyed the fur, turning it over, fingering the silky textures. Dropping the fur as if it burned, Matosapa rose to his full intimidating height.

Night Star cringed as her husband approached, his face deceptively calm as he waved the piece of black fur at her.

"Would my wife like to tell me how she acquired such smooth, shiny beads and furs cut from animals by white men? Your father's village does not deal with traders as ours does. Did you think Matosapa would not be able to tell a fur skinned by an Indian over one done by white men? Does the wife of Matosapa think her husband stupid?" Angrily, Matosapa flung the offending item away.

"What did Night Star give to the trader? You have nothing of value." He waited, but Night Star remained silent. She knew if he found out the truth, he would beat her publicly.

Matosapa stared at his wife's angry, unrepentant face and came to a decision. "Very well. Since I have brought you to my tipi, I thought to give you time to adjust to our marriage, adjust to your new tribe. I have been lenient with you. I have hoped you would come to terms with your life here in my village, but I can see that you are no happier or better off with my gentle handling. From now on, you will act as a warrior's wife. You will be obedient, or I will beat you. You will give no more trouble to the other women, or I will cut your sharp tongue out. Is that clear, wife?'' Matosapa roared, loud enough for those outside to hear.

Night Star's eyes grew round and she nodded, for once truly scared. She had no doubt he was serious. She'd pushed him too far with this last act of rebelliousness. A feeling of sadness washed over her as he turned away and headed for the doorway. When he stopped to fasten the flap securely before turning to face her once more, her heart sped up.

His hand waved to indicate the bounty at her feet. ''All this will be given to those in need in my village.'' With determined purpose, he took several steps toward her and placed his hands on the thong at his waist. ''It is time for you to learn how to please your husband on our sleeping mat. I long for sons and daughters, and perhaps if you are busy with our babes, you will have no time left to cause trouble. Come to me, wife.''

Night Star watched, her heart beating furiously as Matosapa removed his moccasins and untied the length of cording around his waist. When his breechclout fell to the floor, she stared in fear and wonder at that part of him that was growing large before her eyes. Suddenly, she was eager to discover the secrets of womanhood.

''Your husband is waiting, wife,'' she was reminded.

Night Star wrestled with her resentment for a minute longer before she took the first steps toward her husband.

Chapter Twenty-nine

As hot summer winds whisked across the dry grass of the prairies, anticipation swept through the village. Tipi to tipi, family to family, the air sizzled with excitement. Scouts had returned with news of a small herd of buffalo roaming in the lower regions of the Black Hills, not far from the new site of the village. Immediately, a hunt was planned.

Just days ago, the tribe had settled in a deep canyon that provided cooler temperatures and greater safety with steep canyon walls surrounding them on three sides.

Chief Hawk Eyes decided not to uproot the whole tribe to hunt the buffalo. This would be a small excursion, one more for fun, excitement and training. The one or two buffalo they hoped to get would also tide them over until the main hunt at the end of summer when his tribe would be joining others in great numbers to kill all they needed of the fattened prime buffalo to sustain them through the winter.

Hawk Eyes chose his best hunters and a few inexperienced braves. The warriors would take their families with them as the meat would have to be dried on the spot to prevent spoilage.

Time was spent carefully inspecting weapons, sharpening arrows and readying their best buffalo horses. Wives and daughters made sure their knives were sharp and supplies in order. At night, songs to the buffalo rose along the canyon walls while below, bodies danced, honoring the great beasts.

Many prayers were given by the *Wacasa* while the warriors and braves sat in the sweat lodge, purifying themselves, making themselves worthy to kill the great beasts that their people so depended on.

Seeing Eyes woke early, the air cool and gray with shadows. She turned, rolling over to seek her husband's warmth for a last cuddle before duties demanded her full attention.

Her eyes flew open as her fingers encountered a cold empty spot where her husband had lain. Pushing herself up, she shoved her long black hair from her face and blinked the sleep from her eyes as she glanced around.

Spotting Hawk Eyes squatting in shadows cast by the slowly appearing morning light, she rose to her knees. "Husband?"

Hawk Eyes turned his attention from the box resting in his palm and scooted toward his wife. Kneeling beside her, he held out the object that occupied his attention so early that morning.

Carefully taking the carved box with work-worn fingers, Seeing Eyes stared at the exquisitely crafted box with admiration. The tips of her fingers traced the raised edges of the carved symbols. "This is beautiful, my husband. Where did this come from?" she asked, fingering the softness of rabbit fur inside.

Seeing Eyes knew it was not made by her husband. Each warrior's brand of artistic talent was easily recognizable and objects could be identified by the symbols and style of work.

"It belongs to White Wind." Hawk Eyes held out his hand for the box.

Startled, Seeing Eyes would've dropped the box had her husband not had his hand beneath hers. "White Wind?" she repeated dumbly, as if she'd not heard right. Wide awake, she kept her eyes focused intently on her husband. "Since when does my husband call the white girl by name?"

Hawk Eyes straightened proudly. "Did my wife think her husband would not hear of the name she gave to the white girl?"

Seeing Eyes lowered her eyes in shame as Hawk Eyes continued. "White Wind is the name that you foresaw, is it not?" he persisted.

Seeing Eyes raised her eyes. "Yes, my husband. My vision spoke of a white girl who would be known as White Wind," she answered, then waited, certain he would be displeased with her.

"And what else did your vision tell you? Did it tell you that this would be the mate for our son?"

"Yes, husband. That is what I saw. Sarah is to be our son's wife and the mother of his children." Seeing Eyes laid her hand on her husband's shoulder.

Hawk Eyes nodded, reached over to cup the side of her face and asked, "What of White Cloud and the peace agreement?"

"I do not know the answer to give you, my chief. I only know what has been revealed to me."

Hawk Eyes set the carved box down and looked deeply into Seeing Eyes' uncertain gaze. "The name White Wind would make any woman with Indian blood in her veins proud, including the white girl, Sarah," Hawk Eyes announced, cradling her face in his hands.

Seeing Eyes examined her husband's words, not sure if she understood correctly. Staring deep into his eyes, she hesitantly asked, "Are you telling me that Sarah is Indian?'' At his nod, she shook her head. ''How can this be?'' she asked.

Hawk Eyes related the story told to him by Sarah. He picked up the box and handed it to Seeing Eyes while he dug among his things and brought out the necklace as well for her to study. ''I have seen similar work, but cannot say where or whose it is. Have you recognized this warrior's work?''

Seeing Eyes studied the Indian objects fragile with age. That they were made by her people, she did not doubt. Several symbols were of their nation and of great importance. Her eyes closed as she concentrated on the objects in her hands. Love and sadness overcame her.

Looking into her husband's eyes, Seeing Eyes shook her head. ''I too have seen many of these symbols. As I look upon his work, I also feel his sadness carved into this wood.''

Hawk Eyes did not question what Seeing Eyes felt. He accepted her observation as part of her gift of sight. Instead, he stated, ''An Indian's work is individual. It's a mark of that warrior, of his life and his deeds. When our people come together, we will ask others if they can tell us the name of the warrior who made these.''

Putting the objects away, Hawk Eyes pulled his wife close and looked over her shoulder at their sleeping daughter. Seeing Eyes followed his gaze and smiled as she allowed herself to be pulled back to their sleeping mats.

Sarah stood in front of her tipi and watched the commotion surrounding her. To an inexperienced eye, it would seem as if the village had gone wild. But despite the noise of people, horses and barking dogs, she knew order reigned amid the chaos.

A large party of warriors, women and older braves readied themselves. Horses were packed, some with a loaded travois behind them, ready to carry tipis and all of the family's belongings.

Groups of well-wishers, mainly the elderly, sick or very young, gathered to see their friends and relatives off, many shouting last-minute advice.

Sarah turned back into her tipi at Golden Eagle's call, and noted that he too was ready to leave. She flew into his outstretched arms.

Tenderly, Golden Eagle stroked her cheek and met her saddened eyes. "Take care, White Wind. It is best you remain here this time. You are still weak with sickness from our babe. The work is hard. You are not accustomed to it yet.

"You will help when we hunt during the moon-when-leaves-are-brown. Stay close to the village and take care of our growing babe."

"I will be fine, my golden warrior," Sarah reassured him, hugging him fiercely before stepping back. "I will be very busy looking after Two Feathers and Winona," she reminded him.

Looking deeply into her dark blue eyes moist with sadness, Golden Eagle held her head. "It is important for you to stay close. Our village will be vulnerable with many of our warriors and braves gone. There will be a few left to guard the village, but you must not wander away. Always go with the other women to bathe. Never go to the water alone. Make sure one of the warriors goes to guard you. Take Running Bull with you. He is the bravest warrior remaining and can be trusted to watch over you."

Sarah nodded, still wishing she could go, but knowing she would be of more use to the tribe here at the village, seeing to the elders and her two charges.

Sarah cupped his face in her hands and rose on her toes to kiss his lips. "I will, do not worry. You take care of yourself too, my golden warrior. Our child needs his father to return safely."

With one last lingering kiss, Golden Eagle led Sarah out into the sunshine before heading off to ready his horse. Bright Blossom brought over Two Feathers and a parfleche

269

of his belongings. The two women hugged, and Two Feathers squirmed between them and demanded to be let down. Laughing, Sarah set him down and watched as he headed for her tipi, looking for the treats she always kept ready for him.

A short while later, she stood with the others, waving and cheering until the hunting party was out of sight. She turned and along with the remaining women, young children and elderly, set about preparing for the first load of meat and furs that would be sent back. Everyone worked. Everyone shared in the goods.

Glancing around, hands to her hips, Sarah searched for her young charges. Spotting Winona and Two Feathers climbing on a fallen log, Sarah shook her head. Something told her she had her work cut out for her just tending to them. Calling Winona, Sarah instructed the mischievous girl to bring her belongings to her tipi.

A week later Sarah decided to gather some *wazhushtecha,* wild strawberries, for their meal. Leaving Two Feathers in the care of Morning Grass, she grabbed a small hide pouch and started off.

"Sarah!" Hearing her name shouted, Sarah paused and swiveled toward the high-pitched childish voice. She grinned as Winona came running.

The girl's strong brown legs flew beneath her as she neared Sarah, who quickly stepped to one side, stretched out one arm and halted Winona's headlong flight. "Slow down, Winona. I do not want to have to send word to your parents of your injury," Sarah sternly reprimanded her.

Long black braids whipped across her back as Winona hopped up and down. "I want to go with you," she pleaded. "Can I come too? Please? Let me help. I won't be any trouble, I promise."

Sarah laughed and shook her head in resignation as she stared into the seemingly innocent features of her young charge. She knew first-hand how little effort it took for Winona to get into trouble.

Sarah pursed her lips and put one hand to her waist. "I don't know, Winona. You know I promised your parents that I would not let any harm come to you." She hid her smile when the girl's round face fell with disappointment, her lower lip jutting out in an unmistakable pout.

Sarah laughed. Her love for Golden Eagle's young sister grew each day. It was times like this when she regretted having no brothers or sisters. Nodding her permission, Sarah tweaked one long black braid. "You may come, but stay close. We aren't allowed to go far," Sarah cautioned, holding out her hand to clasp Winona's small brown one firmly in hers.

Hand in hand, the two went up the canyon a short distance toward the thick-growing bushes closest to the village. Together they started picking the fresh juicy berries. Sarah glanced over her shoulder to see how the young girl was faring and stopped her gathering.

Sarah placed her red-stained fingers at her waist. She shook her head in mock dismay, her lips trembling with laughter. "You scamp. Look in your basket," she gently scolded. Together they bent their heads, one fair as the sun, the other dark as night.

Winona smiled sheepishly as her basket was nearly empty. She lifted sparkling unrepentant golden eyes toward Sarah. "But Sarah. They taste so good. I can't help it."

Running her finger down the small upturned nose, Sarah gave a playful tweak to the tip and held up her half-full pouch. "I understand, but you must explain to Morning Grass why your basket is so empty. I promised to pick enough for all to enjoy," Sarah replied, seemingly dismissing it from her mind.

Out of the corner of her eye, Sarah watched Winona's eyes grow round as the child stared with regret at the plump berry she was about to pop into her red-stained mouth. Sighing, properly reprimanded, Winona dropped the fruit into her basket and set about filling her basket so she too could share with the others.

A short time later, carrying one basket barely half full and one bulging pouch, Sarah and Winona returned to the busy village. The two warriors who had followed silently and unobtrusively stood guard also returned.

High up the canyon, concealed in thick bushes, eyes followed every movement of Sarah, Winona and the warriors standing guard. Harry's beady eyes glowed with anticipation. He wiped the perspiration off his forehead, replaced his hat and glanced at the bright burning sun.

He was amazed he'd found Willy's ward so quickly and easily, considering the poor directions he'd gotten from that greedy squaw. Once he had found the area, he'd been frustrated and discouraged to find emptiness where the tribe had once been. Following the faint marks made by dragging travois poles, he'd searched until he'd discovered the location of their new camp in the canyon below, well concealed and well guarded.

Harry sat back on his heals in his hiding place. He'd found the village a week ago and dispatched Hank and Red to report to Willy after arranging a place to meet. Each day he came to watch and plan. All he had to do now was wait for Willy and the boys to return. By his figuring, they should be at the meeting place soon, depending on how long it took the brothers to find Willy and Tom.

It sure would be nice if they got here before the rest of the warriors returned from their hunt, he thought. It had been a stroke of luck that so many had left the day after his arrival, leaving the village vulnerable. Walking the considerable distance to where he'd left his horse, he led the animal silently away.

Two days later Harry returned in the early afternoon for his daily spying. He carefully scouted out the village as he always did. To his disappointment, there were buffalo furs pegged to the ground, stretched out to dry. Everywhere he looked, thin strips of meat hung drying on racks, the women below removing the dried meat until needed to make pemmican. And in one corner of the village, a pile of bones waited to be cleaned.

Carefully, he counted the number of people below and sighed with relief. Not all had returned. To his trained eye, it looked as though half of the warriors and their families had returned.

Frowning, he left. Time was running out. Soon all the warriors would be back. When he felt he was a safe distance from the village, he kicked the horse hard and rode swiftly for his camp.

Chapter Thirty

In another area at the base of the Black Hills, several days ride north of Golden Eagle's present village, lay the village of White Cloud. In her tipi, Wild-Flower paced. Peering out the opening of the tipi, she watched her mother tend to the now-ready meal.

The sight and smell of their cooking meal did not interest Wild-Flower. She wasn't the least bit hungry. Over her mother's hunched shoulders, she watched her father and brothers approach. She grimaced in frustration and spun around, wringing her hands.

She needed to talk to her father alone, without interruptions, but every time she tried, something came up. Usually it was one of her brothers who interfered. Today she had to find a way.

Stepping out when her mother called her, Wild-Flower and her younger sister helped their mother serve her father and brothers. Wild-Flower went to a buffalo paunch suspended by four long poles, hot rocks placed inside keeping the liquid hot. She scooped a few pieces of sliced turnips

274

and a couple chunks of prairie chicken from the simmering stew. Wild-Flower sat and shredded the small amount of meat, eating very little of the mouth-watering meal as she mulled over in her head what she wanted to say to her father.

Preoccupied with her thoughts, anxious for the meal to end, Wild-Flower was unaware of White Cloud's watchful eyes on her.

"Are you not hungry this day, daughter?" Wild-Flower started in surprise when her father addressed her. She set her food aside and shook her head as her mother served White Cloud the empty buffalo paunch which had served as their kettle for cooking the stew.

As she watched, White Cloud took what he wanted and passed it to his sons, each taking and passing it around until it came to her. She shook her head and passed it to her sister and mother. "No, my father. I do not seem hungry at the moment."

Wild-Flower stood to ask if they could take a walk so she could talk to him, but her mother reminded her to help her sister in the clean-up. Wild-Flower rose and worked quickly, hurrying her sister. When done, she wiped her hands on her skirt and headed toward the circle in which her father and brothers still sat and talked, but again her mother's voice halted her.

"Wild-Flower. Today would be a good time to work on your wedding garments. You have much sewing to do before the wedding."

Turning back to her mother, Wild-Flower replied offhandedly, "Not today, Mother. I am not in the mood to sew." The last thing she wanted to do was sit and sew garments for a marriage and a husband she didn't want.

Placing her hands firmly on her hips, Small Bird blocked Wild-Flower's path. "Now daughter, time grows short. You have hardly spent any time on them at all. I insist that you spend the rest of today preparing for your wedding. It is your duty to go to Golden Eagle prepared.'' Her mother spoke firmly, catching her husband's eye.

''But. . . .'' Wild-Flower got no further, as her father's voice interrupted her protests.

''That is enough, Wild-Flower. You will do as your mother bids. I did not raise my daughter to be disobedient. You will bring shame to our tribe if you do not remember this. Your mother is wise. Your time grows short. Now, no more words. Go.'' White Cloud pointed toward the tipi.

Lowering her head to hide tears of hurt and frustration, Wild-Flower stormed inside to her hated sewing.

Chief White Cloud stared at the doorway long after his eldest daughter disappeared. Guilt invaded his thoughts. He'd not spent much time with her recently. Lately, he'd bestowed all his attention on his two youngest sons, who required his close supervision as they were ready to leave childhood behind and begin the rigorous training that would transform boys into brave warriors. Thankfully, he had Running Wolf to help with their training, he thought, glancing proudly at each of his sons.

Staring around the family circle lacking only Wild-Flower, he looked upon each of his children with pride. His firstborn, Running Wolf, had grown into a brave young warrior. At nearly 17 winters, he was strong and brave, and already showed signs of becoming a good leader.

White Cloud listened with half an ear as Running Wolf regaled his two younger brothers with some of his tales. At 10 and 12 winters, they stood in awe of their big brother.

His youngest daughter, now 8 winters, was quietly helping his wife. Desiring nothing more than to help her mother, learning all she could about her future role, she was the opposite of her older sister. From the first day Wild-Flower had walked, she had followed her father and older brother everywhere she could.

More out of amusement, White Cloud had secretly taught her to shoot arrows, hunt small animals and many other things girls were not normally taught. Later, whenever he'd urged her to stay with the women, explaining such activities as hunting were for boys and warriors, she'd pout and argue until he relented.

Running Wolf, older by three years, had pointed out that there was no harm in his young sister learning how to take care of herself. He had also taken an interest in his sister's unorthodox training. Running Wolf was male enough to enjoy having a sister who adored him.

Hopefully, she'd not be a handful or too outspoken in her new tribe. She lived up to her name at times, White Cloud mused.

Allowing his gaze to rest on his wife as she emerged from the tipi, he admired the beauty her face still held. Time and five children had done little damage to her body. True, she was older, as was he, but her beauty had only matured over the years. White Cloud closed his eyes and gave silent thanks for his family.

He accepted his wife's nod of thanks for his intervention and frowned. Again he wondered what was bothering his eldest daughter. Even though raised freer than most girls, she'd never been so difficult before.

He shook his head as his sons called to him. Turning, White Cloud left, Running Wolf striding beside him, the younger two boys running ahead.

Several hours later, still wet from his bath, Chief White Cloud entered his tipi and his gaze went to Wild-Flower sitting on her mat, bits and pieces of softened deer and elk hides surrounding her.

Stopping in front of her, he picked up a large folded piece she had laid aside. Pride swelled within his chest as he noted the wide painstakingly cut fringe at the bottom of the long dress and the painted quills and beads across the yoke. White Cloud smiled his approval, setting the nearly white garment aside to pick up a shirt lying in her lap.

Its size suggested a man's shirt. Nodding his satisfaction

with the quality of her work, he fingered the inside lining of fur. "Your husband will be well clothed. This shirt will provide warmth in the cold months," he said in praise, handing the shirt back so she could continue with her decorating of it.

Lowering her head, Wild-Flower hid her eyes, for she'd not made the shirt for Golden Eagle. It had been made with love for Red Fox.

"You have been very busy and quick today, my daughter. Your future husband will be proud to have a wife so skillful," White Cloud complimented her. "You will make Golden Eagle a fine wife, daughter," he added. His thoughts that afternoon had been on Wild-Flower and whatever was troubling her. The only excuse he found to explain her erratic behavior was her upcoming marriage. Perhaps she grew nervous as her joining neared. That, he'd reasoned, was normal for a young girl, and he hoped to convince her that she had no fears on that score.

Taking a deep breath, Wild-Flower carefully set her sewing down and looked into her father's proud eyes.

"Father, I need to talk to you," she began.

Returning his attention to his child, White Cloud watched Wild-Flower rise gracefully to her feet and hesitate before him.

"Speak, Wild-Flower. I have never seen you at a loss for words before," he teased after she had remained silent several moments.

"Do not force me to marry Golden Eagle, my father," Wild-Flower blurted out, not knowing of a more tactful way to tell him.

White Cloud hid his smile. He had been right. It was marriage nerves after all. "Now daughter, I know your mother has talked to you about marriage and the way between husband and wife. It is nothing to become worried over. You will adjust to being wife to Golden Eagle quickly. Then you will see that all your worry was for nothing." White Cloud traced his finger down the side of her cheek. He'd have Small Bird talk to her once again.

"No, Father," Wild-Flower cried out, stepping back. "You do not understand. I do not wish to join with Golden Eagle at all. I do not want him as my husband."

"What?" White Cloud roared, his face suffused with red as anger at his daughter's words grew. "Explain yourself, my eldest daughter," he commanded, arms crossed, posture rigid and angry.

Wild-Flower bravely drew her self tall and proud and met her father's thunderous expression. "I do not love Golden Eagle, Father. I wish to marry for love. Please allow me this," Wild-Flower begged.

Relaxing somewhat, White Cloud stepped forward to gently cup her small delicate face. His eyes searched hers. "Is this all that is bothering you? Love will come in time, my child. When you go to live with Golden Eagle, the love will grow as you get to know each other. Look at your mother and me. Ours was an arranged match. It has worked well."

Twisting away, Wild-Flower threw out her hands, beseeching him as she cried, "But neither of you loved another. We both love . . ."

Staring at his Wild-Flower as if she'd grown two heads, White Cloud heard no more. He found himself trapped between her words and his memories. Hardening his features and heart to her misery and his memories, he glared angrily at his daughter. "No!" he shouted, cutting her off. "You will do as you are bid. You will marry Golden Eagle. Do you mean to cause shame and war between our tribes again?"

"But Father, Golden Eagle . . ."

"No. No more talk of foolishness. It has been decided. You will not mention this again. I forbid it."

With tears coursing down her cheeks, Wild-Flower sobbed. "Love is not foolish, my father," she choked out.

Cutting her off with the downward slash of his fist, White Cloud shouted, "Enough! You will remain in the tipi and

beg to the spirits for forgiveness for your selfishness."
Turning, White Cloud stormed through the doorway. Chief
White Cloud pushed past his people and kept going, heading deeper into the woods. The demons he'd laid to rest so
long ago came rushing at him, the pictures and voices in
his head startlingly clear, as if it had been yesterday. They
taunted him and drove him far from the village.

Cries. Frightened and hysterical cries echoed in his mind.
He dropped to the ground and put his hands over his ears.
But the memories wouldn't go away. Nor did closing his
eyes dispel the pictures that flashed through his mind. He
groaned and gave in to the painful memories and traveled
back in time.

Wild-Flower's words came back to haunt him. "Love,"
he cried out loud. Yes, he had grown to love Small Bird,
but he'd never forgotten his first love. White Cloud saw
her clearly: sun-yellow hair, blue eyes. Those eyes—eyes
that trusted him to care for her, eyes radiant with love.

He remembered how her eyes had held fear and hurt the
last time he'd seen her, for he'd had to leave her behind
when the time came to return to his people. He'd made
certain she would be found, but it had taken several hours.

The memories continued to wash over White Cloud. He
could not stop the visions, especially of those hours when
he'd remained hidden, watching over her to protect her until the white trapper found her. He'd silently kept vigil,
concealed deep in the shadows high on the ridge. His proud
shoulders had slumped in misery and despair as she called
out to him. The hurt, the physical ache of that one final
moment shot through him like an arrow.

He winced, stared at his hand and involuntarily flexed
his fingers as he remembered holding onto a thick branch
for support as Emily had rocked to and fro in misery. Hot
scalding tears had fallen from his pain-glazed eyes and his
lips had trembled with each of her hysterical sobs echoing
through the forest. But he'd had no choice but to close his

eyes and heart against the anguish he'd unleashed.

He'd begged for strength and ignored her pleas, her heart-wrenching cries. He'd had no choice. Over and over he'd told himself that he had no choice. All he'd had to offer the white girl was freedom. The alternative would have been a betrayal to the love they'd shared, which, in turn, would have bred hate.

High on the ridge, he'd watched until she'd finally quieted, her silence more unnerving than her screams. He'd sunk to the hard ground and shared her pain. That day, that scene, was forever etched in his mind and heart, his own silent pain.

Chapter Thirty-one

Two nights later, a sliver of moon floated high above the darkened world. Glittering stars peppered the blackened sky as beams of glowing light fell to the silent earth below.

Tall trees and thick bushes caught the night rays and held them, spreading shadows across the land. Concealed within one of many deep shadows came a slight movement. Hidden by darkness, the nearly invisible shape crouched low, darting from shadow to shadow.

Peering intently, dark eyes scanned the sleeping village. Seeing no movement, Wild-Flower continued to sneak away from the sleeping village.

Reaching a horse hidden a distance away, she reached out and stroked the quivering flesh, her voice softly reassuring the animal with soothing words. The voice was so soft that anyone about would have taken it for the breeze whispering to the trees.

Wild-Flower knelt, gently picked up each hoof and covered it with squares of rawhide. Standing, she picked up a coiled length of rawhide rope made from cutting the hide of a buffalo in a spiral from outside to center. She formed a lead and led the horse away from the village. As she kept to the shadows, the well-trained horse she'd named Flying Dove quietly followed her beloved mistress.

Stopping only to pick up some supplies hidden deep in a hollowed tree, Wild-Flower mounted. Horse and rider trotted off, slowly at first, increasing their pace as they felt safe to do so.

Breathing a sigh of relief, Wild-Flower refrained from voicing her elation over her success in getting away from her father. Keeping Flying Dove to a slow, controlled pace, she thought over her plan once again. A twig snapped under the hooves, bringing Wild-Flower back to the task at hand.

Giving all her attention to picking her way through trees and bushes, Wild-Flower watched and avoided breaking branches. She did not want to leave an obvious trail.

She guided her horse and watched the trail she'd chosen in front of her. The horse's hooves encased in rawhide helped cover any prints left behind and muffle any noises.

Her father would be furious, but she could not marry Golden Eagle when her heart belonged to another. Since her confrontation with White Cloud, they had not spoken. Even her mother had shown her silent displeasure. She had spent all of yesterday making her preparations. And last night she'd simply announced to her mother that her monthly was upon her and gone off to the women's lodge.

As she'd known from checking earlier, the lodge was empty. Her plan was so simple. Away from her family, it would be easy to sneak out of the village, go to Red Fox and convince him to elope with her. They only had to stay away a few weeks.

And as had happened to her grandfather, when she and Red Fox returned, both tribes would consider them married. It was something that didn't often happen, but Wild-Flower was desperate. Surely, this time there would be no bloodshed. Golden Eagle wouldn't allow it. With her out of the way, Golden Eagle and Sarah would then be free to join.

She and Golden Eagle would then convince her father and Chief Hawk Eyes that marriage between their families was not necessary.

Keeping an eye open for possible dangers, Wild-Flower shoved thoughts of Red Fox aside. She needed to stay alert. It would not do for her to come upon an enemy camp unexpectedly.

When the sun showed its face, Wild-Flower, now tired and exhausted, increased her pace. Already she had many hours' head start, but dared not stop yet. During the long day, she stopped only to feed and water her horse. She ate little herself as she was anxious to get as far as she could before the sun lowered.

When nightfall came, Wild-Flower stopped. Unloading her few possessions, she cared for Flying Dove, then took her mat and threw it to the hard ground. Sitting with some dried meat, Wild-Flower ate hungrily. Tonight she would rest. She should reach Red Fox's tribe by evening tomorrow. She knew from years of visits approximately where they would be at this time. Each year a tribe moved in the same basic pattern unless nature or the white man intervened.

Wild-Flower rolled out her mat and decided to rest for a few hours, her mind dreamily focused on Red Fox. What was he doing? Closing her eyes, she wished he was there beside her. She remembered the few short hours spent in his loving arms. Sighing, she turned on her side, weariness bringing sleep.

It was early evening of her second night when Wild-Flower arrived near Golden Eagle's village. She hid her horse high in the hills, finding a cave with a wide mouth that would accommodate both of them until she was able to let Red Fox know of her presence. Stealthily, she made her way down the canyon, toward the neatly laid-out tipis.

Concealing herself, Wild-Flower sat and watched the activities from a distance, but grew worried as there seemed to be no sign of Red Fox or Golden Eagle. She silently groaned in frustration as she realized that many were missing. Her sharp gaze fell on the results of the buffalo hunt and she had her answer. She buried her head in her hands. "Oh, Red Fox, you can't be on a buffalo hunt," she sighed aloud. She knew too well how long he could be away if that was the case. Lifting her head, she carefully studied the small group of warriors sitting around a large fire. When Chief Hawk Eyes joined them, hope rose in her heart that the others would return soon. It would not take long for her father to reach the village.

Walking to the cave, Wild-Flower prepared to bed down. Tonight, she'd sleep and rise early to watch for her love's return. She would also have to find another secure place in case her father showed up tomorrow.

Lying on their backs, heads pillowed by their hands, Golden Eagle and Red Fox bedded down under the same canopy of stars. The buffalo had fled, but not until the skilled warriors had taken down two huge males. The last of the dried meat had been packed and they had traveled since dawn that day. Tomorrow, they would rejoin their friends and family. Most of the hunting party had returned with the chief several days ago.

Watching the twinkling sky above him, Golden Eagle found himself eager to return to White Wind. He still found it incredible to believe that he would soon become a father. His fingers twitched. He was eager to feel his child grow and kick from within White Wind's womb.

Glancing sideways, he noticed Red Fox was still awake. So far, his friend had not made mention of his feelings toward Wild-Flower. He decided to test the waters. "It was a successful hunt, my friend. You shall have a nice warm robe for the winter months this year," Golden Eagle said in praise.

Red Fox turned his head to Golden Eagle. "The spirits were with me when I shot my arrows," he commented, his voice laced with pride. When the women cut into the fallen buffalo, they first removed the arrow that had killed the beast so all would know who had made the brave kill.

"Red Fox will have many hides to give to his wife when he marries," Golden Eagle stated innocently.

Red Fox grunted. "I have no use for another hide. I shall give it away."

"It would make a fine winter robe for Wild-Flower, would it not?" Golden Eagle asked, peering through the darkness. He watched Red Fox take the bait and bolt upright with indignation, his mouth opening before he closed it and remained silent.

Golden Eagle also sat and spoke quietly, keeping his voice low so as not to disturb others sleeping nearby. His friend's reaction was all he needed to confirm his suspicions. "Wild-Flower and I will not marry, Red Fox. Golden Eagle takes as mate the one meant to be his soul mate. He shall marry White Wind."

Red Fox stared dumbfounded. "What of your father and Chief White Cloud. Have they agreed to this?" His voice quivered with suppressed eagerness.

Golden Eagle noticed the spark of interest creep into Red Fox's voice despite his casual question. Cocking his head, Golden Eagle confided, "Wild-Flower and I talked before she left to return to her village. It seems she has also given her heart to another. We both agreed that it would not be right for us to marry."

Golden Eagle tipped his head to the side. "I think that warrior is you, Red Fox. Is it not?"

Red Fox straightened and met Golden Eagle's knowing gaze. Warrior to warrior, only one secret stood between them. Golden Eagle leaned forward and announced, "White Wind carries my child. Soon I will be a father, Red Fox."

Expecting congratulations, Golden Eagle rose to his knees with concern when he heard choking sounds coming from Red Fox. Leaning closer, Golden Eagle saw sweat beading upon his friend's high forehead. He thumped Red

Fox between his wide bronzed shoulders and stared into stricken depths. Understanding dawned when Red Fox reddened with guilt and shame.

"I was expecting congratulations, my friend. One would think you were the one to discover he had fathered a child," Golden Eagle jeered softly before punching Red Fox in the arm, knocking him to the side.

Recovering from the playful punch and unexpected announcement, Red Fox smacked Golden Eagle in return. The two warriors laughed together and after a few moments of horseplay, much of the tension washed away.

Red Fox was the first to recover "Don't be so smug, my friend. Yes, I am the one Wild-Flower loves, as I love her. But none of us is free to marry who we wish." Tipping his head to the sky, he grinned and gave his friend another playful punch.

Laughing, the two wrestled for a bit as they had when they were just young braves. Tired, they both lay back to gaze at the star studded sky.

"So, the mighty Eagle is going to become a father, eh. Congratulations, friend." Holding out his hand, Red Fox grasped Golden Eagle's in a firm handhold. Serious again, he sighed. "Let us hope all works out for us."

Lying back down, Golden Eagle reassured him. "It will. It has to," he declared. "For both our sakes."

Harry swallowed several colorful curses as he felt the sharp sting of yet another bite. Unable to stand it, he gave in to the irresistible urge and swatted the nasty insect. Thank God it was nearing dawn. Just a bit longer and he would be able to return to his camp.

Harry closed his eyes, wishing he were far away from this hateful place. No amount of money was worth living this close to danger. He'd give this job a few more days, then he was heading out. Old Willy could sit here and do his own dirty work.

Willy and the brothers had arrived two days ago. Willy

had become mean as a she-bear with young when he'd seen for himself that there was no way to get into the closely guarded village during the day.

Hank, Red and even Tom had joined Harry in standing up to Willy. He was crazy, they told him, if he thought they could just enter the village and walk out with the girl, even with many of their warriors gone. Willy's face had turned beet-red with fury when they further explained that if he wanted to go into the village after Sarah, he would have to do it alone. No one was worth dying that kind of death.

Willy had no choice. They would have to wait for Sarah to leave the village before they could attempt to snatch her.

But each time Sarah left the security of the village, she was accompanied by at least two or more armed braves or warriors.

"Sure," Harry had said, "we could kill them Injuns with her." But he knew if they weren't careful, one slip, one scream on her part, and the alarm would be sounded. They wouldn't have a chance in Hell of making it out of these hills alive.

As he rubbed his whisker-stubbed face, disappointment over another wasted night left a bitter taste in Harry's mouth. During the last week, before Willy's arrival, he'd seen the girl rise early to wander the village.

Swatting at another buzzing insect, Harry decided to head for camp. He was hungry and dead tired. Daylight would soon break. "Damn," he fumed, "I ain't gonna sit here this close to them Injuns. It's time to get outta here." He'd rather face Willy's wrath than a mob of savages. As he turned to crawl away, a slight movement in the village caught his eyes.

Dawn was still a few hours away, but for Sarah, getting any more sleep would prove fruitless and a waste of time. Each morning she woke long before the others with her stomach churning. Walking in the cool early morning seemed to help a bit.

Absently, she fingered the necklace with her treasured eagle and locket. She'd combined both the finger-smoothed eagle and her locket onto the leather thong with Golden Eagle's blue beads. She knew part of her sleeplessness arose from her anticipation of Golden Eagle's return. The rest of the hunting party should return sometime today. Already the preparations for the feasting had begun.

Deep in thought, Sarah wandered close to the thick grove of trees that blocked the entrance to their village. Eagerly anticipating Golden Eagle's arrival later that day, she never realized that she'd left the safety of the inner village and had gotten too close to the one unprotected side.

When a slight noise from behind penetrated her daydreaming mind, alerting her to possible danger, it was too late. From behind, a large dirty hand closed around her mouth, silencing her cry of fear. Held firmly against her unknown attacker and dragged a short distance up the canyon, Sarah fought, not knowing that the warrior who had been guarding the narrow entrance to the village lay unconscious beneath the bushes.

Sarah struggled and kicked, managing to trip her captor, sending them both down into the dirt. His grunt of pain filled her ears, but still Sarah could not free her mouth to scream for help. Arms banded around her chest and lifted her once more. She tried to resist being dragged further away from the people she now regarded as "her people."

Harry struggled to keep his hold on the wildly kicking and struggling girl in his arms. He grunted, and nearly dropped her a second time when a vicious fingernail made contact with his face, just barely missing his eye.

Harry kept his hand firmly over sharp teeth that were trying to take a hunk out of his hand. Swearing aloud as teeth made contact with flesh, he shoved her roughly to the rocky and twig-laden ground, following to land on top of her twisting body.

Her attacker raised his hand and struck Sarah with his huge meaty fist. Reeling from the blow while struggling to retain consciousness and fight the nausea, Sarah ran out of strength to fight or scream. Her attacker bound and gagged her. She felt herself flung over bulky shoulders before darkness overcame her.

Chapter Thirty-two

Wild-Flower faced East in the early morn, ready to greet *Wiyohiyanpa*, the Spirit of the East which presided over the new day. She hugged her knees close, waiting for the warmth of the new sun to warm her, as she balanced on a large boulder jutting out from the rocky hillside.

Rising before the light of day after a restless night of tossing and turning on the hard rocky floor of the small cave, Wild-Flower had already packed her belongings and lashed them to her horse.

Eating her morning meal of wild plums and fresh berries, she relaxed as she enjoyed the quietness surrounding her. Her horse, hobbled nearby and shielded by a small stand of pine trees and brush, munched the tall grass, its green now turning to brown. Letting her eyes wander, gazing upon the beauty of the hillside, Wild-Flower knew there was no point in going to the village until evening to see if Red Fox had returned.

So lost in thought and daydreams of her love was she that it took a long moment to realize that the ground beneath her was actually vibrating. Wild-Flower quickly leapt from her high perch to flatten and conceal herself on the ground just as the sound of thundering hooves grew near.

With bated breath, she heard Flying Dove, hobbled out of sight, snorting nervously. Wild-Flower risked a peek through the thin barrier of tall brittle grass that grew among the various-sized boulders dotting the hillside. She bit her lower lip as there was no time for her to reach Flying Dove's side to calm the restless mare. Wild-Flower could only hope the approaching rider would not hear her horse and come to investigate.

Staying as low as possible, she watched horse and rider burst through the trees on her right and continue past her hiding place without breaking stride. Wild-Flower sighed with relief. Flying Dove had not given their presence away.

Her relief was short-lived, however, as she stared after the retreating horse carrying two riders. One was an odd-looking trapper, the other a woman slung across the lap of the white man, her long braids dangling, whipping against the horse.

Wild-Flower's mouth flew open, and she resisted the urge to jump to her feet. Her hands smothered her cry of horror. "Sarah?" she whispered softly, shaking her head in denial. But she knew that yellow hair could only belong to Golden Eagle's captive. "I have to do something," Wild-Flower told herself. "But what?"

She rose from her hiding place and paced, stopping to stare at the point where Sarah's captor had rounded a bend. She had deliberately stayed far enough from Golden Eagle's village to avoid possible discovery, and now found she was too far from them to fetch help. She quickly calculated she'd lose precious time trying to alert Golden Eagle's people. If they were delayed, there was the chance the white man would elude them if he knew these hills, or worse, harm Sarah before help could catch up.

In the space of seconds, Wild-Flower had made her decision. She ran to her horse, put her food and water in her pouch and removed the rawhide hobbles. With a flying leap, she sat astride her wide back. Ears perked, the horse flew onward, needing little direction from her young mistress. Trained well, she knew what was expected of her.

Wild-Flower's mind raced as well. She knew what she had to do. Tearing the rawhide thong from around her neck, she tossed it over her shoulder to land in the swirling dust kicked up by her mount's flying hooves as she raced after her friend in need, careful to keep her distance.

Wild-Flower sent a prayer of thanks for the unorthodox training her father and brother had bestowed upon her. She prayed she would remember all she'd been taught and that someone would miss Sarah soon and come after her. She wished she'd been able to smuggle out her bow and quiver of arrows. But her family would have noticed those missing immediately.

Making sure she left an obvious trail so Golden Eagle and his people would not have to spend precious time searching, she pulled bright colorful pony beads from her dress front and let them fall.

Chief Hawk Eyes reclined against his willow backrest, leisurely consuming his morning meal. The daily chores would not be done today. Instead the day would be given over to preparing for a feast and night of celebration. He looked to his right. Upon arising, he'd unrolled his feather bonnets and hung them from a pole to fluff. The feathers fluttered and lifted as the breeze touched them. He studied them. Both were made with the feathers from the golden eagle.

One was a short and simple headdress made with 32 feathers from the eagle's tail placed in a circle around a hide skullcap base. The other was a more elaborate bonnet with two long tails of eagle feathers that stopped short of the ground. Tonight he would wear the one with two tails.

Finishing the last of his meal, he rose and from another pole at the back of the tipi removed his shield and coup stick, a long willow stick with several eagle feathers attached that he used in raids to touch the enemy and count coup. Hawk Eyes closed his eyes, his heart pulsing to the beat of the drums that would soon fill the air. His body quivered in anticipation of the feasting and dancing that would go on all night.

He also anticipated listening to his warriors count coup. The two warriors who had killed the buffalo with such accuracy would regale all with their brave deeds over the roaring fire. Their arrows, dug from the bodies by the women, would be presented for all to see. It was all part of sending thanks to *Wakan Tanka* and *Tatanka,* the Spirit of the Buffalo, for guiding their hunters and allowing them to take the beasts necessary to their survival.

A soft voice intruded on his musing. Calling out his permission to enter, Hawk Eyes returned to his seat as Bright Blossom stepped hesitantly inside the Chief's tipi.

Bowing her head in respect, Bright Blossom turned and addressed Seeing Eyes. "Is Sarah not feeling well today? She was to come to my tipi early to help with the preparations for our feast tonight."

Seeing Eyes raised her brow and looked over at her husband. "We have not seen Sarah this day, Bright Blossom. Perhaps she is still sleeping."

Bright Blossom shook her head in confusion. "I went to her tipi, but there is no answer to my call. I had thought perhaps she was here."

Hawk Eyes rose, his gut tightening, instinctively sensing something was wrong. He knew from experience that if Sarah had promised her help, she would have been there.

Nodding for his wife and Bright Blossom to follow, Hawk Eyes strode the short distance to his son's tipi. He didn't bother waiting for the women as he entered without calling out.

Seeing Eyes entered behind him and slowly looked around. Suddenly, her eyes grew round. Putting a hand to her head, Seeing Eyes fell to the ground, hands covering her eyes, as if to block out a fearful image.

Hawk Eyes stepped out of the tipi and barked orders for the village and surrounding areas to be searched. He turned, realizing Seeing Eyes must still be inside. Swiftly, he reentered and knelt beside his distraught wife. "Come, love, you must help us search." He took hold of her hands, which had turned icy, and pulled them from her face. He sucked in his breath at the stark fear that stared back at him.

Clutching his strong brawny arm in a panicked grip, the older woman shook her head, her voice hoarse with fear. Tears streamed down her wrinkled cheeks. "She is gone. Evil has come for her." Her head slumped forward as she moaned and started wailing. Hawk Eyes lifted his wife, cradled her close and carried her back to his tipi.

Riding into his village just minutes later, Golden Eagle was so eager to seek out Sarah that the unusual behavior of his people did not make any impression. It seemed forever since he had held her, made love to her. As neither he nor Red Fox had slept much last night, they'd woken the others long before daybreak, eager to return. Riding hard when the sun showed her face, they'd made excellent time.

Golden Eagle and Red Fox pulled up short, finally noting the unnatural hustle in the village. Sliding down, Golden Eagle ran to meet his father. The chief's grave expression sent shivers of fear down his spine.

Motioning his son and Red Fox to enter the tipi, Hawk Eyes followed and wasted no time. Walking toward Golden Eagle, he laid shaking hands upon his sun-warmed shoulders and broke the terrible news.

"Sarah is gone, my son. She has not been seen since last night."

A loud buzzing filled Golden Eagle's ears, drowning out all sound. He shook his head, positive he'd not heard right. But one glance at this father's drawn features left him reeling with shock at the news. He fell to his knees, shaking his head in disbelief. To his right, he saw his mother's pale, tear-streaked face. "No! That can't be!" he cried out.

Swallowing hard, he looked at his father. "Are you sure she hasn't gone to the stream? What about Bright Blossom's tipi? She must be here somewhere." Golden Eagle's stomach lurched at the negative shake of his father's head to each desperately asked question.

Quickly, Hawk Eyes told his son of his mother's haunting vision of an evil source that would surround and try to choke out the goodness that was Sarah.

"Her guardian," Golden Eagle shouted. "He's the one responsible for this. I must find her. I leave immediately."

"No, my son. You will not go alone. But first, we must find signs of her and who took her."

Fanning out from the entrance to the village, silent and grim-faced warriors searched the area for signs of a member of their tribe all had come to like and respect. They found the warrior who had been knocked unconscious, but he could not tell them anything.

So intent was their search, the warriors did not notice the approach of a large group of riders until they were nearly upon the village.

Hawk Eyes and Golden Eagle looked to each other in confusion as they stared at the approaching group of grim-faced warriors. Silently they went to meet their unexpected visitors. The search for Sarah came to a temporary halt.

Holding his hand in greeting, Chief Hawk Eyes greeted the stern-faced Chief. "White Cloud, what brings you to the village of Hawk Eyes?"

Running Wolf edged his mount forward and replied for his father. "We come for Wild-Flower."

Startled gasps were heard from curious onlookers. Stepping forward, Golden Eagle asked, "Why would Wild-Flower be here, Running Wolf? She has not been here since the last time Running Wolf and his warriors came to visit."

"Not true, Golden Eagle. She hides here. We followed her trail to your village. She is here." Running Wolf's black eyes flashed.

Ignoring the angry young warrior in front of him, Golden Eagle addressed Running Wolf's father. "Chief White Cloud. I have only returned a short while ago from a hunt. I have not seen nor heard from Wild-Flower."

Unable to remain silent any longer, Red Fox stepped forward. "Why would Wild-Flower be here?"

White Cloud held a hand high to still the questions being thrown at him. "My daughter and I had an argument. Her trail leads to this area. I can only hope that Wild-Flower has come to the village of Golden Eagle. I ask you to tell me if she is here. I ask you to keep this father from further worry over his daughter." Stepping from his mount and stretching wearily, White Cloud strode to his friend, worry lines etched across his weathered old face. "I bid you, Hawk Eyes, friend to this old chief, have you news of my daughter?"

Reaching out to grasp the upper arms of his one-time adversary, Hawk Eyes truthfully replied, "No, my friend. My son speaks the truth. None here has seen Wild-Flower." He led White Cloud to his tipi. "This is a sad day, my friend. We also search for one missing from our village. The white girl has just been discovered missing."

Golden Eagle, entering behind the two chiefs, expressed a thought. "Perhaps Sarah and Wild-Flower are together." He turned to Chief White Cloud. "The two formed a friendship on your daughter's last visit to us."

"Ah, the white captive. I have heard you have one living in your tipi. Perhaps that is the reason for my daughter's unhappiness. Perhaps your white captive is why Wild-Flower felt she had to run away?" White Cloud directed a hard angry glare at Golden Eagle. "Tell me about this white girl and her place in your tipi. My son tells me she is very beautiful."

Unable to meet Chief White Cloud's penetrating and accusing gaze, Golden Eagle stuck his head out of the tipi and motioned for the other warriors to keep searching.

Hawk Eyes took over. "Sit, Chief White Cloud." He indicated the seat of honor. "We have important matters to discuss."

Sitting as well, Golden Eagle received his father's nod and gave a brief summary of the events that led to finding Sarah and his reasons for bring her to his home. Golden Eagle touched lightly upon how they met earlier, and how he had felt responsible for the safety and well-being of the girl. He finished with praise about how well Sarah had adapted to their way of life and his wish to make Sarah his wife.

"So. The stories I have heard are true. And what of my daughter? She is to be put aside in favor of a white woman? What of our need to join the two tribes by marriage?" White Cloud's nostrils flared angrily.

Meeting the angry chief's proud gaze, Golden Eagle tried to explain. "Chief White Cloud, Wild-Flower and I have talked. It is her wish also to marry another. The one she has given her heart to comes from this village. He is brave and worthy of your daughter. Could the two tribes not be joined in this manner?"

Looking down his arrogant nose, White Cloud directed his displeasure at Hawk Eyes. "It was agreed upon that the eldest son of Chief Hawk Eyes would join with the eldest daughter of Chief White Cloud to right the wrongs of my father. If your son chooses a white woman over Wild-Flower, he will have made the same choice as my father when he chose a French captive over your mother," White Cloud reminded the other chief. "Your people killed my father and mother for making such a choice. Wild-Flower's honor would be destroyed. She would be shamed before all."

Golden Eagle's hopes sank. He tried to concentrate on his father's reply, but noise from outside the tipi grew louder, causing those inside the tipi to raise their voices to be heard. The men in the tipi fell into an uneasy silence as each thought of his words before speaking them. The childish voices arguing outside grew loud enough to divert the men from their thoughts as they all looked toward the entrance.

"It's mine!"

"No it's not!"

"I found it, it's mine."

"It was lost, so it doesn't belong to you. I can prove it."

"No, you can't."

"Yes, I . . ."

Jumping to his feet, Chief Hawk Eyes strode angrily to the flap and bellowed. "Enough!" All inside saw two youngsters spring apart as they stared into the angry face of their Chief.

Making no effort to hide his displeasure, Hawk Eyes ordered the two quibbling girls into the tipi with only the flick of one finger. Together, heads hung with shame upon noticing the important visitors, the girls entered. Their feet dragged as if walking toward their mortal demise.

Golden Eagle watched one of the girls sneak a peek at Hawk Eyes and sigh. Hawk Eyes was very, very angry and Winona knew she was in trouble.

"I will know the cause of your shameful behavior and then you will apologize to our guests," Hawk Eyes demanded. He held one palm high. When two voices started speaking loudly at once, he silenced them. "Now, daughter of Weeko, you will tell me what this is about."

Staring at her toes, Spotted Deer asked, "If I find something, it belongs to me, does it not?"

Winona open her mouth to protest, but Hawk Eyes sent her a warning glance. "That depends on what you find, my child. Does it belong to another?" All watched the child's face redden with guilt. "If it belongs to another, it must be returned," Hawk Eyes gently commanded. "Now."

Golden Eagle stifled the urge to pace. He had no time to sit here and watch his father solve his sister's problems. He was sure, with all the fuss, that Spotted Deer had something that belonged to Winona.

Winona's triumphant "I told you so" look did not escape him, and he hid his frustration as his father glared at Winona long and hard. "Remember, daughter, greed is unworthy of the daughter of Hawk Eyes." As with most parents, formal reprimands were rare. But there were times when his young sister pushed the limits.

"But Father," Winona interrupted bravely, "Spotted Deer found Sarah's necklace. As Sarah is gone, I wanted Spotted Deer to give the necklace to me so I could return it when you find Sarah. After all, she is almost my sister," Winona threw out for Spotted Deer's benefit.

Springing to his feet, Golden Eagle approached the girls and hunkered down to their level, his heart racing as hope stirred within him. "This necklace you found, Spotted Deer, give it to me." He held out a trembling hand, and the smooth coolness of the heart-shaped locket and the warmth of the carved eagle was placed on his open palm.

Holding it high for all to see, Golden Eagle closed his eyes in pain. Turning back to the girls, he laid a gentle hand on each shoulder. "It's all right. No one is angry. I will return this to White Wind. She will be pleased with both of you for finding this for her. Now we must have your help. Where did you find this? Take me there."

Winona grabbed Spotted Deer's arm and ran out of the tipi, toward the area where they'd found Sarah's necklace.

Golden Eagle clutched the leather thong to his heart and ran out after them. The others followed close on his heels, all but one.

Chapter Thirty-three

White Cloud remained frozen, eyes glazed, unable to move. He sat, unaware of the departure of the others, unaware of the watchful concerned gaze of Seeing Eyes, who sat staring at his shield as if in a trance.

White Cloud's mind had gone numb with shock. For the second time in less then a week, his past had risen to haunt him. He sat and stared as the glitter of yellow-gold danced in front of his glazed eyes, lurching his mind backward to that other time, that other place, and to the one who had worn that same adornment around her neck.

His pulse quickened, his heart hammered against his rib cage and sweat beaded his head. White Cloud shut his eyes against painful remembrances that flooded his mind and squeezed his heart painfully.

Suddenly, he jumped to his feet and whirled around the tipi. Golden Eagle. Where did he go? He had to find him. He needed to see that golden object up close. Surely, his mind had been playing tricks on him. This was all his daughter's fault, for she'd been responsible for awakening the demons of his past. His shield fell unheeded to the ground as he stumbled into the bright glare of the sunlight.

Rushing through the deserted village, White Cloud followed the sounds of raised voices. He pushed his way through the crowd watching several warriors who crouched and exclaimed over the discovered white man's tracks, near the side of the canyon. There, Golden Eagle studied the signs of struggle on the carpet of leaves, rocks and loose dirt.

Pushing through the gathering, White Cloud pulled Golden Eagle to him. "Must see necklace," White Cloud rasped, his voice hoarse with suppressed emotion and barely audible. "The white girl's necklace. Give it to me."

"Chief White Cloud . . ." Golden Eagle turned as one of the warriors called to him, pointing something out to him.

"Please, son. It's important."

With a puzzled look and impatient sigh, Golden Eagle handed over the locket that had been clenched tightly in his fist.

Taking it from the young warrior, White Cloud held the piece of jewelry tenderly, head bent as he intently examined and fingered the time-worn smooth surface. With hands that shook, he fumbled with the catch that would release to reveal two time-faded miniatures he knew he would find hidden within.

Gasping for breath, White Cloud stumbled to the nearest fallen log and lowered himself, the locket clutched tightly in his fist. Ignoring the concerned stares of those gathered round, White Cloud had eyes only for Golden Eagle.

"This white captive of yours. My son says she has hair the color of the sun and eyes of the sky. Is this so? Is she old or young? Describe her to me."

Golden Eagle gestured impatiently. "Chief White Cloud, the one you ask about has been taken by an evil white man. There is no time for talk. Already we have wasted much time. We must go after her before she is harmed. Already the white man has a good lead on us,'' Golden Eagle stated unnecessarily, turning away.

White Cloud called out and begged indulgence and understanding. "Please, my son, I must know the answer to these questions. They are very important. Her looks . . .''

Turning toward Hawk Eyes, Golden Eagle received his father's silent command to do as told. With suppressed frustration he gave a brief description of Sarah.

At Chief White Cloud's insistence, desiring to be done with the matter in the quickest way possible, Golden Eagle told all he knew of Sarah, including her parentage and where she lived.

"The name of her Indian father, my son. What is the name of her Indian father? Do you know?''

All stared in surprise at the abrupt change that overcame Chief White Cloud. His voice rang out firm and strong, black eyes shone bright beneath shaggy brows, and he stood proud, hand resting on the hilt of his knife, ready to do battle.

Hawk Eyes frowned and stepped forward to intervene. "We do not know the name of her father, my friend. All we have are a few items made by him and given to her mother,'' Hawk Eyes announced, turning as his wife came up behind him.

"Before I left my tribe to join with Hawk Eyes, all young maidens knew of your great skills,'' Seeing Eyes said to White Cloud. "You were called Swift-Foot then.'' Stepping into the circle of confused men, she smiled at an astonished Chief White Cloud.

"I never knew what became of this mighty warrior. It was said his name changed after he'd risked his life to save a small child.'' Seeing Eyes gave him a questioning glance.

White Cloud nodded and stared at the items he'd made so long ago, now clutched in her fingers, and painfully related how he'd rescued his firstborn son, Running Wolf, from a rain-swollen river by lashing himself and the child to the limb of a grandfather tree. There they'd hung under clouds so low they'd hidden the branches. Later, when they both were found, his name had become White Cloud.

Seeing confusion on the faces before him, White Cloud told the assembled group how, before he'd joined with Small Bird, the young warrior Swift-Foot had sought many vision quests to help guide him in his future responsibilities as chief. In each vision he'd heard a cry, but never knew what or who made the cry. Sharing his concerns with the Shaman, he'd been advised to leave his tribe to search for the meaning of these cries. He would marry upon his return.

He recounted how he'd left during the spring to become one with his surroundings, learning and listening to the spirits as they led him where they pleased, waiting for them to reveal the significance of the cry.

One day, while resting on a high ridge, he'd spotted rising smoke from far below. Deciding to investigate the next day, he'd come across a burned wagon. There had been no sign of survivors of the bloody massacre, so he'd left the area.

But late that night, he'd been awakened by the same cry that came to him in his visions. It was a cry of grief and despair. He'd followed the heart-wrenching sobs, and come upon a young white girl who'd managed to hide and survive the fate of her family.

White Cloud's words were for his son. "Though I had the answer to the cries in my vision, I could not return immediately to my village. I traveled across the land, the white woman at my side. By the end of the summer months I had fallen in love with her, but knew I had no choice but to return to my people and fulfill my duties. I left her where she would be found and taken to safety. Before I left, I gave her this box of wood and necklace."

"Father, what does all this mean?" Running Wolf asked. "I saw the white captive. She is young, my age, and cannot be the woman you once knew."

White Cloud looked up from the box and stared into his son's bewildered expression. His own grew grim as he glanced around him. "It would seem, my son, that you have an older sister and I have two daughters to search for. Come, we ride. Fetch our mounts, Running Wolf. Gather the warriors, Golden Eagle. Much time has been wasted!"

Warriors from both tribes ran to their horses at the chief's command. No one dared point out it was his fault that they'd been delayed in the first place.

Relentlessly, Willy drove his gang onward without rest. Staying close to streams, away from deep ravines where they could become trapped, they rode as if the devil himself were on their tail. For they knew if caught, they would fare much better with the devil than the angry warriors.

During a brief water stop, Sarah lay on the hard ground, hands bound, a ragged cloth tied tightly across her mouth. She lay on her side, curled into a tight ball of pain and misery. Her backside hurt where the old trapper had thrown her to the rocky ground, and her face was swollen and hot where she'd been struck.

Thirsty. She was so thirsty, her lips puffed out, her tongue dry and thick. No one offered her a drink. Sarah listened to her captors as they hurriedly gulped water from the stream and cooled the horses.

Footsteps sounded. Nearer. Unable to move, Sarah waited, knowing from the shuffling Willy was coming. A booted foot caught her rib and shoved her onto her back to rest on numb hands, pulling her shoulders from her sockets. Blinking against the glare of the sun and the shooting pain, Sarah glared at Willy as he towered over her.

"Betcha you'd like some water, huh, missy?" Sarah's eyes went to the bent and beat-up tin cup in his hands. Willy lowered his bulk and held the cup inches from her bound mouth. "Say please, bitch. Ask real nice and I might give ya some." Willy's harsh laughter rang out as Sarah turned her head. Rough hands yanked her head around to face him.

"No, huh. Ah, well. Guess I'll just have ta drink it."

Willy gulped the liquid, half of it running down his chin to drip onto his shirtfront. Sarah groaned uncontrollably as Willy yanked her to her feet and shoved her toward his horse. Tossing her on top, uncaring that her fringed skirt had ridden high to expose her thighs, Willy jumped into the saddle. His arms became tight shackles as he held her against his chest. The horse surged forward in answer to the sharp kick in its side.

Many long hours later, Sarah leaned her head against the rough bark of the tree she was tied to. All day and far into the night, she'd been force to ride. She was exhausted, hungry and consumed with thirst.

She swallowed a moan, not wanting to draw attention to how much she hurt. Each time Willy called for a halt, he'd dumped her onto the hard ground, laughing and tormenting her until he was ready to go on.

This was the longest stop Willy had allowed. He and the others huddled off by themselves, arguing angrily. Her head spun, her stomach lurched queasily. She was faint from lack of food and water. Closing her eyes in misery, Sarah forced her thoughts elsewhere and allowed images of Golden Eagle to soothe her fears. He would come for her. She had to believe that help was on its way.

She was so lost in thought she nearly screamed when a faint voice whispered in her ear.

"Not worry, Sarah. Wild-Flower follow. Soon others follow my trail. Cannot free you now, but will try to keep you from harm till warriors arrive. Do not speak. Must go."

All too soon, the voice faded away. Sarah wasn't even sure that it had been real, that it hadn't been her imagination. But then she heard the shuffling and opened her eyes. Willy approached, canteen in hand.

Bending down, he let his hate-filled gaze roam over her. He held the canteen in front of her face and taunted her. "Water, dear girl?" Yanking off her gag, he warned her. "Don't you talk, or scream if you knows what's good fer you." Unscrewing the cap, he held it out to her.

Unable to reach out and take it, Sarah just sat there, daggers shooting from her eyes. Her mouth was so dry, she couldn't have spoken if her life depended on it.

"Oh, don't want any, huh?" Taking the canteen back, Willy said scornfully, "You've been a bad girl anyway. You don't d'serve none. You caused me no end of trouble. Maybe I'll make you wait till mornin'," Willy slurred as he recapped the canteen and staggered back to his buddies, laughing the whole way.

Wild-Flower observed the exchange, and her eyes narrowed and blackened with anger as she made her way back to her horse. Taking her water pouch and keeping to the shadows, she silently made her way back to the tree where Sarah was tied and eased behind the girl, the low-growing shrubbery hiding her.

Sarah jumped when Wild-Flower spoke once again. "Turn head slowly." Doing as instructed, Sarah turned her head, keeping an eye on the drinking men, who were no longer paying attention to her as they passed Willy's flask around.

Carefully, Wild-Flower dribbled small droplets of water onto a large green leaf and tipped the liquid into Sarah's parched mouth without spilling. "I go now." Slinking away, Wild-Flower flattened herself into the shadows and melted away.

Sarah closed her eyes, thankful for the soothing coolness of the water. She refrained from wetting her dry and cracked lips. Any moisture on her lips would alert Willy that she had help nearby. She prayed for Willy to forget to gag her for the cloth dried her mouth out fast. Later, as Willy unbound her from the tree, Sarah also prayed for her friend's safety.

She winced against the bite of hard fingers digging into the tender flesh of her upper arm. Once again, they were on the move.

Chapter Thirty-four

Golden Eagle stood apart from the others, staring out into the inky blackness, fighting the demons of despair. His hands rested on his hips as he tipped his head back, flexing his shoulders in a circular motion, working the tension from the taut muscles of his neck and shoulders.

He eyed the gray blanket above that blocked the light of *Hunwi*. They needed the light from the sky this night. Silently, he sent a prayer to *Wakan Tanka*, the Great Spirit, to watch over his love and keep her safe until he caught up with the evil one that had taken her. Anger filled him, and immediately he concentrated on stifling that emotion. The time would come to give his anger free reign. But right now, he needed to keep a clear head. His mind had to be free to think and plan.

He slumped slightly, leaning against his horse for support. A hand rested upon his shoulder and tore him from his dark thoughts. He turned slowly, and his troubled glance met the equally worried glance of Chief White Cloud.

"Come eat, my son. We will catch them. We ride much

faster then they do. Already we have gained on them. *Wakan Tanka* will watch over my daughters. He would not lead me to the daughter that I gave life to so long ago just to take her from me before allowing me to claim her as my blood and flesh.''

Golden Eagle watched as White Cloud absently fingered the carving of a tiny windflower he said he'd given to Wild-Flower when she'd turned 13 winters.

Soon after leaving the village the band of warriors had come to a complete stop when they'd spotted the necklace in the middle of the trail. White Cloud and Running Wolf knew it was Wild-Flower's way of letting them know she was following White Wind's captors. Soon after, they'd begun to spot the beads she'd been dropping regularly.

''Your daughter is very brave to follow,'' Golden Eagle now said in praise, unable to believe that this was Sarah's, no, White Wind's father.

''Yes. I will praise her for her quick thinking and cunning. Her bravery has saved much precious time. However, my daughter still has some explaining to do as to why she left our home in the night. Although I can guess it might have something to do with a warrior named Red Fox. Is this not so? This warrior seems very concerned about Wild-Flower.''

Golden Eagle started. ''You are very wise, Chief. Red Fox is the one Wild-Flower wishes to marry.'' He looked over at Red Fox, who, like he, was dealing with concern for a loved one.

Nodding his head toward the others, White Cloud took Golden Eagle by the arm, forcing him to return with him. ''You wish to take as wife my daughter known as Sarah?'' he quietly probed.

''Yes, Chief White Cloud. I love Sarah and she returns my feelings. But from now on, you must call her White Wind, the name given to her by my mother. Her vision said this woman would become my helpmate for this walk on Mother Earth. The Great Spirit has crossed our paths not once, but twice. I believe it is for this purpose. I ask that you allow me to take White Wind as my wife,'' Golden Eagle respectfully said.

Stopping suddenly, White Cloud eyed Golden Eagle in his most forbidding manner. Drawing himself to his most imposing height, he replied, ''White Wind is a most fitting name for the daughter of White Cloud. There is no question or doubt that you shall be joined. White Wind is the eldest daughter of this chief. The agreement between our tribes is for the eldest son of Hawk Eyes and the eldest daughter of White Cloud to marry and join the tribes and wipe out the shame of the past. This agreement will be carried out.''

A sparkle deep within his dark eyes took any sting from his words. ''Now, none lose honor. The agreement will be carried out as it was meant to be.''

Chuckling despite the grave circumstances, Golden Eagle followed in the wake of the wise chief and forced food and water past his lips. He would need his strength when they caught up to the white men. Tracks now suggested there were five horses plus Wild-Flower's. All too soon, they were back on the trail, clouds of billowing dust swirled beneath pounding hooves, kicking dirt and small rocks behind them. The dried earth blurred under scorching rays from above. The prairie floor sped by as they thundered onward. Miles were covered quickly, and soon the flatness gave way to denser growth, sloping upward, forcing the horses to slow.

Slowing his spirited stallion, Golden Eagle nudged his horse toward the sound of rushing water as he signaled for another rest. Two warriors dismounted and on foot disappeared beneath the thick low-hanging branches.

They returned a few minutes later with the given signal that all was safe, and the rest of the large group dismounted and led their sturdy mounts to the river.

Refreshing himself after seeing to his horse, Golden Eagle stared as gurgling water rushed past him. They had passed the forked river, and soon this water would join the large river, the one the white man called the Missouri.

He was thankful the trail followed water. As hard as they were pushing their horses, the unlimited water supply was a blessing.

Rising, he surveyed the others as they sat in small circles and chewed pemmican or jerked meat. Silence prevailed as each took advantage of the brief respite from the hard traveling that had started the day before. No one had slept, but a strong healthy warrior could go days without sleep when the need arose.

His eyes fell to his father. He shook his head as he knew his father would not admit to the tiredness he felt. Golden Eagle knew his father would soon step down as chief. Many times had he brought up the fact that the tribe needed fresh young blood to lead them against the rising numbers of whites that were settling along the many rivers leading to their sacred hills.

Pulling out his pouch of refreshment, Golden Eagle too ate in silence. Popping the last bite of dried buffalo meat into his mouth, he rose. Squaring his shoulders, head held high, he called for all to gather round.

Commanding full attention from the others, Golden Eagle drew in the loose dirt with a sharp stick.

Pointing with one finger, Golden Eagle followed the line that was the stream they now followed, showing where it would join the larger body of water. He placed a rock to show where they were. Adding another rock to a small mound of dirt, above the large river, he explained.

"This is where White Wind lived in her white man's wood home. This is where the white captors now head." Golden Eagle marked a path in the dirt connecting the two marks.

"We must separate. There is a shortcut I will take to the white man's home." He grew silent as he marked the way over the ridge in the near distance. "I will be there waiting." He tapped the shortcut he proposed. It would not be an easy trip, but it would be faster. "The rest can follow Wild-Flower's trail along the rivers."

He and all the other warriors had been very impressed with the girl's courage and cunning. Looking at Red Fox as he squatted down to join them, Golden Eagle saw the pride shining in his friend's eyes.

"I have been to this place two times," he continued. "I will lead my warriors there. Chief White Cloud, you and your warriors follow the white men and your daughters."

Chief White Cloud nodded. "It is a good plan. You are as smart and cunning as your father, Golden Eagle. However, I will ride with you. I wish to be there when the white trapper and his band arrive with my daughter."

Speaking up, Chief Hawk Eyes voiced his agreement to the plan. "I will lead the rest of the warriors with your son at my side, Chief White Cloud. We will trap the whites between us. They will not be able to escape us."

Gathering their horses, White Cloud took his spot next to Golden Eagle with fierce-looking warriors flanking them as they raced to reach the ranch before Sarah's kidnappers.

It was well past noon before Willy called another halt. The five men and four horses halted beneath the shade of a few trees.

Tom's horse had gone lame just after the last rest, nearly injuring its rider as it stumbled. Turning the horse free, Hank and Tom had doubled up. They didn't dare shoot the lame beast for fear the gunshot would be heard miles away. Luckily, none had seen the rock that had been fired from a crude sling and had struck the beast in the leg.

"Hey, Willy, do ya think we lost em?" Tom asked the question they all were thinking.

Willy frowned as he looked around. "Don't know. Too early to tell. We rest for only a few minutes." Willy ignored the groans from the others as he refilled his canteen.

His lips curled in anger as he glanced over at Sarah, who sat tall and proud as she fearlessly met his narrowed eyes.

Willy closed the distance between them and stood staring down at her. His eyes traveled over her filthy and torn Indian garb. His fingers reached out and pulled at her snarled and matted hair. "Not so beautiful anymore, are ya, bitch. Ya looks like your mother did the day John brought her home. All filthy and smelly."

Snarling, Willy threw the canteen at her feet. His eyes narrowed as Sarah defiantly kicked the proffered water away.

Picking up the dirt-covered canteen, Willy growled, "I won't have you dyin' or turnin' weak yet, girl. Drink or I'll pour it down your throat. What I have in mind for you ain't an easy death. Dyin' from lack of water is too good for you. By the time me an' the boys are done, you will have wished you'd never gone against me."

Her hands untied, but bound at the waist to the tree, Sarah picked up the canteen and drank. She knew better than to push Willy too far. She had to stay alive for Golden Eagle and their baby.

"You won't get away with this, Willy. Golden Eagle will kill you and anyone else who touches me," she warned him, loud enough for all to hear.

Sarah refused to show it, but she was scared. Willy was insane and therefore unpredictable. In his present state, he was dangerous. But Sarah knew if she cowered before him, it would feed his wrath and hatred, spiraling it out of control. No, she had to stay calm. She was slightly reassured knowing Wild-Flower was following, leaving an easy trail for others to follow.

Sarah refused to meet the calculating glances thrown at her from the others. Her warning brought laughter. The looks she'd been receiving caused shivers of fear to tear at her insides. They wanted her in the most primitive way a male wanted a woman. There would be no mercy from this group. They were like wild animals hunting and feeding on the helpless.

They had the look of hungry wolves stalking a prey that

was trapped against a wall with no place to run or hide.

She knew she was to be their next victim. Willy had been hinting at it all day. He knew that her fear would grow with each hint and barb he tossed her way.

Grabbing Sarah, Willy threw her back onto his horse and swung up behind her. Sarah sat stiffly in front of him. She would not voluntarily lean against him. Willy's temper snapped. His eyes gleamed with evil as he roughly yanked her against his chest. His arm circled tightly around her waist. "It's no good fighting me, dear Sarah. I'll break you, have ya begging for mercy. Soon, you'll see."

Jerking his head to indicate the others behind them, Willy taunted her. "And when I'm done, maybe I'll allow them boys to sample what's left." Willy laughed when he felt Sarah's involuntary shudder.

Placing a hand boldly over her breast, he applied enough pressure to cause pain. Untying the dress at the neckline, he pulled the dress away so he could have an unobstructed view, his hold on her warning her not to fight him.

Slipping his roughened hand inside to maul her tender flesh, Willy laughed when Sarah stiffened.

Sarah swallowed her fear and revulsion. Willy wanted her to fight, to show her fear of him. She needed to keep her mind centered on Golden Eagle. He would save her. Surely he was following and would catch up soon.

She breathed a sigh of relief as Willy's hand left her body, giving up his torment for now as he urged the horse into a full gallop. He'd had his fun for now. Discreetly, she managed to pull the front of her dress closed.

Harry watched the others gallop away, and stared behind them. His instincts told him something was wrong. He'd caught several of Sarah's glances behind them whenever she'd thought no one was watching.

He rode deep into the trees and dismounted. Concealed among the low-growing shrub, he calmly waited.

He didn't have long to wait before his suspicions were

confirmed. They were being followed. He frowned when he saw only one Indian following. A young girl at that. He watched as she disappeared in the wake of the others.

Still, he waited for a few minutes. No one else followed. Grinning, he kept to the other side of the stream. Silently he followed the Indian girl as she kept pace with the others.

When she stopped in the late afternoon, Harry knew Willy had called another halt to rest the horses. The horses were nearing exhaustion from the fast, unrelenting pace. Good thing they were nearing the end of this headlong flight.

Picking up a thick branch, Harry crept on silent feet toward the unsuspecting squaw as she slowly made her way forward.

Wild-Flower crept forward, following voices. As the voices grew louder, she stopped. Stretching, she waited.

The snap of a twig had her whirling about. But it was too late. She never saw the club that knocked her unconscious.

Minutes later, Harry rode in to join the others. He rode right up to Willy and ignored the gasps of excitement from the others upon seeing a woman slung over his lap.

He addressed Willy. "We've been followed. Caught her tailing us. She's probably been following since we took her," Harry finished grimly, nodding his head toward Sarah.

Hank, Red and Tom all grinned and shouted.

"Now, there's more to go around."

"I gets first taste of that one."

"Wow, she's a real beauty." They stared eagerly at the unconscious girl draped over the horse's back as Harry dismounted.

Marching over to the trio, Willy stood, hands on his hips, in disgust at their denseness. "You jackasses. This means that others may be following her."

His eyes narrowed. "I'll decide what's to become of her

later. Old-Timer, take her on your horse. Tie and gag her so she can't yell when she comes to. Also, check her real good for weapons." He'd not take any chances the way Tom's brother had done.

"Hey, why does he get her?" Protest from behind had Willy spinning around. He whipped out his knife from his boot and pointed it at the gawking men. "Any of you got problems with my orders?"

All three hastily backed off, and mounted when motioned to do so. Walking to where Sarah waited, Willy jerked her hard to her feet. "You god-damned bitch! You knew she was followin' all along." A hazy red film framed his vision of Sarah's wide-eyed glance at the unconscious Wild-Flower. Swinging his hand, Willy slapped Sarah hard, knocking her to the ground.

He was about to deliver another bruising blow when Harry's voice stopped him, hand held high, ready to strike. "Come on, Will. We've got to get outta here. We need to be real careful about our trail now. Follow me. Do what you want with her later." Going to the stream, he urged his mount down the middle.

For the first time since her kidnaping, Sarah slumped in the saddle and did not fight Willy. Her face showed the fear she could no longer hide. Her eyes squeezed shut tightly, as if to block out the voice near her ear. Her hands settled over her abdomen as if to protect the tiny life that grew there.

Tears streaked down her cheeks, leaving moist trails in the layers of dust. Her lips moved silently in a last plea to the golden warrior she'd given up hope of ever seeing again.

Evil laughter floated overhead, surrounding and shrouding her in a black blanket of despair.

Chapter Thirty-five

Golden Eagle and Chief White Cloud reached Sarah's cabin by early evening. Using head motions and hand signals, Golden Eagle silently positioned his warriors around the cabins and concealed himself on the hillside to wait.

He shifted to the right as Chief White Cloud joined him, the older man's arm resting on Golden Eagle's shoulder as dark sienna eyes met coal-black ones. Each sent silent reassurances to the other. White Wind would be returned to them.

The squeak of a door opening captured their undivided attention. Golden Eagle stiffened, his eyes trained on the larger of the two cabins, his hand tightening on his bow.

He relaxed somewhat when a small plump woman came through the door. Golden Eagle's eyes widened. Despite the white woman's strange attire, he recognized her as the one who'd greeted the young injured Sarah with much scolding many summers ago. His eyes followed her every movement as she tromped loudly along the wooden porch to the corner of the house. Reaching up, she grabbed hold

317

of a dangling cord and pulled. Loud ringing filled the air as the woman continued to pull the cord vigorously.

The unexpected loud noise startled the warriors. All had their weapons drawn and were ready to defend themselves when several white men approached the area on horseback, shouting and laughing.

Blending into their surroundings, waiting and watching, the warriors relaxed somewhat when it became obvious that the sound was some sort of signal to the white men, calling them to the wood house for the evening meal that had many noses lifting to sniff appreciatively at the teasing aroma of cooked food. Bellies rumbled, reminding all that it had been days since their last hot meal.

As the evening passed, Golden Eagle grew restless. Sarah and her captors should have arrived by now. He leaned to the side to whisper in White Cloud's ear. Receiving the older man's nod, he left his place of concealment, keeping low to the ground, one silent shadow among many in the night.

Reclaiming his waiting stallion, hobbled a safe distance away, he rode off to scout for approaching riders. As he passed through the small secluded meadow, memories stopped him.

He stared into gloomy darkness. The sadness and despair he'd forced aside rose to the surface. The pain of knowing he could lose his White Wind became sharper and more deadly than any pain he'd ever known. He dismounted and strode to the spot where Sarah had once lain injured. This was where it had all started. He closed his eyes and fell to his knees as images of young Sarah dancing among the tall grasses flashed before him, blinding him to all else.

As if it were yesterday, her childish laughter rang across the meadow. Golden Eagle clung to the image of Sarah's wide blue eyes looking upon him with such innocent trust, felt in his heart that she was still alive, again trusting him to help her.

He shook his head and forced his eyes to open to the

318

present, dispelling past memories that only brought pain. Golden Eagle raised a fist to the night sky. "I will find you, White Wind. Do not fear, my sweet one. You will soon be at my side where you belong," he vowed to the heavens.

As he rose and returned to mount Great Star, a small part of him couldn't help but wonder if he would ever see the same innocence reflected in his own child's eyes. Would he hear the same carefree laughter in his daughter's voice, see the same love of life in their children that had drawn him to the woman who would forever hold his heart?

Chief Hawk Eyes stared with mounting frustration at the thick cloud-covered sky above. There was no bright moon to light their path, no twinkling stars to guide them. Returning his gaze to the barely discernible shadows moving about in the dark, he cursed. Unless the moon showed her face, the trail was lost to them until the new day began.

Hawk Eyes joined Running Wolf, who was deep in conversation with one of his warriors. Both warriors stopped and parted to make room for the old chief. Lone Hunter lowered his head in defeat as he shamefully admitted they could do nothing further tonight. Running Wolf squeezed Lone Hunter's shoulder in silent comfort and turned toward the chief.

"Lone Hunter is my best tracker. If he cannot find the trail, none can." Cursing beneath his breath, Running Wolf turned from Chief Hawk Eyes, smacking his fist into his palm. His shoulders drooped. "We can go no further without light from *Hanwi*. What now? The evil whites have my sister." Turning, he corrected himself. "Both my sisters. I can't stay here and do nothing, yet it's too dark to search for their trail without the risk of destroying it."

Chief Hawk Eyes stared into the young warrior's troubled features. He stood silent for long moments, watching Running Wolf clench and unclench his large fists in growing frustration and worry. Hawk Eyes felt the same helplessness assail him. He too did not relish the thought of just sitting around waiting.

Looking around the group awaiting his commands, Hawk Eyes came to a decision. "Prepare to ride, Running Wolf. We will go to the white man's house of wood. My son awaits us." He motioned for Red Fox to join them.

Picking a handful of warriors to accompany him, he commanded the rest, "You will remain here and wait for the clouds to clear. When you find their trail, follow carefully. I want no harm to come to White Cloud's daughters." There was no doubt the warriors would eventually find the trail. It was just a matter of time.

Turning to Red Fox, he commanded, "You have been to the white man's home. You will lead us there now." Red Fox nodded and, with Running Wolf at his side, they ran to their horses and leaped onto their backs, eager for any activity.

Red Fox and Running Wolf rode up to flank the chief. Hawk Eyes eyed the two worried warriors. "We will find them and take our revenge on those who dare to harm our women. Do not forget, the deaths of Standing Bear's daughters must also be avenged," he reminded them, knowing revenge was to be had at last. Silence met his words.

The old chief knew Red Fox and Running Wolf were thinking of the large branch found near Wild-Flower's abandoned horse with traces of dried blood upon it.

But there had been no sign of Wild-Flower. The last few hours their search had slowed drastically. They prided themselves on their ability to track even at night, but none could track in the pitch black of a moonless night. The difficult task required careful and sometimes painstaking work. The faintest of foot- or hoofprints, one broken or torn leaf, or an overturned rock were all they needed to spot the white man's trail.

But the whites had suddenly started taking care to hide their trail since they'd discovered Wild-Flower's presence.

After much searching the pursuers had finally found the tracks where the shod horses had left the stream.

Hawk Eyes shook his head. The shrewd white men kept returning to the stream, and several times they had cunningly split forces and led false trails before coming back together. As dark had fallen, the search had become more difficult, then impossible, with no help from above.

The ground started to rise steeply, and Hawk Eyes returned his attention to guiding his horse up the steep ridge.

Soft morning rays were streaking across the horizon, adding color to the scattered white clouds floating on the breeze.

As he crouched motionless in his place of hiding, worry lines etched deep grooves on Golden Eagle's forehead and around his compressed lips. He glanced at the horizon. Those who had taken White Wind should have arrived long ago by his calculations. His sharp gaze scanned the area, looking for signs of approaching movement. He gave the land his full attention, and his eagle-sharp gaze missed nothing. Gray wisps of smoke rose from the roof of the cabin, rippling in waves as the breeze caught and tore it away. The smell of cooking food once again filled the air.

Sounds of life awakening stirred in the undergrowth and above in the trees. As he had done last night, his sleep-deprived eyes followed several white men striding about the dirt yard before entering the wooden home with mouth-watering aromas emanating from it. Golden Eagle planned his next move. They couldn't remain here much longer. It was too dangerous.

Chirping and flapping overhead commanded his attention as small feathered birds flitted from branch to branch and called a good-morning to one another.

Golden Eagle cocked his head and listened intently to one particular birdcall. He came to full alertness, all tiredness fleeing as he lifted his head, cupped his mouth with his hands and answered.

Standing over the hot stove, Mary impatiently shoved wisps of hair behind her ears as she added slick slabs of juicy blood-red steaks to the sizzling pan. In another sizzling skillet she fried brown eggs gathered from wild prairie chickens, while placing slices of hot freshly baked bread on the table.

Three hungry men sauntered in and joined Ben at the table after filling mugs with strong-brewed coffee.

Opening the shutters in the kitchen, Mary sighed as the refreshing breeze cooled her flushed face and replaced the stuffy, steamy air.

Turning, she placed pans of steaming food in the center of the table. As she straightened, she motioned for Ben to say grace. Ben eyed her impatiently, but Mary stood firm, crossing her arms across her ample bosom. Since Sarah's disappearance, she was taking no chances in offending their Lord.

When the final amen was uttered, she gave the signal for each to begin dishing up. The reverent hush was suddenly broken as hungry men reached across the table, each taking his share of thick slabs of meat, eggs and bread. Forks hit tin as each one eagerly dug in.

Mary knew from experience that the large amount of food she'd spent an hour cooking would be gone in minutes. Taking her seat at the crowded table, she sat back and relaxed with her mug of sweetened coffee. She usually ate after the men left to go about the daily chores.

Plates were emptied, bellies filled and coffee mugs refilled. Ben kept the discussion centered on horses, furs to be readied and traps to be checked. He was careful to keep any mention of their ongoing search for Sarah from Mary.

Mary ignored the men's conversation. As usual, her thoughts centered on Sarah. It had been nearly three months since Sarah had disappeared and no one had been able to find any trace of her girl. She sighed sadly. Catching her husband's quizzical look, she smiled wistfully.

Ben rose, signaling mealtime was over. Mary also rose and walked with Ben to the doorway.

He drew Mary into his arms. "Sarah's alive out there somewhere, love. We have to believe that. She'll come back to us."

Looking over his shoulder into the yard, Mary dabbed at her moist eyes. "I know, Ben. I know. Sometimes I just can't help but wonder where she is and if she's all right. It's not knowin', the uncertainty, that gets to me."

Mary returned Ben's hug. Her arms tightened as she drew courage to face another long day from her mate. For his sake, she would try to be brave. Straightening, she squared her shoulders and gave her husband a weak smile as she pushed him out the door, following. "Now off with you. I'll just bring my cup of coffee out to the porch this morning." She cocked her head. "Why, just listen to them birds this morning, singing and calling to one another. They're one of Our Lord's finest gifts. You know how Sarah loved to sit and listen to them each morning. Why, many a day she'd even eat her breakfast out here . . ."

Ben's head snapped around and he peered outside, eyes narrowing. Holding up a hand to still Mary's chatter, he listened, his bushy brows lowering worriedly. Suddenly, he flew into action. "Get inside. Now! Stay there and don't come out." Giving his woman a shove, Ben ran to the giant cowbell hanging on the corner of the cabin and rang frantically. As he his fellow trappers ran to join him, he grabbed his rifle off the porch where he'd leaned it earlier.

Startled by the loud peals of the bell, Golden Eagle halted in mid-sentence in his conversation with his father, Chief White Cloud and Red Fox and ran toward his vantage point.

Golden Eagle swore when he saw the white trappers running, guns in hand, to join the man pulling on the cord as the old woman had done the night before. Calling for food was not the only purpose of that object, he learned. Somehow, the whites knew they were there.

Chapter Thirty-six

Ben froze in the midst of warning his trapper friends that he suspected trouble was upon them when he caught movement from the corner of his eye.

The others followed his gaze and also froze. Ben wasn't aware of the gasps of shock coming from those surrounding him. He attention never wavered from the force of fierce-looking Indians that came silently and from nowhere. Each horse carried an imposing warrior perched upon its back, bows held with arrows notched and ready. Hanging from their left side or lower backs, each had a quiver of arrows within easy reach if needed. With their knees, they easily controlled their mounts as they slowly but deliberately edged forward in a half circle until they were but several yards away.

Ben swallowed fearfully and studied those who approached. One warrior in the center held up his hand, signaling a halt. Another command and bows were lowered, still within quick access if needed but not so intimidating.

Ben never let his gaze waver from that warrior. Clearly this was their leader.

He lowered his rifle to a less threatening position and motioned the others to do the same. He didn't want to start something by someone making a wrong move. They were far outnumbered.

The silence seemed to go on forever when four more Indians left the safety of the woods and rode up from the rear to join the leader. Ben's eyes widened in alarm. His stunned gaze took in the headdress and attire of not one, but two chiefs who now flanked the lead warrior, bringing the count to at least 15 warriors standing before them.

Holding up a shaky hand, Ben cautioned the others. "Easy, boys. We don't know how many are still hidden. Hold your fire. Nobody fires without my signal. I'll go see what they want, but be on guard," he cautioned.

Silence reigned as men from two different races watched and waited to see who would make the first move. Golden Eagle nudged his horse forward and stopped. The others remained behind him. His piercing gaze took in each white man, and rested on the woman who stepped from the doorway.

Ben handed his rifle to the man next to him and took a few steps forward, hand held in the universal sign for peace. Each of the rough-looking mountain men behind him tensed, ready to defend a man who had the honor of being called friend by all of them.

Ben took a moment to study the warrior who sat his horse as if he and the animal were one. He gulped nervously as he took several steps toward the silent, imposing Indian.

The horse sidestepped impatiently and tossed his sleek head as Ben approached. Ben's gaze was momentarily diverted to the warrior's magnificent beast. A single soft-spoken command stilled the restless stallion, and Ben raised his brows toward the warrior in respect.

As he stared from warrior to horse, fleeting memories

chose that moment to surface. Ben warily shifted his eyes from the warrior back to the golden horse standing several feet from him.

He was known in these parts for his eye for good horseflesh. That was one reason the commander at Fort Tecumseh paid him to breed strong, sturdy mounts. Many of the mustangs he and John had caught and tamed had produced exceptional offspring, fast, agile and extremely hardy. These were much-needed traits out here in the wilderness.

This particular stallion was not only a fine specimen, but also familiar. In seconds Ben had taken note of the glistening coat, the strong broad body, dark flowing mane, strong neck and proud head.

He studied the white star in the center of the horse's muzzle. He'd recognized that horse anywhere, anytime. It was one he'd helped deliver many years ago, one of their best back then. In his excitement, Ben forgot about the possible danger as he approached.

"I remember the day John presented this yearling to his daughter on her twelfth birthday and her joy and love for the young colt."

He frowned and glanced at the watchful warrior sitting above him. "I also remember the night this young colt disappeared. John said it had been stolen, but I saw what happened that night with my own eyes," Ben said loudly.

He remembered his surprise when he'd gone outside for a smoke the night Sarah had sprained her ankle. He'd seen John come out of the barn carrying Sarah and leading the colt. "I followed them, you know. Saw them leave the colt tied to a tree and walk away. I stayed to see just what was going on." Ben shook his head.

"Sure was surprised to see a young warrior come right up, calm the colt and disappear in the night with Sarah's prized horse. Figured you must've done somethin' real special for her to make that kind of sacrifice." No one knew better than he what that horse meant to her.

Cocking his head, Ben looked toward the waiting warrior. He saw the hint of amusement shining from within luminous deep black eyes, despite the grimness of the warrior's features.

As no immediate threat seemed forthcoming, Ben drew even with the stallion and reached out to run his hand down the muzzle, talking softly. "He turned out better than I ever hoped. Sarah raised this young-un herself. You have done her proud. She would have been happy to see what a fine beast he's become."

Putting his hands to his hips, Ben forced himself back to business. "What brings you back to our land? Why have you returned? What do you want from us?" he demanded aloud, more for the benefit of the others. He used hand signals for the Indian, not expecting him to understand him.

Golden Eagle had been amazed when he saw recognition flare in the old man's eyes. Leaning forward, he posed his own question.

"Tell me, old man. Where is Sarah this day? Is she here?" Golden Eagle straightened at the shadow of sadness in the old man's eyes.

Ben drew himself to his full imposing height, his protective instincts bristling, eyes narrowing suspiciously as he answered with a question of his own. "Now why do you want to know about a girl you've not seen in five years? Why are you here? What do you want from us?" he repeated.

Looking toward the restless men armed with rifles, Golden Eagle sought to reassure him. "We mean no harm to you or your people. We search for the one who is to become my wife. She was abducted from our village. I seek your help."

"I'm sorry, son. We know nothing about any Indian girl," Ben answered, relief relaxing his features.

"The one I search for has the name White Wind, daughter of Chief White Cloud of the *Hunkpapas*." He pointed out Sarah's father, who came forward. "White Wind is the future wife of Golden Eagle, son of Hawk Eyes, Chief of the *Miniconjou* tribe." He pointed appropriately at himself and his father.

"White Wind is also known by the white man's name of Sarah," he announced.

A startled cry came from the porch. Mary flew down the worn path, eluding hands that reached out to stop her. She came to stand by her husband's side to hear news of her Sarah.

Ben threw Mary a withering glare. "Thought I told you to stay inside, woman. Can't you ever do as I ask?" he sternly scolded her.

Mary gave her husband her famous "do hush up" look and turned her attention to the warrior. "My girl, she's alive? Please tell me." Mary closed her eyes as if afraid of what she'd hear.

Golden Eagle reacted to the woman's sincere concern. "When last seen, your 'daughter' was alive and well." He motioned his warriors to put away their weapons, and dismounted as Ben likewise instructed his men to put their rifles away.

Ben and Mary stared at the chief, this warrior who claimed to be Sarah's father. "Sarah left us a letter months ago stating she was going to seek safety elsewhere and maybe search for her father. It would seem she was successful." Ben nodded his head toward White Cloud. "We-'ve not heard nor seen her since."

Mary stepped forward. "Where is she? Why is she not with you still?" Her voice trailed off as a new fear took hold. Something horrible must've happened for this many Indians to come searching for her.

Golden Eagle took several deep breaths. His chest squeezed painfully. "We talk. I will tell you all I know."

Ben looked toward Mary, who nodded. "Come," he invited, "We will talk inside." He turned and led the way to the door.

Golden Eagle motioned for Red Fox to dismount. Followed by Red Fox, his father, Chief White Cloud and Running Wolf, he entered the strange large house of wood. Gingerly, he sat at the wooden table, easing himself onto the wooden seat, following Ben's example. The others also sat themselves.

After all were seated, and those who wanted to listen were standing around the edges of the room, a hush fell upon the two groups of men. Speaking clearly, Golden Eagle disclosed all he knew, from his first encounter with Sarah at the stream to how they'd discovered that she was the daughter of White Cloud.

Ben frowned and glared at Golden Eagle. "You took our girl from us, but you kept her from harm. We found out later that good-fer-nothin' Willy had gone to the fort. Lieutenant Smithers kicked him out for bein' drunk and raisin' hell with his men soon after."

Ben slammed his fist onto the table and stared at Golden Eagle. "That bastard. I don't know what to tell you and your people. We will join your search." Ben leaned forward, eyes intently on Golden Eagle. "But I warn you right now, Golden Eagle, if we find her, she returns with me unless she chooses to return with you. It must be her choice. I will not allow her to be forced again."

Golden Eagle met Ben's fierce protective stare with his own. Slowly, he nodded, knowing that Sarah would return with him. "Agreed," he said.

"Hey, Ben," Jacob called out. "Me 'n Sam, well, we may know somethin'." All eyes turned to a stout bushy-faced man standing outside, lounging against the doorway. Flushing as many pairs of eyes suddenly focused on him, Jacob nervously cleared his throat.

"Well, spit it out, for God's sake. What do you know?" Ben demanded.

"Well, I don't know nothin' fer sure 'bout Miss Sarah, but on our last trip to take them horses to the fort for you, we rode by old Clyde's abandoned tradin' post to avoid a roaming party of not-so-friendly-looking Injuns.'' Jacob coughed and cleared his throat nervously as he'd forgotten about their present company.

Motioning impatiently for Jacob to continue, Ben groaned and Golden Eagle rose. "Speak," two voices commanded in unison.

"Well, we saw fresh horse tracks all around the outside, and inside, well, it were wrecked. Could tell by the splinters on the broken chair it were done recently. Looks as though someone's been spendin' time there. Were empty bottles broken all over the place too. Seemed kinda funny someone would be usin' that place. Not many out here know it's there. Besides, one strong wind storm's sure ta bring the rickety old place down."

Ben threw his hands up in anger. "Why didn't you say anything to me, either of you?" he roared, startling those nearest to him.

Swallowing nervously, Jacob's dropped his voice lower as he sheepishly explained, "We, Sam and me, we didn't figure it important. I plumb forgot 'bout it till now."

Golden Eagle started pacing. "Could this Willy know of that place?"

Ben frowned, then leapt to his feet in excitement. "Of course! John and Willy's grandfather Jean helped build that tradin' post and lived there with Clyde for many years. After John and Willy joined him, Jean built this place. A few years later, Clyde died. It's been so long since I was out that way I didn't know that the shack still stood."

Golden Eagle rose. "Tell us how to get there. We must hurry."

Ben compressed his lips grimly. "I'll do better than that. I will lead you there. Jacob, you and Sam come with me. Henry, stay with Mary in case they come this way. Be on your guard."

Before they left, Mary blocked Golden Eagle's exit. "Do you love Sarah?"

Taking Mary by the shoulders, Golden Eagle met her

331

teary gaze with a compellingly honest stare. "White Wind is my heart, my soul mate. I love her, and she loves me. Do not fear, old woman. You shall see her again," he promised.

"Bless you, God go with you." Tears streamed down Mary's wrinkled cheeks as she and Henry watched until only clouds of dust remained.

Warm temperatures and buzzing insects woke Willy. With one eye open, he took note of the mid-afternoon position of the sun. Grabbing his canteen, he held it up and splashed tepid water over his face, shaking the droplets free as he leaned against a huge gray rock peppered with black spots. He pulled a hunk of leftover rabbit that he'd dried over a fire days ago out of his shirt pocket. Working his jaws, he attempted to chew the leather-tough meat. Grimacing as an acrid taste invaded his mouth, he spat the burned meat out and decided to go without.

Next he pulled out his flask, but that too was empty. Throwing the bottle as far as he could, Willy started pacing, kicking stones and twigs. His glance fell to the open doorway of the shack.

He stopped, feet planted apart, arms crossed, as he gave thought to the problem at hand. What to do with his ward and the squaw? Since Sarah was now living and dressing like one of them, keeping her was out of the question. She's no better 'n her ma in her whorin' ways, he thought.

But he still had the problem of getting her money. His lips twitched. If she died, as her only surviving relative, he could legally lay claim to all that had belonged to her.

He stared unseeingly at the wide blue sky. He needed to be rid of the girl without bringing suspicion on himself. His brows drew together as he reviewed and discarded one idea after another.

A picture of her in her Indian garb with her braided hair flashed unwanted before him. "Goddamned squaw. Livin' and sleepin' with them heathen savages. You'll pay for

332

ruinin' my plans,'' Willy swore aloud. A sudden thought occurred to him, and his eyes narrowed to slits as a plan with possibilities began to take form. Willy grinned. ''Damn, ol' boy. You's done it again. All we gotta do is kill her, let Ben find her body and blame the Injuns. Then the money's mine,'' he gloated aloud. ''Even that stupid Lieutenant Smithers will have no choice but ta force Ben ta give me what belongs ta me.'' He laughed.

A movement to his left distracted him as Red sauntered through the bush, supplies in hand. Tom lay sleeping on his bedroll, and Hank stood watch over the girls. Harry had left soon after they'd arrived, saying he had no desire to take part in the fun planned for the evening.

Tossing his ripped and torn hat to the ground, Willy stretched and scratched the top of his head, his hair matted with bits of dirt, leaves and twigs. ''Ah, time to see how my prisoners are faring.''

Chapter Thirty-seven

In broad daylight, the precariously leaning old trading post had a sad, defeated air. Large gaps in the decaying log sides had allowed small animals to squeeze through. The once sturdy door hung limply to one side, propped open by a large rock. Time had taken its toll, allowing nature to reclaim what was once hers.

Inside, years of accumulated dirt, debris and animal matter hid the wooden floors. Leaves scattered from one side to the other with each breath of air that passed through the open door.

Sarah opened her eyes and surveyed her surroundings with forced detachment. Life had started here for her father and grandfather. Was life to end here for her?

She hugged her knees tight to her chest and lowered her head to rest on her knees. Her hands and feet ached with numbness from the constricting ropes binding them. She scooted back and pressed herself tightly into the corner, as if she could make herself invisible from Hank, who stood guard at the open doorway.

She ignored the silken spiderwebs, their tiny owners temporarily scared away. Wild-Flower sat across the room, bound securely to what was left of a sagging bed frame. She lifted her gaze to Wild-Flower's, and once again admired the Indian girl's bravery. Sarah tried to draw strength from her fearless stare, her unyielding pride, but looked away in shame. It was her fault Wild-Flower found herself in Willy's evil clutches.

Lifting listless, haunted eyes to the shabby one-room shack, she searched fruitlessly for a way out, a weapon, anything. But she knew there was nothing. She'd searched every inch of the room countless times since Willy had dumped her and Wild-Flower in here.

No one would think to look here for her. Not many even knew of this old place. Leaning her head back, she caught a glimpse of blue sky peeking through gaping holes in the ceiling. Her thoughts wandered to Golden Eagle and the many questions buzzing in her head, leaving her dizzy as her emotions ranged from stark hopelessness to the belief that rescue was just around the corner.

Had Golden Eagle returned? Had his people discovered her missing? Were they even now searching for her? Had they even found Wild-Flower's trail? And the hardest question that frightened her the most: How long could she hope for rescue before time ran out?

Sarah stole a glance at Hank, slouched over in front of the door, falling asleep. She couldn't see the others.

Glancing once again at Wild-Flower, Sarah couldn't read the girl's stoic expression. Another wave of guilt and fear overrode her optimistic hope of rescue as a single tear escaped.

It could've been hours or just minutes when Sarah lifted her head. The sound of approaching footsteps had her sitting straight, watching the doorway warily.

Willy stood in the opening. "Out with you." He nodded at Hank, thumb jerking over his shoulder to emphasize his command.

Susan Edwards

"Hey, Willy, when does we get one? I could take the squaw outside," Hank eagerly offered, eyes traveling over the Indian girl who remained silent, her stony gaze unwavering.

Willy slapped Hank on the back and grinned as he too looked his fill, tongue snaking out to lick his lips. "All in good time, ma boy. Thinks I'll be the first white man to teach her a thing 'bout lovin'. But don't you worry none. I'll break her in real good for you guys. Now get."

As Sarah watched, Hank left, rubbing his hands in anticipation, and Willy advanced into the small room and towered over Wild-Flower, letting his eyes rove over her enticing curves.

Knees cracking and protesting, Willy bent over, grabbed Wild-Flower's chin and grinned at the burning hatred smoldering in her eyes. "I think you's gonna be a real wild one. Mebe I'll have you first. We'll let Sarah over there watch, and show her what she's been missin' all this time." His head turned as he spoke, staring hard at Sarah.

Grinning, he added. "I hoped there's still some fight left in you she-cats. I like my women with lots of fight in them. They all fight me at first, then they gets all scared. That's when I show 'em who's boss." Willy eyed Sarah over his shoulder. "Just like them two squaws I had. They was real feisty. They fought me real good, but it didn't do them no good. They learned what it means to fear me. Just like you two bitches will."

Willy stood, grabbed the one remaining chair and pulled it around to sit between the girls at an angle so he could look at first one, then the other. His beefy arms rested across the broken chair back and his legs stretched out.

Sarah kept her eyes trained on Willy as he sat and stared at them, beady eyes shifting from one to the other as if he couldn't make up his mind which one to torment first. She knew he was trying to unnerve them and feed their fear. That he was succeeding and knew it made him worse.

Willy's eyes hungrily settled on Sarah, and she swal-

336

lowed hard as his hand lowered to his lap, stroking himself in anticipation. "Ah, dear Sarah. I hope you were able to rest. I's got great plans for us. Such a pity we've never really gotten to know each other. Seems I waited too long. But no matter. By the time I'm done with you, we'll know each other intimately."

Sarah cringed, his cruel laughter jarring her sensitive nerves. She didn't dare close her eyes. Instead, she reached deep within herself, struggling with her fear. She thought of her unborn baby and anger grew, giving her the courage she needed. If she were to die, she'd not cower and beg. "You think you're pretty clever, don't you. What do you wanna bet that by nightfall you'll have an arrow piercing your black, wicked heart? Do you really think you can out-smart the warriors of Golden Eagle's tribe?" she asked scornfully, forcing the trembling fear from her voice.

"Golden Eagle, eh." Willy's lips twisted into a sneer as he glared at her attire. "Ya know, cept for this hair"—he leaned over and tugged cruelly—"you could pass for one of them savages. Is this Golden Eagle your lover?" he asked, hands clenching into large fists as he watched her head lift proudly.

"Golden Eagle is to be my husband," Sarah stated with pride. "If you were smart, you would leave and run. It's the only way to save your worthless hide."

Willy's lower lip dropped as he gave a shout of laughter, one hand slapping his knee. "Yore what? Ya mean ta tell me, girl, you was gonna marry one of them redskins?" A hard glitter crept across his face. "Like mother, like daughter, huh?"

Harsh laughter bounced off the walls of the shack. "So, I won't be your first lover, eh, Sarah. Ah, well, that's all right. I'll just have ta show you what it means to have a real man love you, not some fumbling Injun. And if you thinks your Indian lover will save you, forget it. We made real sure we wouldn't be followed this time."

Sarah lifted her chin and scoffed. "Your brand of loving

is nothing more than the rutting of pigs. You know nothing of love, Willy. You're selfish and evil.''

Sitting helpless before the crazed man, Sarah felt driven to wipe the smug look from his hateful face. ''If that old man you called your guide was so sure he'd left no trail that could be followed, why did he not stay with you? The others are so eager for your planned entertainment, they'd do anything for you. Why not him? Why wouldn't he stay if he felt it was so safe?'' Sarah stopped to let her words take effect.

Willy flushed angrily at her scorn. Unwittingly, Sarah's words hit home. ''He was too tired. Said he wanted to get back.''

''If the old man was so tired, why didn't he stay and sleep as you all did? Hank was the only one who stayed awake, and even he fell asleep. I think your guide decided it was too dangerous to stay. He's probably miles from here. And why did he leave without getting any of the money you promised? The others are waiting for their cut. He's going to be laughing at all of you as he sleeps tonight because he'll be alive and you'll all be in Hell.''

Willy's eyes narrowed as he looked to the open doorway. Sarah's words brought a worried frown to his eyes. Sarah continued to goad him. ''I think he knew there was no way he could hide your trail. He could only make the following harder to buy him time to escape with his worthless hide free of arrows.''

Sarah knew she was pushing Willy to a dangerous point, but she couldn't sit and let him terrorize her. She'd rather he get mad and kill her outright than go through what he had in mind for her.

Willy's temper snapped. In a flash the chair flew over her head, slammed into the weak and rotting wall and shattered into a thousand slivers. Startled at the sudden violent movement, instinctively she cringed and buried her head against her knees as what was left of the chair pelted her.

She tried to scoot away as Willy grabbed a fistful of her

dress front and yanked her to her feet, holding his knife point to her pulsing throat.

Sarah closed her eyes as the tip of the blade pierced her skin, a bead of red appearing. She prayed for a quick death, while regret for what could have been pierced her heart, the pain sharper than any wound the knife could inflict.

Willy's stale breath fanned her cheeks as he snarled, "You'd like me to use this right now, wouldn't ya."

Sarah's limbs went weak with relief when the blade fell away. Suddenly the rope around her ankles gave way and fell to the ground.

As he sliced the bounds around her wrists, Willy mockingly informed her, "Sorry to disappoint you, sweetie. Won't work. You'll die, all right. But only when I've had enough of you." Willy lowered his lips to Sarah's exposed neck. She jerked her head away, unable to look upon his deranged twisted features, as she struggled ineffectively against his strong hold.

"Fight me." Willy grabbed Sarah's hand and forced her to feel his throbbing flesh. "See what you're doin' to me? I'm all hot and hard for you." Willy grinned.

Sarah screamed and kicked as she was shoved to the floor, Willy falling on her as she struggled to fight him off.

Her hands were held above her head as Willy rose to sit above her, grinding his pelvis into her soft contours.

"Tell me again about your lover coming to save you, bitch," Willy taunted her before lowering himself over her, settling his hips on hers.

Sarah saw her chance and raised her right knee, jamming it hard into Willy's crotch. A roar of pain and outrage thundered in the air as she twisted away, unbalancing Willy, who was still groaning from the blow she'd delivered. Crawling, her breath coming in frightened gasps, she ducked her head as curses rang from above her, dropping like hailstones upon her ears.

The air left her lungs in one sobbing whoosh as Willy's full weight crashed down upon her, his labored breathing harsh with pain. "So, ya wants it rough, huh. I'll teach ya to mess with me." His fingers tangled in her hair as he jerked her head back, and his other hand slid up her thigh, shoving her buckskin dress out of his way.

Sarah let loose a piercing scream and struggled for her life.

Chapter Thirty-eight

Silent figures crept closer toward the run-down shack. As each one received his silent orders, he slid into position. With a nod from Golden Eagle, two warriors slipped away to approach the last two whites outside. One lay sleeping, while the other rummaged through saddle packs strewn across the ground next to the exhausted horses. The first white had met his end in the woods, and after these two were taken care of, there was just one left—Willy.

Slowly, bows were lifted, arrows notched and arms drawn back, muscles bulging against the taut pull of bowstring. The warriors took aim. The swift-flying arrows found their marks. Red toppled over with a started jerk, a gurgling choking coming from gasping lips, then silence. Tom never awakened.

The horses shied and pulled at their tethered reins, uneasy with the smell of blood and death. Quickly, two warriors approached and led the three horses away before those in the cabin became alerted to their presence.

Golden Eagle looked around and nodded, satisfied that

all but Sarah's guardian had been killed, and turned his attention to the small wooden building. In the midst of plan-making with Chief White Cloud and Ben, he froze as a piercing scream tore through the air, raising the hairs on his neck as his heart jumped to his throat, pounding with fear. He turned toward the others. "We cannot wait for the white to come out. We go in."

Ben held out his arm, staying Golden Eagle. "I know what you're feeling, son. But ya can't let desperation rule now. If you go stormin' in there, the girls will get hurt. You don't corner a mountain cat without risking injury," Ben cautioned Golden Eagle.

Chief Hawk Eyes stepped forward. "We will force the white man out." Golden Eagle listened intently as Hawk Eyes explained what they would do. He never took his eyes from the wooden shack that separated him from Sarah, his White Wind. His gut wrenched with each cry and his eyes became coals of heated anger, ready to burst into flames with each sound of struggle that reached them.

White Cloud and Golden Eagle nodded their agreement to Hawk Eyes' clever plan. Golden Eagle positioned his warriors and raised his hand high, ready to give the command when all was ready. He looked over at a small group of warriors and Ben as they huddled in a group, coaxing sparks into flames.

Sarah lay gasping for breath, both from her struggles and from the full weight of Willy sprawled on top of her. The fight suddenly left her. Her limbs went limp. She forced bitter saliva past her throat, now raw from her useless screams. Her eyes closed, unable to witness Willy's triumph. As her strength ebbed, hope left her as well. There was nothing and no one to save her now.

Willy laughed, his labored breathing fanning her face. Sarah didn't even have the strength to turn from his foul breath. From deep within, her mind struggled against all odds, still seeking for a way to escape. Her eyes opened.

She would have grinned as Willy swiped the blood from his nose and lips, results of two blows she'd managed to land, but her lips were too swollen, cracked and bleeding as well.

Willy's evil grin distorted his swollen face grotesquely. So sure was he of victory, he released her arms and buried his fingers in her hair. "What's the matter, sweetie? Hope yer not too tired." His hands and eyes roamed her body, in no hurry to quickly take what he wanted.

Sarah caught sight of Wild-Flower from the corner of her eye. The Indian girl sat absolutely still, head tipped to one side as if listening. Her lids fluttered shut, brows wrinkling as she tried to concentrate on any strange noise coming from outside. But the only sound she heard was Willy's harsh breathing. Outside, all seemed silent. Sarah's glance flew to the roof. Earlier, her nerves had been so raw and sensitive to each and every sound that noise from birds and squirrels on the roof had nearly driven her crazy. Where had they gone?

Suddenly, several thuds on the roof had all eyes looking upward, watching, waiting. A strange crackling noise filtered down to Sarah. She held her breath with renewed hope. Soft and faint at first, the crackling grew louder with each passing second. Sarah's nostrils flared as the smell of burning wood wafted downward. Curses spewed forth as Willy jumped to his feet and hauled her up.

Willy grabbed his gun from the holster hanging by the door. "Don't move or yore as good as dead," he hissed near her ear. With one arm wrapped around Sarah's neck, his other hand held the gun to her temple. "Move real slow like. Don't try nothin'," he warned, forcing her to the doorway.

Sarah's heart pounded as Willy pushed her to the doorway of the now-burning building. Out of the corner of her eye, she saw Wild-Flower's frightened look as she struggled to free herself. Sarah bit her lip, tears coursing down her cheeks. There was nothing she could do to save her friend.

"Stop right here," Willy ordered, peering out the door. Stillness greeted them. "They's out there. I can feel them savages," he whispered. His eyes searched, but there was no movement. "Damn," Willy cursed, spying Red and Tom dead, arrows piercing their backs. "The horses are gone too," he choked.

Keeping the gun at Sarah's temple, Willy slowly inched out into the open, eyes shifting nervously as he had no choice but to escape the building's heat and blanketing smoke.

Stopping a few feet from the blazing building, Willy yelled, "Stay away or the girl dies." To emphasize his words, he shoved the gun hard into Sarah's temple and cocked the weapon, eliciting a cry of pain and fear from Sarah.

Willy's eyes grew round and fearful as mounted warriors left the concealing cover of trees and prevented any escape. He broke out in a cold sweat.

"Let the girls go, Willy. You can't escape now," Ben yelled out, stepping forward, rifle held in the crook of his arm.

Willy's eyes widened when he recognized Ben and Jacob standing shoulder to shoulder with the Indians. His eyes shifted wildly as he took in the number of arrows poised and ready to fly at him. He'd become a damn pincushion, he thought to himself, searching his brain for a way out of the situation.

A desperate gleam came into his eyes as he kept a tight hold on Sarah, using her as a shield as he struggled to keep an eye on Indians surrounding him on three sides. "Nothin' doin', Ben. If an arrow hits me, I'll have time to pull the trigger. Keep 'em away, Ben. Get them Injuns where I can see them. Now!" he screamed in desperation.

Golden Eagle motioned all warriors back and they joined him, forming a large half circle in front of Willy but leaving

344

Willy's back clear. No one noticed Red Fox slipping behind the flame-engulfed structure.

Willy glanced around, satisfied that the only threat came from in front of him. "Get me a horse, Ben, and you'd better make sure I ain't followed or them savages try somethin'. This half-breed's my safe passage outta here. I may die, but so will she. You can't guarantee Sarah won't get hit by a stray bullet or arrow, Ben. If she dies, it'll be your fault," he shouted wildly, moving further from the burning shack as large pieces of the rotting roof fell around him and flames claimed the shack.

Behind Willy, spirals of black smoke drifted upward and orange flames danced across the needle-covered logs, dropping down through the rotted openings to spread inside.

Golden Eagle whispered to Ben and stepped forward, slowly leading his snorting and prancing stallion. "That's close enough, Injun. Leave it and back off," Willy demanded, his eyes never leaving the warrior before him.

Golden Eagle dropped the lead rope with a softly spoken command that only the horse heard, but all, including Willy, saw Golden Eagle's ebony eyes narrow with hatred and his jaw clench, which his warriors knew warned of great anger.

Willy inched forward toward the wild-eyed stallion. Harsh laughter rang in Sarah's ears. "That wouldn't be lover boy, now would it?" Willy jeered, and stepped closer to the sidestepping horse. "Too bad you'll never see him again," Willy taunted, longing to put a bullet through the hated redskin. But it was too risky. Soon they would all pay. Sarah's death would be his revenge.

Willy edged closer, reaching the snorting beast, using the animal as a shield to block the arrows aimed at him. Keeping the gun at Sarah's temple, he told her, "Reach out slow like and grab the rope. Any sudden moves and it's all over for you."

Sarah blinked the tears from her eyes and reached for the rope dangling in front of her. "Good. Now, give it to me,'' Willy ordered, the smell and taste of freedom within his reach. He planned to lead the horse into the woods behind him and, with Sarah, make his escape. Willy latched onto the rope and slowly started backing away.

Before he took two steps, a piercing whistle broke the tense stillness, startling Willy as the stallion reared up, flailing his front hooves at Willy, snorting loudly. Willy lost his grip on the rope and stumbled backwards.

Sarah took advantage of Willy's loosened grip to twist out of his arms and fling herself to the ground, rolling several feet forward.

Warriors took aim, but the path to their target remained blocked as Sarah jumped to her feet, ready to flee for freedom. The sound of laughter behind her had Sarah frozen with fear as she turned and stared at the gun trained on her heart. Golden Eagle lunged forward, desperate to get Sarah out of firing range. Golden Eagle raced around his horse shouting. ''White Wind, down!''

Willy's eyes glowed eerily, and a high-pitched cackle rose from his throat. Willy knew death was upon him. His hand lifted, the gun aimed straight at Golden Eagle's heart instead. ''What better way to get my revenge than to kill the one you love, eh, Sarah?''

''NO!'' The scream tore from Sarah's throat. With a strength born of love and desperation, Sarah lunged, flying at Willy at the same time his finger squeezed the trigger.

The sudden blast of gunfire momentarily paralyzed white men whose rifles were clutched tightly in their hands and warriors who stood ready, faces grim, muscles pulled taut as their arrows were notched and ready to fly.

Sarah felt herself falling. How strange, she thought, the ground seemed to be rising slowly to meet her, and without feeling the impact, she suddenly found herself lying on her side, stunned, as a strange lethargy invaded her body.

She was unaware of Golden Eagle dropping down on top of her, covering her body with his as arrows flew overhead with deadly accuracy. She didn't see Willy fly backward under the assault of dozens of arrows that pierced his heart. And she would later be thankful that she'd not seen the evil grin that, even as death claimed him, he still wore.

The sounds of yelling and shouting faded as blessed numbing began to take hold, diminishing the searing pain that radiated from her shoulder. Blackness descended, and her eye lids fluttered and slowly closed as she slipped into oblivion.

Chapter Thirty-nine

Golden Eagle lay panting, and finally raised his head to see that Willy would never bother any of them again. He turned his full attention to the still figure beneath him. He got to his knees, heart pounding as he turned Sarah over onto her back.

"No . . ." Golden Eagle's anguished voice cried out, his eyes fixed on the widening circle of red on her clothing. He gently pulled Sarah toward him, holding his breath as he searched for some sign of life.

Everyone rushed forward at once and chaos reigned. White Cloud halted several feet behind Golden Eagle, tears falling from eyes that had seen much tragedy, but nothing so gut-wrenching or painful as the injury of his own child, his flesh and blood.

Golden Eagle glanced up at Sarah's father. "She's hurt, but alive." Just as White Cloud kneeled beside him, Golden Eagle's glance shifted toward the flame-engulfed building as one side collapsed. Tears fell from his eyes as well. Wild-Flower had been trapped in there.

All eyes seemed to have had that same thought at the same time, and a cloud of heaviness settled over all. There was no hope that Wild-Flower could still be alive in that blazing inferno.

Already Jacob and some of the warriors struggled to contain the fire and keep it from spreading to the dry littered ground beneath their feet.

Golden Eagle laid a comforting hand on White Cloud's slumped shoulders as Ben and Chief Hawk Eyes joined them. White Cloud looked to Ben. "I have lost one daughter. I cannot lose my firstborn."

Ben nodded. He and the others near by knew that White Cloud had just placed his trust in Ben to help save Sarah's life. Cutting away the blood-soaked hide, Ben examined the wound and looked at Golden Eagle and White Cloud. "She's damn lucky. The bullet passed through. As soon as we get this bleeding stopped, we'll take her to Mary. She'll soon have her up and bein' her stubborn self again."

Golden Eagle's head snapped up when he heard Ben's announcement. His hands gripped Sarah's tighter. "No! She goes with us. We will care for her." Golden Eagle was not about to let her out of his sight. He closed his eyes. He could still see her body falling limply, lifelessly to the ground.

A hand shaking his shoulder brought Golden Eagle back to the present. "Son, Sarah is in shock and she's lost a lot of blood. She may not survive the long trip to your village. Bring her back to her home. Let Mary tend her. I know how you feel, Golden Eagle, and you too, Chief White Cloud—after all, she is your daughter—but right now, we need to do what is best for her to speed her recovery."

White Cloud stared long and hard at Ben. He then held up a hand to still Golden Eagle's reply. "You are wise, white man. Without your help, we would not have found my daughter in time to save her life. We return to your home."

Turning to Golden Eagle and Hawk Eyes, White Cloud

added. "She must rest and heal before making the trip to your village. Nothing must stand in the way of her recovery."

Golden Eagle met Chief White Cloud's firm dark gaze. The unspoken command stood between them. Golden Eagle bowed his head in respect. As Sarah's father, the chief had every right to make this decision.

"Mary will be worrying," Ben said. "Let's get her home. She'll be fine. She's as strong and stubborn as they come." He rose and wiped his bloodied hands down the sides of his hide breeches.

Golden Eagle rose and cradled Sarah gently against his chest as he went to his horse.

Gray smoke hung in the air and ashes and sparks fell, covering everything in sight. All eyes returned to the smoldering fire. Ben shook his head, silently giving his sympathy to the old chief beside him.

White Cloud hung back as the two men turned toward the horses. "I will follow later. There is business I must attend to first." His gaze went back to the fire and his grieving warriors stood silent behind him.

Golden Eagle reached out and laid a comforting hand on his soon-to-be father-in-law. "I must leave now and tend to White Wind." Golden Eagle received an understanding nod, and placed Sarah in Ben's arms as he mounted.

As Golden Eagle reached down to take Sarah, a cheer went up from the silent warriors. Everyone stared as Jacob came from behind the burning shack, shouting. "Found 'em. I found 'em. Layin' in some bushes behind the burnin' building," Jacob yelled out, slowly leading Red Fox and Wild-Flower away from the blinding choking smoke.

Red Fox had his eyes closed against heat and smoke, his face red and swollen with burns. He gasped and choked as he inhaled, and his upper arms and chest were covered with angry red welts and blisters.

Away from the intense heat, Red Fox forced his eyes

open, stepped away from Jacob and on weak and wobbly legs, stopped in front of Wild-Flower's joyful father.

Wild-Flower, still coughing and choking, fell into her father's secure arms as others caught Red Fox.

With tears of happiness, White Cloud fell to the ground, where he stroked Wild-Flower's pale soot-streaked cheeks, murmuring his love and thankfulness. He glanced up to give his thanks to the brave warrior, and noticed that Red Fox had eyes only for Wild-Flower.

Wild-Flower turned her head and reached out to clutch Red Fox tightly. With a wry smile, White Cloud handed her back into Red Fox's arms. "You are the warrior my daughter has chosen. She is wise to follow her heart's desires. I see now it would have been wrong to force a marriage between two people who love others. I would be honored to call you son. You saved my daughter's life. I cannot repay the gift you have given to me this day."

Red Fox nodded and accepted help mounting, and finally the large group slowly made their way back to the house, leaving a small group behind to take care of the bodies and keep watch on the smoldering ruins.

Marring the crystal blue sky, thick plumes of steel-gray smoke rose from the distant tree tops. Climbing upward, dark fingers stretched across the horizon, blotting out the sun's bright rays as it rode the strong currents.

The acrid smell of burning wood drifted on the brisk afternoon breeze, while small gray flakes showered the earth with a fine mist of ashes.

Mary stood on the wooden porch, wringing her work-roughened hands, her attention riveted on the billowing smoke in the distance. Stray strands of hair blew across her face. Impatiently, she reached back and smoothed the loosened hair back into the bun at the nape of her neck, securing it firmly against the prying fingers of the persistent wind.

Pacing back and forth, she grew more impatient and worried as minutes slipped into hours. The agonizing wait had been worse the moment she'd spotted the fire in the distance hours ago. She closed her eyes tightly and once again prayed none had been hurt—except for those responsible for putting her baby in danger, she silently amended, not feeling the least bit guilty for that dark thought.

Moving swiftly, Mary went inside, letting the front door slam in her frustration. She shook her head and closed her eyes. "I've got to keep busy, or I'll go crazy with waiting." Clearing her mind of all depressing thoughts, she went to the stove and stoked the smoldering embers, watching with satisfaction as flames eagerly rose to consume the fresh wood.

Grabbing two huge black kettles, she filled them with cold water from the barrel outside the door and set one on the stove to boil and the other over the fireplace. She figured she would need one for hot strong coffee and one for any injuries, perish the thought.

With that in mind, she went to a small cupboard and reached for her cloth bandaging strips and healing herbs, and bustled about the warm kitchen until everything was readied to her satisfaction.

Long before she could see anyone, the ground vibrated and shook, signaling the approach of many horses. Mary grabbed the shotgun by the front door and waited, peering through a small crack in the open door. She also noticed Henry stationed by the barn.

Mary held her breath until the first riders broke through the cover of the trees. Relief relaxed some of the tension from her shoulders. She set her rifle down and opened the door as Ben rode directly to the front of the house.

Running down the wooden steps, Mary nearly collided with him as he swung from his saddle and ran to meet her. "Where is she, Ben? Where is Sarah? Tell me she's safe. Oh, God, why isn't she with you? She's not . . ." Mary choked, grabbing her husband.

Tenderly, Ben held her face and looked into her fearful eyes. "Easy, old woman. Calm yourself. Willy won't bother Sarah ever again. He's dead. Our girl is safe and should be here soon, but . . ."

Mary reached up and wrapped her arms tightly around Ben's neck, choking off his next words as she gave in to tears of joy and relief that Sarah was safe.

Ben grimaced. "Why do you women always have to get so damn emotional?" He tried to pull his wife away from him so he could explain further.

Just at that moment, the others galloped into the yard. Mary looked up expectantly, searching for Sarah. Her tearful smile of welcome faded. Her face blanched and her hands rose to cover her mouth and stifle her cry of horror when she saw Sarah, who lay pale and unconscious in Golden Eagle's arms. Her anguished eyes took in the bloodied and torn dress.

Forcing all thoughts of dread from her mind, Mary concentrated only on tending to Sarah. Pushing impatiently against Ben, freeing herself, Mary admonished him. "Why didn't you tell me Sarah was injured? Out of the way, old man. I must see to her."

Still muttering her complaints, Mary reached Golden Eagle, who was dismounting carefully, trying not to jar the unconscious and moaning Sarah.

Ben shook his head. "Women. Why do I bother tryin' to explain anything?" He stepped quickly out of the way as Mary sprang into action.

Humorously, he watched Mary turn to the fierce warriors and start giving orders, oblivious to their looks of wariness and bewilderment. She paid no mind to their fierceness as she impatiently led Golden Eagle into the house, shouting out orders, turning to make sure they obeyed.

"Gently now. In here. Hurry! Now lay her here. Careful, careful, that's it. Oh, my poor baby. You'll be all right. Mary'll fix you up. You'll see. Oh, dear, oh, dear," Mary moaned as she bustled into the cabin, shutting the door firmly.

Chapter Forty

Golden Eagle shook his head as if in a daze. He'd barely set Sarah gently onto a thickly cushioned platform, drawn a deep breath and leaned down to check her still-bleeding shoulder before a human whirlwind shoved him aside to place a bowl of hot boiled water on a small wooden table next to where Sarah lay moaning. In a flash, Mary flew across the room and returned with strips of white bandaging slung over one arm and several jars and pots clutched against her bosom.

Fascinated, Golden Eagle just stared. He'd never seen another human move so quickly. Shaking his head, he felt dizzy watching Mary dash about. Finally, after one last trip for toweling and bedding, Mary's small feet carried her swiftly to Sarah's side.

Moving back to make room for the woman, Golden Eagle straightened, then cursed the low ceiling overhead as he rubbed the tender spot on his head. Mary spared him a brief glance while picking up an old hunting knife. "This is where her pa use to sleep. Sarah slept upstairs in the loft." Her head indicated the rungs leading to an area up above his head. "It's a bit crowded in this narrow space. Wait."

Mary carried all her supplies to the fireplace. "Help me move that bed out here. It's warmer and there's more room." Carefully, the bed was moved and positioned near the fire. Supplies laid out to her satisfaction, Mary struggled to cut the strong deer-hide dress to remove the bloodied garment.

Coming to his senses, Golden Eagle stepped forward, gently put Mary aside and took his prized hunting knife from a painted sheath at his waist. Part of his war gear included a wide rawhide belt worn at the waist over the thong holding his breechclout in place. From there hung all items a warrior needed in battle.

Swiftly, Golden Eagle cut the dress from neck to shoulder and down each side, leaving two pieces for easy removal. Mary nodded her thanks, but Golden Eagle had already started to remove Sarah's clothing.

Mary's voice rose indignantly. "Here now, this isn't proper. I will tend to Sarah. You can wait outside with the rest of the menfolks. She'll be all right. You can see her later. Now go on, out with you."

Golden Eagle turned to Mary, but before he could speak, she continued, shaking a finger at him. "I have been taking care of this child for many years. You may sit with her after I have seen to her injury. I must get that wound cleaned and dressed quickly or infection will set in."

Golden Eagle spotted the disapproval written on the old woman's face. "White Wind will soon be my wife. I will help with her care. It is my duty to see to her needs." His voice brooked no argument, and his features hardened. He was ready to do battle if necessary to remain at Sarah's side where he belonged.

Even though Golden Eagle greatly admired this woman who wasn't afraid to speak her mind, who knew what needed to be done and got on with it, she'd not force him to leave. No one could.

Mary sighed, recognizing Golden Eagle's firm resolve. Shrugging, she turned away to soak a strip of toweling in warm water. Wringing out the excess water, she sent a stern warning toward Golden Eagle. "Ah, well, I might need help moving and holding Sarah while I tend to her and change the bedding," she stated grudgingly, subtly letting Golden Eagle know she was still in charge.

"With my help, we will finish sooner and that would be better for Sarah, would it not?" Golden Eagle queried, letting this woman know that he wasn't trying to usurp her position in Sarah's life.

His softly asked question seemed to work. Mary's hands fell from her hips as she started washing Sarah's bloodied shoulder, revealing an oozing hole.

"As there are none here who can help me any better, you may remain." Mary carefully bathed, inspected and washed all dried blood away from Sarah's still form. Before applying the bandages, she made a poultice from several herbs in the many jars and pots on the table, and reluctantly added some of Golden Eagle's, taken from a pouch dangling from his belt after Mary closely inspected the herbs first.

At last, Sarah was bathed and donned in a clean white nightdress that hid her bandaged shoulder, her pa's quilt pulled up to her chin. Her head rested on a fluffed-up pillow, and her golden hair was pulled to the side and tied with a length of ribbon.

"Feed her some of this for pain while I clean up and check on the others." Mary handed Golden Eagle a bowl of cooling tea.

Golden Eagle frowned and sniffed the liquid until he saw the tightening of Mary's lips. Straightening, he did as told, dribbling small amounts past Sarah's colorless lips. Setting the bowl down, he sat beside her, stroking his fingers up and down her wan cheeks as he murmured words of love and encouragement.

His eyes never left Sarah's colorless face. His hand clasped hers. Hours or mere minutes could have passed, but Golden Eagle forgot about everything and everyone around him. He paid no attention to the comings and goings as he willed his White Wind to heal. Fleetingly he wondered if their baby could possibly survive the boot kicks she'd received. He'd seen the ugly bruises covering her ribs and abdomen when he'd removed her clothing.

Soon her skin had the pink flush of fever, and Golden Eagle bathed her, kept her cool and when she moaned in pain, gently lifted her head and forced the pain-relieving liquid down her throat. His eyes glazed and he held his arms overhead, stretching weary and stiff limbs.

Mary thrust a cup of steaming liquid under his nose. "Here. Take this," she said. Golden Eagle glanced up and saw the older woman with two mugs of steaming brew in her hands. "It's coffee. Same as I gave all the others. Go ahead, drink it. It won't harm you. You look like you need it."

Golden Eagle took a tentative sip and found it strong, bitter but not unpleasant. He nodded his appreciation as Mary joined him, taking a seat on the other side of Sarah.

Golden Eagle raised his head as a thought came to mind. "Red Fox and Wild-Flower, have their burns been seen to?" he asked, realizing he'd neglected to ask about them in his worry over White Wind.

"I dressed their burns." Her eyes narrowed and she gave a snort. "Acted as if they didn't trust me either. They insist on remaining outside with the others."

Mary rose to her feet, setting her coffee down. Pacing, she stopped, folded her arms across her ample bosom and stared down at Golden Eagle. "I would have a promise from you, young man," she began.

Golden Eagle glanced up and found her uncompromising stern gaze leveled at him. He lifted his brows as her tone suggested he might still be a young brave, instead of one of the most powerful warriors in his village.

But he smiled indulgently and nodded for her to continue. "Speak Healing-Woman."

Mary seemed to startle when addressed with an Indian name. "I wish to attend Sarah's birthing. You must bring her here for the birth of the babe, or allow me to come to her when her time is ready. I want to see the safe delivery of her child."

Golden Eagle had just taken a large gulp of the still-hot coffee, and now he choked, sputtering as he stared in amazement at Mary. "How did you know White Wind carries my child?" he asked, wide-eyed. "Do you have the gift of sight, old woman?" Golden Eagle eyed Mary uneasily.

Mary grinned and relented. "I have sewn Sarah's clothes for many years. I watched her grow into womanhood. There are certain changes in a woman's body when she is with child that another woman would be instantly aware of."

Understanding dawned, and Golden Eagle grinned as he looked toward Sarah. He had not seen her for several weeks due to the buffalo hunt, and today he had been more concerned with her bullet wound and had not taken notice of her swelling abdomen.

Suddenly, concern clouded his face. "Tell me, Healing-Woman, has the child been harmed this day?"

Setting her empty mug down, Mary shook her head. "Sarah is young and healthy, despite her injuries. Your baby is well protected within her womb and I do not think you have anything to fear on that account." She glanced at Golden Eagle before she resumed speaking.

"I have seen for myself your love for her. You also saved her life and this I will remember always. It would make this old woman very happy if allowed to come and visit and to have her and her children visit here. This is still her home. It will always be here for her children and their children." Mary sat and waited, hands twisting her plain white cotton hanky with shaky fingers.

Golden Eagle sighed in relief. He would promise this and more if necessary to ease this woman's mind. After all, his White Wind loved this woman as a mother and their children would know her as another grandmother.

"I love Sarah and will provide all she needs. She is happy with my people, has earned their respect and friendship. She works hard and is always looking out for those in need. You have raised her well, Healing-Woman. She will be well treated and cared for. I will bring her to see you as often as is possible and will send for you before the birth of our child. Sarah would wish to have you with her."

Mary rose wearily and patted Golden Eagle on the shoulder. The long day of worry and waiting had taken its toll on her aging body. "Thank you. I will leave you as I have much work to do yet."

Afternoon quietly gave way to evening. Golden Eagle stood at the window of Sarah's cabin. Pushing the shutters further open, he glanced out and noticed the large circle of warriors not far from the buildings. Chief Hawk Eyes and White Cloud had accepted Ben's invitation to stay the night.

Most of the warriors, though, had gone into the woods to camp for the night, being too uncomfortable in the presence of white men and their wood structures.

This new friendship and blood tie between his people and Sarah's would take time to forge, but he was confident that these people of Sarah's were good, and therefore worthy to be called friends.

Wearily, he stretched, standing on tiptoe, rubbing a hand across his jaw as lack of sleep nearly overcame him. Turning, he started toward the ladder leading to the loft. Mary had told him Sarah had slept there. Because of her injury, they'd decided to leave her by the warm fire, but Golden Eagle felt the need to see where White Wind had once slept. Besides, he was so tired. If he didn't get up and move about, he was going to fall asleep where he stood.

Slowly he ascended and pulled himself up. Standing, he glanced up and remembered to duck his head as the ceiling was low. He stood by another set of closed shutters and opened these too, needing to have nature's light, air and sounds around him.

He looked out and far below. It was an odd sensation. Golden Eagle leaned against the wall and studied his strange surroundings. Her bed, much like the one down below, was covered with a bright blanket, a quilt the old woman had called it. The squares of material had been sewn in an eye-pleasing pattern.

There was one square wooden object to one side of the bed with an unlit candle resting on its surface. Reaching down, Golden Eagle pulled on the wooden knob and revealed a hidden compartment filled with Sarah's collectibles. There was another larger wooden box within this hidden space. This held white women's clothing. He shook his head. Why did whites have so many different pieces of clothing?

Scanning the rest of the darkened room, he smiled when he saw the blank stares of well-cared-for dolls and the soft shapes of various animals. He pulled one down. He stared down into a face lovingly stitched into an irresistible smile. Grinning back, he carefully replaced the soft doll. He thought of Winona. His sister had never seen dolls such as these and would love to see these white girl's toys.

A noise from below caught his attention. Looking over the railing, he saw Sarah twisting and flailing under her covers. Golden Eagle quickly scrambled down the ladder and returned to her side. He put his hand to her forehead. She was warm, but not too hot. Picking up the cool cloth Mary insisted he use, he wrung out the excess water as she'd instructed and wiped Sarah's face and neck. Dropping the cloth, he trailed his finger down her pale cheek. Closing his eyes, he prayed to the Great Spirit to heal his love.

"White Wind, will you not awaken? How long must you sleep? I love you, little one. When you are well, we will return to our home and I promise to keep you and our child safe.''

Golden Eagle continued to croon soft words of encouragement to Sarah. Speaking aloud to her was his only way to black out the terrible visions of her being held at gunpoint and then falling to the ground to save him from a bullet.

It was the only way he had to keep from scolding and lashing out at her for risking her life for his once again. Golden Eagle knew how close he'd come to losing White Wind forever. He shuddered, knowing he would have nightmares for weeks.

The door opened softly, admitting Chief White Cloud. He looked into the dark room and stopped beside his daughter. "Go rest, Golden Eagle. I will watch over White Wind. I have slept, you have not.''

Golden Eagle started to refuse, but had second thoughts. This was White Wind's father, a father who'd not known of his daughter's existence and then had nearly lost her. Golden Eagle respected White Cloud for giving him much time with his daughter. Now he must give White Cloud time alone with her as well.

Golden Eagle nodded. "I will rest.'' He gave White Cloud the same instructions Mary had given him, but still he hesitated to leave her to go outside. His hand stroked her hair one more time.

He glanced up and pointed for White Cloud's benefit. "I will sleep up there. I will be close if she awakes and calls for me.''

At the chief's nod, Golden Eagle made his way to the loft once again, but this time he stretched himself out on the feather-stuffed bed. Before Golden Eagle could worry over the prospect of nightmares, the warriors outside or even the excessive softness he sank into, he was asleep.

Chapter Forty-one

White Cloud leaned forward, elbows on knees, head resting in his hands. No one needed to remind him of his good fortune, that Sarah and Wild-Flower had survived their ordeal at the hands of the white men.

He lifted his head, one hand rubbing the weariness and shock as if to wipe it away. If only he had known before leaving her that Emily would give birth to a child conceived that wonderful summer so long ago. His face pinched with pain. His lungs contracted painfully and his breath came in shallow gasps. He shook his head because in his heart, even if he'd known, his fate had been sealed. He could have done nothing different.

White Cloud stood and leaned over the bed, gathering the courage to study his newfound daughter, something as yet he'd not been brave enough to do. Tears formed in his eyes. His heart hammered, the pulse echoing in his ears as his mouth worked silently. He stared in amazement as he studied each and every delicate feature. White Cloud drew a raspy breath. Sarah's features were so like her mother's, the years melted away and he beheld his lost love again.

Tears coursed down his wrinkled leathery cheeks as he remembered the gentle young woman he had loved and cared for. Their time together had been short, but Emily had meant so much to him that thoughts of her rekindled an ache in his old heart, even after all these years.

Looking upon Sarah, White Cloud knew he would never forget that summer with Emily. He also hoped Small Bird would accept White Wind into their family as his eldest child, for he knew he would never turn his back on her. Wild-Flower already looked upon White Wind as her sister, and Running Wolf did not seem to mind that he now had an older sister, and was even showing signs of brotherly protection, much to Golden Eagle's annoyance.

As the minutes ticked by, White Cloud became immersed in long-buried memories, became the young man he had once been. Taken in by his father's brother when his parents were brutally murdered, he had grown up with tribal warring. And when he'd become old enough to participate, he'd gone on raids, become part of the vicious cycle of tribe retaliating against tribe.

And then, scenes from that wondrous peaceful summer when he'd roamed at will flashed across the lids of his closed eyes. The miles of earth he'd walked across, the long, solitary hours spent on top of a mountain, listening to the wind, and the nights sleeping out in the open, the tall prairie grass hiding him from his enemies, the dark sky filled with bright flickering light.

Suddenly, he frowned, the stars in his mind obscured by the thick smoke from the burned wagon. In quick flashes came the image of the white girl, curled in a fetal position, crying, alone and frightened.

As long as he lived, he knew he'd never forget those months shared with the white girl. That summer had been one of the happiest times of his life. Their love grew stronger each day, unlike anything he'd ever known, but it was not destined to be. His arranged wife-to-be awaited his

363

return. The pain of leaving Emily was as sharp and piercing today as it had been 18 years ago.

A moan reached his ears, followed by another. White Cloud's eye's flew open, his mind cleared of past memories when he realized the soft moans were coming from White Wind, not from him.

Sarah tossed restlessly, her covers twisting around her hot body, whimpers of pain escaping her gasping lips, as her body fought the return to consciousness. White Cloud picked up the cloth that Golden Eagle had laid aside and gently wiped her face, squeezing some moisture onto her parched lips.

"Come, daughter, leave the dream world behind. Open your eyes. You are safe now," he coaxed his daughter in a trembling husky voice.

Eyes the color of snow-fed streams flickered open, glazed with fever, and quickly closed as another spasm of pain racked her young body.

White Wind's pain became his as he reassured both of them, "You will heal quickly, daughter. You are strong and brave. Do not fight the pain. Breathe deeply. That's it. Slowly now."

Slipping his arm carefully beneath her head, White Cloud gently raised her head and coaxed her to drink a few sips of the cool pain-numbing tea.

White Cloud held his daughter until she relaxed, the herbs numbing her pain and easing her fever.

Sarah opened her eyes again as the pain subsided to a dull throbbing and stared at the stranger leaning over her. She blinked her eyes, but couldn't seem to focus or think clearly. She didn't even know where she was, but there was something she desperately needed to know. If only the clouds hovering over her would stay away until she thought of what it was.

Her hand went to her throat, but the necklace was gone, her eagle. "Golden Eagle," she croaked, nightmarish flashes of the scene with Willy coming at her fast and furious. The last thing she remembered was Willy aiming his gun at Golden Eagle.

She panicked and tried to rise, but a cry of pain escaped as her shoulder, stiff and sore, protested with sharp, piercing throbs. Gasping, tears blurring her sight, Sarah sobbed in barely audible words, "Golden Eagle. Golden Eagle. Where are you?"

Strong hands gently held her still, urging her to remain calm. She tried to fight, but had no strength. The desire to yield to the fog surrounding her was overwhelming as the herbs worked to claim her mind once again. Her eyes closed against her will. Her pain eased. Sarah struggled to focus on the words being spoken near her ear.

"Rest easy, daughter. Golden Eagle is well. Your actions this day have saved his life. Soon you will be strong and see for yourself. Sleep now."

Relief flowed through her. Safe. The stranger's voice kept whispering over and over. Her hands gravitated toward her middle. "My baby," she whispered weakly.

"The child within you is safe. Now hush, daughter. No more questions. When you are well, we will talk. Sleep now," the soothing voice commanded.

Sarah let her body relax to the soft harmonic crooning. But something kept tugging at her. He called her daughter. That wasn't right. Her father was dead. No, her pa was dead. Her brows wrinkled in confusion. She didn't know her father yet. But why . . .

White Cloud rose as Sarah's breathing deepened and once again she fell into a long, deep, healing sleep.

All the next day Sarah slept, waking only for brief moments to accept water, teas and soup that were spooned into her mouth. She slept, oblivious to hands that bathed her with cool rags, and never heard any of the commotion of people coming and going.

Mary allowed Golden Eagle to take over Sarah's care, relieving him so he could eat and rest. Many times White

Cloud and Hawk Eyes also came in to sit at her side. For two more days, heat raged through Sarah's body as she fought off infection.

On the evening of the third day, the outside door opened tentatively to admit Wild-Flower and Red Fox. Gingerly, they stepped into the darkened room, casting a warm glow onto the shadowed wall as they entered, Wild-Flower carrying a candle-lit lantern.

Wild-Flower glanced around in curiosity as she set the lantern down. "Healing-Woman asked me to bring you this light-flame."

With Red Fox at her side, as she'd been nervous about entering the large wooden house, Wild-Flower's eyes grew round as she took in a way of life she'd only heard about, but never seen.

"How is White Wind, my brother?" Red Fox inquired, noting Sarah's pale, drawn features.

Golden Eagle sighed deeply. "She is resting, my friends. The Healing-Woman says exhaustion is causing her to sleep so long. She says the wound is healing and the heat seems to have left her body. I will wait for White Wind to awaken and show me she is recovering," Golden Eagle declared.

Wild-Flower approached and looked down at the sleeping white girl. Sitting on the opposite side, she put her hand over her sister's relaxed fingers. "Father has told me we are sisters. I like this idea of being sister to your White Wind. An older sister is welcome, and I will be aunt to your children as well."

Grinning mischievously, Wild-Flower added, "Our fathers sit under the full moon planning our weddings and discussing their first grandchild. You were right, Golden Eagle. The *Wakan Tanka* showed our fathers his true path."

Sobering, she looked to Red Fox, love shining brightly as she grasped his hand, careful of the bandages Healing-Woman had insisted on applying. Wild-Flower shuddered as she recalled just how close she'd come to being trapped in that burning building.

After Sarah had been taken out by the white man, sparks and burning pieces of the brittle dry roof had fallen in, igniting everything they touched. Bound to the wooden bed frame, Wild-Flower could not flee the hungry flames. Desperate, she'd managed to retrieve the knife that Willy had dropped and forgotten.

But it took her too long to cut the ropes. By then smoke filled the room, making it impossible to see the doorway.

In her dreams she still saw the flames licking at the old mattress, heard the crackling and popping noises made by the fire as it consumed the entire space around her.

Just when she'd given up hope, sounds of ripping and tearing had her searching the smoke-filled room, her eyes burning and her lungs near to bursting for air. Red Fox had ripped off the rotting boards at the back to lead her out. She'd never forget the relief that had surged through her when she felt his strong arms lift and carry her, coughing and gasping, past angry flames to safety. Even now, she had to fight her apprehension at just being in a wooden building again.

A light touch brought her eyes up as Golden Eagle's strong hand helped her to her feet. Wild-Flower nodded her head in silent acknowledgment. "We leave you now. I will tell Father that White Wind still sleeps."

Golden Eagle watched Red Fox and Wild-Flower leave, happy that things had worked out so well for them. Turning back to White Wind, Golden Eagle carefully stretched out beside her and closed his eyes.

Chapter Forty-two

A dull throbbing ache invaded Sarah's safe warm cocoon, bringing her out of her deep sleep. She attempted to snuggle closer to a warmth that even in her unconscious state she knew represented safety and comfort, a haven from nightmares and pain.

Her movement, slight though it was, brought a sharp stab of pain to her shoulder, causing eyes clear of fever to fly open. Black shadows lurked on walls of wood, thrown there by the lone low-burning candle. Sarah took careful calm breaths until the pain subsided as one of her dream voices had instructed.

A puzzled look entered her shadowed eyes. Had it been a dream? She was still groggy and disoriented and she knew she had been hurt, but where? Experimentally, she moved each limb.

First she moved her legs, one at a time. She sighed. They were a bit stiff, but otherwise all right. Likewise, she could move her right arm, but when she attempted to move her left arm, burning shafts of fireballs tore through her, causing her to bite her lower lip until she tasted blood. She forced herself to remain still, and continued the slow deep breathing until the pain returned to a dull throb.

Opening her eyes again, Sarah moved only her head as she looked around, trying to get her bearings. Her eyes fell on a crudely made corner chair with its embroidered pillow—her first attempt at embroidery, she fondly recalled. She relaxed as her eyes lit upon item after item of familiarity. She was home. A soft smile tilted her lips and she sighed. Home. What a sweet sound that had.

Wait. This wasn't home. Not anymore. Home was a pallet of furs on the ground, walls of sewn-together buffalo hides. Home was Golden Eagle's tipi. Where was he? Sarah panicked, and just then felt movement beside her. Fearfully she turned, and found herself nose-to-nose with the most wonderful sight of all. Golden Eagle!

Lifting her good arm to his smooth face, unable to see clearly, Sarah spoke, her voice hoarse with disuse. "You weren't hurt? Willy didn't shoot you? I'm not dreaming, am I?"

"No, my sweet one. I am unharmed." His brows drew together suddenly. "Except for the scare you gave me. Do not ever step between me and my enemy again. I forbid it," Golden Eagle commanded as he slid off the bed and gently lifted her head, careful not to jar her wound and cause undue pain. Placing a cup of cool water to her dry cracked lips, he urged her to sip. When she had her fill, he carefully laid her back and checked her shoulder dressing for signs of fresh bleeding.

Sarah sighed with relief, but thoughts of Willy made her look anxiously around. Her chin was tipped toward Golden Eagle. "You will never have to worry about the one who caused so much pain to us all," he reassured her. "He will never bother anyone again."

Sarah closed her eyes and shuddered, blocking out the horrible nightmare. She was thankful that she'd never have to worry about Willy again, but a small part of her was sorry that it had had to end the awful way it did.

"No regrets, White Wind. Your guardian chose his path," Golden Eagle said, recognizing the look of sorrow on Sarah's face.

"I know." A fragment of a dream came back to her and she concentrated, drawing her brows together as she tried to remember. Her father? She'd dreamed her father had sat here beside her. Was that possible? No, she must've been dreaming. "Some dream. I just wish it had been true," she said more to herself than to Golden Eagle.

"What dream? What are you talking about, White Wind?" Golden Eagle asked.

Sarah smiled in the semi-darkness and spoke softly. "I had a dream. A strange wonderful dream."

Receiving a nod of encouragement, Sarah continued. "I dreamed my father sat here, holding my hand, talking to me, but how can that be? We don't even know who he is yet or if he still lives," Sarah sighed regretfully.

Golden Eagle got to his feet and tucked the covers gently around her shoulders. "I'll be right back," he promised.

A few minutes later, the door opened, but the bed was back under the loft and Sarah couldn't see who entered.

Golden Eagle reappeared, and behind him stood three people. She recognized one. "Wild-Flower! You're safe," she exclaimed, struggling to sit. Golden Eagle helped her sit and sat behind her, supporting her.

Sarah leaned back, fighting waves of tiredness but not wanting to sleep anymore. Wild-Flower came and stood at the foot of the bed grinning. "It is good to see the sister of Wild-Flower awake."

Before Sarah could reply another person came into view. After a few moments, Sarah recognized him to be Wild-Flower's older brother. "This warrior is very happy to see both his sisters alive and well. Running Wolf welcomes White Wind as his sister."

Sarah nodded in return, perplexed. But before she could question his odd statement, an older man came forward, tears in his eyes. But unlike Wild-Flower and Running Wolf, he came right to the side of her bed and reached for her hand.

Golden Eagle leaned forward. "White Wind, this is Chief White Cloud, father to Running Wolf, Wild-Flower and . . . to you. This, White Wind, is your father."

Sarah stared speechlessly. "How . . ."

White Cloud spoke. "It is a story that I will tell you when you are stronger. For now, know that we are your family and welcome you, firstborn child to Chief White Cloud." He motioned Running Wolf and Wild-Flower to join him.

Tears welled and spilled down Sarah's cheeks. She lifted a corner of her blanket to wipe her eyes as she stared from one face to another, always returning to her father's as the talk turned to general news. Sarah did find out that she had one more sister and two more brothers. A family! She now belonged to a large family.

White Cloud rose as Sarah struggled to keep her eyes open, and her mind focused on the talk around her. He motioned his two children out. "There has been enough excitement this day. White Wind must rest now." He held his hand up to still Sarah's protest. "Do not fight your need to rest. And do not argue with your father. Your eyes keep drooping," his voice chided gently.

"You'll be here tomorrow?" Sarah asked, half afraid that he would be gone in the morning.

"Yes, daughter. When *Wi* shows her face, I will return to your side," White Cloud promised as he turned and left.

Sarah sighed and leaned back, her strength gone. "Oh, I'm so tired, but I don't want to sleep. I'm afraid I'll wake up and find out it was just a dream."

Golden Eagle got up and stretched out beside Sarah, tucking her close beside him, mindful of her injury. "It's no dream. Your father is here. Hush now. Let us rest."

Nodding her blond head, Sarah relaxed next to her golden warrior, and before she knew it she had fallen asleep, her heart lightened by the prospect of seeing her new family on the new day.

Six weeks later, Sarah paced restlessly across the wooden porch, her boots thumping in agitation as she stopped to scan the countryside. But seeing nothing of interest in the watery-blue horizon, she gave a sigh of impatience and resumed her pacing.

Standing just inside the doorway, Mary shook her head in exasperation. Stepping outside, clucking her tongue, she gently scolded. "It will do you no good to get so worked up, young lady. Your husband will be here any day for you, and your pacing and pathetic sighs will not bring him here any faster. Now sit and eat. What will he say if he finds you in ill health from all this needless worry?"

"But Mary, it's been such a long time already. What if something happens to him? What if he doesn't return for me?" Sarah worried aloud, chewing her lower lip. Her fingers tangled in her necklace as she worried the beads, eagle, locket and the newest addition—a small wooden carving of feet with outstretched wings.

Mary pulled forth a rocker with a thick padded seat and waited for Sarah to seat herself. From her first day out of bed, Sarah had taken to spending most of her convalescing hours sitting on the porch, claiming she felt closer to Golden Eagle as she imagined him staring at the same blue sky.

"That's enough, Sarah. Golden Eagle will be here before you know it. Why, it took all of us to convince him to leave you here for your own good, so you could recover and get back your strength when the time came to return with his people. He'll be here any day, you mark my words. Now sit and eat. I have my chores to do yet and cannot stand here holding your lunch all day."

Sarah flung herself into the chair, took the proffered tray of bread, meat and fruit and watched Mary retreat into the house. She would miss Mary when the time came for her

372

to leave. Tears gathered, and her eye lids drooped with sadness. With a determined shake of her head, she put her depressing thoughts aside. Tears, it seemed, came easily to her these days.

Sarah forgot her sad thoughts as her stomach growled, reminding her of her hunger. She quickly ate every morsel of the meal Mary had prepared for her.

Fully recovered from the gunshot wound, she now only experienced a bit of stiffness and tenderness. As each day of her recovery passed, her appetite grew, as did her belly. The baby was growing rapidly and becoming stronger each day.

Looking at her bulging abdomen, Sarah smiled, and laughed aloud when the tray resting against it moved ever so slightly, threatening to tip over. Removing the tray, Sarah patted her belly. "Won't your father be surprised to see how you have grown?" She leaned her head back, closed her eyes and took a few moments to rest.

The movements of the baby had become much more noticeable in the last few weeks. Last week a definite kick had startled her, causing her to drop and break a bowl she'd been washing.

A short time later, Sarah rose, unable to sit any longer in the weak warmth of the sun. What to do now? As Golden Eagle was due any day, she had already packed her things.

Leaning against one of the supporting pillars, Sarah frowned as she remembered the day he'd left to return to his home without her. It had been decided, not by her, that she would stay and remain under Mary's care to heal and recover her strength before making the long trip back to the Black Hills.

Golden Eagle had been reluctant to leave her, but Mary had pointed out that she was safe in her own home now, and she and Ben would nurse Sarah back to health so she could make the journey without endangering their baby.

The two chiefs had also agreed. They each needed to get back to their tribes and prepare for the moves down to the prairie for the summer celebrations. The summer celebrations would also include a combined wedding feast between the two tribes.

Sarah and Wild-Flower had decided they wanted to be married in a double ceremonial, but as Sarah was to remain behind to heal, Golden Eagle and Red Fox had convinced the two chiefs to perform a simple ceremony at the house, allowing Mary and Ben to take part in Sarah's wedding. A more elaborate ceremony and the celebrating and feasting would follow upon Sarah's return to her tribe.

So here she sat waiting impatiently for her husband to fetch her. It was mid-September, over a month since Golden Eagle had left.

Already nature had changed her seasons. The leaves were turning color and the air was much cooler in the mornings. Soon the rains would turn to snow.

"This is ridiculous! I can't sit here any longer," Sarah exclaimed as she pushed open the door and went inside. In the small kitchen area she helped Mary in an attempt to keep busy, but as her mind was not on the chores, she was more in the way.

When Sarah's absent-minded fumbling caused her to drop a heavy cast-iron pan onto the floor, startling Mary, who nearly cut herself peeling potatoes, Mary's nerves snapped.

"Out! You're nearly as bad as Ben in the kitchen today, child. Out with you till you can keep your mind on what you're doing," she ordered the sheepishly grinning girl.

"Oh, Mary. I'm sorry. What can I do? I'm going crazy just sitting and waiting. I'm not used to this. At Golden Eagle's village there is so much to do that this waiting is killing me," Sarah wailed as she apologized.

Mary shook her head. Oh, to be young and in love again. She had an idea and snapped her fingers. "Why don't you go for a short ride before dinner? Ben is somewhere out in the yard working today. Ask him to go with you," she suggested.

Sarah's eyes brightened. "What a wonderful idea, Mary. What would I do without you?" Sarah sobered as her words hit home. "What will I do without you, Mary?"

Mary blinked her tears away and replied gruffly, wondering what she'd do without Sarah around, "You'll do just fine, young lady. I didn't raise you to be attached to my apron strings, now did I? Now, away with you, you scamp. I've got dinner to see to. Don't be late now," she instructed as she shooed Sarah out.

A few minutes later Sarah rode leisurely toward the meadow, leaving Ben to follow behind at his own pace. Slowly, she guided her horse to the center of the field and looked around.

Dismounting, she led the horse to the tree where she and her pa had had their last picnic together, and tethered the animal loosely so he could nibble at the grassy shoots.

Ben, she noticed, had remained at the edge of the woods, still seated on his horse, whittling on a piece of wood, chips flying in all directions. Sarah thought of all the intricate wood carving Ben had done for her to give to her new families.

She smiled as she pulled out her necklace, the number of dangling objects increasing. Just before leaving the barn, Ben had presented her with a new charm. The miniature of Great Star left no doubt in her mind that Ben was competing with Golden Eagle and her father.

Ben's eyes never left Sarah's wandering form for long. He knew Mary would skin him alive if anything further happened to Sarah. A movement in the woods behind Sarah caused him to reach for his rifle.

Recognition dawned in his craggy old face when he caught sight of the warrior still hidden in the woods. His face broke out into a welcoming grin. Silently, he gave a wave of acknowledgment, and quietly took up his reins to head back the way he'd come.

Chapter Forty-three

Unaware of Golden Eagle's arrival, Sarah continued to wander, remembering many of the good memories she'd forgotten. Her hand rested on her swelling abdomen, caressing the growing life there. Would Golden Eagle be pleased or would he view her swelling body with horror and not want anything to do with her? So lost in her worries and thoughts was she, that when words were spoken, Sarah thought at first she was hearing voices of the past.

"So, we met again, my pale-haired love," Golden Eagle called out, grinning and dismounting. Sarah squealed, her face lighting with joy. All worries were forgotten as she raced across the grassy meadow and flung herself into his outstretched welcoming arms. "You came back. You're finally here," she cried out, tears of happiness running down her healthy pink cheeks.

Tipping her chin with one finger, Golden Eagle gently wiped her tears as he tenderly inquired, "Did you doubt that I would return for you, wife of mine? We belong to each other, and nothing could have prevented me from coming for you." His head lowered as his lips claimed hers.

Sarah locked her arms around his powerful shoulders, sliding them around his neck, and stood on her toes to eagerly meet his lips with hers. With a deep welcoming sigh, she opened her lips to his probing tongue.

Golden Eagle's hands lovingly traced her curves down to her rounded bottom, where he tucked her into the cradle of his hips. His tongue delved deeper into her receptive cavern, tasting and exploring. At Sarah's insistence, he allowed her the same freedom, groaning as her small thrusting tongue dueled with his.

With reluctance, Sarah pulled away, fully aware of where this would lead. "How I wish we could make love here in this special place," she sighed.

Golden Eagle reached out to cup one swollen breast and asked, "What is there to stop us, my love?"

Sarah reached up to caress his bronzed face. "We can't. We must stop. Ben awaits me in the woods," she explained.

Golden Eagle grinned. Teasingly he inquired, "And if Ben were not waiting in the woods, what would be your wish, my sweet White Wind?"

Blushing, Sarah lowered her eyes to his gleaming chest and shyly stated, "If we were truly alone, I would wish for my golden husband to love me here and now." She looked directly into his eyes as she finished seriously, "I have missed you so much, Golden Eagle. It seems forever since we last shared our love for each other. I ache for you in a way that I've never known before. My love grows stronger each day."

"My heart has longed to hear those words these many days of separation," Golden Eagle whispered. "It has been long since I have touched you as a man touches his wife. I too suffer a great ache. I need you, White Wind. Feel how much this warrior needs you." Golden Eagle placed Sarah's hand over his throbbing loins.

Sarah glanced between them and grinned. "Your breechclout does not hide your need from eyes, Golden Eagle. Let us hope Ben does not notice!''

Golden Eagle leaned down to nuzzle her throat. "We are alone, little one."

Sarah sighed. Her breathing grew shallow and rapid with desire. "No," she said, "Ben is here." Sarah twisted in Golden Eagle's arms, looked back to where Ben had been and saw nothing. "Where is . . ." Turning back to Golden Eagle, she caught his teasing grin, watched his eyes dance with laughter.

"He's gone, isn't he? He knew you were here and left," Sarah said, then laughed with joy. "That's a rotten trick, Golden Eagle." Her eyes lit up with impishness.

Sarah slid her hand down his chest and stopped at the leather ties. Quickly the knot was undone and her fingers were threading through springy black curls.

Golden Eagle sucked in his breath. Mesmerized by Sarah's playful behavior, he'd not stopped her from removing his breechclout, nor had he stopped her fingers as they threaded through his thick mat of curls. But when her hand closed around his turgid manhood and stroked his soft velvety flesh, a groan escaped his lips.

"So, my golden warrior likes to tease, does he?" Sarah stepped away, her soft chuckle filling the air.

Golden Eagle opened his eyes as her hand stilled and fell from his pulsing flesh. He glanced into eyes of blue that sparkled with mischief.

Sarah saw the exact moment Golden Eagle realized she'd repaid him by teasing him in a most unfair manner. She took a step back. He advanced. Sarah laughed, and ran when a low growl erupted from his throat. Laughing and chasing each other, Golden Eagle and Sarah played as children in the shadows of the quiet meadow.

Not even winded, Golden Eagle caught Sarah, who sat gasping for breath, and lifted her high into the air. Under the sheltering trees, Golden Eagle lowered them both to the tall grass as they gazed into each other's eyes, all laughter and teasing gone.

Golden Eagle slowly undid her plain blue dress, allowing it to pool at her feet. Piece by piece, each of her under garments fell until she was revealed to him in the dusk of the evening.

Sarah watched Golden Eagle stare at her bulging belly and swollen breasts, and blushed uncomfortably. "I'm afraid our baby is already making his mother fat and unsightly," she whispered, embarrassed.

Golden Eagle ran his palm over Sarah's belly and reassured her. "Do not worry, my love. To me, you grow more beautiful each day. You are the mother of my child and I look forward to seeing him or her grow big within you."

Golden Eagle ran his finger gently over the puckered, scarred flesh of her shoulder. "Do you still have pain from your wound?"

Sarah shook her head. "Not much. It is nearly healed." Sarah leaned into Golden Eagle, her expression reveling in the wonderful feeling of flesh meeting flesh. "Please, Golden Eagle, love me."

They sank to the ground as one, and their lips meet and hands roamed freely as each sought to quench the fires of desire.

Sarah moaned as Golden Eagle teased one swollen bud, then the other, the flesh especially sensitive to each caress. Her hips lifted and his lowered, moving in small circles to an age-old rhythm as Golden Eagle brushed his pulsing shaft against her.

Unable to wait any longer, Golden Eagle positioned himself over her and thrust deep. Their hips rose and fell, meeting and parting, as all movement became frenzied and all breathing labored.

"Golden Eagle," Sarah cried as deep shudders went through her. Golden Eagle heard her cry and answered with his own. "White Wind, my love." And with his final thrust, his cries joined hers and their bodies throbbed as one.

The next day dawned bright and clear. Sarah and Mary hugged each other tightly, tears streaming down their faces as they bid each other good-bye.

Golden Eagle stood with Ben, making sure that their horses were ready and the supplies on the two packhorses were tied securely. Ben and Mary had insisted they take various staples such as flour, sugar, coffee and dried meats as well as cloth, sewing threads and Sarah's favorite, a Dutch oven. Most would be given as gifts. Sarah had also packed her childhood toys. Some for her children and some for Winona, Spotted Deer and Two Feathers.

Ben and Golden Eagle shook hands and walked over to the tearful women. "Come, White Wind. We must leave now. We have far to go this day," Golden Eagle reminded her, anxious to get under way and to be alone with her for a few days.

Embarrassed, Golden Eagle allowed Mary to hug him tightly. "Rest assured, Healing-Woman, that I will keep my promise and send for you before the babe is born."

Sitting on her horse, Sarah allowed herself to be led away as she waved her good-byes until the trees swallowed Ben and Mary from sight. "Come now, wife, dry your tears. We will see them again soon."

"I know, husband. You made them very happy with your gifts. I saw Ben practicing with his bow and arrows this morning, and Mary loved the parfleche your mother made her, as well as the warm moccasins and buffalo robes they sent."

"Your family is ours. Come, let us ride now," Golden Eagle stated, proudly patting the English-made dagger sheathed at his waist.

For the next few days, Golden Eagle kept the pace slow. He stopped often, making sure White Wind rested and ate.

When they came to streams, they would stop and bathe, frolicking in the water till they were tired. Their few days turned into two weeks.

Every moment was spent talking, touching and learning from each other. The pace of village life had not allowed this luxury. After their long separation, each had much to say.

Sarah listened to Golden Eagle's ideas to keep his tribe safe from the rising numbers of white men, and his hopes for his people and for them and their family.

Golden Eagle learned about her life with her stepfather, her dreams and her idea to teach the children of his tribe English as the trapper had done before her.

She, like him, felt it would be needed in the future. She would also teach the customs and history of the white man. All of this would make these people stronger in the future, for she knew in her heart that someday the whites would outnumber the Indians.

Their love grew, previous barriers crumbled and they were free to build a firm foundation for their future. They spent their last evening on the trail locked in each other's arms. Golden Eagle explained what to expect when they arrived on the new day.

"Your father, new mother and brothers and sisters and all of their tribe will be there. Our marriage as well as the marriage of Red Fox and Wild-Flower will be held again in three of your days. We will have no more time alone. You will stay in the tipi of your family until we are married again."

Sarah glanced up in surprise. "But we were already married and even sharing the same tipi before that. Why is this?"

"We are now man and wife as are Red Fox and Wild-Flower, but those of both tribes will expect to witness the marriage between their future chief and his wife. And Wild-Flower and Red Fox have chosen to wait for your return, so we will have a formal double ceremony for all to behold.

Afterwards, there will be many days of celebrating between the two tribes. Remember, not only will we be married, but our marriage officially ends all hostilities and rights the wrongs of the past. As for remaining in my tipi, my people knew that while you were my captive the sharing of my tipi was expected. But since you are the daughter of a respected chief, all normal courtship rules must now apply.''

Sarah lifted herself on one elbow and asked, ''If I am to be kept away from you until we marry, how is it you were allowed to come for me alone?''

Golden Eagle chuckled. ''Your father is a wise man, my love. He knew nothing short of tying me up would have kept me from coming after you. But he made it quite clear that the moment we set foot in the village, his wishes would be respected or I would answer to him.''

Sarah smiled and lay back down, pulling Golden Eagle to her. ''You can be very stubborn when you choose. My father is indeed wise if he recognized this in you.''

''Hmm, I seem to know another who perhaps matches my stubbornness. We seem to be well matched, little one,'' he commented as he covered her from above. ''Well matched in more ways than one, don't you think?'' he asked, not bothering to wait for an answer as he proceeded to show her just how well matched they were.

Chapter Forty-four

Sarah sat before a warm fire, looking about her, studying her handiwork with a frown. Everything had to be perfect. To her eye, all appeared ready. The sleeping mats were laid and she kept the small fire going at all times. Some of her cooking utensils and food hung in decorated parfleches, ready for their expected guests.

Adding another small log to the glowing embers, she braced herself for the task of rising. First, she rolled to her knees, then began the difficult job of getting to her feet. The sudden appearance of a hand under her elbow guided her to her feet effortlessly.

"If this baby gets any bigger, I won't be able to get up at all," Sarah wailed.

Golden Eagle laughed at the familiar complaint. "I guess you will just have to stay in bed and let all think Golden Eagle has a lazy wife," he teased, slipping his arms around Sarah, holding her close, as close as was possible with her swollen belly. "Hmm, that doesn't sound so bad to me," Golden Eagle said, reconsidering.

Sarah playfully socked him in the stomach. "Oh, you! Will you be serious? There is much to be done yet," she stated as she once again surveyed the newly erected tipi.

Golden Eagle sighed in mock disappointment. He too glanced around. "You have done well. Healing-Woman and Woodcarver-Who-Lives-in-Woods will be pleased. But it is time for you to return to our tipi. All is ready here and I wish for some time with my wife on this cold day. Your family will not arrive for at least another day."

Golden Eagle took Sarah by the hand, draped a heavy robe of buffalo fur across her shoulders and lifted the flap to usher her out into the bitter cold, helping her across the frozen ground, last night's snowfall nearly gone.

As Golden Eagle opened the flap to their tipi, warmth rushed out to greet them, and once inside, Golden Eagle removed her heavy buffalo robe, a devilish glint flashing from eyes as black as night. "There is another fire my wife needs to see to. It burns hot and strong."

"And will I be able to put out this fire, my husband?" she joked, still in awe over how little it took to flame the fires of their love.

Golden Eagle grew serious and cradled Sarah's face between his hands, giving her such a long loving look that Sarah felt as if she'd just caught on fire herself and would quickly melt into a pool of molten heat at his feet.

"No, White Wind. As long as we live, my fire will burn hot for you. It will never die, but continue to grow stronger each day. There is none in this land who can put out the flames of my desire, for to do so would be to destroy me. I would become nothing more than a cold empty body without you at my side each and every day. I love you, White Wind. You are the fuel that feeds my fires."

Sarah's eyes misted over. The strength of their love never failed to amaze her. "And I love you, my golden warrior."

The days that followed were long and hard for all. Winter had raged its fury on the small village. As a result, most kept to their tipis, venturing out only when necessary.

Sarah stared at the surrounding walls in frustration. She was cooped up and needed to get out, but both Golden Eagle and Mary had forbidden her to leave the tipi without one of them, and then only if it was necessary. She might slip or get too cold, or too wet, she was told repeatedly.

She longed to go visit Bright Blossom or Wild-Flower. She was desperate enough to even put up with Night Star's company. She and Matosapa had arrived to winter with Striking Snake, afraid he might not survive another harsh winter. Night Star had changed, had mellowed and had even managed to make new friends within her old tribe.

Sarah frowned as she thought of Night Star. Within days of their arrival, the other girl had followed her down to the stream and had confessed that she had been responsible for the white men who had kidnapped Sarah. With tears in her eyes, Night Star had begged Sarah to forgive her and keep her evil deed between them. She now loved her husband, was to bear his first child and seemed eager to put the past behind her. Sarah had agreed.

She had known that it would have only been a matter of time before Willy had found her anyway, and she too was eager to put the past behind them. Night Star had presented her with several finely crafted infant garments which had been meant for her babe but which she insisted Sarah have. She, Night Star, would have time to make new ones for her own babe, she'd stated.

Sarah sighed, letting out her pent-up breath, and looked down at herself. She was sick of this unwieldy condition. A strong kick to her ribs alerted her to the baby's restlessness. Her hand covered her belly protectively.

"So you are restless too, hmm. Well, there's not much to see or do this day, I'm afraid. We are both to be prisoners of our surroundings for yet another day. Your ma's been in such a bad state with her temper that your pa went out to brave the horrible weather to get away," Sarah complained aloud.

"Can't say I blame him, though. I have been in a rotten mood lately," Sarah groaned, automatically rubbing her belly to calm her little one before putting her hand to her lower back to ease the stiffness.

Golden Eagle stood outside listening to White Wind talk to the baby. For the last two days, she'd been moody, emotional and hard to be around. Healing-Woman and Seeing Eyes just smiled and nodded knowingly. It was to be expected, they told him.

He shook his head, confused. Why were females so difficult to understand? Taking a deep breath, he adjusted the smoke flaps of the tipi and let himself into the warmth inside, going to the fire to warm his cold hands. He kept an eye on Sarah, watching warily as she continued to pace. She reminded him of a she-cat about to pounce.

Enough of this, he decided. He'd been told by all that she should remain inside, quiet and calm, until the babe came, but he couldn't stand any more of this. His wife was far from calm and her agitated pacing was driving him crazy.

He strode over to the pile of furs and held her robe out in front of him. "Come, we are going for a walk. I cannot stand another day of this," he ordered.

Sarah allowed Golden Eagle to bundle her in several warm layers. "Thank you, Golden Eagle. I promise to be careful." Turning her back on him, Sarah hung her head in shame. "I'm sorry I've been so out-of-sorts lately. I don't mean to be, yet I just can't seem to help it, and being cooped up all day doesn't help," she apologized.

Turning her to face him, Golden Eagle tilted her chin and planted a light kiss on her lips before leading her out. "I know. This is a difficult time for you. But soon, the air will warm and our babe will rest in our arms. Now come, perhaps we will call on Red Fox and Wild-Flower. Seems Wild-Flower is just as moody since she became with child. We cannot stay long, though," he warned. "Another storm brews and already the winds grow strong.'' Hand in hand, Sarah and Golden Eagle walked along the river to the tipi of Red Fox and Wild-Flower.

Hours later, warmed by a meal of hot soup and bread brought to them from Mary, Golden Eagle sat on his pallet of furs and watched Sarah ready herself for bed. Outside the tipi, winds howled with growing fury, while inside, hot embers glowed brightly, keeping the cold at bay.

Golden Eagle grew concerned as he noticed Sarah rubbing her lower back. Rising, he led her to a pile of furs and helped her to a comfortable sitting position, then took her brush and lovingly stroked her blond hair until it crackled and shone as bright as the moon. Deftly, he re-braided the pale strands into a single plait down her back before easing her onto her side so he could rub her back. His fingers firmly loosened the tight muscles. "What's wrong, White Wind?" Golden Eagle inquired as Sarah moved restlessly.

"It is nothing, Golden Eagle. My back is stiff as a board, but it will pass," she answered.

Golden Eagle rose to his knees. "Perhaps Healing-Woman will prepare a cup of soothing tea for you," he suggested. He and the members of his village had come to respect the woman who knew much about nature's power of healing.

Mary had arrived three weeks ago with Ben, whom they had named Woodcarver-Who-Lives-in-Woods for all the wood carvings he'd made as gifts. Since her arrival, Mary had set out to learn all she could about the herbs the Indian women used, and in turn shared her knowledge of herbs and healing with them.

"No, don't disturb them. It's late. The discomfort will pass as always." Sarah sighed, Golden Eagle's hands soothing much of the stiffness and discomfort. She was drawn close to Golden Eagle, her back spooned to his front as he drew covers over them, stroking her back until they fell asleep.

Later, low moans woke Golden Eagle. Looking around in the darkness, Golden Eagle spotted Sarah hunched over as if in great pain. Another gasp escaped her clenched lips. Golden Eagle sprang to his feet. Only the glowing embers shed light on White Wind's pinched features as black storm clouds hid all light from *Hanwi*.

"The baby, is it time, White Wind?" At her nod, Golden Eagle quickly donned his shirt, leggings and moccasins before running to fetch his mother and Healing-Woman.

A short time later, Golden Eagle stood bewildered and frustrated as his White Wind was led into the birthing hut. He could hear her cries and moans of pain, but could not help her. Ben, Chief Hawk Eyes and Red Fox tried to distract Golden Eagle by joining him in his father's tipi.

As another loud cry rent the air, Golden Eagle jumped to his feet. "She's going to die in there!" he exclaimed, fearful that he'd never see or hold her again.

A hand on his shoulder held him back, and he realized he had started for the door. He looked into the knowing eyes of his father. "No, my son. White Wind is strong. The spirits are with her. She will give you a strong child, but you must not interfere. Leave her to the women. This is a difficult time for fathers, but you must have courage. It is the way of the world. Go now and rest. There is nothing you can do for her at this birthing time. She will need you strong when the new sun shows her face," Hawk Eyes counseled.

Golden Eagle looked out into the storming night sky. Wind howled through the tree tops, sending sheets of rain in every direction.

Golden Eagle needed to be alone, needed to beg the powerful spirits to watch over his loved one. He let himself out, unaware of the chilling wind or the water seeping through his leggings. The only chill he felt was deep within, brought on by his helplessness to ease White Wind's pain.

Climbing the steep rise that protected one side of his village, Golden Eagle fought the elements. The wind-driven rain pushed against him, sending him stumbling down the slick muddy earth. Time and time again, he picked himself up, struggling to reach the top. Exhausted, he stopped just short of the top of the ridge. Raising his arms to the clouds above, he prayed. His chanting grew loud as he asked *Wakan Tanka* to spare White Wind and his child.

The storm drew near, thunder rolled closer, flashes of white illuminated the eerie darkness.

Suddenly, Golden Eagle found himself thrown to the ground as a loud crack rent the air, followed by a loud crackling hissing noise close by. Stunned by the suddenness, Golden Eagle rose to his knees and looked around, blinking the moisture from his eyes. He sucked in his breath, for there at the very top of the ridge a giant tree lay split down the middle, flames sizzling as rain pelted the burning wood.

Tears streamed down his face, mingling with the rain. This was a sign. Slipping and sliding down the hill, he made his way to the hut where Sarah lay. He froze when a piercing scream rang out into the night air. Silence followed. Even the storm seemed to have been stilled for a brief moment by the cry.

Then, from within the birthing hut came the cry of a newborn baby filling his lungs with air for the first time. Golden Eagle grinned, the cry music to his ears, even though he knew the babe's cry would be silenced by the women inside as the baby received his first lesson. No crying.

Safety for the village depended on a child not crying and giving them away to their enemies, so babies were taught moments after birth not to cry. In return, they quickly learned there was no need to cry, for their every need would be tended to promptly.

As Golden Eagle stood waiting, Seeing Eyes stepped out and motioned him inside. Golden Eagle immediately went to White Wind, who lay exhausted but with a glow of happiness surrounding her. Bright Blossom and Wild-Flower stepped back, allowing Golden Eagle a few moments with his wife.

"Are you all right, White Wind?" he asked, kneeling beside her.

"Yes, my golden warrior. You have made me very happy this day." Sarah looked over at Mary, who handed her a small bundle.

Sarah took the small squirming bundle and placed it carefully in Golden Eagle's arms. "Our son, my husband."

A son! Gingerly Golden Eagle peeled the fur blanket open and looked into the splotchy-red face of his son. With awe, he gazed upon the tiny perfect features. His fingers hesitantly touched the baby's cap of thick black hair. When he stroked one soft cheek, he grinned when the tiny pink mouth tried to latch onto his finger.

Golden Eagle beamed. "He is hungry already. He will grow to be strong." A look of wonder overcame him. "I'm a father. Thank you, my wife. Could a father ask for a more beautiful child?" Golden Eagle leaned over and tenderly kissed White Wind.

A tap on his shoulder, and he rose to meet his mother's understanding gaze. Seeing Eyes spoke to Sarah. "You need to rest now. I know of a certain grandfather who is eager to see his grandson. Wait, that's two grandfathers!" All laughed, knowing that Ben also would be a fiercely protective grandparent. All were astonished at the wooden cradle he'd made the babe, having never seen such wooden furniture.

Golden Eagle and Sarah exchanged secret looks, knowing their children would have the best from both worlds.

Chief Hawk Eyes came forward to see his grandson with Winona, Ben and Red Fox following the moment Golden Eagle and Seeing Eyes stepped into the warm tipi. Taking the small bundle from his son, the chief demanded, "Have you thought of a name fitting for the first grandson of Hawk Eyes?"

Golden Eagle thought of the storm on the hill and nodded

decisively. "He shall be called Striking Thunder. He shall strike his enemies in the dark of night and in a flash be gone, leaving only his fire behind as a sign of his greatness."

Hawk Eyes nodded, pleased. "You have chosen well, my son, has he not, wife?"

Seeing Eyes nodded. "Yes, he shall be a great warrior someday, greater than even his father or grandfather," she stated, looking upon her grandson. Golden Eagle and Hawk Eyes glanced at one another. Each knew by her words that the child named Striking Thunder would indeed become a mighty warrior.

Epilogue

Fluffy white clouds rode the gentle breeze across the deep blue sky. One lone eagle soared the currents, keeping a watch on the earth below. Movement on the Great Gray Rock sent the majestic bird spiraling higher, his cries echoing across the land, as though protesting the human intruders.

A hand appeared from below the top, then another as a figure pulled himself up. Standing from the high perch, Golden Eagle gazed down at the valley floor far below him. His feet were planted apart in an arrogant stance as he lifted his hands to the sky as if to embrace all that he could see before settling on his lean hips.

Sounds of scrambling came from behind him, and he strode over to the edge and helped White Wind over the top before returning his attention to the view below.

White Wind sat a moment and caught her breath. When Golden Eagle had suggested that they take a day and go off by themselves, she'd had no idea he wanted to climb a mountain.

She bestowed a look of love and wonderment at the man she proudly called husband. Framed by the sun's rays, he looked every bit her golden warrior, so magnificent and powerful.

She was proud to be his wife. Despite the hard life they led, she and their six-month-old son lacked for nothing.

Rising silently to her feet, she came to stand behind Golden Eagle, wrapping her arms around his firm taut waist. She rested her chin upon his warm shoulder and took in the glorious sight from the top of their world.

The breeze played with her unbound hair, wrapping silky sun-bleached strands around Golden Eagle. White Wind laughed softly as he pulled her into his protective embrace.

"It's beautiful, Golden Eagle. It was worth the climb up. Look, our home is there below us," White Wind said, awed by the sight below.

"This land is ours. I do not know how long we can hold it from the white man, but it matters not where we go as long as you are at my side."

A cry below had them both looking down. Another eagle soared, staying close to the cliff. An answering cry sounded from above.

Golden Eagle and White Wind, entwined in each other's arms, watched as the eagle above them flew straight up into the clouds and disappeared.

Turning toward Golden Eagle when the bird failed to reappear, White Wind, eyes the color of the sky, mused, "I wonder where he went."

Golden Eagle cupped her chin and lowered his head as he whispered, "He's flown in search of a mate." Once again he surveyed the scene below.

"Come White Wind," he said, "while this land is ours, let us be like the eagles above us. Let us also ride the wind together."

Dear Readers,

I hope you enjoyed reading about Sarah and Golden Eagle's tale as much as I did writing about them and the rest of the cast of *White Wind*.

The Indian culture, particularly that of the plains Indians, has always interested me. In doing the research for this book, I began to understand what these proud people suffered and lost with the intrusion of the white man. I tried to portray the Indian's way of life before alcohol, starvation, guns, wars, and reservations destroyed forever this proud nation and their culture.

I would enjoy hearing from readers and will personally answer all letters if a self-addressed stamped envelope is enclosed. Write to me at:

PO Box 766
Los Altos, CA 94023-0766

THE ANGEL & THE OUTLAW

MADELINE BAKER

Bestselling Author Of *Lakota Renegade*

An outlaw, a horse thief, a man killer, J.T. Cutter isn't surprised when he is strung up for his crimes. What amazes him is the heavenly being who grants him one year to change his wicked ways. Yet when he returns to his old life, he hopes to cram a whole lot of hell-raising into those twelve months no matter what the future holds.

But even as J.T. heads back down the trail to damnation, a sharp-tongued beauty is making other plans for him. With the body of a temptress and the heart of a saint, Brandy is the only woman who can save J.T. And no matter what it takes, she'll prove to him that the road to redemption can lead to rapturous bliss.

_3931-1 $5.99 US/$7.99 CAN

Dorchester Publishing Co., Inc.
65 Commerce Road
Stamford, CT 06902

LEIGH GREENWOOD

"Leigh Greenwood is a dynamo of a storyteller!"
—Los Angeles Times

Jefferson Randolph has never forgotten all he lost in the War Between The States—or forgiven those he has fought. Long after most of his six brothers find wedded bliss, the former Rebel soldier keeps himself buried in work, only dreaming of one day marrying a true daughter of the South. Then a run-in with a Yankee schoolteacher teaches him that he has a lot to learn about passion.

Violet Goodwin is too refined and genteel for an ornery bachelor like Jeff. Yet before he knows it, his disdain for Violet is blossoming into desire. But Jeff fears that love alone isn't enough to help him put his past behind him—or to convince a proper lady that she can find happiness as the newest bride in the rowdy Randolph clan.

_3995-8 $5.99 US/$7.99 CAN

DEVIL IN SPURS

NORAH HESS

Bestselling Author Of *Winter Love*

In the rugged solitude of the Wyoming wilderness, the lovely Jonty Rand lives life as a boy to protect her innocence from the likes of Cord McBain. So when her grandmother's dying wish makes Cord Jonty's guardian, the young girl despairs of ever revealing her true identity. Determined to change Jonty into a rawhide-tough wrangler, Cord assigns her all the hardest tasks on the ranch, making her life a torment. Then one stormy night, he discovers that Jonty will never be a man, only the wildest, most willing woman he's ever taken into his arms.

__3936-2 $5.99 US/$7.99 CAN